PRAISE FOR TOWNSEND RECIPE FOR DISASTER

"I savored this heartwarming and delicious tale filled with family roots, twisty secrets, and mouth-watering food! Shauna Robinson taps into the longing we all share to find our people and our place in the world and gives us a soul-satisfying story that will linger long after the last page."

—Rachel Linden, author of *Recipe for a Charmed Life*

"Hilarious and heartwarming, this book is like a warm drink on a cold winter day. Shauna Robinson stunningly explores our perceptions of family and race and if what divides us is more important than what brings us together. An indispensable read for anyone who has tried to figure out their place in spaces where they never quite fit and a beautiful meditation on accepting yourself and accepting the people you love with your eyes and heart wide open."

—Alex Travis, author of *The Only Black Girl in the Room*

"A heartwarming story about belonging, family secrets, the breaking of generational curses, and forging of new bonds, Shauna Robinson's *The Townsend Family Recipe for Disaster* will have you reaching for the people you love and holding them close."

—Shirlene Obuobi, author of *On Rotation*

"*The Townsend Family Recipe for Disaster* is infused with the warmth and humor that readers have come to expect from Robinson's work. Shauna has always excelled at building worlds that readers want to spend time in and writing characters they want to spend time with, and the Townsends are her best yet. This book is a moving delight, satisfying as a summer barbecue."

—Eva Jurczyk, international bestselling author of *The Department of Rare Books and Special Collections*

"*The Townsend Family Recipe for Disaster* is a heartfelt story of finding identity amidst complicated families and untold secrets. Robinson's writing brought Mae's journey to life, a perfect mix of deeply sad moments and laugh-out-loud inner monologue that kept me turning pages well into the night. True to real life, our histories—familial and racial—hold the best and worst of memories. This story doesn't shy away from hard topics. Rather, it approaches them through a unique, sincere character who wins hearts from the start. More than just a feel-good read, *The Townsend Family Recipe for Disaster* will leave readers cheering for Mae, hoping the best for humanity, and longing for a taste of Southern food! Kudos, Shauna!"

—Michelle Stimpson, author of *Sisters with a Side of Greens*

PRAISE FOR *THE BANNED BOOKSHOP OF MAGGIE BANKS*

"A sparkling bookish story about rules just begging to be broken... I couldn't get enough!"

—Abby Jimenez, *New York Times* bestselling author of *Part of Your World* and *The Friend Zone*

"Shauna writes for the girls without dream jobs, the pandemic babies who moved back in with their parents and are just trying to figure it out, and the extroverts who find purpose in bringing people together. This novel is a booklover's dream, with subtle social commentary to boot."

—Iman Hariri-Kia, author of *A Hundred Other Girls*

"*The Banned Bookshop of Maggie Banks* is a charming rom-com about finding your own path and never being scared to break the rules. It's also an uplifting celebration of the power of books to change people's lives. Visit your favorite bookstore, curl up in a comfy chair, and savor every word!"

—Freya Sampson, author of *The Last Chance Library*

"Delightful and deeply felt, *The Banned Bookshop of Maggie Banks* is one woman's instantly compelling search for herself woven into a celebration of how stories enliven and inspire community. It's the perfect book for booklovers."

—Emily Wibberley and Austin Siegemund-Broka, authors of *The Roughest Draft*

"Consider me an official member of the Maggie army! I found myself rooting for every character in this warm, welcoming tale of a woman coming into her own. If you've ever found comfort in a book—or a bookstore—then you'll enjoy watching Maggie discover how powerful the right story in the right hands can be."

—Lucy Gilmore, author of *The Lonely Hearts Book Club*

PRAISE FOR *MUST LOVE BOOKS*

"*Must Love Books* is a heartfelt and exciting debut. With a relatable protagonist in Nora, frank discussions of the millennial experience, and pitch-perfect sweetness, Shauna Robinson puts forth a wise and honest story of how it feels to be a young woman in search of yourself."

—Taylor Jenkins Reid, *New York Times* bestselling author of *The Seven Husbands of Evelyn Hugo* and *Malibu Rising*

"A book for booklovers that takes a hard look at the predatory approach of the corporate world with a heroine who's easy to love and root for. I enjoyed all of the inside look at the publishing industry from the perspective of a young woman scraping together all of her wits just to get by. It's impossible not to root for Nora!"

—Jesse Q. Sutanto, bestselling author of *Dial A for Aunties*

"Honest, relatable, and real, *Must Love Books* is a tender reflection on finding your person while you're still desperately searching for yourself rolled up in a thoughtful novel about the changing work world."

—KJ Dell'Antonia, *New York Times* bestselling author of *The Chicken Sisters*

"A compelling love story, dishy publishing goss, and a chic urban setting? Yes, yes, yes! But like the works she shepherds through publication, Shauna Robinson's true-to-life story of a struggling editorial assistant is much more than the sum of its parts. Within the pages of *Must Love Books*, the lucky reader will find themselves on an poignant journey of a young booklover with too little support and too many dreams—a place we've all been at one point or another. With emotional honesty and a surprising wit that I found addictive, Robinson's debut is everything a book-about-books fan wants in a novel."

—Kelly Harms, *Washington Post* bestselling author of *The Overdue Life of Amy Byler*

"Readers will be rooting for Nora from the first page and experiencing her grand highs and heartbreaking lows with their entire heart. Get comfy because you won't be able to put this book down!"

—Sajni Patel, award-winning author of *The Trouble with Hating You*

ALSO BY
SHAUNA ROBINSON

Must Love Books
The Banned Bookshop of Maggie Banks

The Townsend Family Recipe for Disaster

SHAUNA ROBINSON

sourcebooks
landmark

Published by Sourcebooks Landmark, an imprint of Sourcebooks
P.O. Box 4410, Naperville, Illinois 60567-4410
(630) 961-3900
sourcebooks.com

Cataloging-in-Publication Data is on file with the Library of Congress.

Printed and bound in Canada.
MBP 10 9 8 7 6 5 4 3 2 1

For my family—by blood, love, and marriage; those I've met and those I haven't; stateside, down under, and everywhere in between.

CHAPTER ONE

Mae didn't realize she was drunk until she nuzzled the peony.

Her future mother-in-law, Susan, paused mid-sentence to watch Mae across the table. Tracing a petal down her cheek, luxuriating in how velvety it was, Mae wondered if Susan had lost her train of thought, and Mae was going to say *You were talking about*—except she couldn't remember. It was something to do with the centerpieces, a debate about roses versus peonies, and then Mae had plucked a petal from the peony in front of her and wondered how that surprising softness might feel on her face. Were peonies good for the skin? If jade rollers were a thing, there had to be a market for face-flowers. What would she call it? Flower facial? Petal peel? Floratherapy? The name needed workshopping, but she was onto something.

But now, staring into Susan's baffled blue eyes, it occurred to Mae that perhaps that look had nothing to do with center-pieces and everything to do with Mae. Mae glanced at Connor, her fiancé. He was watching her, too, except the corner of his lips twitched in the hint of a smile.

In an instant, Mae noticed the warmth in her face, the floating in her head, the flower on her cheek, and realized she might have hit the cabernets too hard. They'd all tasted about a dozen wines that afternoon and yet Mae was the only one fondling flowers. Then again, Connor's parents owned a winery, and she guessed wine-tasting expertise ran in their blood. Even Connor had probably swirled and sniffed from a baby bottle before he'd taken his first steps. Mae, on the other hand, had made it to thirty-one without grasping the basics of wine appreciation. While they went on about hidden flavors and aromas she never picked up on—apricot, mushroom, tobacco, wet gravel, as if anyone in their right mind would want to drink something with notes of *wet gravel*—she'd guzzled every glass, just trying to get the acidic taste over with.

If only today had been a pizza tasting. She was great at appreciating pizza.

Mae lowered her hand to her lap and studied the petal, now patchy with grease. Susan resumed speaking, gushing about the timelessness of peonies, and Mae let the petal flutter to her feet. Her mind was still drifting past the cloud of conversation, but that was how all wedding planning discussions felt. For the last year, talk of table settings and color schemes had swirled around her in words she couldn't quite grasp. Who cared about irrelevant details when her wedding might be the catalyst that finally brought her estranged family together?

"But you don't need to worry about the cost," Susan was saying, her voice faraway.

"I know," Connor said. "But if Mae and I don't care about the flowers, then what's the point of splurging?"

John, Connor's father, laughed like it was the silliest question he'd ever heard. "Because we can."

"You prefer the peonies, don't you, Mae?" Susan said.

Mae snapped to attention. Three expectant faces watched her, waiting for signs of life. Even the fountain behind them, which normally brought a soothing sound to John and Susan's patio, seemed to silence its steady trickle. Mae should say something smart, something relevant at the very least, but her last competent brain cell was busy designing colorful T-shirts stamped with *TOWNSEND FAMILY REUNION*.

Her gaze darted around the table for a distraction: empty wine glasses, assorted flowers, one of Susan's three-ring binders. It was open to a glossy page showing leaves running down a white backdrop. "What's that?" she asked.

Susan perked up. "It's a vine wall, like the one we're doing for the wedding. If we're agreed on peonies for the centerpieces, I was thinking we could put some on the wall too. I have a picture of that somewhere." She licked a finger and flipped through a never-ending funhouse of themed walls: sunflowers, balloons, glowing light bulbs.

Of course Susan had a wall binder. This wedding was serious business for John and Susan Rutherford. It was decreed long ago that their only child's wedding would be held at their picturesque winery. With a coveted venue at their disposal, and their many contacts in the wedding industry, the Rutherfords were determined to make this wedding the event of the century. And Mae and Connor would be there, too.

"Wait," Mae said when she caught a glimpse of food. "What was that one?"

"This?" Susan turned back to a page where colorful donuts hung on wooden pegs. "Oh. This is a donut wall we did for a wedding a few years back."

"The Harrington-Chambers wedding," John said. "May 2019."

Mae always thought it was impressive that John could remember every wedding. Though he could just be spouting off random names and dates for all she knew. He could have said, *The Crumpet-Trolleybottom wedding, January 1593*, and they would have all nodded knowingly. The thought made her laugh, and John gave her a puzzled look, and she cleared her throat and went back to staring at the donut wall.

"I love donuts." Mae rested her elbows on the table with a dreamy sigh. "I love when the glaze hardens and gets a little bit country." She frowned. "Crunchy." Yes, that was it. Her head swimming with glazes and sprinkles, she gasped and turned to Susan. "Hey, what if we did a donut wall? Instead of the vines?"

Susan did a double take, looking from Mae to the binder. "You…want to do a donut wall?"

Mae couldn't tell what Susan found more surprising: that Mae was finally expressing a wedding-related opinion after a year of nods and shrugs, or that a wall—and not flowers, or music, or anything else Susan had a dedicated binder for—was the one detail Mae chose to speak on.

But donuts were delicious. Mae could go for a donut right now. And maybe her dad's side of the family liked donuts too. In fact, maybe this whole, elaborate wedding wasn't so absurd if the spectacle of it drew them in.

"Yeah," Mae said. "Is that possible?"

"It *is*. It's just…" Susan's brow pinched. "This was for a morning wedding. Donuts went with the breakfast theme. But your wedding's in the evening." She spoke like there was something unspoken in her words.

"I'd eat donuts day or night," Mae said. She glanced around the table. John was squinting thoughtfully into the distance, the temple tip of his glasses between his lips, like he was trying his hardest to imagine a world with night donuts.

But Connor, smirking at Mae, was already in that world with her. "Let's do it," he said. "Donut wall."

"Donut wall!" Mae echoed, lifting her water glass. Connor clinked his glass against hers, his eyes dancing with mirth.

"Okay." There was a touch of pain in Susan's voice. She tucked a blond flyaway into place, surveying the two of them uncertainly. "Let's have a donut wall...at night."

"Night donuts!" Mae raised her hand for a high-five.

A range of emotions passed over Susan's face: confusion, surprise, maybe joy? Susan gave a delighted laugh and slapped her hand neatly against Mae's in the demurest high-five Mae had ever received.

"I didn't know you liked donuts so much," John said. "We could have picked some up for you today."

Alarm bells sounded in the small part of Mae's brain that hadn't succumbed to the wine fog, flashing a bright-yellow caution sign, slow down, yield to oncoming intimacy.

For years, she'd curated the perfect balance of geniality and distance around Connor's family. Semi-regular lunches and dinners with Connor and his parents? Sure. Pedicures with Susan? No, thank you—she was busy that day. Coming over to admire the Rutherfords' kitchen remodel? Certainly, and she'd even gift them some fancy olive oil to mark the occasion. Being left alone with them when Connor had to step out to take a call? Oh, actually, she had to use the bathroom for the exact duration of Connor's call, please excuse her a moment.

There was a logic behind her avoidance. Mae knew that if she let her guard down around his parents, they would do the same around her—and that was when the danger set in.

Yet, John's donut offer and Susan's high-five excitement had Mae's resolve crumbling a little, as it always did when their kindnesses caught her off-guard. She studied John and Susan, searching for traces of Connor. With that gray hair lining the sides of John's bald head, he didn't much resemble him—but those warm brown eyes were the same. Susan's hair was lighter and thinner than Connor's honey blond, but her crooked smile mirrored his. Mae could choose to believe in them, accept that John and Susan might be every bit as good as their son.

"That would be great," Mae said. "We'll have to get donuts sometime."

A strangely fuzzy feeling came over her as she took in John and Susan's pleased expressions. Was this growth? Had she really overcome her fears about Connor's parents *and* invented flora-therapy (patent pending) in a single afternoon? She should get drunk more often.

While John and Susan debated potential donut vendors for the wedding, the talk of flavors and toppings had Mae's mouth watering—except someone must have taken the snack platter inside. The old Mae might have politely toughed it out around the Rutherfords, but she was evolved now. She was Cabernet Mae. CaberMae, if you will.

"I'm gonna grab a snack," she announced, standing abruptly. "Can I get anyone anything?" A wave of dizziness washed over her. She gripped her chair to avoid swaying.

"You good?" Connor asked, watching her closely.

"I'm great," Mae assured him. She even believed it.

One foot in front of the other, and she was walking fine. So, she wasn't falling-down drunk, just does-weird-things-with-peonies and high-fives-with-abandon drunk. She crossed the patio and entered the Rutherfords' house, where air-conditioning provided a welcome respite from the muggy, June heat. She ran her fingers along the living room wall, fantasizing about what she might find in the kitchen.

Kitchens had souls, personalities. The Rutherfords' kitchen was like a pristine gourmet market, neat cupboards and marble countertops brimming with expensive snacks and drinks. Her parents' kitchen had been more like a 7-Eleven, stocked with foods meant for microwaves, like Hot Pockets and canned soups. And she knew from her dad's stories about his childhood that his family's kitchen was equal parts playground and paradise, where his mom made tantalizing feasts while he and his three siblings hovered around her, asking when dinner was ready, sneaking tastes from bubbling pots of peppery gravy or creamy mashed potatoes, scampering off in a giggling panic if they got caught at the stove. Mae always loved that image, a kitchen swarming with curiosity, laughter, activity.

The Rutherfords' kitchen had none of that, but it *would* have those seed crackers they'd served several wines ago, which were sure to quiet her growling stomach. They'd been crunchy and nutty, with sunflower seeds and flaxseeds and a hint of garlic. She'd meant to ask what brand they were, but then John busted out the malbec and Mae returned to knocking back wines she didn't like.

Murmurs were coming from the kitchen. She started to make out the words as she drew closer.

"...uneven," Connor's aunt Laura was saying. "Most of the

guests are from our side. I don't think Mae's invited more than sixty—oh, hi, Mae!" Laura's eyes briefly widened before she broke into a grin. "We were just talking about the guest list."

Connor's uncle Rob flashed her a smile too wide for his face. "How's it going out there?"

Something familiar and unpleasant pulled at her. "Great," she said, throwing on a smile too, for this was clearly the thing to do. "I was just getting a snack." She scanned the counter: green olives, mango compote, truffle almonds that tasted like salty dirt—the seed crackers! She lunged for them, grabbing a handful and holding them up like a trophy.

Laura and Rob chuckled awkwardly. Mae lingered in the uncomfortable quiet, racking her brain for something to say. "Found 'em."

Laura's eyes traveled to the crackers in Mae's hand, and Mae felt an urge to set them down and back slowly out of the room. But that would be worse, wouldn't it, now that she'd already touched them?

Fleeing was the only option. Mae stammered something about the bathroom and got the hell out of there.

In the safety of the bathroom, she turned the lock and leaned against the door. She ignored the floral potpourri smell and stuffed a cracker in her mouth while her mind spun with regret.

This was why. This was why she'd worked so hard to keep Connor's family at a distance. Why she couldn't let herself get swayed by donuts and innocent smiles.

Laura and Rob hadn't done anything wrong. Her guest list *was* paltry compared to the Rutherfords'. But walking in on them talking about her unlocked a feeling she'd spent her adulthood trying to forget. A squirmy instinct that she didn't belong.

Mae knew that feeling well. At every family function she'd attended with her white mother's extended family, Mae and her dad had grown accustomed to being the only Black people in the room. They exchanged knowing looks when Mae's aunt felt the need to specify the race of the waitress who got her order wrong. They tiptoed through conversations about politics and pop culture. When they walked in on her uncle speculating that half the Black population of east Bakersfield was part of a gang, they'd shared a glance over the way he startled when they entered the room.

Mae's mother was quick to challenge any noticeably ignorant remarks, but she didn't catch them all, and Mae and her dad had a more detached approach, anyway. It was easier to treat these occurrences like private, fleeting club meetings: a shared look or a stifled laugh, and then the minutes were taken and they adjourned until next time.

Mae had always longed to expand their club. Her dad's stories about his childhood, growing up in North Carolina with his siblings, cousins, aunts, uncles, neighbors, painted a picture of an extended family with a boisterous closeness that made her ache with curiosity. Instead of uncomfortable moments at perfunctory holiday meals, his family had Sunday dinners packed around the dining table, passing plates while five conversations went on at once. She used to pepper her dad with questions, usually when holidays rolled around and her desire for belonging intensified. *What did you eat for Thanksgiving? Did you bake cookies for Santa on Christmas Eve? Tell me again about the time your neighbor's dog ruined the Easter egg hunt.*

Mae, feeling so far away in California, had hoped that one day something would bring them all together. No matter that her dad's parents hadn't approved of him marrying Mae's mom. Naturally, they weren't thrilled about their son becoming a father at twenty-one and running off to California with the white woman he'd gotten pregnant. But so much time had passed since then. They had to move past it sometime.

As a kid, Mae had dreamed her wedding would reunite her family. Her dad would walk her down the aisle, she'd exchange vows with—well, back then it was Eric from *Zoom*; his smile made those science segments worth watching—and at the reception, her dad would introduce her to all their North Carolina relatives, and she would finally feel like she belonged.

She hadn't expected that the occasion to finally get them all in the same room would be her dad's funeral.

It wasn't the heartwarming reunion Mae had anticipated. Their two-day visit was brief, they stayed in a hotel, and Mae, then fifteen, had been too busy fighting back tears to make a meaningful connection with them beyond dim smiles and answering their questions about what grade she was in and how she liked school. And then the visit was over, they went back to North Carolina, and Mae never saw them again.

So she'd swallowed her grief and accepted the reality that her club's membership had shrunk to one. When she headed off to college at Howard a few years later, she thought she'd never have to experience that odd-one-out feeling ever again.

And then she went and fell in love with a man as white as mayonnaise.

She couldn't help falling for the cute white guy who made her laugh at her friend's birthday party nearly five years ago. That stupid pun he'd made about his Midori sour (*it's one in a melon*), the endearing way his eyes crinkled when her laugh rang out amid a sea of groans, how he'd raised his glass at her like they were the only people with taste, and she was a goner.

But she *could* control her relationship with his family. She refused to let the Rutherfords get close to her and start feeling comfortable enough to say ignorant things around her the way her mom's relatives always had. She'd thought she could manage it, but their impending wedding intensified her creeping fears tenfold. Spending the rest of her life behind a wall of polite formality, attending those club meetings all by herself, was too achingly lonely a prospect to bear. Something had to change.

And so, late last year, Mae had tapped right back into that childhood fantasy and invited every single one of her North Carolina relatives to her wedding. She'd pressed her mom for the Townsends' addresses until she relented and emailed her the few she had, warning that they might not be up to date. From there, Mae cross-checked them against Zillow to see who might have moved. When in doubt, she defaulted to her grandmother's address. Zillow showed that her grandmother's split-level home hadn't been sold in decades. It felt like the surest bet. She just needed her grandmother to put aside her disapproval and get the invitations into the right hands.

Mae had sent the save-the-dates in December, then the invitations in May. Surely now the Townsends would remember Mae existed, feel terrible about their three decades of ignoring her, and show up with hugs and apologies at the ready. Mae would take them in with open arms and donuts aplenty, and all would be forgiven.

She hadn't gotten a single RSVP from them.

But they still had a week. Maybe CP time applied to RSVPs.

Mae pulled out her phone and checked the app for the wedding website Connor's parents made them use. No new RSVPs. She sighed through her nose and swiped to Instagram instead. All she had to do was type *S* in the search bar and Instagram did the rest, knowingly suggesting *Sierra Townsend*.

Her cousin Sierra mostly posted pictures of her baked goods, from unassuming cranberry oat muffins to cakes swathed in shiny ganache and immaculate frosting dollops. But sometimes, she shared pictures of friends and relatives, too. Mae liked to scan their faces for familiarity, read captions for references to their family. And, lately: search for clues that Sierra might be planning a trip to DC for a wedding next month.

Mae checked the latest post—nothing since the lemon bars last week—then scrolled to find the old picture of Sierra with Mae's father. Sierra had posted it last month with the hashtag *throwback*. She could tell from the wooden backyard fence, the red checkered tablecloth behind them, and the red paper plate he held, that it was from the Townsends' big Fourth of July barbecue—the one holiday her dad flew back to North Carolina for every year. Mae used to hover around him while he packed his suitcase, asking what he was most excited about doing and eating when he got to Hobson. And when he came home blissfully jet-lagged a week later, he'd patiently answer Mae's questions about what he ate, who he saw, and what their relatives were up to.

Sierra probably didn't even know what a privilege it was to attend that legendary barbecue. In the picture, Mae's dad had one arm around Sierra while the other held a plate piled with ribs, corn on the cob, potato salad, mac and cheese, and baked beans. Sierra, who must have been about twelve at the time, grinned patiently at the camera, as if this were the third or fourth time someone had tried snapping the shot.

Sierra's eyes were rounder than Mae's, her skin darker and cheekbones higher, but Mae's gaze always gravitated to Sierra's nose. It was the same as Mae's: wide and flat, tapering up to a narrow bridge. It grounded her, this knowledge that she had a whole other family, and some of them had her nose. It felt absurdly unfair that Mae had grown up with just her relatives in Bakersfield when, many miles away, were the Townsends, who Mae knew would never make her feel out of place. You didn't alienate someone who had the same nose as you. It just wasn't done.

And, okay, there were some hurdles to work past. Her dad's parents disapproving of his marriage to Mae's mom. The way her dad had gone to those Fourth of July barbecues alone, even though she begged to go with him. How the Townsends' one and only trip to Bakersfield was riddled with tension. Mae remembered exchanging a puzzled look with Sierra, then nineteen to Mae's fifteen, as their mothers got into a heated whisper-fight half an hour before the funeral.

Mae never found out what that fight was about, but she always came back to that look she and Sierra shared, a reminder that she wasn't alone in wondering why the hell their family was so fragmented. It made her certain, even all these years later, that she could at least count on Sierra to come to her wedding.

Mae washed down the crackers with a mouthful of water from the sink, then wiped crumbs from the corners of her mouth. CaberMae might have worn these crumbs blithely, but it would be all the invitation Susan needed to brush them away, hypnotize Mae with maternal affection, and then gleefully grab a fistful of Mae's 3c hair to see what it felt like, or whatever weird thing Susan was secretly dying to do.

Mae checked her teeth in the mirror, swished water around her mouth to rinse away the purplish wine stains, fluffed her curls, straightened her posture, and eyed her reflection with resolve. May CaberMae rest in peace.

When Mae returned to the patio, she was the picture of poise. She listened and nodded at appropriate intervals, answered questions with precisely calculated amounts of warmth and charm, doled out one-point-five-second hugs as she and Connor took their leave. The minute she slid into the passenger seat of Connor's Prius, she let her head loll back, her spine curve, her legs stretch. Every undignified mannerism she'd suppressed all afternoon was hers to embrace again.

"You seemed to enjoy the wine," Connor teased when he got in the car.

Mae laughed. It wasn't the dignified chuckle she contrived for his parents but the shameless kind that made the muscles in her stomach contract. "Maybe I'm too polite to spit in front of people."

"You *are* a very polite drunk," he conceded, lightly kissing her nose as he dropped something in her lap.

She looked down to find a large Ziploc bag of seed crackers. "Where'd these come from?"

"Aunt Laura said you liked them."

"Oh." She chewed the inside of her lip and stared at the bag. Was it an innocent suggestion, an *I packed these for Mae*, Aunt Laura just doing aunt things? Or was it steeped in mockery, a *Mae sure demolished those crackers, that greedy drunk*, and they were gossiping about her in the kitchen right now, staring through the window?

Instinctively, she sat up straighter. Mae rubbed her eyes,

ate a cracker despite herself. Dissecting every little thing the Rutherfords did was exhausting. But she didn't know how to stop.

"You want to go anywhere?" Connor asked as he started the car. "We could drive around and look for *For Rent* signs. Adams Morgan. Lanier Heights." He was practically singing the neighborhoods, like he was suggesting a tropical vacation and not an apartment-hunting chore.

Mae held his gaze, met the hopeful spark in his eye, and shook her head. "I'll pass."

"Fine." He pretended to grumble, but that spark never left him. "But our lease is gonna be up soon." He eased the car down the Rutherfords' driveway, stopping when they reached the road. The coast was clear, but he didn't move. He glanced at Mae. "You love DC."

"I love Baltimore too," she said with a shrug. Admittedly, DC's free museums, blooming cherry blossom trees, and eclectic variety of cuisines within walking distance had mesmerized her since college. But it would be hard to keep his parents at bay if she lived two miles from them. Baltimore put an hour between them, offering so many more excuses for avoidance.

Connor studied her a moment longer, searching her face for truth, but Mae held firm. She couldn't unload her spiraling fears on him and explain how her line of thought could possibly travel from *I do love DC* to *I'm worried your family is secretly racist*.

"We'll figure it out," he said. "We still have some time."

He slipped his hand into hers and squeezed, sending a ripple of love through her. The gesture was enough for Mae to push her lurking thoughts aside and relax the rest of the way home.

Mae felt lighter as Connor parked in their usual spot, down the street from their row house. The sun was golden, they'd narrowed down wine pairings and invented night donuts, and her Rutherford obligations were over with. Now she could change into sweatpants, collapse onto the couch with Connor, maybe order a fennel and onion pizza from their favorite pizzeria. Her mouth was dry and sour-tasting from too much wine, but a tangerine La Croix from the fridge would take care of that.

And when Mae stopped to check the mail and found a gold-colored envelope with *Sierra Townsend* in the return address, her hopes skyrocketed.

She flipped it over and slowly peeled open the envelope, heart pounding. Suppose Sierra wrote a note on the RSVP card? Something like *Can't wait to see you, cuz!* Mae's best friend Jayla called her cousins *cuz*, and Mae had been struck by that, how cool it sounded. But a note wasn't necessary. They could catch up all they wanted at the wedding.

Mae saw the check mark first. Sierra had selected the box for *Declines with regret*.

She willed herself not to feel the plummeting disappointment, reminded herself that asking a near-stranger to travel three hundred miles for your wedding was a tall order, cousins or not. At least Sierra took the time to fill out the RSVP and send it back. That was kind of her.

Except…

Mae peered closer. She'd thought there was a stray mark on the card, or maybe a hair, but no. In a straight, decisive line of ink, Sierra had firmly crossed out the *with regret*.

This wasn't a kindness. It was a calculated attack.

CHAPTER TWO

Surely there were seating charts in hell.

It was a torture all of its own, trying to decide where three hundred people should sit. Made harder by the fact that Mae was slightly in denial about which relatives were coming to the wedding.

That Sunday afternoon, Mae, Connor, and his parents sat at the small, round table in Mae and Connor's kitchen, moving colorful page markers around a posterboard with the intensity of generals crafting a war plan. And Mae did her best to dodge the questions Connor's parents lobbed at her.

"Have you decided who you want at table one yet?" John asked.

Mae's gaze drifted to the circle at the top of the board. Table one was half-populated with lime-green page markers representing a selection of Connor's family members. The other half had just two neon-yellow strips side by side: one for Mae, one for her mother. The blank space beside them threatened to swallow the table whole.

"Maybe Jayla?" Mae picked up a blue strip with her maid of honor's name on it.

"Table one's usually for family. There's no one you want to add from here?" Susan swirled a finger around the army of yellow page markers who hadn't yet been assigned a seat.

Suddenly color-coding felt supremely rude. Susan had touted its benefits, explaining how easy it was to see things at a glance: green for Connor's family, yellow for Mae's; pink for Connor's friends; blue for Mae's. So easy to look at the posterboard and instantly note the abundance of green and all the sad yellow tags huddled in the corner, not yet seated, as if they'd been shunned from society.

Some of these were Parkers, from her mom's side of the family. A few had agreed to come despite Mae's best efforts at dissuading them. When Mae's cousin Madison had called her to squeal about the invitation, Mae told her she had no expectations for Madison or any of the Parkers to make the trip for such a small, slapdash affair (while crossing her fingers that Susan and John would never hear her call their ornately planned wedding, which included a twelve-piece orchestra and four different chocolate fountains, *slapdash*).

"Don't be silly!" Madison had cooed. "I'm coming. I haven't seen you in forever."

And Mae hadn't known how to say there was a reason for that. She and Madison had been close as kids, having sleepovers and playdates and all the intimacy that came with living just a few blocks away from one another. Along with Mae's maternal grandparents, Madison and her family had been the only Parkers Mae saw regularly, not just on holidays. It wasn't unusual for Madison's mom to babysit whenever Mae's parents had to work, or for their grandma to take Mae and Madison out for ice cream to celebrate good grades.

But over time, she came to realize just how alienated Madison's family made her feel. Not just the little comments from Madison's parents that Mae and her dad might share a look over. Madison's remarks were personal, spoken with enough conviction that Mae used to think Madison was doing her a favor. Like the time Madison came over on Mae's hair wash day when they were nine and wrinkled her nose in disgust when she learned Mae washed her hair once a week. *You're supposed to wash your hair every day*, she'd said.

(Mae then started washing her hair in secret, every night for two weeks, until her hair was dry and brittle and her scalp so itchy that she gave up and went back to weekly washings. She never again told Madison anything about her haircare routine. She learned to tell Madison less and less as they grew older.)

So, after Mae left Bakersfield for college, she kept her visits home brief. She'd see her mom and stop by her grandparents' when they were still alive, but that was it. No more formal holiday dinners with the whole Parker crew, no more hangouts with Madison. Keeping her distance wasn't a perfect system, but it had worked well so far. Until Madison and her parents sent in their RSVPs and said they couldn't wait to be there.

Mae didn't know what to do with their yellow tabs. The simple solution would be to put them at table one—where they belonged, in theory. Except Mae refused to put up with microaggressions at her own wedding.

The remaining unseated yellow tabs belonged to the Townsends. The RSVP deadline had come and gone this week, and all she had to show for her North Carolina-bound invitations was a wall of silence and Sierra's lone, painful response. After Laura's comment about her small guest list last week, Mae couldn't stand the thought of telling the Rutherfords that the only family members attending would be her mom and a smattering of Parkers. They'd probably pity her, sad little orphan Mae, and then say god-knows-what behind her back, just as Laura and Rob had done. Just as the Parkers used to do.

So, if she needed two more people at table one, then screw it.

"My cousin Sierra and my aunt Barbara can sit at table one," Mae said. She stuck their tabs firmly onto the seating chart.

"That's...a choice," said Connor, who had listened to Mae complain about Sierra's RSVP and the Townsends' lack of response all week. She returned Connor's inquiring look with an unapologetic shrug. All was fair in love and war and seating charts.

"What do you mean?" Susan asked, leaning over to inspect the chart.

"No, I said *Good choice*," Connor said quickly. "Table one looks good." Mae exhaled in relief. Bless Connor and his willingness to lie for her with no context.

"Sierra Townsend and Barbara Townsend," Susan read slowly. "Did I miss their RSVPs?" She started rifling through the binder at her side.

"They came in a little late," Mae said. "Is that okay?"

"Certainly!" Susan jotted something down in her binder, then looked up at Mae with a grin. "I'm glad they could make it."

"Me too," Connor said, mischief in his eyes. Mae buried a laugh and studied the outline of table one. What a happy, fictional family they all made.

And it wasn't like Sierra and Barbara were total strangers. They were the only Townsends she'd met outside of her dad's funeral. Mae had once come across a Polaroid of herself at age three, sitting at a small table with the young Black girl with her same nose. Her mother had explained that that was the year Sierra and Barbara visited for Thanksgiving. Mae and Sierra had looked so happy in the photo, Mae's mouth open mid-cackle, Sierra smiling cheerily at the camera, tiny cup in hand from Mae's plastic tea set. If Mae was three then, Sierra would have been about seven. Looking at that Polaroid (which she'd plucked from the photo album and tucked into the back of her Hello Kitty notebook for safekeeping), the idea cemented in Mae's mind that she wasn't really isolated from her dad's side of the family because she was clearly close with her cousin Sierra.

Her dad never had much to say when Mae asked him about Sierra. A niece he saw only once a year didn't draw up the same nostalgia as his childhood memories. But that didn't stop her from spinning fantasies whenever Madison bothered her. If Sierra had been the one living three blocks away, Mae would think, Sierra wouldn't get weirded out by Mae's hair-washing routine. Sierra wouldn't insist on being banker every time they played Monopoly. Sierra wouldn't pout until Mae agreed to switch bowls with her just because Mae's scoop of ice cream had more cookie dough bits than hers. Sierra was the best cousin anyone could ask for, as far as Mae's imagination was concerned.

Which tinged Sierra's RSVP a special shade of cruel.

Table one done, Mae and the Rutherfords moved on to filling out the other tables. She shoved Madison and her parents at table eighteen, in a corner by the restrooms. Susan gave her an odd look but didn't comment.

"Have you decided on the song for your first dance yet?" Susan asked when the seating chart was complete.

Mae and Connor shared a look, silently deciding who would

break the news that they'd once again neglected their duties. He held strong at first, until she quirked a brow.

"Not yet," said Connor, shooting Mae a playful glare.

"Well, you'll have some help now," Susan said, her eyes bright. She turned to John. "Honey?"

"Christopher Walker is going to choreograph your first dance!" John announced. He'd started speaking slowly, as if to build suspense, but the words spilled out in a rush of excitement.

"Christopher Walken?" Connor said.

"Walker," Susan corrected. "I know you're self-conscious about your dancing, and we thought it might make you more comfortable to work with a choreographer."

Connor scratched the back of his neck. "I wouldn't say self-conscious. We just didn't think a first dance was necessary."

"It's more than necessary," John said. "It's tradition. And Christopher Walker is the best you can get. He was a guest judge on *So You Think You Can Dance*."

"Oh, wow," Mae said. She bit her lip. "That's amazing. But you don't need—"

"We *wanted* to," Susan said, beaming at Mae. "You're going to his studio the Wednesday after next."

"What if we had plans?" Connor asked.

"For Christopher Walker, you cancel plans," John said.

Mae could see Connor's mind working in the way his eyes roved around the room. When his gaze settled on Mae, he raised his eyebrows in a silent question. She responded with a subtle shrug. She couldn't be the one to tell the Rutherfords the thought of taking dance lessons made her want to sink into the floor. The refusal had to come from their son.

"Okay," Connor said slowly. "If we have to."

Mae dropped her eyes to the table. Connor's willingness to do whatever his parents asked did make her wonder who he'd be loyal to, if it came down to it. If his parents made one of those careless comments the Parkers always made around Mae, would he call them on it? Or would he let it slide? It was hard to be sure.

As John and Susan chattered about how they came to meet Christopher Walker, Mae felt Connor nudge her foot under the table. She looked up.

Paris, he mouthed.

Her disappointments quickly dissipated. Paris was their bright spot at the end of the aisle. When the wedding plans escalated past the point of reason, somewhere around talk of multiple ice sculptures, Mae and Connor hunched over his laptop one night and decided to splurge on something for themselves. The promise of a Parisian honeymoon worked to brighten their spirits. Mae felt she could make it through anything if her reward was two weeks in Paris with Connor.

So, Connor's quick acquiescence was probably just that, another obligation to tack onto the list. Probably.

Spouting off more of Christopher Walker's credentials, John pulled up a video of the choreographer in action. They all sat there staring at a phone screen as a muscular man roamed a dance studio giving orders, correcting dancers' positions, and breaking into an intricate pose whenever a demonstration was needed. Mae had to wonder just how much money Susan and John were paying him to lend his expertise to two uncoordinated duds.

While John searched for another video that he wanted to show them, Mae checked Instagram to pass the time. She swiped through the pictures on her feed: Jayla's cat napping in a square of sunlight, her bridesmaid Krystal's new colorful tattoo of a parrot, an artsy shot of a pregnant belly that Mae quickly moved past. Madison had been posting about her pregnancy nonstop. Worse, she expected Mae to fly to California for her baby shower in October. But Mae hadn't figured out how to say no yet. Somehow a cross-country flight did seem easier than explaining how a childhood of microaggressions had dug their way into her, leaving invisible pinpricks beneath her skin and a confused notion of what family was. What it meant. What you were supposed to tolerate. Where the limit was, if there was one at all.

Mae kept scrolling. She wouldn't solve all that today.

She stopped at a post from Sierra. A small plate held a neat, square dessert: perfect layers of wafer cookies, banana slices, and pudding, topped with browned meringue and cookie crumbs. It looked like a fancy version of the banana pudding her dad used to get from a bakery in their neighborhood. He'd told her his mom rarely made dessert, but that this pudding was one of the few she did make. It was always a momentous occasion, he'd said, to come home and see a box of Nilla wafers and a bunch of ripe bananas sitting on the counter.

Mae eagerly scrolled down to read the caption.

Banana pudding is the first dessert I ever learned to make. My grandma taught me how when I was six. Watching pudding thicken over the stove, layering Nilla wafers and banana slices, whipping egg whites into stiff peaks, I fell in love with baking.

My grandma died yesterday. The first thing I did after she passed was make this dessert, just the way she taught me. For a second it was like she was there in the kitchen with me again. This one's for you, Grandma.

Mae tried to make sense of the words, the picture, the iron heaviness landing in her stomach. Her grandmother was dead. Her grandmother was dead, and she'd never known her. Her only memories of her were a firm hug at her dad's funeral, a stone-faced expression, the scent of jasmine, a no-nonsense voice, a Southern accent more pronounced than her dad's. That was it. Five details gathered over two days to describe a woman she should have known for a lifetime.

Mae had told herself it was just the grief that colored their meeting. She'd thought that one day, in the future, she'd be able to see her grandmother on better terms. Then maybe she could really get to know her and get a glimpse of the woman from her dad's stories.

But now, she would never know that version of her grandma. The lioness who stared down her dad's principal until he cowered and admitted that perhaps her son hadn't cheated on his math test after all. The drill sergeant who threw open her kids' doors every Sunday morning without fail to announce it was time for church—and yet was also the first to take the lord's name in vain in uniquely foul ways at every minor inconvenience. The secret softie who had shed a tear at her daughter Phyllis's piano recital, then adamantly denied it and claimed she'd never cried a day in her life.

Mae couldn't decide what this heavy feeling was—if she was sad, if she was sad that she wasn't sadder, if it was possible to mourn something you never had. Getting Sierra's RSVP last week had been proof that her grandma had done her part and passed Mae's wedding invitations to the rest of the Townsends. Her grandma had done her that kindness, helped Mae take a step toward forging a connection, and then she'd gone and died.

Mae swallowed past the growing lump in her throat. John hit play on the next Christopher Walker video, but she could only stare at the seating chart, a corner still speckled with discarded paper tabs. There she was, a neon-yellow *Althea Townsend* who would never make it to the wedding. Mae reached over and peeled it off the board, then studied it, stuck to her finger.

"All right, let's get some lunch," John announced, snapping her out of her thoughts.

Mae followed them out the door in a daze. On the walk down St. Paul Street, she held Connor's hand and half-listened as John raved about Christopher Walker's many talents.

In Mae's other hand, she fiddled with the sticky paper tab on her finger. Her thoughts swam with whipped egg whites, banana pudding, and one hazy Thanksgiving many years ago.

CHAPTER THREE

Going through the motions of a normal workday felt impossible when Mae's mind was miles away.

She spent the next few days in her home office, doing her work as a remote project manager for a marketing firm. She led calls with clients, adjusted schedules, and used the word *deliverable* more often than she would have liked.

But throughout the day, she'd snatch pockets of time to indulge in her new daily habit: searching for scraps of information about her grandma. An obituary, funeral details, anything. She hoped it would give her closure somehow, help her make peace with the heavy realization that she'd never know her grandma. She could even put the funeral on her calendar, think of her at the same exact time as the Townsends, feel like they were all united in something for once.

On Wednesday, she turned up a page for Althea Townsend on the Bethel Family Funeral Home's website. Mae read the obituary eagerly, soaking in the minimal details about Althea Townsend's roots in Hobson, her love of feeding her family, the profound impact she had on the people she met, that she was survived by a list of names that did not include Mae. She accepted this omission, letting the disappointment take root but refusing to dwell on it.

She scrolled further down, seeing funeral details at the bottom of the page. Friday, June 16, 10:00 a.m., at the Grace Community Church. Jackpot.

But as she added it to her calendar, she felt nothing. She imagined her calendar popping up with a notification on Friday, cheerily announcing *Time to mourn Grandma!*

A quick mourning between meetings wouldn't make her feel more connected to the Townsends, she realized. It would just make her feel further away.

But she couldn't just...go to the funeral.

Could she?

No. She had work tomorrow and Friday. And she hadn't told Connor a thing about her new search obsession. Ever since informing him of her grandmother's death, he'd been especially attentive all week, asking her *How are you feeling today?* as soon as he got home from work. Faced with his sympathetic brown eyes, Mae had shrugged it off and launched into the drama of a client's dissatisfaction with an ad campaign. It was easier that way. She had no reason to be anything other than fine.

And yet, she'd spent ten minutes crafting a text to her best friend Jayla on Monday, taking great care to show she didn't care, sharing the news like a mundane discovery, like that time she'd gone all day wearing her shirt backward and hadn't noticed.

Oh, yesterday I learned my grandma on my dad's side died, she'd written. She briefly added a confused-face emoji, then decided that little yellow icon with its sad, crooked half-frown was too revealing and deleted it.

Sending the text made Mae feel like she was fishing for something, except she didn't know what.

JAYLA: You ok? I'm free now if you wanna talk

Panic rose in Mae as all the feelings she'd tried to squash threatened to reveal themselves. She typed out a hasty response before she could change her mind.

MAE: Oh haha yeah I'm fine haha! Just thought it was random, that's all haha.

That was definitely too many *hahas* to use when discussing a death. Any more than zero was too many. Jayla just reacted with a heart, thank god, and that was that.

Mae channeled that maniacally unaffected version of herself now as she sifted through emails. She wasn't going to take tomorrow off work to drive five hours to North Carolina and attend a funeral she wasn't invited to. She'd just been looking for the funeral details to give herself peace of mind. Now she had the details. Ergo, her mind was at peace.

Except she couldn't sleep.

Mae laid awake that night thinking about how Grace Community Church was probably a big space. It had to be, to make room for the community and all. She imagined herself slipping into a pew in the back, hair up, eyes down, and no one would recognize her.

She rolled onto her stomach and buried her face in her pillow. She turned to one side and came face-to-face with a snoozing Connor, getting a whiff of his sleeping breath. She turned to the other side and stared at the hamper piled high with laundry. She'd have to do laundry tomorrow. (Assuming she was here tomorrow, a small voice said, and Mae killed the thought.)

Finally, she slipped off her bonnet, pushed back the covers, and eased out of bed. There was only one place where she could make sense of the jumble in her mind right now. She shut the bedroom door gently behind her and crept through the dark hallway. When her feet reached the cold linoleum of the kitchen, she turned on a switch and the room flooded with light. On the counter, she spotted a box of Cheez-Its, her usual late-night snack.

But mindless snacking wasn't enough tonight. She needed to make something, get lost in the meditative act of cooking. Mae stared into the fridge, looking for possibilities. Half-empty takeout containers of rice and Szechuan shrimp from when they'd ordered Chinese two days ago. A carton with two eggs remaining. Half a lemon from the fish tacos she'd made on Saturday. A bunch of grapes. A quarter of an onion wrapped in foil. A half-used block of extra-sharp cheddar.

Somewhere amid the culinary equations running in her head came a memory: sitting in a red vinyl booth at the Skyline Diner with her dad on the Saturday mornings when her mom was working a shift at the hospital. Mae always ordered blueberry pancakes; he always got scrambled eggs and bacon with a side of grits. But every time the grits arrived, looking pale and glue-y, he'd lean toward Mae and whisper, like a secret, *My mom makes 'em better.*

Mae, then wrinkling her nose at that bowl of mush, had been mystified to learn his mom's version often included cheese and shrimp. He'd once explained grits to her by comparing them to oatmeal, and the prospect of cheesy, shrimpy oatmeal was beyond her childhood imaginings. It didn't sound *good*. But her dad had taught her enough to know that her grandma made the best food in the world.

Mae let the fridge door swing shut as a bolt of inspiration struck her. Grits. She could make grits. Nothing she'd ever made or eaten before, but it felt like the perfect use for this restless late-night energy coursing through her.

She crossed to the bookshelf they used as a pantry, nudging aside dried beans and sushi rice until she found the cornmeal. Not grits, but they were both made from corn, right? The logic checked out.

Mae pulled up a recipe on her phone for Southern-style cheese grits and fluttered about the kitchen, her mind clearing with purpose. She put cream and water in a saucepan, then shook in the spices. As the mixture warmed on the stove, she measured out the cornmeal and grated the cheddar. Then she hovered over the saucepan, breathing in the simmering liquid. She could picture her dad as a kid, smelling this savory aroma, coming into the kitchen with his siblings to bombard their mom with questions and sneak a taste.

She couldn't help it—she dipped her finger into the pot, even though she knew it was basically just spicy, watered-down cream at this point. Surely her dad had taste-tested a few dishes too early in his day.

The cream mixture was warm but not scalding. Mae sucked on her finger and closed her eyes. The rich cream mellowed out the cayenne's heat, but she could feel its pleasant sting in the back of her throat.

"What are you doing?"

She opened her eyes. Connor leaned against the doorway in his rumpled white shirt and boxer-briefs, brow knitted in curiosity.

Mae pulled her finger from her mouth as casually as she could manage. "Just making grits."

Connor scratched his head, leaving his sandy hair even more disheveled, and peered into the saucepan where the cream mixture bubbled away. He turned back to her, his eyes slow-blinking and sleepy. "At two a.m.?"

Mae dumped the cornmeal into the saucepan and started stirring. "I couldn't sleep."

"Any reason?"

Mae kept stirring, breaking up lumps with her wooden spoon. Finally, she glanced up at him. "Is it weird to miss someone you never really knew?"

The crease in his brow relaxed. Mae supposed he'd been waiting for this, waiting for her to stop insisting she was fine. Connor loved talking about feelings. Mae liked to bottle them up, slap a cork in them and let them age like the wine in his parents' cellar. Connor liked to lay them out in the open, sort them into little piles until everything made sense, like transforming a mountain of useless pennies into a neat roll of coins.

"Not at all," he said softly.

The cornmeal mixture was angry now, spitting at her for turning away. Mae kept stirring, trying to get it as smooth as the hissing bubbles would let her. At last, she lowered the heat and covered the pan, then turned around to face Connor, leaning against the counter.

"With the wedding coming up, I've been thinking about my family more. Like…this barbecue my dad flew to North Carolina for every year. How come he never let me go with him?" She tapped her nails on the counter, thinking. "And I get that his side of the family wouldn't want to come up for the wedding since we don't really know each other, but why would Sierra go out of her way to send that RSVP just to hurt me?"

All traces of sleep had left Connor's face. He was watching her intently, listening and processing. "What are you thinking?" he asked. Like he knew there was more she wasn't telling him, more she was gathering courage for.

Mae picked a shred of cheddar cheese off the pile on the counter and rolled it into a ball between her fingers. She could ask herself these questions forever and still never know the answers. Pretending she didn't care got her nowhere when she'd spent so much time googling her grandma's name, stalking Sierra's Instagram, cobbling together fragments to form the tiniest pinhole glimpse into her family. She had to break the pattern, take a bigger step.

Mae sucked in a breath and looked up. "I want to go to the funeral."

"Then you should," he said, like there was nothing to it. "Do you know when it is?"

"I found it online. It's Friday morning."

"Then go. You should see your family."

His words were validating, like it wasn't a ridiculous idea at all. Like it actually could be this easy, to just get in her car and drive. She turned to check on her not-grits and give them a stir. "But they don't know me."

"They'll know you if you go."

Mae suspected garnering a reputation as a funeral-crasher might not be the best way to connect with her family. But it might be her only option. "Okay," she said, feeling lighter already. "I'll go."

"Good." He slid next to her, putting a hand on her back and leaning toward the pan. "How's it looking?"

"Almost there, I think?" Mae scooped up a spoonful and watched it fall to the pan in thick ribbons. "Hopefully this is looking right."

When the mixture took on a creamy consistency, she removed the pan from the heat and stirred in the grated cheddar, then a pat of butter. While Connor looked on, she poured the makeshift grits into a bowl, dumped the leftover Szechuan shrimp on top, and finished it off with a flourish of freshly ground black pepper.

"Shrimp and grits," she announced, gesturing to the bowl with fanfare. "Sort of."

"Looks good to me." Connor handed her a spoon. He contemplated his own spoon as they took seats at the table, bowl of faux grits between them. "Do you want me to come with you?"

Mae pictured it, showing up to a funeral with Connor in tow. The exiled Townsend and her white fiancé in the flesh. "I think it's bad enough that I'm crashing a funeral. I should probably go alone."

"I could still drive you," he offered. "I'll hide out in the parking lot."

"That wouldn't be creepy at all." She took his hand across the table, squeezed it with a silent thanks—for his offer, for being so thoughtful that he'd volunteer to drive five hours for her family's funeral, while she was too paranoid to spend five minutes alone with his parents. "I'll be fine," she said, digging her spoon into the grits. "But thank you."

The grits were lumpy, but the flavor was incredible: the garlic and onion powder, the cayenne's heat lingering after every bite, the creamy tang of the cheddar. It had all the savory, carb-laden richness of mashed potatoes, but better. If this dish was anything like her grandma's, no wonder her dad was so disappointed by the Skyline Diner's pale imitation.

"I'm amazing," she decided.

"Of course you are."

She grinned and went for another bite, this time with the shrimp. She doubted her grandma's shrimp and grits involved Chinese takeout, but it sort of worked, the sweet, spicy shrimp and the creamy grits. "It's supposed to be grittier," she admitted. "And less Szechuan-y. But I had to improvise."

"Tastes great to me," Connor said. He hefted another large spoonful into his mouth, then considered her thoughtfully. "Why did you tell my parents Sierra's coming to the wedding? And there was someone else, wasn't there?"

"Barbara," Mae supplied automatically. "Sierra's mom. She's the oldest of my dad's siblings. The responsible one, he always said."

He nodded slowly. "Why'd you say they were coming?"

Mae let her spoon sink into the bowl. He'd probably held off on asking, in light of her grandma's death, but she'd known he'd question her eventually. She tapped the side of her bowl in thought. "I guess...I didn't want to admit that I don't have a lot of family coming. It's too pathetic."

He softened. "No, it's not."

"I'll figure something out. I could hire actors. Or maybe I can get Amber to come," she said, naming her favorite Parker cousin. "She's teaching English in Japan for the summer, but maybe she'll sign a written statement for me. 'Mae isn't pathetic,' something like that."

"Very convincing." Connor studied her for a moment, then tipped his head back, thinking. "What if Sierra and Barbara came down with the flu two days before the wedding? Wouldn't that be a shame?"

A smile slowly came over her. "Really?"

"My parents always partner with a shelter to donate leftovers after weddings anyway," he said. "They'll just get a couple more donations than usual. Everybody wins."

"Everybody wins," Mae repeated. She held his gaze, feeling a rush of appreciation, and leaned over to kiss him. She pulled back, met his boyish grin, and went back to her grits.

Her plans solidified as they ate. They decided she would make the drive tomorrow, attend the funeral on Friday, keep Saturday open to spend with her relatives, and drive back Sunday in time to get back to work and make their dreaded first dance lesson with Christopher Walker next week. She was entitled to two bereavement days for extended family, so she could make the trip without touching the PTO she'd earmarked for Paris.

It was strange how something she'd spent two days agonizing over could be resolved in a simple conversation over fake grits at nearly 3:00 a.m. on a weekday. Connor had a way of doing that— cutting through the thoughts tangling in her head and offering simple solutions. She felt the impulse to give him the other issue she'd been wrestling with, confess her fears about being the odd one out in his family.

But she didn't want to go there tonight, or this morning, or whatever she could call this magical in-between time that had them pretending they didn't have responsibilities tomorrow, didn't owe loyalty to that meal called breakfast. They'd solved one problem, and she could worry about the next one later. For now, they could sit at the kitchen table and keep doing this: eating cheesy quasi-grits and cold Szechuan shrimp, wondering how Christopher Walker felt about cowbells, and debating how many patisseries they could visit once they made it to Paris.

When Mae went back to bed, sleep pulled at her eyelids just as easily as Connor's arm slotted around her waist. In a little over a day, she would be attending her grandmother's funeral, meeting the Townsends, and taking her first steps toward building a bridge to her distant relatives. Some of them might even want to come to the wedding once they got to know her. And how convenient that her lie about the seating chart opened up a couple of spots for them.

And she wasn't really crashing the funeral. The funeral home had posted the details. It was public knowledge. She was the public.

It would be fine, Mae assured herself. That tangled mess of worries was still somewhere in her head, waiting to ensnare her, but she ignored it. She would drive to North Carolina and meet her family and everything would be fine. She was sure of it.

CHAPTER FOUR

The strange thing about Grace Community Church was that it looked like an ordinary church.

Well, put like that, it didn't sound all that strange. Obviously, a church looked like a church. It was a one-story brick building with a slanted roof and a white steeple. Mae wasn't sure what the point of a steeple was, but churches had them, and this one was no different.

But that was the thing, she realized as she swung her car door shut and started across the parking lot. She'd *expected* it to be different. She'd expected a lot of differences since arriving in Hobson yesterday. As the place where the elusive other half of her family lived, she'd built up Hobson—and North Carolina by extension—in her mind for so long. Growing up in California, North Carolina had felt a world apart. So, in her head, it *was* a world apart. It was supposed to be every depiction of the South she'd ever seen in movies and on TV. The second she crossed that border into North Carolina, she was supposed to smell the smoky, sweet aroma of barbecue. A banjo would inexplicably start playing in the distance. The water in her Hydro Flask would miraculously transform into sweet tea—or maybe moonshine. One or the other.

But it was all so ordinary. No barbecue, no banjo, no moonshine. It was definitely a good ten degrees warmer here— right now it was a balmy eighty-three and it wasn't even 10:00 a.m.—but the humidity here felt the same as it did in Maryland. The motel she'd checked into looked like an off-brand Motel 6. And Grace Community Church was any other church.

Except her family was inside.

The thought sent a nervous thrum through her middle. She ran a hand up the nape of her neck, already sweating in the heat. Just ahead of her, a pair of old, Black ladies in wide-brimmed hats stepped out of a weathered sedan. Mae fell into step behind them, not minding that she had to slow her stride. She watched a strand of gauzy ribbon on the woman's hat in front of her, observed how it swayed with every movement. She was close enough to hear the women talking, notice that at least the Southern twang in their words was a difference between here and Baltimore, and then one of the women said they had to stop by CVS after this to pick up a case of Cokes for the reception.

Mae's heart thudded. So, there was a reception too. But it wasn't the time to wonder where it was and how to get there, because now the church's open doors were coming into view, and she could see the throng of people filling up the pews. People who had no idea she was here. People who might take her presence badly if the Townsends' years of silence toward her was anything to go by. Suddenly, Mae wished she had a hat to hide under, too.

That rush of confidence she'd felt making these plans with Connor the other night was nowhere to be seen now. It had escaped the moment she'd crossed the border into North

Carolina yesterday, seen the welcome sign with its image of the state flag billowing carefree in an invisible breeze, and known it was a lie, because she couldn't be welcome if no one knew she was coming.

Her worries multiplied the deeper she drove into North Carolina, and by the time she reached her motel room, a massive bundle of nerves sat unmoving in her ribcage. She perched on the edge of her bed and called Jayla.

"I made it," she said.

"Good. How was the drive?" Jayla's voice was always soothing. Jayla could be held hostage and she'd still sound like a yoga instructor heading into downward-facing dog. Mae loved this about her right from the moment they'd first met, in a study group for an anthropology course, their sophomore year at Howard. While Mae's response to getting a C on her first midterm was creating a thick deck of flashcards, making an alphabetized twelve-page study guide, and assembling a study group, Jayla had been the one to make sure they took snack breaks and got home at a reasonable time.

"It was good," Mae said half-heartedly, kicking her shoes off. She rolled her stiff ankles in small circles, then paused and looked down at the damp spots on her socks. The carpet was wet. How wonderful. She hoped it was only because the cleaning staff had just given it a vigorous shampooing. With a shampoo that happened to smell like a musty old tablecloth.

"Really?"

Mae sighed and laid back on the bed. The mattress squeaked in indignation. "Well, I kept trying to imagine what the funeral would be like."

"You've been to funerals," Jayla pointed out.

"Yeah, my dad's and my grandparents'. But this is Black, in the South, in a Baptist church."

"And it's your family," Jayla reminded her softly. "It's not gonna be as different as you think."

"I don't know. The research I did was pretty wild."

"You did not do research."

"I watched *A Madea Family Funeral* this morning," Mae confessed.

A beat of silence, and then Jayla erupted into laughter. Mae followed suit, giggles loosening her knot of nerves. The conversation fell into lore about the Madea cinematic universe, Jayla describing the gory gift her cat had left her that morning, Mae walking her through every detail of her mildewy motel room. Mae had gone to bed that night feeling again like there was nothing to worry about.

But now, there was the sun, her sweat, the slow shuffle of the women ahead of her as they inched ever closer to the church—all blending into a whisper that she didn't belong, that neither Jayla's calming words nor Madea herself could save Mae from this slow-motion disaster she was surely barreling toward.

The ladies hobbled their way inside and Mae crossed the threshold at last. She quickly side-stepped into the back row, sliding all the way in.

Once safely nestled in the corner of her pew, Mae let out a quiet sigh and relaxed into her seat. She'd done it. She'd made it to the funeral and the world hadn't imploded. She scanned the room, looking for faces she might recognize, bringing forth mental images of her relatives: the tear-stained blur of her dad's funeral, faded photos in her dad's old albums, profile pictures from social media accounts, the smattering of non-food photos on Sierra's Instagram.

She studied faces across the aisle, but from her spot in the back, she didn't see anyone familiar. Her dad's immediate family was probably in the front. So she leaned forward and inspected the backs of heads instead.

Could that woman in the front row, in the purple top with dark, relaxed hair in a bob, be her Aunt Phyllis, who won the district spelling bee at age twelve? Could the man beside her with the ring of graying hair surrounding a bald head be her Uncle Wendell, who once got a bee sting on his tongue while eating a Popsicle at the park? Wendell had had hair the one time she'd met him, but maybe he'd started balding in the last few decades.

Mae knew these questions were fruitless, that anyone could be anyone, but she couldn't stop herself. The fact that she was related to at least some of the people in this room practically had her skin buzzing with excitement. The only person who seemed more curious than Mae was a boy who looked about two years old, standing in the pew across from her. The woman next to him had one arm around his waist, trying to keep him still, but he squirmed in every direction, large brown eyes searching the room restlessly. When his eyes met Mae's, she instantly felt a sense of camaraderie with this little boy, whoever he was, who *got* it.

She waggled her fingers in a wave. He squealed and buried his head in his mom's shoulder, then popped back up an instant later. He squealed again, and Mae grinned. At least someone was glad she was here.

After he wriggled in a different direction and found a new distraction, Mae went back to searching. The people entering the church paid her no mind, kept walking until they found a pew closer to the front. But then Mae spotted a face that was undoubtedly familiar: a woman about her age with round eyes, curly hair pulled into a low ponytail, and a nose like Mae's.

Sierra.

Mae swallowed and averted her gaze. The last thing she needed was the author of the unregretful RSVP confronting her to deliver a harsher message in person. Mae faced forward, focusing all her attention on the large picture of her grandmother at the front of the room. It was strange to reconcile this woman, with the short, gray curls and the wrinkles and the laugh lines, with the sad, serious version of her Mae had met at her dad's funeral.

But it wasn't long before Mae cheated a glance to the side, looking for Sierra once again. The lure of her in this room was too strong to ignore. She scanned the pews, looking past possible Aunt Phyllis and maybe Uncle Wendell to all the rows behind them. She spotted the back of Sierra's head—that low ponytail— leaning in toward a woman already seated. Sierra was taller than Mae expected, maybe somewhere around five-foot-nine to Mae's five-five. She wore a silky, collared black blouse tucked into black slacks. There was something commanding about the way she stood, one hand on the pew, the other on her hip.

Mae faced forward when a man rose to the lectern at the front and gave an opening statement that morphed into a prayer. Mae went along with it, bowing her head when everyone else did, even though her parents had never taken her to church in her life. Then the woman Sierra had been speaking to stood from her pew and moved to the lectern. Mae studied her face, a flash of recognition coming to her. This was her aunt Barbara. She could still picture her at the back of the church at her dad's funeral, eyes narrowed in indignation, whisper-fighting with Mae's mom. But she'd been kind to Mae. When Barbara had flown in for the funeral, she'd given Mae a tight hug and said, *It's been too long, sweetheart.* She'd been the only Townsend who'd launched into affection right away instead of delivering an awkward introduction.

Up at the lectern, Barbara gave a long look to the framed photo of Mae's grandma, then began her eulogy.

It was strange to feel nostalgia for something Mae had never experienced. But as Barbara spoke about Althea Townsend, sharing memories about her snarky humor, her iron-willed resolve, and her fierce love of her family and community, Mae wrapped herself in these stories like a blanket, wistful with the knowledge that she could have been part of these memories, too, in another life. She could have nodded knowingly when Barbara described the time Althea doggedly kept the church's food pantry open during a townwide power outage after a bad storm, or how Althea argued with a car salesman for six hours until he relented and gave her the price she wanted for the 1974 Toyota Corona that would faithfully see the family through twenty years of memories, from beach trips to Emerald Isle to driving lessons for the teenage Townsends. She wouldn't wonder why people laughed when Barbara referenced a raggedy purple shawl that Althea claimed could dress up any outfit, because she'd get it. She'd be in on the joke, too.

A shiver crawled down Mae's spine when Barbara described Althea's passion for cooking. She described the scatterbrained way Althea stored her recipes, jotting them down on scraps of paper she kept around the house, then graduating to storing them in an empty margarine tub. Mae thought back to all the times she'd written recipes on Post-its as a teen, because it was easier to take a Post-it to the kitchen than a heavy cookbook. Maybe, without even knowing it, she'd gotten that from her grandmother.

The thought opened a gate in her mind, a desperation to know everything about this woman, any other traits Mae had unknowingly inherited from her. But then Barbara was wrapping up her eulogy, and the minister was leading them in another prayer, and Mae was back to bowing her head and pretending.

When the minister concluded the service, Mae's throat tightened at the thought that this was the closest she could ever expect to feel to her grandmother—until he uttered a reminder that sent hope fluttering inside her: there would be a reception at Barbara's house immediately after the service.

People rose from their seats with purpose and started moving down the aisle. Mae eased out of her pew, then stood uneasily in the back debating her next move. Coming to the funeral service was one thing; the details had been posted publicly. But the reception was another matter. She had to score an invite, get the address. She had to talk to Barbara.

Mae waited by the doors, letting more people pass. Barbara was by the lectern, Sierra at her side. Then Barbara put her arm around Sierra and the two of them started walking toward the doors. Mae's heart thudded faster the closer they came.

Sierra noticed her first. Just a few feet from the exit, her eyes caught on Mae and held. Her stare was searching, like she was solving an equation. When her brow wrinkled, Mae gathered that Sierra had done the math and didn't like the answer.

"Mae?" Sierra said. Her penetrating voice seemed to ring throughout the church.

Barbara turned to stare at Mae too, a light of curiosity in her eyes. "Rodney's Mae?"

Just hearing her dad's name made her eyes sting. "Yeah," Mae said quietly.

"What are you…doing here?" Sierra asked.

It was a fair question. Politely asked, even—cautiously, like Sierra was afraid of any sudden movements Mae might make, as if Mae's surprise appearance had established her as completely unpredictable. But it stung anyway, the notion that showing up at her own grandmother's funeral was cause for interrogation.

Mae swallowed, searching for her voice. "I-I'm here for the funeral," she managed to say.

"But…why?" There was something existential about the way Sierra asked it, like she was demanding a truth deeper than any answer Mae was prepared to give.

As Mae shuffled through possible responses, she started to think she didn't have an answer at all. She'd spent the past few days trying to convince herself this wasn't important, trying to see reason in her unreasonable idea, this need to drive five hours to attend a funeral for a woman she didn't know. But there wasn't clear logic attached, only a pulsing need to be here, to be part of this, to know what it felt like to truly be a Townsend before she married into something else entirely.

Mae lifted her head to meet Sierra's eye, mustering as much resolve as she was capable of. "She's family."

Sierra was silent, studying Mae. She opened her mouth, but before she could speak, Barbara pulled Mae into a hug.

"Sweetheart," she whispered. The word curled around Mae, warming her inside out. Barbara pulled back, a hand still on her shoulder. "You have his eyes." A sad smile came over her. "You've always had his eyes."

Mae's throat felt thick and heavy. Not just from the mention of her dad, but the *always*, this small sign that Barbara had thought about her enough to invoke perpetuity.

"Thank you," she whispered. Under Sierra's cautious gaze and Barbara's wondering stare, Mae felt an urge to say more. "Your eulogy was beautiful. I wish I could have known her."

Barbara gave a sad chuckle. "She was a force."

A silence fell upon them. The church had nearly emptied now, and Sierra was wringing her hands, looking past them through the open doors with a detached impatience. Mae needed to spit it out, ask about the reception, but her mouth wouldn't form the words.

Althea wouldn't have had this problem, Mae guessed. The woman who could run a food pantry during a power outage and refused to leave a car dealership until she got the price she wanted could probably demand what she wanted with no hesitation.

If Mae and Althea shared a love of cooking, who was to say some of Althea's other traits weren't lying dormant in Mae, just waiting to come out?

"We should get going or everyone's gonna beat us there," Sierra told Barbara.

Seeing Barbara check her watch, a sense of urgency took over. "The reception," Mae blurted. "Can I—would there be room for me to come?"

A flash of hesitation crossed Barbara's face, but a warm smile took over so quickly that Mae wondered if she'd imagined it. "Sure," she said. "You came all this way. We'd love to have you."

Mae let out a relieved breath. Barbara recited the address, and Mae waved as they left through the exit. Barbara waved back. Sierra didn't.

She wouldn't be able to hide in the back and observe at the reception—and, deep down, she didn't want to. She wanted to talk to more people, hear them call her *Rodney's Mae*, listen to stories about Althea and her dad. While the thought of walking into a room of near-strangers and pulling them into conversation one by one made her want to duck under a pew, the alternative— coming all this way and leaving with nothing but a eulogy and a hug—was worse.

The reception was an opening. And it might just be wide enough for Mae to squeeze herself in and find a way to belong.

CHAPTER FIVE

The more relatives Mae spoke to at the reception, the more she dwelled on that flicker of hesitation she'd glimpsed on Barbara's face after the funeral. She was starting to suspect it wasn't just in her head.

It started with Aunt Phyllis—the real one, who Mae learned was not the lady in the purple top but a pleasant-looking woman with shrewd, serious eyes and relaxed hair pulled into a neat bun. Barbara had taken the time to introduce the two, telling Phyllis, "Rodney's daughter Mae came out here for this." Phyllis's smile stiffened immediately. And then Barbara, Mae's only ally, said something about needing to put out the deviled eggs and fled the scene, leaving Mae to try to interpret and disarm that uncomfortable look on Phyllis's face.

"It was a beautiful service," Mae tried.

"It was." Phyllis glanced around, as if looking for an escape. Defeated, she settled her gaze back on Mae. "It was nice of you to come down. From—where, again?"

"Baltimore," Mae supplied.

"That's right." Phyllis stared into her plastic cup, and Mae scrambled for something to say.

"I drove down yesterday. I'm here until Sunday. I'm staying at the Mossy View Motel." Mae didn't know why she name-checked the motel, as if it gave her more legitimacy. The Mossy View was not a place for anything legitimate. The chain on her door was broken, every inch of the carpet was slightly damp, and the parking lot had a strange, chemical smell she couldn't name.

"Good." After a long pause, Phyllis took a sip from her cup and asked, "How's that family of yours?"

Was that a dig? Mae tried to get a read on her face, as if a look alone could tell her whether that comment was aimed at Mae's mother, the Parkers in general, or the Rutherfords.

"They're good," Mae said timidly. She opened her mouth to ask Phyllis about her family—she had two sons, if Mae was remembering correctly—but then Phyllis said someone was calling for her and left Mae standing alone. When Mae looked over her shoulder, she couldn't see anyone waving Phyllis over—but she did catch sight of Phyllis slipping into the kitchen.

Well. Mae chewed her thumbnail and tried to assess. Phyllis hadn't led with a hug like Barbara, but the conversation had been cordial, mostly. Maybe Phyllis was just a terrible conversationalist. Spelling bee winners weren't renowned for their social skills.

Deciding she'd earned a snack break, Mae moved over to the refreshments table. She slowly walked along it, taking mental inventory: a whole sliced ham, its edges dark and shiny. A colorful macaroni salad speckled with chunks of tomatoes, bell peppers, celery, and carrots in a creamy dressing. Deviled eggs loaded with filling and a healthy shake of paprika. Chunky potato salad a deep shade of golden yellow. Seeing it plucked a string in her chest. Her dad, who considered himself a potato salad connoisseur, said a sign of a good potato salad was what color it was. *If it's white, it ain't right*, he used to say.

She loaded her plate with a little of everything—and an extra-large scoop of potato salad. Mae brought a forkful to her mouth, tasting a sharp zing of mustard and sweet pickle relish. It was creamy, tangy, and so much better than the pale, bland potato salad Madison's mom made every Easter.

When someone brushed past her to grab a fork, Mae realized she was in the way and stepped aside. Beyond the clusters of people filling Barbara's living room, standing and talking to everyone except Mae, she noticed a series of framed photos on the wall by the bathroom. Mae moved closer, seeing several pictures of Sierra at various ages. An elementary school-aged Sierra smiled into the camera for her school photo, and then a teenage Sierra stood in the kitchen, proudly holding a pie. There was a picture of Sierra, Barbara, Althea, Phyllis, and others sitting around what looked like a Thanksgiving spread. Above that was an older, black-and-white photo of Althea with Mae's grandfather, who she remembered was named Herb. Her dad had a copy of that same picture in his photo album.

While Mae peered closer at the pictures, snippets of conversation floated in her ears. "Remember when she went after the head of the HOA when they said her grass was too tall?" a man was saying. Mae turned around, seeing a man of about fifty talking to a group standing by the sofa. His face was familiar— like her dad's, but familiar in another way too. This was her Uncle Wendell, she realized. He wasn't the bald man in the front pew after all. His hair was cropped closely against his head, and he had a goatee with graying stubble. She edged closer, inserting herself into the outskirts of the group.

"They never fined her again," he finished with a sad laugh. Mae laughed too, anything to belong. He rested his eyes on Mae, watching her with a scrutiny that jostled her nerves. She busied herself by shoving a large bite of potato salad into her mouth, which she instantly regretted.

"You're from the California contingent, aren't you?" he said. There was a touch of judgment in the way he said *California*.

"Mmhmm," she said, chewing desperately. She tried to make a joke of it, pointing to her mouth with a helpless smile, but his serious expression didn't change. At last, Mae gulped the food down and said, "I live in Baltimore now, but my mom and her side of the family are still in Bakersfield."

He gave a hum of acknowledgment, looking into his drink. "Your wedding's coming up, isn't it?"

A thrill zipped through her. Maybe he was planning on attending and had just forgotten about the RSVP deadline. "Yeah. Three weeks from tomorrow."

"Congratulations! That's very exciting." There was a slight warmth to his words, but he mostly sounded preoccupied. His eyes shifted somewhere off to the wall as he spoke. Mae followed his gaze to a blank square of wall next to the television. Maybe he'd learned all his conversational skills from Phyllis.

"Thank you." She hesitated, waiting for him to say whether he'd be coming to the wedding. He stayed quiet. "So the invitation reached you okay? I started to get worried when I didn't hear back."

"Oh." Wendell cleared his throat, looking pained. The man standing between them took a small step backward. "I won't be able to attend. I'm sorry."

She swallowed and glanced between him and the others in their group. This was her chance to explain herself, say why she'd invited them, why she'd come. "That's okay. I know it's a long drive. I just wanted to reach out to you all and—"

The woman next to Wendell leaned in and whispered in his ear, and he nodded like he was remembering something. "Sorry to interrupt," he told Mae, "I've got to check in with Barbara." The pair stepped away, leaving Mae with the two men standing near them. One busied himself with cramming a deviled egg in his mouth, while the other drained his can of soda like he was chugging a beer at a frat party. Mae sighed and went back to the refreshments table.

So it went every time Mae tried to insert herself into a conversation. If they weren't relatives she'd invited to the wedding, they were family friends who had clearly heard of her, because they would clam up as soon as she joined them, and the topic of conversation would suddenly change. After enough stiff expressions and polite nods, Mae gave up and went back to the refreshments table for another slice of ham. She was, coincidentally, very full now.

All she'd wanted was a chance to know her dad's relatives the way he had. Sunday dinners full of overlapping conversations, the bustling kitchen where people came to gather, the warmth and intimacy. The Phyllis who'd stayed up long past bedtime helping Mae's dad with his malfunctioning volcano science project couldn't possibly be the same Phyllis who panicked at the idea of being alone with Mae. And how was Wendell, the baby of the family, often painted in her dad's stories as the trusty sidekick, so willing to ditch Mae mid-conversation? Weren't sidekicks famously loyal?

She'd known seeing the Townsends at a funeral meant she once again wouldn't be catching them at their best. But this discomfort was something else entirely. Whatever kept her family apart had to run deeper than the story her parents always fed her. Althea disapproving of Mae's parents' marriage couldn't be the reason no one could handle talking to her for more than sixty seconds. There had to be something else. Something big.

If Barbara had been sympathetic enough to let her come to this, maybe she could shed some light on whatever Mae was missing. When Mae didn't see her in the living room, she started for the kitchen. She could pretend to be looking for a trash can for her empty plate, and when she ran into Barbara, she could compliment her on the deviled eggs, say she had a lovely home, and ask for an itemized list of Townsend family secrets. Easy-peasy.

When she drew closer to the kitchen, she paused at the sound of voices.

"Did she tell you she was coming?" a woman asked.

"No, she just showed up at the church," another woman—Barbara?—responded.

"What do you think she wants?"

"Maybe she's trying to recruit us all for her Pinterest wedding," said a different voice, one younger than the others. It sounded like Sierra. Several laughs rang through the room.

Mae's face burned. She took a shaky breath and retreated to the living room. So this was what it was going to be like around the Townsends. Just like the Parkers, just like the Rutherfords, she'd walk in and hear them talking about her. No matter what family she was part of, she'd always be on the outside looking in.

Rob and Laura's conversation about Mae's small guest list felt so innocent now compared to Sierra's wedding remark. What an absurd idea, that she could just show up out of the blue and they'd instantly welcome her with open arms because, what? They were all Black?

Evidently her Black family could alienate her just as well as her white family. At least they had that in common.

Mae eyed the front door across the room. Part of her was tempted to leave now, just take her empty plate and go. Her relatives clearly wanted nothing to do with her.

She glanced at the refreshments table, a plan forming in her mind. One more scoop of potato salad—hell, maybe she'd steal the whole platter; no use bothering with social norms anymore—a quick stop at the Mossy View to collect her things, and then she'd drive home today, sobbing and stuffing potato salad in her mouth all the way down I-85. As one does.

A familiar laugh pulled her out of her thoughts. She turned to follow the sound. Coming down the hall, being carried in a young woman's arms, was the two-year-old boy who'd sat in the row across from her. The boy who, once again, felt like her only friend here.

Mae gravitated toward the pair before she knew what she was doing.

"Who's this?" she asked, her voice pitching helplessly upward when she met the boy's large, brown eyes.

"This is Ethan," the woman said. "I tried to put him down for a nap, but he wanted to explore." She tapped his nose, which made Ethan giggle, and looked up at Mae. "I'm sorry, I don't think I know you."

Mae almost laughed. She knew how this would go. She'd say

her name and the woman would get weird and find an excuse to leave. "I'm Mae. Rodney's daughter." When the woman still looked at her blankly, Mae added, "Althea was my grandma."

"Your grandma," she repeated, like she was trying to piece it together. "Oh! Scott's uncle Rodney, the one who..." She grimaced and shook her head, dark curls bouncing with her. "Yes, okay, I've got it now. Sorry. I'm Desiree, Scott's wife."

Awkward rambling was a refreshing change from uncomfortable silence. Mae warmed to her instantly. "And Scott is... Phyllis's son?"

"That's right." Desiree's smile was kind and genuine. Probably because she'd married into the family and didn't know about whatever rift ran deep in the Townsend lineage. But that was fine. They could be ignorant together. "Where are you from?" Desiree asked.

"I drove down from Baltimore," Mae said for what felt like the twentieth time that day. The words were tired. She was tired. "It's a long story," she said with a wave of her hand. "More importantly, Ethan's the cutest baby I've ever seen."

Desiree lit up, and they were off. Desiree told her all about Ethan's latest obsession: grabbing potatoes out of the pantry and running around the house with them. Which, as far as Mae was concerned, obviously meant he was a genius. Potatoes were one of the most delicious carbs in existence.

They moved to the couch, where Ethan made a game out of toddling between the pair, demanding excessive cheers every time he reached one of them. Mae got caught up in sharing amused looks with Desiree and hyping up Ethan, letting herself relax into the couch—until a man came up to Desiree, an infant on his hip.

"Amara just had her most dramatic blowout yet," he said, an urgency in his words. He gestured to the baby, who couldn't be more than a year old, her lower half loosely wrapped in a navy-blue towel. "She needs a bath. So do I, frankly."

This had to be Mae's cousin Scott. His untucked black collared shirt and crooked glasses, apparent effects of his blowout struggle with Amara, clashed with his otherwise neat appearance. His hair and beard were closely cropped, and the cuffs of his pressed pants sat so precisely at his ankles that Mae guessed they were tailored.

"On that note!" Desiree said to Mae. "I was just talking to Mae," she told Scott.

Scott glanced at Mae, the briefest of knowing looks passing over him. "Hey," he said. "I heard you came down. It's good to meet you."

It was hard to know how much he meant it after seeing whatever flickered over his face, but Mae had to hope he was as genuine as Desiree. "You, too."

Desiree stood to follow Scott, hefting Ethan into her arms, then stopped and turned back to Mae. "Maybe I'll see you at the dinner tomorrow."

Mae didn't have it in her to reveal that she hadn't been invited to whatever this dinner was. But she relished the thought that Desiree—a Townsend in name only, but a Townsend all the same—wanted her there. "Yeah, maybe."

She watched Desiree and Scott walk toward the front door, Ethan and Amara in their arms. They couldn't go more than a few feet without someone stopping them to coo at one of the babies or chat them up. An elderly woman who had been tight-lipped when Mae introduced herself now leaned in to straighten Scott's glasses for him with a casual affection that made Mae's heart twist. When they finally made it through the door, everyone in their path resumed talking, reminiscing, expertly ignoring Mae.

Mae leaned against the couch. She couldn't bring herself to intrude on conversations anymore, but fleeing didn't feel right either. If she'd given in to her impulse the first time, she never would have had that moment with Desiree and Ethan. She had to believe another family moment was waiting for her here. She stayed where she was, silently observing, taking it all in.

Over time, the crowd thinned. As people trickled out the door, Barbara emerged from the kitchen and began walking around the living room collecting plates.

"I can do that," Mae piped up. Anything was better than the activity she'd been preoccupying herself with for the last several minutes, which was counting the number of pieces in the framed hummingbird puzzle on the wall by the window. She'd lost count somewhere after ninety-three anyway.

Mae half expected Barbara to give her one of the forced smiles the Townsends and their friends had perfected. Instead, Barbara said, "Okay. All the used plates and cups can go in the kitchen trash."

Mae slid into her new role like a second skin. Having something to do felt good after idling for so long, but it was more than that. Walking around this room with purpose, weaving between people and stacking plates and cups abandoned on the coffee table, the end table, the TV stand, she could let herself pretend helping out at her aunt Barbara's house was something she did all the time. Let herself imagine a world where her face appeared in one of those framed photos on the wall, where she'd hunched over the coffee table to help put together that hummingbird puzzle on a rainy Sunday, and she'd know exactly how many pieces it had because she'd done it.

She brought the plates and cups into the kitchen with that same energy, immediately zeroed in on the garbage can and stuffed everything in without hesitation. She took a step back, lungs swelling at the feeling of accomplishing something, being useful, no longer a lonely lurker in the corner.

Mae glanced at Barbara, busy scooping leftover macaroni salad into a plastic container. The kitchen was empty. This was her best chance to build on whatever tentative connection they'd forged.

"I was hoping to get to know some of our relatives today," Mae began.

"It's a funeral, not a party," came a voice behind her. Mae turned to see Sierra had joined them, a stack of small, ripped pieces of paper in her hand.

Mae pursed her lips, letting Sierra's remark wash over her. It sank deep into her skin, joining the comment she'd overheard about her Pinterest wedding. She took a breath, working out how to set the record straight. "It's more that...I hated that I never got a chance to get to know her before she died. I came here today because I wanted to hear what she was like. And I wanted to meet you all before..."

"Before we die, too?" Sierra supplied. There was a glint in her eye, and Mae couldn't tell whether she was mocking her or joking.

"Something like that, yeah," Mae said, managing a diffident smile. She watched Sierra sit at the table and start laying out the scraps of paper. "I'm not imagining it, am I?" Mae asked. "People seemed to not want anything to do with me."

"No, you're definitely not imagining it," Sierra said lightly.

"Sierra," Barbara warned.

"She asked!" Sierra protested, glancing between Mae and Barbara, her mouth slightly upturned. Mae realized she was enjoying this, addressing her questions in the bluntest manner possible, maybe even finding it funny. Something about Sierra's straightforward manner was refreshing. At last, a seed of truth after an afternoon of cold politeness.

"Why?" Mae asked. Sierra had now laid out all the paper scraps and was moving them around like she was completing a puzzle.

"Maybe it's weird to show up at a funeral unannounced," Sierra said.

"Is that all it is?" Mae pressed. "There's no other reason?"

Sierra tilted her head like she had answers she wasn't interested in sharing. But Barbara, closing the fridge on a mountain of Tupperware, heaved a sigh.

"Barbara?" Mae prodded. "Or—Aunt Barbara? I don't know what to call you."

Barbara chuckled. "Barbara's fine." She studied Mae for a few moments, then shook her head. "Some people hold grudges for longer than they should."

Mae held still, trying not to visibly react to this new piece of information. She carefully asked, "Why do they have a grudge? And who against?" Already her mind was reeling with guesses. Her mom? Her dad? All of them?

"Just things people probably should have moved past a long time ago," Barbara said with a wave of her hand.

Mae waited for Barbara to elaborate, explain, say something that didn't rival her old Magic 8 Ball in vagueness. Though at least Magic 8 Balls encouraged you to ask again later. Pressing Barbara any further felt like too much, too soon.

Barbara moved on to wiping down the counter in silence. Mae suppressed a sigh and glanced at Sierra, her reliable truth-teller. But Sierra was still focused on her bits of paper. She was tapping her nails on the table, looking through the paper scraps.

"What are those?" Mae asked.

"You and your questions," Sierra said.

Mae drew closer, bending down to peer at the tiny words written on the ripped scraps of paper. Most of the pieces were no bigger than a Post-it. *Smothered chicken. Shrimp and grits. Lamb chops. Fried chicken. Black-eyed peas. Chicken pot pie. Oyster dressing. Corn casserole. Barbecue sauce.*

Seeing these felt like being reunited with an old friend. The tiny handwriting was unfamiliar, but the dishes jumped out at her like memories. Her dad had talked about some of these. He'd told her about shrimp and grits on those mornings at Skyline Diner. And he'd mentioned oyster dressing and corn casserole once when Mae had asked him what his family ate at Thanksgiving. The barbecue sauce might have been something Althea made a big vat of for their annual Fourth of July event.

Mae studied every scrap, every word, for any trace of her grandma she could find. Under each title was a list of ingredients and a series of arrows pointing to one or several ingredients. Next to each arrow was a direction: *Combine, sear, sauté*. Some ingredients included quantities, but many didn't. They seemed more like mental notes for the recipe writer rather than an actual written recipe for someone to follow.

"Were these..." Again, Mae couldn't decide what to call her. *My grandma* was too possessive. *Our grandma* suggested a bond stronger than what she and Sierra actually had. *Althea* was too formal. "...her recipes?"

"Yeah," Sierra said, sounding distracted. "Bee, I still can't find the mac and cheese."

"That's everything from the margarine tub," Barbara said, taking a seat across from Sierra.

Mae flickered a glance between Sierra and Barbara—or *Bee*, as Sierra had called her. There must have been some cute story behind that nickname. Mae ached to understand it, be part of it. Instead of being so ostracized that the words *aunt* and *grandma* sat like hurdles for her to trip over.

Sierra caught her staring and gave her a puzzled look. Mae blinked and trained her eyes on the recipes, hurriedly searching for something to say. "You said you were looking for mac and cheese?"

"Yes," Sierra said, still eyeing Mae suspiciously. "I've been organizing Grandma's recipes. I want to get them into a system that's better than...this." She swept a hand over the recipe confetti. "But I can't find her mac and cheese recipe anywhere."

"But you have so many others," Mae said gently. She refrained from pointing out how lucky Sierra was to have a treasure trove of recipes before her, even if one was missing. If Sierra wanted to make their grandma's shrimp and grits, she wouldn't have to pull a recipe from a random food blog and hope for the best. She could just pick up a scrap and start cooking.

"Yeah, but..." Sierra straightened the scrap recipe for *Chicken pot pie*. "Mac and cheese is different." There was such finality in her tone that all Mae could do was nod and pretend she understood.

"What Sierra means is she's a vegetarian," Barbara supplied.

"Mom's mac and cheese was one of the only things she could eat at holidays. She always made sure it was on the table for her."

"That's sweet," Mae said. "She must have really loved you." That was possibly sucking up too much, but Mae was going for broke.

Sierra, who might have seen straight through Mae's words, only grunted. "She probably just loved guilting me. Remember?" She looked up at Barbara, faraway nostalgia in her eyes. "If I didn't clean my plate, she'd start going on about how she made it just for me and I wasn't showing my appreciation enough?"

Barbara chuckled. "That woman guilted every one of us. Making us show up at her house every damn holiday. 'I made a whole feast just for you!'" she said, assuming a croaky voice. "'Don't make me waste it!'" Barbara and Sierra laughed, but there was a sadness in their wistful expressions.

Mae, meanwhile, was staring at the recipe scraps, wishing she could commit each one to memory. Their reminiscing made her wish, more than anything, that she could have experienced Althea's guilting tactics for herself. Even just once.

A quiet fell upon the three of them. Mae imagined they were all thinking of Althea: Barbara and Sierra reflecting on everything they missed. Mae tallying all that she'd missed out on.

"I'm gonna go home and put these away," Sierra said, starting to pick up the recipe scraps. "Let me know if you find any more recipes," she told Barbara.

"Wait," Mae said. "Do you mind if I take a picture? I've heard a lot about her food, and I'd love to be able to try it."

Sierra hesitated. She picked up another scrap, stared at it, scratched her jaw. Then she peered at Mae, like she was weighing her trustworthiness. "Okay," she said at last. She returned the scraps she'd picked up back to the table, laying them out again. "Thanks." Mae stood and hovered over the table, positioning her phone's camera over as many recipes could fit in frame. She took a picture, then moved her phone around, getting a shot of the rest. No one spoke as she worked. She felt like she was intruding somehow, taking something she didn't have a right to. Like she was a documentarian capturing footage of a group she'd never belong to.

But she refused to feel weird about taking these recipes. Althea was her grandmother too. These recipes, this love of cooking and food they shared, were her birthright too.

Sierra collected the recipes and headed out, giving Mae nothing more than a cursory wave.

Left alone with Barbara, Mae stared at her hands. She knew she needed to excuse herself. But it was hard, forcing herself to leave a relative she'd spent her whole life wondering about. She glanced at Barbara, who was idly scraping at a mark on the table with her fingernail. Her dad's stories about Barbara had played up how she was the eldest, the sensible one their parents trusted most, who always caught him and Wendell when they were up to no good—like attempting to build a bonfire in their backyard, or plotting to jump from the roof to the tree outside their house—and kept them out of trouble. But there was more to her than that. The way she called Mae sweetheart. The hug she'd given her. The kindness she'd shown today while Mae waded through so many dead-in-the-water conversations. Mae couldn't help but wonder what else there was to know about Barbara—about everyone—if she only had the time.

"Thanks for inviting me today," Mae said. "Even if it didn't really go how I hoped."

Barbara sighed and leaned back in her chair, looking thoughtful. "A funeral's a hard time to get to know someone."

Mae nodded. Her dad's funeral had taught her that well enough. "I'm glad I got to meet everyone, at least. And see those recipes. My dad talked about your mom's food like it was gospel. He was always going on about how her grits were better than any he could get in a restaurant."

A misty smile overtook Barbara. "Rodney loved her grits. He'd beg her to make it and then complain if there was no shrimp. And then she'd lecture us about the price of shrimp and the value of a dollar."

Mae laughed, a little dazed and a little dazzled. All those stories her dad told about his family and now she got to hear one of them reminisce about him. "I tried to make her shrimp and grits a couple of nights ago," she confessed. "I wanted to know what they were like. Except I didn't have a recipe, or grits, and the only shrimp I had was leftover Szechuan."

"And how did that taste?" Barbara asked, letting out a surprised laugh.

"Weird. But good too." Mae pulled up the picture of the recipes on her phone and zoomed in on the one for shrimp and grits. "I'm excited to try again now that I have the real thing. I'm excited to make all her recipes." When she set her phone down, she looked up to see Barbara watching her with interest.

"You cook, do you?"

"I love cooking. I love *food*."

Barbara laughed again. Still, she studied Mae, looking her over pensively. "You know, Phyllis is having a dinner tomorrow night. Why don't you come along?"

Mae's breath hitched. An invitation. Barbara offered it like it was nothing, but to Mae it might as well have been written in calligraphy and presented under a shiny silver cloche.

"I—yeah. Yes. I would love to," she stumbled out.

"All right. Give me your number, and I'll text you the address."

Mae's heart thrummed with possibility when she left Barbara's that afternoon. The dinner invitation meant another chance to get to know her family and break past the shield of detached politeness they'd put up around her.

Beyond all that was one more reason to feel hopeful: Barbara's number in her phone. No matter what happened at dinner tomorrow, Mae had a way to get in touch with at least one Townsend now. A way that wasn't sending a wedding invitation into the void and hoping for the best. She and Barbara might be able to text or have the occasional phone call, even if it was just on holidays and birthdays. (Mae made a mental note to find out when Barbara's birthday was.)

Mae felt like she'd been handed a lifeline. She just needed tomorrow's dinner to go well enough that Barbara didn't regret it.

CHAPTER SIX

It wasn't lost on Mae that she was technically crashing an event. Again.

Standing amid the many plants adorning Phyllis's front porch, Mae consoled herself with the knowledge that at least Barbara had invited her this time. Then again, Barbara wasn't the one hosting this dinner. Phyllis might not even know she was coming.

At least Mae knew she had the right house. Several cars were parked in the driveway and on the street outside Phyllis's two-story craftsman home, and Mae could hear voices coming from inside. If yesterday's reception was any indication, those voices would probably deaden to silence as soon as she stepped inside. But if she stood in this sweltering heat for a minute longer, she'd sweat through her sleeveless top, and then she could add body odor to the list of things the Townsends could talk about behind her back. She summoned her courage and nudged a fern's leaves aside to ring the doorbell.

Within seconds, the door swung open.

"Hello!"

Mae found herself face-to-face with a tall, bald man. For a brief moment, they both stared at one another, pleasant faces firmly pasted on, each trying to figure out who the other was. She thought she remembered seeing him at the reception, but they hadn't spoken.

"I'm Mae," she offered. "Rodney's daughter. Barbara invited me."

"Ah!" He thrust out a hand. "Jeremiah, Phyllis's husband. I guess that makes you my niece."

"Good to meet you." Mae shook his hand. It was warm, rough, and inviting.

"Come in, come in." He stepped to the side and ushered Mae inside. "Did you bring something?"

Mae glanced down at the tray in her arm. She'd spent her afternoon holed up in her motel room hunched over her phone, zooming in on her pictures of Althea's recipes and trying to decipher her scratchy handwriting, hoping in vain to stumble upon a dish that could work within her motel room's limitations. She didn't have an oven or a stove, but she had...a coffee maker. A blow-dryer. An iron. In Mae's freshman year at Howard, she'd become an expert at making grilled cheese sandwiches in her dorm with the aid of an iron and a sheet of aluminum foil.

Somehow Mae doubted the Mossy View's iron was up to the challenge of doing Althea's chicken pot pie recipe justice.

Mae then spent an hour wandering the aisles of the Harris Teeter down the street from her motel. Cornbread was a classic side, but what if it didn't pair well with whatever Phyllis was making? Or suppose Phyllis was making her own cornbread, and then Mae showed up with the same thing? It was practically challenging her to a duel.

Mae had finally settled on a tub of hummus and a bag of pita bread, which she'd dropped onto the conveyor belt with a resigned sigh. Ina Garten would never, and she was pretty sure Althea Townsend wouldn't, either.

"It's hummus," she told Jeremiah. "Store bought. I haven't tried this brand, so I don't know if it's any good. I'd normally make something myself, but for all its redeeming qualities, the Mossy View Motel doesn't have kitchens in their rooms."

Jeremiah gave a hearty chuckle. "I'll make sure to let them know," he said. "Why don't we go to the kitchen and put this on a plate?"

Mae relaxed into a puddle of goo as she followed Jeremiah down the hall. Whatever grudges the Townsends held, Jeremiah evidently had no part in it. Then again, Jeremiah married into the family, so he wasn't technically a Townsend at all. Between Desiree and Jeremiah, Mae was two for two with the by-marriage crowd. Not quite the goal, but every infiltration had to start somewhere.

Mae didn't know where to look when she entered the kitchen. Phyllis stood at the stove pan-frying what smelled like fish, its breading turning a golden brown. Down on the tile floor, a twentysomething man she hadn't met was sitting with Ethan, the two of them engrossed in stirring a wooden spoon around an empty Dutch oven while Ethan chattered about potatoes. At the other end of the room, Scott sat at a long dining table bouncing a babbling Amara on his knee.

"Look who I found!" Jeremiah boomed when they entered the kitchen. Bless Jeremiah for serving as her emcee. "Barbara invited Mae, and she brought hummus. She'd normally make something, but she's staying at the Mossy View, so she had to improvise with store bought." Jeremiah had a wonderful way of making Mae's ramblings sound completely normal, delivered in a teasing but friendly tone.

Mae forced a smile. "Hey." Her voice came out shyer than she planned.

"Good to see you again, Mae," Phyllis said. Her expression was taut, like she was straining every muscle in her face to keep from grimacing. "Barbara told me you were coming."

"Thanks for having me," Mae said. She watched Phyllis lift a sizzling fish fillet out of the oil and place it on a plate lined with paper towels. "Can I help with anything?"

"I'm all right, but thank you." Phyllis didn't look up from the stove when she said this, but Mae decided she just took fish-frying very seriously.

Mae turned to Jeremiah, hoping he might know what to do, but he was busy at the counter, cutting a large pan of cornbread into neat squares. At least she'd been right about that.

Glancing between Ethan and the man on the floor, and Scott and Amara at the table, Mae felt like she was at the reception again, looking for a group to insert herself into.

"What's going on down here?" Mae asked, kneeling on the floor.

"Soup," Ethan replied matter-of-factly, stirring a wooden spoon around the empty pot.

"Potato and ketchup soup," specified the man, looking up.

Meeting his eye, Mae recognized him as the one who had chugged his soda to get out of talking to her at the reception. "I didn't catch your name yesterday. I was worried you might have died of thirst."

He broke into a sheepish smile. "Tyrese."

That sounded familiar. Mae remembered her dad mentioning a Tyrese occasionally. "Phyllis's son?"

"Yeah. And sorry, I didn't mean anything by it. I just can't deal with awkwardness."

Mae sat with that statement, wishing she could stop tiptoeing around these references and outright ask what the hell the Townsends had against her.

"Ty, another potato," Ethan directed.

"You got it." Tyrese hovered his fist over the pot, then opened the fist with a dramatic explosion sound.

Ethan burst into laughter. "More."

Tyrese and Ethan fell into a cycle of more explosive potatoes and Ethan's giggles. Mae, looking on next to them, hands sitting uselessly in her lap, started to feel like a third wheel. When Desiree entered the room, she waved brightly at Mae on her way to join Scott at the table—but before Mae could follow, the doorbell rang.

Jeremiah went off to answer it and returned with a posse behind him: Wendell, a woman who must have been his wife, and two teenage girls who, Mae gathered, were their daughters. The older one surveyed the scene, round eyes peeking from under her curly bangs, then poured her attention into her phone. The younger one, who looked to be about thirteen, her hair in cornrows dotted with bright-blue beads, shrieked at the sight of Ethan, who abandoned his wooden spoon and ran over to her. Tyrese took the chance to stand up, taking the empty soup vessel with him. Which left Mae, sitting alone on the kitchen floor for no apparent reason. Wendell gave her a curious look.

Mae stood slowly, brushing off her knees while kitchen hubbub swirled around her. Tyrese helped Jeremiah carry plates of food to the table. Desiree coaxed a fussy Amara into a high chair. Scott pulled plates from the cabinets and started setting the table. Wendell and Phyllis stood by the stove talking about something to do with plumbing. Somewhere in the mix, Barbara and Sierra entered the room. Unlike Mae, they didn't stand around awkwardly wondering what to do. Barbara joined in on the plumbing conversation, and the older teenage girl sidled up to Sierra to show her something on her phone.

Mae stood by the counter, invisible and yet so exposed, the only person standing in the corner while family happened around her. She smoothed down the front of her shirt just to have something to do, but her eyes stayed on the scene unfolding before her. This was the busy kitchen that had been at the center of so many of her dad's stories—she just wasn't really part of it. It was a lonely feeling, but a strange fascination captured her, too, in that same documentarian way she'd felt when she was taking pictures of Althea's recipes yesterday. This was what a Townsend family dinner was like. At long last, she was finally here.

"Roll call!" Jeremiah announced. All at once, the room quieted. Mae's head swiveled back and forth, searching for a cue. Was she supposed to raise her hand and say *Present*?

"Sprite," Scott said.

"Coke," said Tyrese.

"Water," said the older teenager.

One by one, every Townsend named a beverage. Watching Jeremiah root around the fridge and set drinks on the counter, Mae pieced together that this must be their way of taking drink orders. In the brief time she had as people rattled off drinks, Mae debated what she would say. Play it safe like the older teenager and ask for water? She wasn't about to stand out even more by being the only one to request La Croix, even though she'd caught a glimpse of it in the fridge.

It was then that she noticed the room had gone quiet. She blinked to attention. Everyone was staring at her, beverages in hand.

"And you, Mae?" Jeremiah prompted helpfully, one hand still on the open fridge door.

"Oh. Yeah. I'll take, um…" She darted glances around, settling on the slender glass bottle in Wendell's hand with a red label she'd never seen before. "Whatever that is," she said, pointing.

"You don't know what Cheerwine is?" the younger teenager asked.

"Ariel, be nice," her mother warned. "She's not from here."

Mae internally deflated at the reminder. As if anyone here could forget.

"It's like a cherry soda," Jeremiah said, handing her the bottle.

Mae made a point to sound enthusiastic about this comparison. Even though cherry-flavored things always tasted like cough syrup to her.

Mae and her medicinal Cheerwine joined the others on their way to the table. She lingered at the end, watching Scott, Tyrese, and Ariel settle into seats without hesitation. Only then did she appreciate the genius of the Rutherfords' color-coded seating chart. Seating charts were brilliant. Seating charts saved you from awkwardly standing around like a sweaty statue.

"Anywhere's fine," Desiree whispered as she brushed past her. Mae gave her a grateful look and pulled out a chair near one end of the table. As people took their seats, no one seemed to want to take the empty seat next to Mae—until Jeremiah, nonplussed, filled in. He caught her eye as he pointed to her hummus and pita on the table between them. The pita was cut into triangles, artfully fanned out on the plate.

"I watch a lot of *Chopped*," he said conspiratorially, making her smile.

Snippets of conversation floated through Mae's ears as the family piled food on plates: Phyllis asking Desiree how Amara was coping with teething, Ariel telling Wendell she needed a posterboard for her summer school project.

Deciding to focus on food before trying to join the conversation, Mae put a little of everything on her plate: fried catfish, cornbread, braised greens, coleslaw. Her hummus seemed an out-of-place accompaniment to the meal, but Tyrese had some, and so did Phyllis and Leah, which Mae learned was the name of the older teenager. Jeremiah quickly polished off five pita triangles piled with hummus—which must have been a waste of stomach space given the many more delicious things at the table, but Mae liked thinking Jeremiah had done it to show support.

When Mae reached for another fish fillet, her fork almost collided with Phyllis's as they both went for the same piece. Mae paused, they shared an awkward smile, and Mae selected a different one.

Mae turned her fork over in her hand. She hadn't spoken since they'd started eating, and this small moment with Phyllis was as close to an opening as she might get.

"The catfish is delicious," Mae said, speaking up to be heard over Ethan's babblings and Ariel and Tyrese's conversation about an anime series. "Do you use smoked paprika?"

"And about fifteen other spices," Jeremiah said.

"My in-laws use one spice at a time, so I think this would be a shock to their system," Mae said. The comment slipped out, like she was grabbing lunch with Jayla and not sitting at a dinner table surrounded by near-strangers. She looked up to gauge the reaction, nerves loosening when Jeremiah, Wendell, and Barbara laughed. Mae then sent a silent apology to the Rutherfords for putting their bland cooking on blast. But she wasn't that sorry. Anything that got the Townsends laughing was well worth it.

"How *are* your in-laws?" Wendell asked. The emphasis in his words suggested he wasn't asking how they were doing. There was a scrutiny to them. A hidden meaning.

"They're...good," Mae said uneasily. "They're nice."

Wendell took a bite of coleslaw. "You and that white boy want kids?"

Mae squirmed, feeling everyone's eyes on her. "Yeah, maybe in a couple years."

"Is white boy up to the task of raising mixed kids?" he asked. "Does he know what that involves?"

Mae's face grew warm. "Yeah," she lied, hearing the falter in her voice. "We've talked about it."

"You have?" Sierra asked.

How could Sierra tell when Mae was lying? Mae met her gaze. "Yes," she said with more confidence than she felt. She and Connor *had* talked about having kids. But they'd never talked about the race question, not really. They'd danced around it—Connor knew why she slept with her hair in a bonnet and kept a jar of coconut oil in the bathroom. But there were other things he didn't know.

He didn't know about the time at the beach a few summers ago, when they'd gone to Rehoboth with his parents. Connor and his dad had gone into the water while Mae and his mom lounged on the beach. As Mae slathered sunblock on her skin, Susan had asked, *How dark does your skin get in the sun?*

Mae had halted, then recovered and resumed rubbing her

shoulder until the streaky white sunblock faded into an oily sheen. Still, she kept on rubbing, stalling, parsing through the words. What sort of question was that? Was there a fear behind it, a worry that Mae might go from light-skinned to dark-skinned in the course of an afternoon? Like it was acceptable for Connor to date Mae so long as she passed the paper bag test, but she'd be out on her rear if she got a shade too dark?

Or was it an innocent question, a naïve curiosity about how Black skin functioned in the sun?

It was probably the latter. Mae told herself it was the latter when she gave Susan a non-answer of *It depends.* Even so, the question crawled under Mae's possibly too-dark skin and made a home there, popping back into her mind every chance it got. When Mae tried on wedding dresses and Susan suggested ivory might look better against Mae's skin, she was back on that beach, dissecting Susan's words, wondering how much time Susan spent thinking about the color of Mae's skin.

(The ivory *had* actually looked better on Mae, but that wasn't the point. It was never the point.)

Even if Mae applied the most generous interpretation to Susan's question, it seemed like an omen of things to come. Like the Parkers, the Rutherfords also might loosen their tongues and say whatever came to mind. Maybe Susan would also tell Mae one day, while the Olympics played in the background, that Black people were *so* good at sports. Maybe John would lean across the dinner table one Thanksgiving and tell a story about working with a vendor he suspected was an affirmative action hire.

And what would Connor say in the face of comments like these? They'd once gotten a rude remark from a white man in Eastern Market who saw them holding hands, and Connor hadn't hesitated to calmly respond *Go fuck yourself*, like it was second nature. Connor, being bi, had plenty of experience with comments like that. He'd told Mae that even just standing too close to his ex-boyfriend had resulted in everything ranging from pointed looks to threats. He was an expert in letting rude remarks from strangers roll off his back.

But what about digs from his family? Remarks that weren't meant to be rude, weren't meant to be racist, that might sound innocent if you hadn't spent your entire life hearing them? Connor hadn't dated anyone Black before, and he probably wouldn't recognize the subtle ways people could express their racism, unknowingly or not. Would Connor be as quick to respond then? Or would he think nothing of it and drink his pinot noir without a care in the world?

That, Mae knew, was what Wendell was getting at with his question. But she didn't have an answer for him. Not an honest one.

"Marrying into a white family can be tough," Wendell said. "You ready for that?"

"She better be," Sierra said. "Her wedding's three weeks away, right?"

Mae pasted on a smile. "It's coming up. I'm definitely ready."

The conversation moved on to Tyrese's job hunt, and Mae took a long gulp of water when the heat was off her. Jeremiah, who seemed to pick up on her shaky nerves, gave her a reassuring look and took another pita triangle.

She played with a lemon wedge on her plate, Wendell's words reverberating in her mind. *Marrying into a white family can be tough.* He couldn't have been speaking from personal experience— his wife Dawn was Black. But there was a clear cognizance in his voice. Like he was speaking about someone else. Possibly her dad.

Part of Mae wanted to bring the conversation back to Wendell's question, get it out in the open, force herself to steep in the awkwardness. But the rest—the part that sat back and listened to Phyllis recount a run-in with an old neighbor they'd grown up with, the part that was happy just to be here, just to be included— let the moment pass. She'd done enough today. She'd had her first ever Townsend family dinner, met more relatives, and even gotten a laugh out of them. She didn't need to face hard truths tonight.

As the evening continued, Mae jumped back into the conversation when she could. She learned Ariel was an aspiring artist, that Leah had made the colorful striped top she was wearing, that Desiree had an extensive vinyl collection. She did her best to memorize every detail, capture the feeling of sitting around a table with family who looked like her.

"Did anything you made today come from your mom's recipes?" Mae asked Phyllis. "I hear she had a pretty extensive recipe collection."

"She really did," Phyllis said. "Not that she'd share them with any of us. Any time we asked her how to make something, she'd always say—"

"'It's all up here,'" roused Barbara and Wendell in unison with Phyllis, all three of them tapping on their heads in an imitation of their mother. Mae let out a small laugh that was part wistful, part marvel.

"And if we *could* get a recipe out of her, it was always, 'A little of this,' 'A little of that,'" Wendell recalled. "I was following that woman around the kitchen with a notepad begging for quantities."

"'You don't measure love,'" Phyllis said, assuming the croaky voice of an older woman.

"She was impossible," Wendell said, shaking his head.

"Couldn't get her to give us measurements, but try to pry a calendar out of her hands and it was a whole other story," said Barbara.

"The Sunday dinners," groaned Jeremiah.

"*Every* Sunday," added Tyrese.

"And every holiday," Barbara continued. "Always had to be a big thing at her house. Remember the year Dawn wanted to go on that cruise over Easter?" she asked, pointing at Wendell's wife.

Dawn chuckled. "She acted like I was trying to tear the family apart."

"Guess nothing's stopping us from going on that cruise next year," Wendell added. He said it lightly, but a quiet fell over the table when the meaning of his words set in.

"And our Sundays are free now," Barbara murmured. She dabbed at her eyes with her napkin.

Mae took a sip of her cherry-forward Cheerwine. She couldn't help but feel responsible for the sudden mood shift. She was the one who'd brought up the topic of Althea in the first place. Food was probably a safer choice.

"What was her mac and cheese like?" Mae asked. Sierra shot her a questioning glance.

Phyllis gave a long hum. "So rich, it should be illegal. The sauce was already full of every kind of cheese you can imagine, and then she'd pour it into a pan and pile a mountain of cheese on top."

"So, it was oven-baked?" Mae guessed.

"Yep. She'd let the cheese on top get bubbly and brown on all the edges," Barbara said.

"Holidays weren't holidays without it," Phyllis said.

She'd unearthed one clue, then. "Do you know what cheeses she used?"

"What are you up to?" Jeremiah asked, giving her a nudge with his elbow, squinting at her in playful suspicion.

"I'm curious! I heard you don't have the recipe and I was wondering what it tastes like."

"You haven't been able to track it down?" Phyllis asked Sierra, a line of worry creasing her forehead.

"Not yet, but I will. I'll find it by Thanksgiving." Sierra looked down at her plate, becoming very interested in her coleslaw.

"You'll have to let us know how it is," Scott said. When Sierra gave him an inquisitive look, he explained, "Desiree and I are spending Thanksgiving with her family this year. Since..." He stopped, not seeming to want to finish his sentence. "It just didn't make sense to keep coming back here for holidays after we moved."

"Moved?" Mae asked.

"We moved to Asheville last year," Desiree said. "We're just in town for the funeral."

"Oh." Disappointment burrowed in her gut. It figured that one of her only allies didn't even live in Hobson.

"I don't know why I said Thanksgiving," Sierra said. "I probably won't even be here for it."

Mae turned from Desiree to Sierra, a sense of dread rising in her. "Why?"

"My job. They want me to move to Seattle in the fall. They're promoting me to an executive position."

"Oh." Her dad's stories had given her a dated, frozen-in-time view of Hobson and the Townsends. The idea that some of them might leave this town and start lives that had nothing to do with

Hobson or each other took some getting used to. Now she had to rework her mental map of her family, add pins scattering in new directions. Directions that, in Sierra's case, were even further from Mae than before. Not that it mattered, she reminded herself. It wasn't like she and Sierra had made plans to hang out any time soon. Or ever.

"I wouldn't be surprised if we had a quieter Thanksgiving this year," Phyllis said. "Unless someone's feeling up to hosting."

Again, the table was silent. Mae watched the others look around, a melancholy sort of hope in their eyes. For all their complaining about Althea's holidays demands, they looked sad to let the custom go, sad that the person who used to push them into keeping up tradition wasn't around to do it anymore.

"We were thinking of going down to Savannah for Thanksgiving this year," Dawn said. "See how Leah's settling in at her dorm."

"Dorm?" Mae echoed, turning to Leah.

Leah nodded, a shy smile lighting up her face. "I'm starting at the Savannah College of Art and Design in the fall."

"Congratulations," Mae said. The word came out more chipper than she felt. Another pin on her mental map moved from Hobson to Savannah. Even more miles separating Mae from another one of her relatives. She buried the thought and went back to channeling that upbeat tone. "That's amazing. Are you excited?"

"Yeah. Mom's taking me down there for a few days next month to attend an orientation session and explore the city."

"I don't see why you can't take me too," Ariel grumbled.

"Whose fault is it that you have summer school?" Wendell said.

"Mrs. Gruell's!" Ariel insisted, eliciting laughter around the table (from everyone except her parents, Mae noticed).

After Ariel's heated account of the many ways her pre-algebra teacher was out to get her, conversation meandered to summer plans. Tyrese said he was going to a concert in Raleigh next weekend. Dawn ran through the dorm essentials she and Leah needed to buy. Phyllis shared that she and Jeremiah booked a room at Falls Lake for the Fourth of July weekend.

"Fourth of July?" Mae repeated, looking up from her plate. "What about the barbecue?"

"Hmm?" Phyllis said.

"Don't you always do a barbecue every Fourth of July?"

"Well…" Phyllis trailed off. Looks went around the table. "Yes. Your grandma would throw a few barbecues over the summer."

"Memorial Day was the big one," Jeremiah explained. "It was how she liked to kick off the summer."

"Oh." Mae had to do some rapid adjusting to process the fact that there was a barbecue bigger than the one she'd always heard about. The Fourth of July one must have just been her dad's favorite. Perhaps it was more intimate, a better opportunity for catching up with his family the one time a year he saw them. "But there's normally a Fourth of July one, too, right?"

"Yes," Phyllis said slowly. "But…I'm not sure we're feeling up to taking that on without Mom."

Mae registered the downcast eyes and drooping faces surrounding her. She was starting to piece together how much was changing in the wake of Althea's death. Family traditions were falling by the wayside, succumbing to grief and a reluctance to take the helm. But Mae hadn't realized just how quickly these changes were happening. If the Fourth of July barbecue was canceled, that meant tonight might be the last time the Townsends were all together. Scott and Desiree would be going back to Asheville in a day or two, and then soon enough Leah would be off to college, Sierra to Seattle. Without Althea around to coax people to visit and gather, Ethan and Amara might never know the Townsend traditions Althea had worked so hard to form.

And deep down lived the part of Mae that had always wondered about that Fourth of July barbecue. Now that she was finally here in Hobson, attending the barbecue and fulfilling a lifelong curiosity was tantalizingly within reach. Except—it wasn't. Not if it wasn't happening.

Unless someone stepped up to the plate.

"I'll do it," Mae said. "I'll throw the Fourth of July barbecue."

Phyllis and Barbara exchanged a skeptical look. Sierra tilted her head, like she was waiting for a catch. Desiree was busy keeping Ethan from stealing her butter knife, but she briefly glanced up to watch Mae.

Wendell, drinking the last of his Cheerwine, slowly lowered the bottle. He regarded Mae with doubt as he set the drink on the table. "*You'll* do it?"

"Why not?"

"It's a lot to organize," Barbara warned.

Mae could have laughed. If anything, Barbara was helping her make her case. "I'm a project manager. Organization is my life."

"Where would you have it?" Dawn asked.

Mae hurried to think. The Mossy View parking lot certainly wasn't an option. She reflected on what she knew from her dad's pictures and stories. "It's usually held in my grandma's backyard, right? I could hold it there."

"The yard's a mess," Wendell said. "The whole house is. We're still trying to get it in shape to sell."

Mae played with the napkin in her lap as she turned over this new piece of information. This was an extra challenge, but not enough to stand in her way. Every major task was always composed of smaller subtasks. If she was going to throw this barbecue—and she *had* to, now that she'd spoken the idea aloud, started to think it through, watched it begin to transform from a wispy hope into concrete reality—then she was going to do it right. In her grandma's backyard, where it was supposed to be.

"I could help with that," she said. "Clean it up enough for a barbecue."

"We already booked our room at Falls Lake," Phyllis said, glancing at Jeremiah.

"You can go to Falls Lake any time," Mae said. She wasn't completely sure if that was true, given that she'd never heard of Falls Lake before tonight, but she pressed on. "When's the next time you're gonna see Ethan and Amara, if they're spending the holidays with Desiree's family? Sierra said she's moving to Seattle in the fall. And this is Leah's last summer here before she goes to college, right? She could have an internship next year. I think it's important that we get together while we can."

She knew this was ironic coming from her, the person who hadn't been to a single Townsend get-together until now. Sierra seemed to know it too, going by the wry look she gave her. But Mae hoped they could hear the sincerity in her words. As she looked around the table, she could see them consider the idea more seriously. Ariel scrunched her lips to one side in thought. Wendell absent-mindedly rubbed his goatee with the back of his hand. Desiree and Scott seemed to have a silent conversation: he lifted his eyebrows in a question, and Desiree gave him a small shrug.

"It won't be the same," Tyrese said.

"It won't," Mae agreed. "But I'll do my best." Remembering what Phyllis had said about Althea's mac and cheese being a holiday staple, Mae perked up and said, "I'll even make her mac and cheese. I'll figure out the recipe."

That got their attention. Ariel paused, her fork mid-air. Sierra's eyes sparked with interest.

"How?" Wendell asked.

Mae scratched the back of her neck. "I'm a pretty good cook. I've figured out recipes before. It just takes some trial and error to get there. If I had access to a kitchen—maybe my grandma's, if I could stay in a spare room at the house or something while I get the place ready—I could make it work. The fact that I've never had her mac and cheese makes it a little harder, but…you could be my test subjects."

"Isn't your wedding on July 8?" Leah asked.

Mae's first thought was to ask how Leah could have her wedding date memorized if the Townsends were such a united front on ignoring her invitations, but she pushed it aside.

"Yes," she admitted. "But I can do both." Not that she had any idea how. But this barbecue was so important, so necessary, that she was certain she would find a way. She needed to make it happen. She needed to make sure the Townsends didn't all go their separate ways as soon as Mae entered their lives. She needed to be part of this barbecue for once in her life.

"All right," Phyllis said, sharing a look with Jeremiah. "We'll go to Falls Lake another time."

"Yes!" Mae cheered. She looked around at the others. "You'll all come?"

Slow nods and agreements went around the room. Sierra hesitated before she confirmed that she would come. But a yes was a yes.

After dinner, Phyllis handed Mae a set of keys to Althea's house. Even after dropping them into Mae's hand, Phyllis held onto the key ring for a few extra moments, as if she still might change her mind. But she let go at last, and Mae closed her fingers around them before she could change her mind, meeting Phyllis's intense scrutiny with a sunny smile.

Mae was practically skipping on her way back to the Mossy View that night. The Fourth of July barbecue was happening, and she was going to be part of it.

She just had to figure out how to host a barbecue four days before her wedding.

CHAPTER SEVEN

Mae's first act when she stepped inside her motel room that evening was to open her laptop and pull up Excel. As a project manager, timelines were her forte. Before committing to a deadline, it was important to see if it was even feasible. The Fourth of July was her deadline, the barbecue one giant deliverable. If she couldn't make this work, she'd make an apologetic call to Barbara and carry on with her original plan to head home tomorrow.

If her rough timeline sketch showed this was possible...then Connor was in for a surprise.

In Excel, she listed every to-do she could think of. Recreate the mac and cheese recipe, which involved a host of subtasks: scour recipes, ask the Townsends more questions about the mac and cheese, make trial batches, hold taste tests, make tweaks until she got it right. Then the barbecue logistics: visit Althea's house, find out what kind of state it was in, and get the house and backyard in shape for company. Put together a preliminary list of attendees and ask the Townsends who else to invite. She knew from her dad that family friends and neighbors often attended holiday events, but she didn't have any names to go off of. Finalize the menu. She jotted down the barbecue staples she could remember from stories and pictures: corn on the cob, ribs, burgers, potato salad, baked beans, obviously the mac and cheese. Figuring out the rest would involve asking the Townsends. And, while clearing out the house and yard, look for the things she'd seen in pictures and heard about through years of stories and retellings: the red checkered tablecloth, the mismatched lawn chairs, the spindly-legged blue grill. Every feature, every detail, she wanted present and accounted for to do this barbecue justice.

She logged onto her work's HR portal to run the numbers on her remaining PTO. She'd been carefully saving her limited time off for her honeymoon, but she wouldn't need to dip into much for this. If she worked during the day, attending meetings and completing critical tasks, and used her lunch time and an hour or two of PTO here and there to cover any time she needed to spend on barbecue prep, the numbers added up. She could do extra work in the evenings to make up for it. As long as she kept her PTO use to a minimum, didn't use more than she'd accrue in her next couple of paychecks, she'd be fine.

She added more notes, thoughts, timeline considerations. Looking it over, she forced herself to set aside her optimism and think pragmatically. Was this really possible and not just because she wanted it to be? Could she throw a barbecue in two and a half weeks and make it home in time for her wedding just four days later?

She felt the answer before her mind could work it out. It felt right—simple as that. It felt possible. It felt *necessary*. She could do a barbecue and a wedding four days apart. She could make this work. In her head, she could already see it working.

Which meant she had to add one more item to her list of to-dos, highlighted in an urgent neon-yellow: *Call Connor.*

Connor was understanding, as Mae knew he would be. It was one of many reasons why she was marrying him.

"If you need to stay longer, I want you to stay longer," Connor said when she gently broached the idea of spending more time in Hobson. "But we should figure out when you're coming back, because I had lunch with my mom today and…Mae, she made another binder."

Mae pulled her head back, almost hitting the headboard. "Another one?"

While Mae was more of a spreadsheet-and-organization app sort of planner, she could respect Susan's binder-based approach. It was the use for wedding planning that frightened her. No wedding should need that much preparation, at least not any wedding Mae had envisioned for herself.

"I'm serious. It's a binder of everything we need for the next three weeks leading up to the wedding. Let me get it." There were rustling sounds on the other end. When Connor finally spoke again, it was a whispered, "Oh god."

"What?"

"It's two binders. One for the next three weeks, and then the other binder is just for the wedding day. It's an inch thick. Hold on, I'm gonna FaceTime you. You need to see this."

Connor spent several minutes showing Mae the binders, flipping through the pages and bemoaning his mom's liberal use of paper tabs. Only after he read Mae the table of contents word-for-word, lingering on subsections like *boutonniere maintenance* and *guest in white dress contingency plan*, did he get the conversation back on track.

"How long are you staying for?" he asked, paging through a binder. "We have our first dance lesson on Wednesday. It looks like you have your final dress fitting on Saturday. I can cover for you at the dance lesson, but I don't think I can do your fitting. I have a terrible hip-to-waist ratio."

Mae laughed. "Um…" She scrolled through her spreadsheet, scanning the column where she'd put tentative dates for her tasks, though a bounty of question marks accompanied each one. "Well. I need to be here on July fourth."

Connor shook his head, as if he'd simply misheard. "But that's right before the wedding."

"I know, but they're not doing their Fourth of July barbecue for the first time ever because my grandma isn't around to host it. No one wants to take it over, but I can tell they all *want* it to happen, and I spent my entire life watching my dad fly out for this barbecue every year and now I finally have a chance to go, so I *had* to volunteer to throw it," she finished breathlessly.

Connor gave a delirious chuckle, followed by a sigh. He pressed the heel of his hand to his forehead, probably regretting his decision to marry someone who was incapable of sticking to her own itinerary. "So, I'm not gonna see you until, what, a few days before the wedding?" he asked.

"I've thought about it, and it really just depends on how soon I can crack the mac and cheese recipe."

Connor lifted his head, blinking blearily. "The what?"

As Mae explained how she'd used the promise of Althea's mac and cheese to convince the Townsends to come, she could see Connor flashing back to all the other times she'd gotten carried away with a project. How finding tomatoes on clearance at Safeway had ignited a quest to make a different tomato recipe every day for a month, from spaghetti bolognese on day one all the way to tomato ice cream on day thirty. How buying a box of Thin Mints outside of Target and overhearing a frazzled parent say their troop treasurer left them in the lurch had turned into Mae taking on the role even though she had no affiliation with the Girl Scouts whatsoever.

Connor had never complained. He'd eaten her chewy tomato leather; he'd stayed up late helping her proofread the annual finance report she'd needed to compile for her troop. He did ask once, as he watched her lay out her troop's receipts on the kitchen table one morning, why she'd volunteered for the role.

"Were you a Girl Scout when you were a kid?" he'd asked.

Mae, peering at a receipt for camping equipment, looked up to meet his inquisitive face. "No. But I knew I could do it. So, I said I would."

He'd nodded and gone back to his cereal, but still he'd watched Mae with interest as she went on organizing receipts and jotting notes about overdue reimbursements. She could tell he didn't completely understand, but she wasn't sure what there was to grasp anyway. Taking on odd projects wasn't always logical. It was more that a shiny vision of the final outcome entered Mae's mind whenever a project idea first came to her, and that was what she was drawn to. Mae as a master of tomato cuisine, serving up a feast of creative dishes and becoming so skilled she could just look at a tomato and it would fall into perfect slices. Mae in a Girl Scouts uniform saving an overwhelmed troop from financial ruin, submitting a report so perfect they'd enter it into their hall of fame and offer her free cookies for life.

True, the visions never quite reflected reality. Tomatotember, as she and Connor referred to that month of tomato overload, had been more exhausting than she'd anticipated. Mopping up the kitchen floor when her SodaStream spilled fizzing tomato soda everywhere. Not having dinner until past 10:00 p.m. when long workdays and complex recipes got the best of her. And while the financial report had been a success, the work was disappointingly tedious. Not cookies and camping trips so much as financial policies and account numbers. She'd stepped down after two years, when a parent with accounting experience joined the troop and expressed interest in the role.

But Mae could never resist that glossy vision that lured her in. And she could see this next one so clearly. Standing in Althea's backyard while the Townsends talked, laughed, and ate. The summer heat, smoke rising from the grill, the smell of barbecue char in the air. Sierra biting into her mac and cheese and declaring it perfect. The Townsends enveloping her in a group hug and declaring their undying love for her.

Mae scrolled through her spreadsheet as she explained the logistics to Connor. "If I figure out the recipe, and get the barbecue prep stuff done in time, I could be home by next weekend. I'd have a whole week to help you out with wedding stuff. And then the weekend after next, we could drive back down to Hobson, have a quick little barbecue, and be back with plenty of time before the wedding." She braced herself, hoped he wouldn't bring up Tomatotember, Girl Scouts, or any of her other questionably ambitious ventures as proof of how quickly plans could veer off course.

His dazed expression softened around the edges. "We?"

She pulled a pillow into her lap, met him with a hopeful

smile. "Well, yeah. You're obviously invited. If you want to come." Now that Mae was in charge of this barbecue, she'd make certain no one would be excluded from it. She liked the idea of Connor being there, meeting her family. Growing up, family was something strictly segregated: the Parkers in Bakersfield, the Townsends in Hobson. She refused to let this pattern continue. The Townsends may not be coming to her wedding, but Connor would get to know them one way or another.

And so would she.

Though the Rutherfords could stay in DC, she decided, feeling uneasy at the image of Susan wandering around the barbecue asking Phyllis about her skin color.

"I'd love to come," Connor said. "But...do you have the PTO for that? I thought you had to save everything for the honeymoon."

"All good," she promised. "I already checked. I'll still work remotely, and any PTO I do use won't be enough to affect the honeymoon."

"Okay," he said. "We have a plan. And maybe we just..." He closed the binder and tossed it somewhere off-camera, sending a laugh through her. He returned his gaze to Mae. "So, I got some good news today."

"What?"

"I got an interview at Kaufman and Stout." His tone was nonchalant, but his eyes were bright with excitement.

"Really? That's great!" And it *was* great. Connor had been wanting to leave his job as in-house junior counsel at a small finance company for a while now. He'd grown tired of updating boilerplate templates in Track Changes and drafting fintech agreements, and he'd started pestering his friend from law school, an associate attorney at the renowned firm Kaufman and Stout in DC, for news of job openings. His pestering had clearly paid off.

The problem was, it raised the DC question. It was only a matter of time before Connor brought it up again. When Connor was in law school, interning at a firm in DC that had him commuting up to ninety minutes each way in traffic, they used to talk dreamily about moving to DC after he graduated. Connor wouldn't have a slog of a commute, and Mae could metro to her favorite ramen place any time she wanted.

But she'd never thought they would actually follow through with it. She'd thought they were just daydreaming, so she'd ignored real-world considerations—like the very real fact that living in DC would put them uncomfortably near Connor's parents.

"Yeah?" Connor said. "Maybe we can start looking at apartments in DC when you get back. If I get the job."

"You'll definitely get the job," Mae said, because she was excellent at deflecting.

Connor's smile relaxed into something easy and content. "I miss you."

The yearning that tugged at Mae when he said this was quickly replaced by a trickle of guilt for the doubts she'd felt when Wendell asked about Connor at dinner. Surely he understood the nuances of marrying a Black woman, raising mixed kids, standing up for his family. And all it would take to confirm that was a simple conversation. Mae just needed to say the words. She stared into Connor's attentive eyes, took a breath, and spoke.

"I miss you, too."

Later. She'd tell him later.

Mae pushed those thoughts aside after the call and returned to her Excel sheet. She marked the *Call Connor* task complete.

She clicked over to her work inbox and drafted an email to her project teams, stating that she'd be working on and off this week because she was still tending to family matters here in North Carolina. It felt like a brag, boasting to the world that she had *family* here to spend time with.

Next up: barbecue preparations, mac and cheese recreation, and clearing out Althea's house—all while working remotely during the day. Doing all these things at once did feel a smidge impossible. A single snag—the recipe taking longer than expected to figure out, a client emergency, getting a call from the ER that Connor had been crushed under the weight of Susan's meticulous wedding binders—could throw this enormous undertaking wildly off the rails.

Mae started a new Excel sheet and got to work on the invite list. She could handle going a little off course if it came down to it. She could handle anything if it meant finally being part of Townsend tradition.

CHAPTER EIGHT

A sense of wonder came over Mae when she pulled into Althea's driveway.

This house was the setting of so many of her dad's stories. The tall, sprawling dogwood tree out front was home base whenever her dad and the neighborhood kids played tag. Just behind the rickety wooden fence was the backyard where the Fourth of July barbecue took place. So much of her family history happened here, in this split-level house that had seen better days. The brick that formed the two lower levels had dark, spotty patches of dirt and discoloration. The vinyl siding on the upper level was spattered with gray splotches that muddled the yellow color underneath.

Her eyes fell on the one-car garage on the side of the house. It might hold a lot of the things she needed for the barbecue: chairs, tables, probably that blue grill. But a bigger temptation called to her.

She jingled the keys in her hand on the walk up the front steps, dragging her suitcase behind her. What a strange notion, that she could just unlock that front door and enter this mythical home after all this time. When she inserted the key Phyllis gave her, it slid right in, turned with ease, and the door opened to welcome her inside.

The first room that greeted her was a small living room: a red-and-beige plaid couch with lumpy cushions on one side of the wall, a TV on top of an overstuffed cabinet on the other, and a chipped coffee table in the middle. She pictured her dad here as a kid, maybe sitting on that same couch, watching a television that was smaller and chunkier. The house probably smelled different then, Mae thought, noticing the stale air filling her nose. She stepped over the dark-teal carpet and trailed a hand along the couch's textured, cottony fabric as she moved farther into the house, desperate for more details she could match against her dad's stories or the picture of Althea still forming in her mind.

Althea had made the most of the narrow dining room. A long, wide, wooden table with rounded ends filled the entire room, chairs crammed around it. The lines in the middle revealed where leaves had been added in the center to extend it. Growing up, Mae's mom only extended the table for special occasions, Thanksgivings and Christmases when it was their turn to host the Parkers. But Althea kept the table wide and yawning all year long, always prepared for a banquet.

In the kitchen, Mae took her time. If her grandma was anything like Mae, this was the place where she felt most sure of herself. This was the place where anything was possible, where family gathered and talked and watched ingredients transform into feasts. At the stove, she pictured Althea stirring a simmering pot of something delicious while her kids perched on these faded yellow countertops and whined that they were starving. Pictured her dad stealing piping-hot tastes of food while Phyllis distracted their mom, ever-responsible Barbara maybe snatching a young Wendell from the stovetop to keep him from burning a finger. This was exactly the sort of vibrant, lively kitchen she'd imagined when she was a kid back in California, watching the microwave count down the seconds until her TV dinner was ready.

Mae opened one of the wooden cabinets above the counter, not surprised to see it crowded with spices. Unlike her own alphabetized spice rack, these had no order she could see. Cinnamon next to paprika next to sesame seeds. But she was willing to bet Althea knew exactly where to find each one. Behind a nearly empty jar of garlic powder, Mae found a brand new one, its top still sealed in plastic. She felt a pang at the thought of Althea buying this refill, never knowing she wouldn't get a chance to use it. Mae put the spices back, gently closing the cabinet.

She set her sights on the upper level next, anticipation rising within her at the thought of seeing her dad's childhood bedroom, finding another piece of him. The first room she found at the top of the stairs was a guest bedroom with a neatly made bed and an old antique dresser. When she spotted a tree branch in the window by the dresser, she raced up to it in victory. Her dad had talked about how the sound of the tree's leaves rattling against the window during thunderstorms used to terrify him as a kid, and how Phyllis hadn't helped matters by convincing him it was a tree monster coming to visit.

Mae knelt on the carpet and propped her elbows on the windowsill, staring at the view. She could imagine this scene staying much the same as it had been some fifty years ago. The dogwood tree, the grassy front yard, the broad stretch of asphalt where her dad would have ridden his bike through the neighborhood. A sense of accomplishment wafted through her as she sat there, even though she hadn't done a single productive thing yet. But there was something powerful in exploring this house for herself. Like she'd cemented her dad's memories and stories in stone, prevented them from waning with time. All she'd ever had to keep his retellings alive was faded recollections of his words, but they took on new vibrancy now that she could see his child-hood home for herself.

Eager to unearth more memories, Mae stood to keep explor-ing. She walked down the hall and peered into the room beside her dad's. This would have been Phyllis and Barbara's room, but now it had the makings of an office: a desk cluttered with papers, a file cabinet, overflowing bookcases. She scanned the shelves, seeing mass-market paperbacks, cookbooks, a bible, encyclope-dias, backyard gardening guides, books about growing your own vegetables. She remembered her dad saying his father, Herb, had been an avid gardener, then felt a twinge of guilt that she hadn't asked the Townsends more about him. Herb had been more on the periphery of her dad's stories, dependably in the background, rarely the star. When Althea yelled at Mae's dad for letting Wendell sit on the handlebars while he rode his bike down a hill, Herb was the one quietly bandaging Wendell's knees. The one watering his plants in the backyard while the kids pestered Althea in the kitchen.

She almost reached for one of Herb's gardening books, but a row of tall, dark-green hardcovers on the bottom shelf caught her eye. They were all the same style, the same shiny gold writing on the spines, like they were out of a series. She turned her head sideways to read one. *Newton High School, 1982–1983.*

A thrill rocketed through her. There had to be one for every Townsend kid, for every year they attended high school. She ran her finger along the spines, doing mental math to figure out which years her dad would have attended. Mae pulled one out and flipped it open. Messages on the inside cover were scattered about, all addressed to Rodney.

Have a great summer!

Stay cool, Rod-man.

Can't believe we survived Mr. Klein's class. We're free!

She thumbed through the pages, searching until she found her dad's square yearbook photo staring back at her. There was a wide smile on his face, hair sculpted into a tall, asymmetrical high-top fade, a stark contrast from his usual short, close-cropped style. She found herself mirroring his grin, swelling with satisfaction at finding something new about her dad, this little square she could add to her finite collection of bits and pieces of him.

A wistful longing came to join that feeling, an urge to go back in time and tease him about this. He'd probably cackle and defend his teenage hairstyle, point her to all the yearbook inscriptions as proof of how cool he and his hair were.

Even if she couldn't tease him about it, she could at least laugh about the photo with Connor and Jayla. Mae took a picture and texted it to them both, taking comfort in their jokes about '80s trends. She stayed where she was long after the texting ran its course, still flipping through pages, looking for more traces of her dad.

A knock at the door pulled her from her perusing. On her way down the stairs, Mae wondered if it might be Phyllis, Barbara, or Wendell stopping by to say hello, give her a proper tour, and tell her about all the memories kept within these walls.

But she quickly discovered that the hard-eyed man on the other side of the door had no interest in any of that.

"Hi," she greeted him, her smile tentative but hopeful.

An older Black man in a striped polo shirt gave her a long, serious once-over. "Can I ask what you're doing here?"

Vaguely, Mae knew she had every right to ask him the same question. But there was such authority in his stare, in his voice, that she stammered out, "I-I'm helping out at the house."

He craned his neck to peer behind her. Bizarrely, Mae found herself wishing she had some concrete evidence in hand to support her claim, like a pair of rubber gloves or a duster.

"No one told me about this."

Mae hesitated. "Should I have?"

"It never hurts. As head of Watchful Neighbors, if I see a car I never seen before"—he pointed to her Kia—"I write down the plate number and I start asking questions." He held up a small, spiral flip notebook with a worn cover.

"Oh. Sure," Mae said, trying to match his gravitas. "So, is Watchful Neighbors like Neighborhood Watch?"

He scoffed. "*No.* I don't trust Neighborhood Watch."

"Right." Mae guessed there wasn't a lot this man trusted. Several silent seconds passed, in which he stared at her expectantly. She had to fight the urge to pull out her wallet and show him two forms of ID. "Well," she began slowly, "I guess you might want to know that I'm throwing a barbecue here on the Fourth of July?"

"That's not yours to throw," he said, his brow knitting.

"It is this year." When his suspicion still didn't ease up, Mae tried a different approach. "You're welcome to come."

He seemed to weigh this invitation, tilting his head a moment, until he made up his mind with a curt nod. "Fine. I'll be there. And I appreciate the notice. Althea never did seem to respect my position."

It was hard to imagine anyone having as much respect for this man's self-imposed authority as he himself did, but Mae nodded gravely all the same.

"I didn't catch your name," he said, his eyes narrowing into slits. "I'm Brian Posey."

"Mae. Townsend," she added.

"Townsend," he repeated. "I thought I knew you all."

"I'm Rodney's daughter," Mae said through a sigh, dreading what would come next.

"*Oh.*" And there it was. His voice even rose higher at the discovery. He pulled a pen from the pocket of his polo and jotted something down in his notebook. Mae leaned forward an inch, trying to divine what sorts of observations he wrote in there. Probably things like *Saw squirrel with strange twitch—what does it know? Postman eight minutes behind usual route; report this to Post Office tomorrow. Bill's garbage has unusual volume of orange peels this week; must investigate further.*

"Interesting," Brian said, snapping Mae out of her thoughts. He gave her a knowing look as he tucked the pen back into his pocket, like learning her name told him everything he needed to know about her.

"What's interesting?" Mae asked, but he just turned and began strolling down the steps.

She called after him louder, frustration bleeding into her words. "What's interesting?"

Halfway down the driveway, Brian stopped, turned. "Everything's interesting when you're head of Watchful Neighbors," he said. Then he carried on his way, never looking back.

Mae groaned. Brian seemed like the sort of person who thought life was an action movie and cast himself as the hero.

She closed the door and leaned against it, running a hand over her curls. She couldn't take it anymore. The strange looks, the knowing remarks. Was this how it would be at the barbecue, too? The barbecue she'd just disrupted her plans to throw? Would she spend it standing stock-still in the backyard, mumbling *Rodney's daughter* to everyone who came up to her, mentally cataloging their reactions while Brian took notes in the corner?

Somewhere in this house, there had to be a clue to the mystery surrounding her family divide. Even if it took her all day, all night, if she had to turn over every inch of this house and steal Brian's notebook for clues, it didn't matter. She'd find it.

The mystery stopped here.

CHAPTER NINE

Sleep was for quitters.

This was what Mae decided when midnight struck and she'd come no closer to unraveling the thread of the family fallout. Since Brian's departure, she'd systematically gone through every room. The file cabinet in the office had seemed like a promising place to start, except it held nothing but tax returns dating back to the '90s and old mortgage documents. The master bedroom on the top level, which housed a queen bed with a floral blue comforter, a wobbly dresser, and two nightstands, didn't turn up much either—at least, nothing related to the family.

The nightstands were a dead end, stuffed with pens, loose papers, empty notebooks, an address book full of names she didn't recognize. But she did uncover old issues of *Piquant*, Mae's favorite food magazine. The first one on the stack was *One Pot Wonders*, a March issue from a few months ago. Mae remembered getting the digital edition in her inbox that spring. She'd made a ginger salmon rice dish from that issue. She thought about Althea getting the magazine at the same time, pictured her flipping through it. The two of them reading the same magazine in different formats hundreds of miles apart, completely unaware of just how connected they were. The thought filled Mae with longing—and then she set the magazine down and carried on with her search.

By midnight, her eyelids were heavy with sleep. But she couldn't give up when there was still one place she hadn't yet tried.

A chorus of chirps and croaks filled her ears as she stepped down the front stairs and crossed the driveway to the garage. The humidity instantly made her skin feel sticky and damp, and in the short walk to the garage door, she had to slap her arm, leg, and ankle to ward off the mosquitos that descended to feast on her.

She tried the keys on her ring until she found one that unlocked the garage door, then quickly shut it behind her to keep hungry mosquitos out. In the darkness, she felt around the wall until she found a light switch. The room lit up with a hazy yellow glow, revealing stacks of cardboard boxes and plastic storage totes, trash bags heaped on the ground, and a clutter of miscellany. A pile of paint cans sat under a table, which held several chairs precariously stacked on top of it. In the corner nearest Mae was an old chest of drawers, an upturned wooden dolly with a broken wheel, and a dusty box for a dehumidifier.

Staring at the overwhelming expanse of junk to sort through, she realized with heavy disappointment that this was going to be much harder than searching file cabinets and dresser drawers. Her tired eyes pressed her to give up then and there. But she refused to stop now. And, once again: sleep was for quitters. Mae took a deep breath and waded into the clutter.

Confined within the walls of this hot, musty garage, Mae lost all sense of time. She weaved carefully through tangled extension cords and precarious piles, stopping to rifle through every box she came across. Most held junk—rusty toolboxes, an old rotary phone, a deflated soccer ball. These boxes she moved to a corner, figuring the Townsends could go through them the next time they came by and confirm what could be thrown out. Every now and then, though, she came across something useful for the barbecue: a pair of coolers, the red checkered tablecloth, lawn chairs, a long table. She set them aside for later and carried on with her search.

Mae expected more junk when she dragged a plastic storage tote toward her and pulled the lid off. Instead, she found a shoebox containing a pile of letters, all addressed to Althea Townsend. She sorted through them, checking the names in the return address field—none she recognized. But when she came across a letter with her dad's name in the return address field, her heart thudded. She pulled it from the pile and examined it keenly. It was postmarked just a few days after she was born.

Mae carefully unfolded the letter, and a picture fell into her lap. She picked it up and studied it. Herself as a newborn, her face red and squished. On the back, in her father's handwriting, were the words *Mae Janine Townsend.* She swallowed and went back to the letter.

Dear Mom,

We have a baby girl! Her name is Mae Janine Townsend, and she was born on October 20. She came in at six pounds, three ounces, and she has a very healthy set of screaming lungs. She's so beautiful.

Tears pricked at Mae's eyes. Her dad went on to recount the story of Mae's birth, which she'd heard him tell many times before—how they had gone to see a *Nightmare on Elm Street* sequel in theaters, and as soon as Freddy Krueger popped up on the screen driving a bus, her mother gasped. Her dad hadn't thought anything of it until her mom gripped his hand and dragged him out of the theater. Her dad had always said he'd felt so unsettled never seeing the rest of the movie, until he rented it months later. He'd called Mae his little horror fan, telling her she must have loved the movie so much that she'd needed to come out and see it for herself. He went on to show Mae every movie in the series, despite the questionably not-age-appropriate content. *A Nightmare on Elm Street* was still one of Mae's favorites.

The next paragraph was one Mae had to read twice.

We're settling into life in Bakersfield well. I hope you and Dad can visit us one day. I would love for you to meet Mae. I know Doris was awful to you, and I know nothing can change what you went through, but I promise Stacy is nothing like her. I really hope you can give her a chance.

The mention of Doris gave her an odd jolt. What was her maternal grandmother's name doing in a letter to Althea? Her brain struggled to reconcile the two. It was the same sort of jarring feeling she got when she ran into a teacher at the grocery store as a kid. Teachers stayed at school, and the Parkers stayed in Bakersfield. That was how it was supposed to go.

She zeroed in on the word *awful*. Whatever Doris had done, Mae had a creeping feeling that this was a particular kind of awful, far beyond a few impolite words at the dinner table.

In fact, this could be *the* Big Awful Thing. Exactly what Mae was looking for.

Every ignorant word Mae's grandparents had ever uttered

whirled around her in a haze. Her grandpa casually using the n-word before correcting himself that the word was *jury-rigged* now. That time when Mae was twelve and she'd done her hair in two braids with a pink bandanna over her head, just like she'd seen on *That's So Raven*, and her grandma had squinted at her and said she looked like a thug.

Mae had always thought it was interesting that all four of her grandparents were from North Carolina. Her grandpa had grown up in Southern Pines and then met her grandma Doris at Duke. But Doris had always said she was from Durham—the city that neighbored Hobson.

Goosebumps chilled her skin.

Mae's first instinct was to call her mom and demand answers, but even with the time difference, her mom would be fast asleep by now. Carefully, she put Althea's other letters back in the tote, closing it with a gentle motion. But her dad's letter she took into the house with her.

Phyllis had mentioned while handing over the keys that she and the others might be weaving in and out of the house over the next few days, organizing Althea's things for an estate sale they were planning and making small repairs to the house as they got it ready to sell. Plenty of opportunities for Mae to ask about the letter.

Mae stuck the letter to the fridge with a magnet, hanging it between a church potluck flyer and a year-old invitation for Desiree's baby shower. She wasn't going to let them dodge her questions anymore.

———

Mae's head snapped up at the sound of the front door opening.

She blinked at the idle laptop screen in front of her. The last thing she remembered was closing her eyes for a few seconds after a weekly project meeting. Somehow that had turned into an early afternoon nap right here at the dining room table. Between scouring the house for that letter and getting used to the strangeness of sleeping in the guest room of her late grandmother's empty house, sleep had come fitfully last night.

"Hello?" she called. Split-levels had their charms, but the lack of an open floor plan made every visitor a guessing game unless she was standing by the front door.

"It's me," a woman's voice said. Mae could have laughed at the idea that she'd be able to recognize the Townsends by voice after a couple of days. It had to be either Phyllis or Barbara. She went ahead and guessed Phyllis.

"Just here on lunch," Barbara said when she rounded the corner.

Mae decided she'd guess it right next time.

"I'm having an electrician take a look at the circuit breaker out back," Barbara continued, setting her purse on the kitchen counter. "He here yet?"

"No." Mae yawned and stretched her arms over her head, debating whether a third cup of coffee might cure her drowsiness. The first two hadn't done a thing, but there was that saying about doing something three times, if her brain would function enough to remember it.

"What's this?"

Mae opened her eyes to see Barbara standing in front of the fridge, that bomb of a letter in her hand. Her brain jolted to attention. She'd hung it up with such determination last night, but now the prospect of having a serious talk about family secrets when she was still fighting the lure of sleep felt impossible.

Especially when she had a sinking feeling those secrets were going to permanently change the way she saw her maternal grandmother.

"I found that in the garage last night," Mae said. She watched Barbara move her lips as she read. "I wondered about that paragraph at the bottom," Mae said tentatively. "Do you know what that's about?"

Barbara's brow furrowed. "You don't know?"

"Know what?"

"I know you had some questions at the reception," Barbara said, crossing the kitchen to join Mae at the dining table. "But I thought you at least knew this story."

"I don't," Mae said. "They only ever told me your mom didn't approve of my parents' marriage."

Barbara laughed bitterly. "That's a mild way to put it."

Mae breathed a quiet sigh. It was getting tiring, people assuming she had the same special prior knowledge of Townsend family lore that they did. She may have known about the tree monster, and Wendell's bee-stinged tongue, and Phyllis's spelling bee win, but evidently the serious things—the important things—her dad kept to himself. Just as he'd left her out of that barbecue all those years, he'd left her out of this, she thought with a jab of indignation.

"How would *you* put it?" Mae asked.

"Typical of Rodney to make this my responsibility," Barbara grumbled. But when she met Mae's eyes, her features relaxed. "Okay." She folded the letter and handed it back to Mae, then clasped her hands on the table, growing pensive. "You know your mom's mom, Doris, grew up here in Hobson too, right?"

"She always said Durham."

Barbara rolled her eyes. "People from west Hobson always say Durham to make themselves sound fancy. Well, one day when Mom was fifteen, she went to the pharmacy for a soda and a pack of gum. As she was on her way out, *Doris* shouted, 'That'"— Barbara lifted her eyebrows and gave Mae a serious look for her to fill in the blank—"'just stole from the register.'"

Just the idea of her grandma saying the word Barbara had so deliberately omitted sucked the air out of Mae's lungs. And yet she wasn't entirely surprised. She'd known her grandparents were from a different time. She'd always been a little afraid to know what they might have been like *in* that time. And here was confirmation that her grandma Doris—who baked cookies for her and taught her to knit—was an undeniable racist. Not the oblivious kind of racist, where they said the wrong thing sometimes, but their heart was in the right place. This was the kind of racism you couldn't argue against, couldn't see it differently if you squinted.

"Mom denied it," Barbara went on, "but Doris was insistent. Someone called the police, who came and brought Mom to the station for questioning. No parents, no lawyer, just a couple of cops and a fifteen-year-old girl scared out of her mind. They didn't arrest her, but the damage was done. It was in all the papers, all but calling Mom a thief and praising Doris for having...a strong moral character, I think they called it." Her brow arched. "Neighbors took sides. The story died down eventually, but Mom had a hard time for a few years. Even just going grocery shopping. There were already eyes on her all the time just for being Black. But once she was branded a shoplifter, that was a hard reputation to shake." She paused, fixing grim eyes on Mae. "She never stole *anything.*"

"I know," Mae murmured.

"Doris moved out of town a few years later and Mom had an easier time of it. She married Dad, got involved in the church, started getting the respect she deserved. And then, thirty-some years later, Rodney met your mom when she came here for college. Our mom figured out who her mom was, and all hell broke loose. She forbade Rodney from seeing her."

"But he didn't listen," Mae supplied. This much she knew from the sanitized story she'd been told. Her grandma had disapproved of the marriage, and Mae—then six when she first heard the story—had assumed it was because Mae's dad was Black and Mae's mom was white. Mae had thought it was so romantic of her parents to bridge the divide anyway, a real-life Romeo and Juliet. And she'd thought that if only her grandma could be a little more open-minded, they could all get along. It made her nauseous to remember that assumption now, to realize she'd spent decades pinning the blame on the wrong grandparent.

"No, he didn't," Barbara agreed. "He thought Mom would come around once she got to know your mom. But Mom refused. She couldn't stand the idea of Rodney marrying into the family that made her life hell. She wanted no part in it."

Mae took a shaky breath. The translation, it seemed, was that Althea wanted no part of *Mae*. It felt selfish to think, to make this story all about her, but it was a thought she'd always had, mental math she'd worked out a long time ago. Her dad's mom didn't approve of her parents' marriage; therefore, she didn't approve of Mae.

Mae gave Barbara a weak smile. "Well. Now I know. Thanks for explaining."

"They should have told you." Barbara's voice was firm and

disbelieving. She watched Mae with probing eyes. "Do you have any other questions?"

"Not until I find another letter with more family secrets," Mae mumbled. To her surprise, Barbara let out a chuckle. Mae looked up, already plotting ways to extend the moment. "Have you had lunch?" she asked. "I was just about to get some."

Barbara looked like she was considering the offer, but a knock on the door interrupted the moment. "That'll be the electrician. I've gotta show him into the yard and get back to the office." She stood, then paused, giving Mae a half-smile shrouded in pity. "But maybe another time, okay, sweetheart?"

Mae nodded. Even though Barbara had tempered her rejection with sympathy, disappointment still pulled at her as Barbara left. She heard the front door open and close, caught a glimpse of Barbara and a man through the kitchen window overlooking the yard. She went back to her laptop and dutifully clicked through the new emails she'd received while she'd been busy learning the secrets of the Townsend-Parker divide. Meetings and Gantt charts seemed so inconsequential in comparison.

Mae opened a slide deck she needed to prep for a client, but she found herself staring blankly at the first slide, Barbara and the electrician's distant voices drifting into her ears. Finally, she gave up and called her mom. Part of her hoped she wouldn't answer, that she'd picked up a Monday shift at the hospital where she worked as a nurse, and Mae could postpone the discussion until she had a better handle on how to find the words.

"Hey, hon!" Mae registered the note of surprise in her mother's voice. She didn't normally call in the middle of a weekday. "What's going on?"

"Um." She wound a curl around her finger, gathering the

resolve to voice the question pushing forth. She finally had a detail to press them on, proof that the story was more complicated than her parents led her to believe. "Why didn't you ever tell me Grandma was awful to Dad's mom?"

There was a long silence. "Who told—"

"I'm in Hobson," Mae said. "Dad's mom died, and I came down for the funeral."

"Oh. Oh, Mae. I didn't know."

"You didn't know what?"

"I didn't know she'd died," she said quietly. "How was the funeral?"

"Well. Weird," Mae said with an ironic laugh. "Since no one knew me. But I met a lot of family."

"That's good." Mae knew her mom was probably also sorting through a spinning wheel of questions she didn't know how to ask. She could picture her at home, maybe sitting on the tufted green couch in the living room, brown hair down instead of the ponytail she always wore at work, one finger tapping her coffee mug in thought. "What made you want to go?"

"The same reason that made me want to invite them all to my wedding. I was tired of not knowing my family."

Her mom was quiet for a moment. "And did someone say something to you about Grandma?"

"No. They just said something about grudges." Mae paused, waiting to see if her mom would offer up anything. When she was met with silence, she continued, "But I volunteered to throw the Fourth of July barbecue at...well, my other grandma's house, and I found a letter Dad wrote her when I was born." She picked up the letter and started reading.

"I remember him sending pictures," her mom said when Mae

finished reading. Her voice was soft, a little stunned. "I didn't know he wrote that letter."

"Why didn't you tell me about what Grandma did?" Mae asked, setting the letter down. "I had to hear it from Barbara."

"What did Barbara say?" her mom asked quickly. The note of defensiveness in her voice stung at Mae. As if her mom had any right to take umbrage at Barbara telling Mae something her parents should have told her years ago.

"The *truth*," Mae said. "I showed her the letter and she told me about Grandma accusing dad's mom of stealing, and how she was treated like a thief everywhere she went. And how dad's mom didn't approve of you guys getting together. How come I never got the full story?"

"I-I didn't know how to tell you," she finally said. "Your dad didn't, either. We didn't want you thinking your grandma would ever do anything to hurt you. We thought it might be better if you didn't know."

Mae traced a crease along a fold in the letter. On second thought, now she wasn't sure if she'd have preferred to know. It would have put a wall between her and her grandma, certainly. She would have held her at arm's length, would have never looked forward to their trips to Dairy Queen, where she'd treat Mae and her cousin Madison to Oreo Blizzards. It would have robbed her of being close to the only grandmother she'd ever known.

But what if that knowledge had sent her in the opposite direction? What if it had compelled her to reach out to Althea and bridge the divide? They could have gotten to know each other over phone calls, maybe even visits. Mae could have joined the Townsends when they recounted stories about her grandma, could have recited one of her notable quotes right alongside everyone else. That one shred of knowledge could have saved her from feeling like a stranger among her own family.

"You should have told me," Mae said.

"I'm sorry, Mae," her mother said softly.

"Was that the reason why I never knew Dad's family?"

"Initially, yes. Your dad's mom made it very clear she didn't want anything to do with me or my family."

"But there were other reasons?" she prodded. In the pause that followed, Mae traced a dent in the table, suddenly not sure if she wanted to hear the answer.

"There was that Thanksgiving we had with Barbara and Sierra when you were three. I think it became obvious then that this wasn't something we could work past." Her mother was speaking slowly, like she was choosing her words with great care.

"Why?" Mae asked.

"Nothing in particular," her mom said. "I don't think anyone was at their best that night."

"Okay." Mae moved her cursor aimlessly around the slide she was supposed to be working on, letting the silence engulf them. Her mom had to have been holding something back, but Mae couldn't bring herself to call her on it. Her hesitation, coupled with her use of *we*, had Mae wondering if her father had something to do with it, something her mom wouldn't want to reveal.

It was hard sometimes, tiptoeing around his memory. He wasn't perfect. He couldn't be on time to save his life; Mae had gotten used to being the last kid picked up from sleepovers when her dad was tasked with the job. He could be arrogant too, so sure he knew everything that he'd defend his stance even when proven wrong.

But they didn't want to dwell on that after he died. He was

perfect 99 percent of the time, and it felt like a lie to focus on that 1 percent of him that was human.

If there *was* something about that Thanksgiving she should know about, she didn't feel like pressing her mom on it now. She'd had enough surprises for today.

"I have another question for you."

"Okay," her mom said warily.

"Did dad ever talk about his mom's mac and cheese?"

Her mom's laughter came readily, amusement flooded with relief. "I don't think so. Why?"

"I've been told it was legendary, but no one has the recipe. I'm trying to find it, or recreate it. He never said anything? Did he ever make mac and cheese?"

"Your father? Cook?"

Mae laughed. Her dad knew how to make exactly one dish: chili on Fritos. Mae's love of cooking had stemmed partly from her dad's stories that painted the kitchen as a magical place, but mostly from being so tired of the few dishes in her parents' repertoire that one day she'd checked a cookbook out of her middle school's library and taught herself how to make something that wasn't chili or Kid Cuisines.

Her mom said she'd go through his old things and see if she could turn up anything, then asked Mae if she remembered the odd-flavored batch of chili he'd made the time he'd accidentally used cinnamon instead of cumin. They talked a few minutes longer, letting the familiar story ease the strangeness between them.

Even so, her grandmothers' dispute still pressed on her mind as the day passed. Barbara and the electrician left not long after Mae got off the phone with her mom, leaving Mae and her thoughts to spiral in solitude. She spent some time sorting through more junk in the garage, trying to channel her feelings into organization. But stepping back and seeing the neat piles she'd formed of things the Townsends might want to either keep, toss, or donate didn't rouse even an ounce of accomplishment.

Dinner that night was pure comfort food: a sausage and onion pizza from the closest pizza place that cropped up in her search. She didn't even do her usual dance of comparing restaurants, reading reviews, scouring websites for menus and getting swept into the excitement of trying a new place. Tonight, she couldn't be bothered.

She settled onto the living room couch, turned on the Food Network, and propped her feet up on the coffee table. Not the politest thing to do in Althea's house, but Mae dared Althea to come back and haunt her for it. Althea's ghost was probably working hard to give her the silent treatment even now.

She was well into her second slice when Wendell dropped by. As he closed the front door behind him, Mae gave him a wave without putting down her pizza. She couldn't muster the energy to stand and greet him properly.

"Don't you look right at home," he commented.

She raised her eyes, expecting a judgmental look. But he was smiling.

"Mom hated it when we put our feet on the coffee table," he said. "Your dad was worst of all. He'd put his stinky bare feet on that thing and Mom would riot."

Something in Mae softened. She remembered the way her dad would rest his feet on the coffee table sometimes, though thankfully he'd outgrown the bare feet part. And now this memory of him doing it as a child was something she could add to her collection.

She turned down the TV and pointed the remote at the pizza box. "Do you want some?"

"I shouldn't," he said, eyeing the box. "I'm just here to fix a faucet upstairs, and then I'm having dinner with Dawn and the girls." But he moved closer, lifted the lid, and took a slice. "I do love sausage." He settled into the armchair against the wall.

For three minutes, they ate their pizza and watched TV in silence. When a judge on the baking competition made a snide remark about a weeping meringue, Mae and Wendell both laughed. She glanced at him from the corner of her eye, felt a tug of satisfaction, and went back to her pizza.

She chewed thoughtfully on the end of her crust. Lamenting about the divide in her family wouldn't change anything. This moment here with Wendell, this companionable silence that felt like home, was something worth chasing. The Townsends were starting to warm to her, little by little. And as for how to get through to them, she had the answer right in front of her. One offer of pizza and Wendell had voluntarily sat down to eat with her.

Althea had taken that same approach, really. That was basically what the Townsends said at the family dinner the other night: Althea coaxed them to come over for holidays and Sunday dinners by saying she'd made a feast for them and couldn't let it go to waste.

No wonder Althea had to go to such lengths to get the family together. The Townsends probably wouldn't take the initiative otherwise.

Mae took her feet off the coffee table, suddenly remorseful for her rudeness. She couldn't be disrespecting Althea's furniture. Althea was the only person she understood right now.

She picked up her phone to swipe through her pictures of Althea's recipes. Mae had a family dinner to plan.

CHAPTER TEN

MAE: Hey everyone! This is Mae. You're all invited to dinner tonight at Grandma's. Smothered chicken with rice, vegetarian black-eyed peas, collard greens, corn fritters, and peach cobbler for dessert. Dinner's served at 7!

ARIEL: Not Mae forcing us into a group chat

WENDELL: How are you texting? We took your phone away

JEREMIAH: What a feast!

ARIEL: I can text from my laptop

DESIREE: Wish we could be there! We drove back home to Asheville on Monday

BARBARA: That sounds delicious. Can we end the group chat?

LEAH: Group chats never end

TYRESE: Just had breakfast but suddenly I'm starving

JEREMIAH: Ethan left his caterpillar here! [Picture attached]

PHYLLIS: How did you get this number?

DAWN: How can I text from my laptop?

ARIEL: I'll show you if you give me my phone back

BARBARA: Leave group chat

Barbara was probably regretting giving Mae all the Townsend phone numbers she'd asked her for that morning. Mae hadn't said anything about a group chat. But it was easier that way. Mae took any excuse to throw people together into the same chat. The first thing Mae had done when she had to pick bridesmaids for the wedding was start a group chat with Jayla and two friends from college and call it *Here come the bridesmaids*. They were less than thrilled.

Mae was feeling one with Althea as she got started in the kitchen. Just pushing her cart down the aisles of the Food Lion up the road earlier that day had made her feel connected to Althea. But now, standing in her kitchen, pulling out the same spices and pots and pans Althea used, Mae had never felt closer to her grandmother.

Prepping for the dinner was an exercise in multitasking. While sitting in meetings, she turned the camera off and sliced onions, every so often pausing to check her phone when it went off with more rambles and grumbles from the Townsend group chat. (The latest was from Dawn, sending a test text from her laptop.) Then she'd enlarge her pictures of Althea's recipes, looking to see what she had to prep next, and start in on the garlic. And when her boss, Kevin, IM-ed her with a budget question, Mae had to wash her garlicky hands and hurriedly type a response to him quickly enough that he didn't catch onto how distracted she was.

Mae took a break from her flurry of activity to have a quick lunch: a prepared chicken salad sandwich she'd grabbed at Food Lion. She sat at the dining table, eating and scrolling social media posts, her mind running calculations on what time she should start cooking each dish to make sure everything was ready by seven. She kept scrolling, seeing posts without really seeing them.

The scroll slowed on a post from Madison. Predictably, she was sharing more pregnancy content. Today's post was a column graph about maternal mortality rates, accompanied by the caption:

> This makes me so sad. Growing a human is hard
> enough. We shouldn't have to fear for our lives on top of
> that.

Mae frowned. The graph was cut off. It showed rates for *All*, *White*, and *Hispanic*, but there was a sliver of what looked like another bar on the far right. Under it, the only part of the word that didn't get cut off was *Bl*.

Ordinarily, Mae wouldn't have wasted any time on this. It was just Madison being Madison, thinking of herself and no one else. But after learning about her grandma Doris's racist past yesterday, it was hard to look past anything about the Parkers anymore.

A reverse-image search turned up the original article, titled *Black women three times more likely to die in childbirth than white women*. The full graph showed that the column for Black women towered over the other columns Madison had posted.

Anger and annoyance rising within her, Mae returned to Madison's post and started typing.

> You'll be fine. If you'd read the article and shared the full
> graph, you'd know the point of the piece is that Black wom-
> en are way more at risk. Or do you not care about that?

She hit send before she could change her mind.

This grenade she'd just lobbed at her own flesh and blood

gave Mae another activity to add to her list. Between prepping dinner, working, and checking the Townsend group chat, she monitored Madison's post for responses.

Amber, another cousin on her mom's side, had liked Mae's comment. At least Amber could see reason.

Madison, evidently, could not.

This isn't a race issue, Mae. This is a women's issue.

Mae wanted to laugh at the absurdity that an article about Black women wasn't about race. She hit reply, started typing a tirade. But three ranting sentences in, she stopped, deleted her words. Waging a war over Madison's ignorance wouldn't get her anywhere.

She did take a screenshot of their exchange and send it to Jayla, her usual recourse with Madison's ignorance.

JAYLA: lmao typical white feminist bullshit

JAYLA: idk how you still have the patience for her. The unfollow button is free 😉

Mae sent back a laughing emoji, then paused, her thumb hovering over her phone. Turning her back on family felt wrong. Family was something you put up with. For better or for worse. Even if so many of her interactions with the Parkers seemed to fall under *worse.*

Mae swiped back to Instagram. Her thumb hovered over the Unfollow button on Madison's profile.

But she still couldn't do it.

By seven o'clock, Mae's multitasking narrowed to just one focus: wait for the Townsends.

The smothered chicken and gravy, collard greens, and the black-eyed peas she'd modified to make vegetarian for Sierra were ready and warm on the stove. The rice waited patiently in the rice cooker on the counter. The corn fritters were warming in the oven. The peach cobbler, fresh out of the oven, cooled on the counter next to a dish she hadn't told the Townsends about, which she'd covered in foil until it was time to bring it out. The entire house smelled heavenly, from the savory garlic and onion to the rich chicken-gravy to the cobbler's sweet cinnamon spice.

Mae breathed it in from her post by the living room window, waiting for a car to turn into the driveway. She tapped her nails on the windowsill as a car passed by. Suppose no one showed up? Or, suppose they did and everything would be different now that she knew what her grandma had done to Althea? She'd been so blissfully oblivious at the last family dinner. Did she need to say something to acknowledge what she now knew? Recite a formal statement when they were gathered around the table? Bow her head and apologize for having a racist grandma?

She checked her phone. No new messages in the group chat since Ariel last used it to crowdsource answers to her math homework an hour ago.

Mae wandered to the kitchen to check on the food. Suddenly this all seemed like...a lot. An embarrassing amount of food. She could eat this for every meal for the next week and still have leftovers. This was probably karmic retribution for her seating chart lie.

Then the doorbell rang.

Mae spun on her heel and rushed to the door. There on the doorstep stood Phyllis and Jeremiah.

"You came!" Mae exclaimed.

"With that menu? We wouldn't miss it!" Jeremiah said, greeting her with a hug.

"Thank you for inviting us," Phyllis said. Her smile was a touch perfunctory, but she could have been openly scowling for all Mae cared. She was *here*.

High off of Jeremiah's hug, Mae opened her arms to Phyllis in what was very much a high risk, high reward move.

Phyllis hesitated a second, then accepted the hug, giving Mae two quick pats on the back and pulling away.

Reward it was.

Jeremiah, already in the kitchen, raved about how good everything looked, and Mae decided if she ever needed a hype man, Jeremiah would be a top candidate for the job.

More Townsends trickled in after that: Wendell and his family, Tyrese, Barbara, and even Sierra, to Mae's surprise. Sierra was the one person who hadn't acknowledged the group chat at all. But here she was, standing around in the kitchen with the rest of them, eyeing Mae's peach cobbler while Leah and Phyllis chatted about a horror novel they were reading and Tyrese updated Wendell about a job interview he had that day.

Mae caught herself edging further away, bit by bit, until she backed into the dishwasher. It beeped to life, she whipped around to silence it, and when she turned back, the Townsends were all watching her. She leaned her elbows on the counter behind her, aiming for cool and casual as her mind searched for something to say. Bringing up her grandma discovery felt like throwing ice water on the glowing, familial fire sparking here in Althea's kitchen.

"Can I get you all something to drink?" Mae asked. "Or," she said, an idea coming to her, "maybe I should just say...roll call!" She looked around the room, seeing only confused looks. Her smile faltered. "What?"

"We only do that at Uncle Jeremiah and Aunt Phyllis's," Ariel explained.

"Just something silly that started with Tyrese and Scott when they were little," Jeremiah said. "I don't think your grandma ever really understood it."

Mae's cheeks burned. It was only fitting that she'd somehow missed the nuance and done it wrong. The Townsends and their secret traditions and their exceptions to the traditions were exhausting. She stuck her hands in the back pockets of her shorts, squirming under the horde of eyes on her. "Well, *I* don't understand it either," she said.

Dawn laughed. "None of us do."

That eased her embarrassment a little. Phyllis told a story poking fun at one of Jeremiah's family's holiday traditions involving a glass boot of eggnog, and Mae went around serving drinks in the normal, boring, non-roll-call way.

At the table, Mae ended up sitting between Leah and Tyrese. People served themselves, Mae watching anxiously to see how they liked it. Althea's recipes had been vague, just ingredients and arrows and monosyllabic directions. There was probably much more left between the lines that she'd missed. She watched Barbara take a bite of chicken, trying to get a read on her face as she chewed.

"It's wonderful," Barbara said with an approving nod.

"Fritters are great," said Jeremiah.

Mae had to stop herself from doing a fist-pump. "Really?"

"What's the green stuff?" asked Ariel.

"Oh, I went a little off-script with that," Mae explained. "I made a cilantro sauce that I thought would pair well with the fritters."

Leah gave an uncertain hum.

"I like it," Phyllis said, licking a dab of sauce off her finger.

"The black-eyed peas are vegetarian?" Sierra asked.

"Yeah. No bacon. And I used veggie stock instead of chicken stock."

A small smile crossed Sierra's features. "Thanks."

Mae watched her spoon a large scoop on her plate, a ribbon of joy running through her. Now, while everyone was enjoying the food, was the time to bring out the surprise.

"There's another reason I invited you all over today," she said. Meeting their curious looks with a mysterious grin, she darted into the kitchen, coming back with the foil-covered dish she'd left off the menu. She set it on the table between Leah and Tyrese, peeling the foil back in a slow reveal. "It's the first batch of mac and cheese for you to taste test!"

Seeing them warily eye the dish, Mae began to regret all the fanfare she'd sprinkled into this moment—but not enough to back down. Even as she took her seat, she gestured obnoxiously to the square dish, as if they could have possibly missed it.

"It looks different," Ariel said.

"Looks can be deceiving," Mae replied. Though she was fairly certain this was not one of those times. She'd drawn from a recipe from one of Althea's cookbooks, modifying it to add a baked cheese topping. It looked fine enough, but it was still a stab in the dark and they all knew it.

Tyrese was first to volunteer. He scooped a small spoonful

onto his plate and took a bite. A few others followed suit, spooning tiny amounts onto their plates.

"Well?" Mae prompted. He gestured to his still-chewing mouth, and she fought off an impatient sigh.

"It's okay," Tyrese said. "There's nothing wrong with it, but it's definitely not Grandma's."

Mae chewed on her thumbnail. She knew she wouldn't have gotten it right on the first try, but some part of her still hoped she could have miraculously done just that. The Townsends would praise her, call her a culinary genius, say Althea's spirit lived on in her. They'd also add that they'd decided to come to her wedding after all.

Wildly unrealistic, but she was allowed to dream.

"How is it different specifically?" she asked.

He shrugged. "It's bland."

"So…more salt?"

"More *flavor*," Wendell said, taking a bite from the dish.

"What flavors?" Mae prompted. She typed a string of notes into her phone. "Garlic? Onion? Something else? Or does it need different cheeses?"

"I'm not sure." Wendell took another bite, frowning as he chewed.

"The texture's not right," Leah volunteered. "It should be creamier. But also…less saucy. It should stick together better."

"Anything else?" she asked. Her eyes fell on Sierra. Mae could see from the noodles on her plate that she'd tried it, but Sierra said nothing. Mae's shoulders drooped. It was going to be hard to get the recipe right if the person who cared most about this dish refused to cooperate.

With the mandatory taste test over, Mae dug into the food

on her plate as people talked. The mac and cheese may have been a miss, but the Townsends had approved of everything else (Leah and Ariel's reservations about the cilantro sauce aside). She ate knowing that this was what her grandma's cooking was like: rich, hearty, and full of flavor.

Some time after the peach cobbler was doled out, Mae began to see the signs that people were itching to leave. The conversations around the table died down, and the primary sound in the room was metal clinking against ceramic as people finished the last of their cobbler. Phyllis was checking her watch for the third time, and Leah had been scrolling on her phone all throughout dessert. Mae searched for an excuse to raise a new topic.

"Is there a list of people I should invite for the barbecue?" she asked.

"You're still set on that, are you?" Phyllis replied, giving her a bemused look.

"Well, yeah. I'm not gonna miss my chance to see the famous family barbecue."

Ariel snorted. "It's not famous."

"It's famous to *me*," Mae said with a laugh. "I always wished I could join my dad when he flew out for it every year."

Sierra, head down as she prodded at her cobbler, scoffed.

"What?" Mae said, defenses rising. If Sierra had something to say, she wished she'd just come out and say it. Or say anything at all.

Barbara and Phyllis exchanged a look. Wendell's eyes skittered between Mae and Sierra. Tyrese took great interest in his can of Sprite.

"It's pretty straightforward," Barbara said quickly. "It'll be some family, friends, and neighbors. I can work on a list."

"Okay." Mae waited to see if Sierra would speak, but she stayed focused on her cobbler. "Brian stopped by yesterday and I invited him," Mae said, a silent *so there* punctuating her statement. See, she knew people. She belonged here.

"Who's Brian?" Barbara asked, cocking her head to the side.

"Brian Posey." Watching them exchange surprised looks around the table, Mae decided she wouldn't let herself feel *too* superior about being closer to Althea's neighbors than the Townsends were. It just felt good to finally know something for a change.

And then Ariel shrieked, "You invited Nosy Posey!" and the entire table burst out laughing.

"Mom *hated* him!" Phyllis gasped between laughs.

"Always getting in her business, writing in that damn notebook," Wendell wheezed.

Mae, shrinking in her chair, resigned herself to embarrassed silence. Sierra was laughing too, because why wouldn't she be. Leah had her napkin pressed against her mouth, her shoulders shaking. Even Jeremiah couldn't help himself, falling against Phyllis as he laughed.

"I can uninvite him," Mae mumbled into her plate.

"Don't," Tyrese said, putting a hand on her arm. "It's funnier if he comes."

"What did he say when you invited him?" Dawn asked.

Sheepishly, Mae recounted how he'd knocked on the door and started interrogating her. "I mostly invited him because I didn't know what to say," she admitted.

"He knows how to trip you up," Barbara agreed. "Mom was the only one who could call his bluff."

"Remember when he passed around a sign-up sheet to get

people to volunteer for shifts to watch the neighborhood?" Phyllis asked, eyes shining at the memory. "And Mom signed up for every single one and then did nothing?" More laughter. "He was furious!"

"Nosy Posey in Mom's backyard," Wendell said with a contented sigh. "Never would have imagined it."

"What do you think he'd even eat?" Jeremiah mused, wrinkling his nose.

"Jell-O," Sierra said.

Mae's laugh came unexpectedly, surprising even herself. When the Townsends turned to her with befuddled expressions, she said, "Because it's see-through, right?"

Sierra, with a smile growing across her face, nodded.

While the table broke into a mix of groans and laughter, Mae kept her eyes on Sierra, who was still watching her with that smile. Mae had to press her lips together to keep from breaking into a satisfied grin. She could feel a thaw start to set in between them, a soft but steady glow warming her from within.

Mae's embarrassment about the Nosy Posey incident washed away as the Townsends carried on. It was worth her faux pas to hear these new details about Althea. She listened to them share more memories of Althea and her grudge against Nosy Posey, laughed along with them when they joked about more foods and drinks Nosy Posey probably consumed, just so he could spy on people through them whenever the need arose: broth, lemonade, weak tea, donuts and bagels, and anything else with a hole he could stick an eye through.

As the Townsends trickled out the door still chatting among themselves, Mae stayed put. She opened her Notes app and reviewed what she'd jotted down earlier:

Bland. Add spices? Garlic/onion? Different cheeses?

Needs to be creamier and "less saucy"

She could do some brainstorming tonight to figure out what tweaks to make for the next batch. But first, she swiped to the note titled *BBQ Menu* where she'd put down a few initial thoughts. At the end of the list, she added *Jell-O.*

Traditions were sacred, Mae knew. The barbecue was certainly sacred to her, even though she'd never been.

But new traditions were important, too. Mae never would have anticipated that Nosy Posey and Jell-O, of all things, were going to be her great contribution to the Fourth of July barbecue. But remembering the laughter tonight, the way an entire room of still-grieving relatives had gotten the giggles imagining an elderly man spying through a Jell-O mold, she couldn't be prouder of the strange, new custom she was creating with this year's barbecue. And who knew? Nosy Posey and Jell-O—and Mae—might become family barbecue fixtures for years to come.

CHAPTER ELEVEN

MAE: Good morning! Reminder that I'm planning the BBQ invite list. Who else should come? Besides our bestie Nosy Posey?

SCOTT: Why is Nosy Posey coming???

TYRESE: This is what happens when Mae's in charge

PHYLLIS: Neighbors to invite are Richard, Marlene and Joan, and the Sandersons, Ortizes, and Davises

BARBARA: And the ladies from the church. Harriet, Patty, Diamond, Charlotte, Rhonda

ARIEL: Except not Patty

BARBARA: No, invite Patty

ARIEL: Patty's a bitch

DAWN: ARIEL. You know better than that.

ARIEL: It's true!

BARBARA: Patty is particular, but she was a close friend of your grandma's and we have to invite her

ARIEL: Is "particular" code for bitch?

WENDELL: Ariel, that's enough.

BARBARA: Yes

Mae yawned into her coffee as she sat at the dining room table watching the texts come in. She waited to see if Phyllis or Barbara might specify where to find these neighbors and church ladies. But when the conversation derailed to speculation about what secret ingredients Richard must put in his homemade cider, Mae let the chat carry on and decided to see what she could dig up on her own. That address book she'd found in Althea's nightstand a couple of nights ago flashed through her mind. She raced upstairs to retrieve it.

Back at the dining table, she flipped through Althea's address book, running her finger down weathered pages, parsing through blue-inked script for entries that matched the names Phyllis and Barbara had texted. Unlike her cramped scrap-paper recipes, Althea's address book handwriting was clear and intentional, large, swooping letters spelling out names and numbers. Mae could gauge Althea's feelings about each person by the shape the entry took. Entries for the church ladies and some neighbors were more detailed—birthdays, anniversaries, phone numbers for their spouses or kids, phrases like *Run RDC* or *Veggie House* that Mae couldn't make sense of but assumed meant something. The entry for *Brian (Nosy Posey)*, meanwhile, was bare and obligatory besides the taunting nickname, just basic details and nothing more.

Mae started with Richard, who lived two doors down. His entry had included the oddly cryptic phrase *Jelly Kraft*. As she approached his house, a split-level like Althea's, she checked the exterior for signs that he had some sort of jelly obsession, but the shiny white vinyl siding told her nothing.

Richard, a kindly, dark-skinned man with frizzy white hair and glasses in bright-blue frames, raised an eyebrow when Mae introduced herself, but he warmed to her when she told him about the barbecue. He agreed to bring his homemade cider, even making her wait at the door while he ran into his garage to hand her a bottle to try.

"It's really good," she said, taking another drink. It was fresh and crisp, less sweet than the store-bought ciders she'd had. When she lowered the bottle, a black Labrador with a wagging tail had come to stand beside Richard, sniffing inquiringly in Mae's direction. The silver tag dangling from its collar read *Jelly*.

"Jelly?" Mae said. Both Jelly and Richard fixed their gazes on Mae.

"You know my dog?" Richard said, eyeing her in confusion.

Mae smiled into her bottle. "My grandma had a note next to your name in her address book. It just said 'Jelly Kraft.' I didn't know what it meant."

Richard frowned. "Craft?"

"Kraft, with a K. Like the cheese."

"I don't—" Richard stopped, eyes roving with thought, and then he burst into laughter. "That woman's been sneaking food to my dog!" Seeing Mae's puzzled expression, he explained, "Jelly always came running whenever I opened a slice of American cheese—that plastic crinkle. I always figured whoever had Jelly before me used to feed her Kraft singles." He shook his head. "Explains why Jelly was always jumping fences to get into Althea's yard. She raised such a fuss over it, telling me to control my dog. Come to find it was all her fault!"

Mae laughed, delighting in the dichotomy between Richard's indignant tone and his sentimental smile. "That sounds like her," she said, feeling a ripple of satisfaction at having enough of an inkling to say this.

"That woman's a con artist." He crossed his arms and leaned

against the door frame. "I was falling over myself apologizing, bringing her cider, mowing her lawn, trying to make it up to her." He glanced toward Althea's house. "I hope you're doing something about that yard before the barbecue. My days of mowing that lawn are over."

Mae followed his gaze. She hadn't paid much attention to the backyard, come to think of it. She'd caught glimpses of tall grass through the kitchen window but hadn't yet gone into the yard. She mentally moved *Mow lawn* up her to-do list.

"I can mow it," she said, keeping her voice even despite the doubt coiling in her. "I remember seeing a mower in the garage." Subtask: *Watch a tutorial on how to use a lawnmower.*

"Don't bother with that old thing," Richard said with a wave of his hand. "Borrow mine. It's electric. Way better." He disappeared again, and it wasn't until Mae heard the rumble of his garage door opening that she realized she was supposed to come around and meet him there.

And then Mae was carefully wheeling a lawn mower down the sidewalk with one hand, a bottle of cider in the other, and a charger and cable wedged between her elbow and her side. From a porch across the street, a pair of older women stared at her. Mae noticed the numbers on their house and discerned that they were Marlene and Joan. She stopped and lifted her hand in a wave. The one on the left, a Black woman with a book in her lap, was first to wave back, and the other, a white woman in an oversized T-shirt and loose shorts, soon followed. Mae smiled to herself and continued pushing the mower to Althea's. One introduction down, and the next was already off to a promising start.

With the mower safely in the garage, Mae dashed inside to

check Althea's address book. Marlene and Joan's entry included the phrase *Veggie House*, her next mysterious clue.

Marlene and Joan greeted Mae with welcoming smiles and invited her to join them on the porch. As they poured her a glass of sweet tea and plied her with thumbprint cookies, Mae asked if *Veggie House* meant anything to them. Marlene and Joan shared a surprised look.

"It's my nephew's vegan restaurant," said Marlene, setting her book on the small wicker table between them. "He opened it a couple years ago. I asked Althea if she'd want to go sometime, and she said it was too crunchy for her. She really wrote it down?"

Mae nodded. "I get the idea that she cares more than she lets on," she said. Her voice caught as the idea struck her that Althea just might have cared about *Mae* more than she was willing to admit, too.

That afternoon, Mae threw herself into making introductions, issuing barbecue invitations, and dropping revelations that delighted Althea's friends and neighbors. On the Sandersons' doorstep, she learned *Abby Lorna* referred to their youngest daughter's love of Lorna Doone shortbread cookies. Frank Ortiz explained with wide-eyed wonder that *Run RDC* was the website for the marathon he ran several years ago, noting that Althea must have followed his race-day progress on the site, even though she was always lecturing him about heatstroke whenever she saw him running outside.

Mae learned from calling Althea's church friends that they felt no such surprise at learning what Althea knew about them. She quickly gathered that this was a tight-knit group. There was something endearing in knowing her grandma had a squad. Still, the notes proved useful in dispelling the bemused distrust they emitted on hearing Mae's name. She wished Harriet a happy belated birthday, asked Diamond how her husband Owen was doing, listened to Charlotte explain how Althea's *No seafood* note told a story of an allergy, a church potluck, and a mislabeled tub of crab dip. Patty was the only friend Mae couldn't soften. True to her reputation, she said in a clipped voice that it was rude to extend an invitation at such short notice. But even she, like all the others, agreed to attend the barbecue, and Mae ended the call awash in triumph.

She came away with more than triumph, actually. She didn't notice it until she sat at the dining room table to join her two o'clock weekly meeting, but the table was scattered with offerings and notes she'd collected from her door-to-door canvassing and calling. Marlene and Joan had given her a Veggie House menu, suggesting she visit the restaurant and drop their names for a discount. Abby Sanderson gave her a packet of Lorna Doones. Frank Ortiz, shooting Mae a look of concern when she admitted she didn't exercise regularly, handed her a flyer for a gym he belonged to. Charlotte had Mae write down the time and address of her group's weekly bible study sessions and told Mae she had a standing invitation. All signs of the steadfast community Althea had built here.

Mae could only half-listen during her meeting. While talk of timelines and marketing plans floated through her ears, the rest of her crunched on buttery Lorna Doones, read through the Veggie House menu, and basked in the quiet contentment of feeling like she was well on her way to becoming part of Althea's community.

––––––––––

Mae stared down Richard's electric mower, as if she could intimidate it into looking less terrifying. Shiny and green, robotic and unblinking, it stared right back at her in a silent challenge.

She tied her hair up with a scarf, stalling as she hyped herself up. She could do this. The tutorials she'd watched had all bizarrely assumed Mae at least knew the basics of lawn-mowing, which. She didn't. But there was only one way to figure it out. She pushed the mower into the front yard—waved at Marlene and Joan again, who were still there on the porch, ready to witness her every mistake—and let the mower roar to life.

The neat, parallel lines Mae had planned in her head soon gave way to crooked uncertainty, but she wiped the sweat off her forehead and kept going. She also realized, nearing the dogwood tree, that she wasn't entirely sure how close she was supposed to get. She stopped in place and tried to think over the mower's impatient snarl. The tutorial had said to cut at an angle around trees, but what did that even mean? And how was she supposed to navigate around the giant tree root running through the yard?

"Mae!"

She looked up. Marlene was waving her down from the porch. Mae silenced the mower's roar.

"Everything going okay?" Marlene called.

"Yeah," Mae shouted back. What her voice lacked in certainty, it made up for in volume. Marlene gave her a thumbs up. Mae returned it, grimaced at the mower, and powered it back on.

This turned out to be far from the last interruption. Marlene called out to her again a few minutes later, when Mae stopped to furiously scratch a mosquito bite on her calf, to ask if she wanted any sweet tea. Mae politely declined, then spent the next few minutes regretting her politeness. The sun beat down on the back of her neck, her throat became a desert, and sweat seeped through her shirt. She was starting to understand the South's sweet tea fixation. It wasn't just a drink; it was a cold, caffeinated elixir for staving off sticky heat. Sweet tea was a miracle, and she was an idiot for turning it down. While she continued mowing uneven stripes of incompetence into the front yard, she fantasized about pouring Marlene's pitcher of sweet tea over her head and luxuriating in the cold.

As she moved on to the task she'd put off—attempting to angle the mower around the tree—Joan slowed her green hatchback to a stop in front of the yard, sticking a large plastic cup out the window. "I got you a Baja Blast."

Mae could have kissed her. She accepted it gratefully and spent a few serene minutes sitting in the driveway, drinking her Baja Blast, watching Marlene and Joan dig into Crunchwraps and conversation on the porch. Sunshine and asphalt conspired to make her skin sizzle, but she felt impervious to it as long as she had this cold, sugary drink coursing through her system. Not the sweet tea she'd been fantasizing about, but it tasted like relief all the same.

Mowing the backyard had its own interruptions. Richard happened to be in his yard playing catch with Jelly, and even from two fences over, he tried to backseat mow. He yelled helpful instructions Mae couldn't hear over the sound of the mower and then mimed advice to her in incomprehensible gestures—until she turned the mower off, and then he'd call out, "Perimeter first!" or "Overlap!" Mae didn't know what this last one meant, but she made a big show of nodding and thanking him before carrying on with her fumbling.

She stopped the mower when she came to a small corner of backyard where she noticed the remains of a garden, grass giving way to a patch of mulch with square, wooden raised beds. The beds were overrun with weeds, but the Popsicle sticks peeking through the dirt hinted at the form this garden might have taken once upon a time.

"Did the mower stop on you?" Richard shouted, leaning over the short fence separating his yard from their shared neighbor's. "Check the air vents!"

"No, it's fine!" Mae called back. She knelt down, her knees sinking into prickly grass. The writing on some of the Popsicle sticks was dark and smudgy, but she could make out others: CUCUMBER, TOMATO, RADISH. This had to be where her grandpa had done his gardening.

Spotting his gardening books in the office had been one thing, invoking a nebulous impulse to ask about him. But seeing the neglected remains of his garden, his careful, all-caps Sharpie lettering, a wave of longing washed over her. These neatly organized plots, the perfect lettering, the labels—it was exactly the sort of thing she would do, if she had a garden.

Mae rifled through her fleeting memories of meeting her grandpa at her dad's funeral: his tall figure and quiet voice, that gentle smile he'd put on when he'd asked Mae what her favorite subject in school was. He'd died nine years ago, she remembered from an obituary she'd found in Althea's office. She could understand why the Townsends' conversations had been so Althea-centric—he'd been gone for longer. But she swore that this time she wouldn't let herself forget to ask her relatives more about him, this kindred spirit with a green thumb and a flair for organization.

"Lawn looks nice," spoke a quiet, hesitant voice.

Mae turned to see Phyllis stepping through the sliding back door. She almost didn't know how to handle a simple compliment after all Richard's commentary. "Thank you."

"Little early to mow it now, though, isn't it? Won't you have to do it again closer to the barbecue?"

Mae's shoulders sagged. None of the tutorials she'd watched—nor Richard, practically a real-life tutorial—had explained how frequently lawns were supposed to be mowed.

Phyllis stepped further into the yard until her brown sandals came into view beside Mae.

"Been a while since I thought about this garden."

Mae looked up, seeing her soft expression. "Was this my grandpa's?"

"He called the yard the 'Herb garden.' I think that joke is the only reason he went by Herb instead of Herbert," she said with a fond eyeroll. "He did love this yard, though. He planted vegetables here, the rose bushes on the side of the house. He taught me how to look after plants."

Mae rose to her feet and brushed off her grassy knees. "What did he do with the vegetables?"

"He loved making 'Herb salad,'" Phyllis said, a gentle mockery touching her voice. "That's what he always called it. Just cucumber, tomato, and parsley. A little bit of lemon juice and salt. Mom said it was a sin to make salad without dressing, but he loved it."

A quiet laugh bubbled out of Mae. Any salad she'd ever seen her dad eat was studded with bacon bits and drenched in ranch. It was starting to make sense why he never rhapsodized about Herb salad. Though the salad sounded familiar for a different reason. Goosebumps swept the back of her neck when a Tomatotember recipe flashed into her mind.

"I've made something like that," she said. "A few different ingredients, but the same concept. The salt draws out the liquid, so it kind of makes its own dressing."

"That's what Dad said," Phyllis said incredulously. "And Mom would tell him no salad should have to dress itself."

She smiled. It was easy to picture Althea asserting her culinary opinions. She wondered what Herb would have said in response. What he would have thought about her Tomatotember exploits. "What was he like?"

Phyllis slapped at a mosquito on her arm, then let out a pensive sigh, lifting her eyes to the cloudless blue sky. "He was more introverted than Mom. She liked throwing big dinners and volunteering at the church and visiting the neighbors. He liked hiding out with a puzzle. He was very composed, never raised his voice. Mom could yell for twenty minutes straight if we spilled juice on the rug, but he was more calm about everything. Nothing could rattle him."

Mae gave a thoughtful hum. That sounded a lot like her dad, actually. He always knew how to keep his composure, even at those family dinners with the Parkers.

"He wasn't even rattled when he found out my dad got my mom pregnant out of wedlock?" she asked, half-joking.

Phyllis opened her mouth to say something—but then she seemed to think better of it, her eyes roaming like she was looking for a script. She pursed her lips. "He was surprised," she said. From Phyllis's tone, it sounded half like a question, half like a statement. But she didn't elaborate. Instead, she asked, "How's the mac and cheese coming along?"

Mae tried to read Phyllis's face. That sudden turn into discomfort was like those moments at the reception. She'd thought they'd all moved past that by now, but apparently any subject that touched upon her parents' courtship would spark awkwardness. It was dejecting, seeing how deep this ran—and knowing she couldn't do anything to change it.

"Fine," Mae replied dimly. "It's a work in progress." Which summed up everything, really. The barbecue. The yard. Her attempts to weave into this family. The frustration of it made her want to let out a growling sigh, throw a tantrum, demand answers.

Instead, she looked down to the garden at her feet. She surveyed the dry, caked-over dirt, the weeds cropping up, the crooked Popsicle sticks. This garden wasn't complaining, yelling, fussing. It just sat here, quietly fading, expecting nothing. Even though it deserved more.

Gingerly, she bent to her knees and tugged at a weed until it gave way and broke off in her hand. She kept going, reaching for more, both hands grasping for every imperfection crowding the garden Herb had worked so hard on.

Phyllis walked off not long after, but Mae kept going. There was something satisfying about using her hands, channeling her frustration into these weeds that couldn't avoid her.

She jumped when a rusty trowel dropped into the grass beside her. Mae looked up to see Phyllis holding a trowel of her own, a wrinkled orange towel and a pair of gardening gloves in her hands. Phyllis shook out the towel and laid it on the grass, then knelt next to her and handed her a glove. Mae followed her movements: scooting onto the towel, putting on a glove, using the trowel to dig under the roots of the weeds, scooping them up intact and dropping them into an ever-growing pile.

Mae got no more answers that afternoon, no explanation for that awkward moment she still didn't understand. But she liked to think Herb would be proud of what they did here, if he could see them. She couldn't fix the past, couldn't fix her family, but she could fix this garden. In this moment, that simple truth felt like the only one that mattered.

Sitting on the couch looking up gardening tutorials on her phone that night, Mae noticed her search history perfectly encapsulated the range of her meandering ambitions that day.

How to mow a lawn
How to start a lawn mower
How to mow around a tree
Sweet tea recipe
Mosquito bite remedies
How to get family to like you
How to start a garden

Then the screen changed, her phone buzzed, and Connor's flashing name jolted her with a reminder that there was a whole other life she'd been putting on pause to pursue these exploits.

"Everything is happening at once," Connor announced when she answered. He looked like he was fiddling with something off-screen, which already wasn't a good sign. Connor got fidgety when he was stressed. He always insisted he didn't and ignored the stress balls and fidget toys she'd tried gifting him over the years, but then he'd pick his fingernails until they bled or obsessively flip the pages of Mae's Post-its back and forth until the entire stack had a permanent curve.

"What's wrong?" she asked.

"The favor boxes arrived." He held up a small, flattened square of plain white cardboard. "I meant to start folding them into boxes tonight, but I never got past this one. It's actually kind of fun to play with." His hands manipulated the cardboard, expanding it and then flattening it again, first one direction and then the next.

"Something up?" Mae asked, eyeing the cardboard's worn creases.

"Just…the interview tomorrow. I keep trying to prep for it, but there's only so much I can do." Back and forth the cardboard folded. "And then getting these," he added, lifting the cardboard. "I'm already gonna be spending tonight obsessing over the interview, and then my dad springs on me that I have to assemble three hundred tiny boxes. And I have my first dance lesson tomorrow night and I don't know what shoes I'm supposed to wear, and I also have four meetings tomorrow, and it's all just a lot."

Mae ached to pull that cardboard out of his hands and lace her fingers through his. She knew, even though he wasn't saying it, that her absence was a stressor too. If she'd been there, she could have helped fold the favor boxes, helped him prepare for his interview, handed him one of the many stress balls she'd bought him, be there at the dance lesson. Instead, she was here, causing more stress.

"Your interview's gonna go great," she said. "The favor boxes can wait. Maybe wear your dress shoes to the dance lesson?" Mae frowned, realizing she wasn't sure either. "And bring your gym shoes just in case? If Christopher Walker is as great as your parents say he is, he should be able to teach you in anything." She ran her tongue along the underside of her teeth. "And I'm sorry about all the meetings. You should get that hazelnut coffee thing you like on your way to work tomorrow."

His folding movements slowed. "Everyone else in the office drinks black coffee."

"Everyone else is boring. That's why you're leaving! Ask Kaufman and Stout how they feel about hazelnut mochaccinos. I bet they love them."

Connor laughed. "I'll add it to my list of questions."

"I'm sorry I'm not there with you."

"It's okay." And he did look more okay now. He'd set the cardboard down and was staring wistfully at the camera. "Are you getting close with that recipe? I could really use you here."

Mae scratched a bite on her arm. Between inviting Althea's neighbors and church friends to the barbecue, mowing the lawn, checking in at work, weeding the Herb garden, and paging through his gardening books to learn the basics of planting, she hadn't made any progress on the recipe today.

"I made the first test batch a couple of nights ago. And it wasn't close. But I'll be working on it more tomorrow," she rushed to say. "I just had to deal with...other stuff."

Connor, bless him, didn't even fault her for it. He just said, "What kind of stuff?" and listened, chin cupped in hand, while Mae recapped her encounters with Althea's neighbors, her lawn-mowing efforts, the mosquitos eating her alive, and working on the Herb garden with Phyllis.

"I still feel like there's something else going on that nobody's telling me," she confessed, mentally replaying that awkward moment with Phyllis. Hearing the words spoken aloud, she groaned and ran a hand down her face. "I sound like a conspiracy theorist."

"I'd believe your conspiracies," he said, his smile warm and genuine. "I think it's just gonna take some time."

"I don't *have* a lot of time." She scratched frantically at the bite on her arm. "I know I need to get back, and I promise I'll spend all day tomorrow working on the recipe so I can—"

"It's okay. I get it." His calming tone had her letting out a long breath and relaxing a little more into the couch cushions.

"Thank you," she said. "I swear I'll try to be home soon."

"I'm sending you some lotion for the mosquito bites."

Mae laughed. "I'm sending you a fidget toy."

"Deal," he said with a grin.

After they hung up—and Mae ordered him a fidget cube—she revisited her notes from the first taste test. Connor had been sweet and patient, but she needed to make real progress on the recipe soon if she had any chance of getting home before the barbecue. Connor didn't deserve to deal with all the wedding preparations on his own.

But if there *was* another family secret, she couldn't help thinking as she pulled Althea's cookbooks off the shelf, she didn't deserve to be left in the dark.

Mae settled in for an evening of flipping through cookbooks to find a lead on the mac and cheese recipe. The back of her mind, meanwhile, kept turning over that moment with Phyllis, wondering what else the Townsends might be hiding.

CHAPTER TWELVE

Watching smoke billow from the hood of her car was not on Mae's to-do list for the day.

All she'd planned to do that morning was take a trip to the Publix in Durham, which she hoped would have a wider selection of cheeses than the small, deserted Food Lion by Althea's house. One of Althea's cookbooks had recommended a two-year aged cheddar, and picking up some of that—and whatever other cheeses caught her eye—could help edge her closer to the recipe.

But a mere five minutes from her destination, she noticed a strange smell, like something was burning. Seconds later, plumes of smoke started rising from the hood of her car, and Mae had to pull over to the side of the road.

She stood in front of her car, hands on hips, utterly at a loss. If she'd known this was going to happen, she would have looked up a tutorial for what to do when your car starts smoking.

Mae sighed and looked around. At least this happened on a multilane road with space to pull over. But she was miles from Althea's, the car hood was so hot she couldn't touch it, she didn't know what she could have done if she *had* been able to lift the hood, and—most tragically—she hadn't even had breakfast yet.

After calling to arrange a tow and getting an estimated wait time of an hour, she paced the strip of grass on the side of the road. She tried calling Connor, but when she reached his voicemail, she checked the time and remembered he was in his Kaufman and Stout interview. Next, she texted Jayla a string of complaints. Jayla replied sympathetically, but said she was about to head into a meeting and couldn't talk until after.

She scrolled further down her recent contacts and saw Barbara's name. The word *sweetheart* floated into her ears like a familiar melody, wrapping her in a cocoon of comfort.

Suddenly, her phone was calling Barbara's. Mae took in a sharp breath, found the end-call button…but her thumb could only linger above it, refusing to press down.

"Hello?" Barbara sounded confused, but not indifferent. Mae clung to that strand of interest and let the story spill out, her voice growing more confident as she spoke. If Barbara didn't care, she wouldn't have picked up. Family relied on one another, didn't they? Had they finally reached that point?

"I'm at work," Barbara said, piercing Mae's airy hopes with reality. "But let me see what I can do."

Mae was left to lean against the side of her car and hope Barbara didn't forget about her while she was—well, Mae didn't know what Barbara did for a living. Somehow they'd never gotten around to discussing the basics. *What do you do?* probably wasn't something most relatives needed to ask each other.

Twenty minutes later, a silver Honda pulled up behind Mae. Sierra, dressed in a wrinkled gray T-shirt and loose black joggers, got out of the car.

"How'd you know where I was?" Mae asked.

"Bee said you were on the Clarendon Turnpike and that you could see a Hilton from where you were." She pointed at the multilane traffic next to them, then at the hotel in the shopping center across the road. "Clarendon Turnpike. Hilton."

It was hard to reconcile her snarky tone with the kindness of her showing up here at all.

"You didn't have to come out here," Mae said. "The tow's not coming for another forty minutes at least."

Sierra joined Mae by the side of her car, keeping a healthy distance between them. "I didn't want you waiting alone."

Mae had to restrain herself from calling attention to this, asking Sierra if this meant she cared, asking why she'd been so aloof before. Instead, she swallowed her feelings and stuck to a simple *thank you*.

A silence stretched between them, punctuated by the whir of cars speeding by. Mae watched the cars for a while, then snuck a glance at Sierra. She was staring at her phone, her thumb swiping at the screen. Mae breathed in a sigh through her nose, accidentally getting a whiff of her car's burning smoke in the process. She coughed violently into her elbow, cleared her throat as if nothing happened. Sierra lifted her head long enough to visually confirm that Mae hadn't died, then went back to her phone.

They did this dance for a while, Mae watching cars and shuffling her feet in the dirt and peeking at Sierra from the corner of her eye and trying her best to maintain the silence Sierra clearly wanted; Sierra ignoring the antsy mess next to her. Mae knew she could have busied herself on her phone like Sierra, but it felt like giving up. Like any second now, Sierra was going to put down her phone, see the interest written all over Mae's face, and initiate a spontaneous heart-to-heart right here on the side of the road.

When Sierra let out a sigh and tucked her phone into her pocket, Mae turned to her, ready for soul-baring conversation.

"How much longer do you think they'll be?" Sierra asked.

Oh.

Mae checked the time, then forced a sunny smile. "Shouldn't be much longer now." Sierra moved on to examining her nails, and Mae raced to prolong the exchange. "So, um…are you excited about moving to Seattle?"

A dark and bitter laugh tumbled from Sierra. "Not especially."

"Why?"

Sierra looked down at her sneakers. "I don't know. I don't love my job, and my life is here."

"But?" Mae prodded.

"I guess…I see my friends settling down and starting families and *doing* something, and I'm…" She shrugged. "Maybe a change wouldn't be so bad."

A thousand questions sprang to Mae's mind, about Sierra, her life, her job, her friends. She waited a beat, then selected one follow-up. "What do you do?"

"I'm a financial analyst."

Mae nodded. Waited. Carefully put forth another question. "And you don't like it?"

"It's stressful. They act like the work we do is the most important thing in the world, and…" She wrinkled her nose. "It's not? We're helping rich people make more money. So we can make money off their money. There's nothing important about that."

"I try not to think about the big picture, honestly," Mae said.

"I'm a project manager for a marketing agency. All we do is help clients spam more customers. But I like the work I do. Keeping track of schedules and budgets. I love a good spreadsheet."

Sierra chuckled. "At least you like it. I have to bring in a set number of new accounts every quarter, and some of these people are just entitled dicks."

Mae's eyes went back to Sierra's casual outfit. "How come you're not at work now?"

"Oh, um." Sierra ran a hand up her scalp, lifting her curls and letting them fall back into place. "I've been on leave for the last few weeks," she admitted quietly. "I couldn't be in that place anymore. When Grandma died, something in me just...broke, I think."

"Because you were close?" Mae asked.

"Yes and no," she said, staring at the cars passing by.

"What do you mean?"

Sierra shook her head, still watching the turnpike. "I was closer with my grandpa. He got me in ways Grandma didn't." She turned to Mae with a watery smile. "Thanks for weeding the Herb garden, by the way."

Mae's breath caught. "You...how did you...?"

"Phyllis told me."

Mae was quiet a moment, soaking in these discoveries. There was too much to marvel over. Sierra thanking her. Phyllis telling Sierra about their moment in the Herb garden. Finally starting to feel like she was doing something right. "I'm still figuring out how gardening works, but I want to plant some seeds, try to start something."

"He would have loved that," Sierra said, her eyes shining.

"I can't promise it'll go well," she warned.

"Nah, he's easy to please. Not like…" Sierra's smile faded, her gaze clouding over.

"Your grandma?" Mae guessed.

"It's not like she was trying to be difficult, but…what she wanted for me was different than what I wanted for myself. She was always hinting that I needed to meet someone and get married, which I have no interest in doing." She tossed a discerning look at Mae. "And when she got your wedding invitation, she held it up and was like, 'See, Mae's getting married! Look how happy she is!'"

Mae let out a surprised laugh. "She did?"

Sierra chuckled. "Yep. Passed 'em out at Sunday dinner. I don't think she expected anyone to go, but she wanted us to know. She *especially* wanted *me* to know," she grumbled.

Suddenly Sierra's RSVP started to make more sense. Sierra's slumped shoulders quickly extinguished Mae's spark of joy at picturing Althea passing out her wedding invitations at the table. "I'm sorry," she said. "I wasn't trying to make anything harder for you."

"It would have been hard either way," Sierra said with a shrug. She crossed her arms and let out a sigh, her forehead wrinkled in thought.

When Sierra didn't speak, Mae tentatively pressed on with another question. "What are you thinking about?"

"I feel like we wasted so much time arguing. We were just too different."

"But you also have some pretty big similarities," Mae cut in. "You're both passionate about working with food, and you're so good at it. I've seen all those desserts you post on Instagram. That red velvet cake a few months ago, with the frosting swoops and the crumbs sprinkled all around the edges? I've eaten a *lot* of red velvet cake, and that's the prettiest one I've ever seen."

The corner of Sierra's lips perked up slightly. She seemed torn between taking the compliment and dismissing it. "It's just experience. Red velvet's my favorite flavor, so I've made a lot of it over the years."

"Mine too!" Mae exclaimed. "I get it for my birthday every year."

Sierra nodded, returning Mae's excitement with a smile. "Cool." She grew thoughtful as her gaze turned back to the turnpike. "But I bake *desserts*. Grandma wasn't really a dessert person. And the one time I tried to help her out in the kitchen, I burned the gravy, and she teased me about it my whole life. So, I'm basically useless."

"Yeah, you'll never attract a man with burnt gravy," Mae said. Immediately she regretted the joke, worried she'd gone too far—until Sierra laughed, and Mae's worry dissolved into relief.

"Thanks," Sierra said sarcastically. "I just still have her voice in my head, and I know if I told her I was quitting to do something else, she'd say I wasted my time working in this job and not being married, and jumping to a new career won't solve anything."

Mae nodded slowly. "Maybe a better way to think about it is that she wanted you to be happy. She thought getting married was the answer, and it's not. But *you* know what would make you happy. Maybe it's as simple as that. Or it should be," she added.

Now her grandma Doris was creeping into her mind. Her grandma had never pressured Mae or belittled her ambitions, but Mae had been struck by guilt for the way she'd limited her visits to Bakersfield. If she wasn't such a bad granddaughter, she'd told herself, she'd have visited her grandma more, could have been with her in person those last few months instead of over phone calls. Mae had feared she was blowing the whole thing out of proportion, selfishly putting her own needs first.

But if Mae took her own advice, she could see it a different way. Her grandma wouldn't have wanted Mae to feel uncomfortable around her family. Her grandma never knew she was part of the problem, but if she had, Mae had to believe she would have wanted her to do what was best for her.

"I never thought of it that way," Sierra said. She crossed an arm over her waist, looking pensive.

"Me neither," Mae admitted. "So what would you do if you quit your job?" When Sierra shrugged, Mae pressed, "Something to do with baking?"

Sierra turned to Mae in surprise. "I've thought about starting a bakery."

"And?"

"And starting a business is risky. And expensive. A lot of new businesses fail in the first year."

As the tow truck came rumbling toward them, Mae turned to Sierra and said, "That doesn't mean yours will."

Mae didn't want to read too much into anything, but she suspected Sierra might have been considering her words. While Mae was speaking to the driver and filling out the paperwork, she occasionally stole glances at Sierra and saw her staring into the distance. Not on her phone, not watching the passing traffic. Just thinking.

"Decided to open your bakery yet?" Mae asked when the tow truck took off.

Sierra gave a disbelieving laugh. "No." She spun her key

ring around her finger and moved toward the driver's side door. "Come on."

"Then what were you thinking about?" Mae asked, opening the car door.

"Just wondering what you were doing out here in the first place."

Mae gave her a doubtful look as she slid on her seat belt, but she offered up the answer anyway. "I thought maybe getting some specialty cheeses from Publix could help me figure out the recipe."

"There's your first mistake. She didn't use fancy cheese."

"Neither did I in my first batch, but you all said it sucked," Mae mumbled. "So I'm trying to get creative."

"It didn't suck," Sierra said, laughter in her voice.

"Then what am I doing wrong?"

Sierra gave Mae a considering look. "Are you saying you want my help?"

"Is that an option? Yes."

"Me? The gravy burner? The person who's banned from being within fifty feet of Grandma's stove?"

Mae was practically bouncing in her seat, the poor seat belt straining to keep her in place. "*Yes.* A hundred percent."

Sierra turned to survey Mae, like she was waiting for a catch. Finally, her mouth perking up at the corners, she faced forward and started the car. "Okay."

"Okay." Mae tried to match her casual tone, but a thread of disbelief still wound through it.

With Sierra's help, cracking the recipe, planning a barbecue, and getting home in time to save Connor from wedding stress was starting to feel the slightest bit more doable.

CHAPTER THIRTEEN

There was something special about the batch of mac and cheese Mae set before her taste testers that night. It was the first batch she and Sierra had worked on together. It was cousinship incarnate in a square metal tin.

That didn't stop the Townsends from ripping it apart.

"It's overcooked," Phyllis said. "I wonder whose fault that is." She fixed her playful stare on Sierra across the table.

Even though Phyllis was joking, Mae caught the way Sierra's face fell. Sierra was so traumatized from the gravy-burning incident that she'd insisted Mae be the one to stir the cheese sauce. Mae had tasked her with cooking the macaroni, hoping an easy task might boost her confidence. But Sierra, not realizing the macaroni would finish cooking in the oven, had let the noodles boil for slightly too long.

"That's my fault," Mae piped up. "Sierra brought over this brand of macaroni our grandma uses, and they're like twice the size of regular macaroni, and I thought they'd need to boil for longer." Sierra shot Mae a grateful look.

"At least the *size* of the macaroni is right," Wendell conceded.

"And you have Sierra to thank for that," Mae said.

"I don't need a defense attorney," Sierra said, but she was smiling when she said it.

"How's the flavor?" Mae asked. In response to the comments that her first batch was bland, she and Sierra had gone through the jumble of spices in Althea's cabinet, settling on garlic powder, onion powder, and paprika.

Jeremiah took another bite. "Flavor's better. It tastes like *something* now. But..."

"How do you mess up mac and cheese?" Ariel let her fork fall into her bowl with a disappointed clatter.

"Ariel," Wendell warned.

"No, I get it," Mae said. She rested her elbows on the table and looked at Ariel, sitting across from her. "Figuring out the right recipe means we have to make a lot of wrong batches in the process. Trial and error. What don't you like about it?"

Ariel looked down at the bowl in front of her with disdain. "You should be able to taste cheese when you're eating mac and cheese."

"Okay. We'll make it cheesier." Mae swiped to her notes and typed *Change cheese proportions? Less Velveeta, more sharp cheddar? More cheese, period?*

"How many more times are you gonna make this?" Ariel asked.

"Until we get it right," Sierra replied. Mae nodded in agreement, reveling in the feeling of having Sierra on her side.

Even more Townsends showed up the next night. Mae found that cooking with Townsends swarming around her was quite a departure from her kitchen at home, where the only sounds primarily came from food—the sizzle of onion, the bubble of boiling water. In Althea's kitchen, she was surrounded by a whole cacophony coming from different parts of the house. Jeremiah grunting single-word directions to Tyrese as they carefully moved a heavy, wooden desk down the stairs. The intermittent sound of a shower turning on and off upstairs as Wendell fixed a faulty diverter stem. Dawn and Ariel talking over a show they were watching in the living room while Leah shushed them. And, in the kitchen, Barbara and Phyllis offering unsolicited critiques to Mae and Sierra. It wasn't the exact scene Mae's dad had always described, but it was close enough to that bustling kitchen tableau she'd come to associate with the Townsends. To be here experiencing it for herself was so joyously surreal that even Barbara and Phyllis's heckling sounded like music.

"Remember not to overcook those noodles this time," Barbara said when Mae set a pot of water on the stove to boil.

"No promises," Mae quipped, shooting her a wink on her way back to the counter.

"Is that all the Velveeta you're using?" Phyllis asked, gesturing to the bright-orange block of cheese Sierra was cutting into cubes.

"Yes..." Sierra looked to Mae, as if for backup.

"It seemed like plenty to us," Mae said. The boxes of Velveeta stacked in Althea's pantry had been proof enough that Althea held the processed cheese in high regard—but for Mae, any Velveeta at all felt like too much.

Barbara scoffed, sharing a look with Phyllis. "You sure?"

"It's not like it's gonna help with the flavor," Mae said, picking up a cube of the too-bright, too-shiny stuff. "It's practically plastic."

Barbara and Phyllis burst into cackles. "If Mom ever heard

you say that!" Phyllis said. "Remember when I sent Mom an article that said Velveeta was unhealthy?"

"'It's called liquid gold for a reason,'" Barbara said in her imitation of Althea, making them all laugh. "Or when I brought her that queso I made with low-fat cheese," Barbara said. "She was standing all the way over by the sink and said, 'I can tell just by looking that it's missing Velveeta.' She gave me a whole lecture about it. Which is why I can tell you," Barbara said, pointing at Mae and Sierra, "that you need to add more Velveeta."

"All right." Mae gave a resigned sigh and updated her notes. "Let's add more. But we're adding more cheddar to make up for it."

"Sink in the master's looking good," Wendell said on his way down the stairs.

"Good, because there was nothing wrong with it," Phyllis muttered.

"It was draining slowly!" he insisted. "And I fixed it. Fixed the shower diverter stem, too." He sidled between Mae and Sierra, pinching a clump of shredded cheddar between his fingers and dropping the whole thing into his mouth. Sierra, still grating, gave him a disapproving look. He raised his hands in a show of innocence and backed away, making Mae laugh.

"I should call a real plumber over here one day just to see how much crap you make up," Phyllis said.

Mae turned to face him. "You're not a plumber?"

Wendell's chest puffed out, but before he could speak, Barbara and Phyllis fell into laughter.

"You just made his day!" Phyllis said.

"Dad *loves* pretending he's a plumbing expert," Leah called from the next room.

Wendell narrowed his eyes and gave a disapproving grunt.

"I work in insurance sales," he told Mae. "But I know a lot about plumbing too."

"I believe it," Mae said. "And I noticed the bathroom sink wasn't draining great, so thanks for fixing it."

"Suck up," Sierra whispered.

"You're *welcome*," Wendell said. "Oh, I wanted to give you something." He reached into his pocket and pulled out a small red packet labeled *Cajun spice blend*. "I didn't see it here, but she used this a lot. I saw it when I was at Harris Teeter today. Thought it might be useful."

"Thank you." Mae turned it over, her heart filling with love. She was going to think of Wendell and her grandma every time she saw this spice packet in the grocery store.

Mae added the packet in with the spices she and Sierra had measured out—but when the Townsends gathered around the table for the taste test, Wendell was the first to declare that the seasonings were all off. Mae rolled her eyes and crossed out *Cajun spice blend* in her notes. But the Townsends' feedback suggested this batch was decidedly cheesier, though the flavor was still missing something, and it wasn't as creamy as they remembered.

Mae finished updating her notes, then glanced at the stove, where a pile of dishes awaited her. This time last night, after the taste test had come to a close, the Townsends took their leave, and she'd gotten to work scrubbing pots and pans in an empty house. But tonight, they were still lingering around the dining room table. Sierra, Ariel, and Leah were making plans to go shopping the next day. Wendell and Dawn were gushing over a picture Jeremiah had shown them of baby Amara. Barbara was telling Phyllis and Tyrese about a sale at West Elm.

Mae smiled and set her phone down. She hadn't even had

to summon them all here with the promise of a feast like she'd done for the family dinner earlier this week. Just a simple text saying they were welcome to come over to try more mac and cheese. Not even a whole meal—just a few measly bites each, since making a dinner-sized batch would be a waste at the testing stage. But still that had been enough. Mae couldn't be sure what was really drawing them: the chance to help get Althea's mac and cheese right, or the opportunity to be around each other, to gather here at this home the way they used to before Althea passed. Either way, the fact that Mae was part of it warmed her from the inside out.

"Isn't that the shirt you wore yesterday?" Ariel asked, her eyes zeroing in on Mae's top. "Doesn't it smell?"

Mae had forgotten how brutally honest thirteen-year-olds could be.

"It is," she said, looking down at her red V-neck. "But it's clean. I only packed enough clothes for a few days, so I've been washing my clothes almost every day."

Ariel gave Mae a look of judgment mixed with concern. "Not very well."

"What do you—" Mae stopped herself when she spotted a small splotch on her chest. She pinched the fabric and lifted it for a sniff. "Balsamic vinaigrette," she said, as if anyone asked for a forensic analysis of the food she was wearing.

"Oh my god," Ariel muttered through a weary sigh. "Just come shopping with us tomorrow. This is too tragic."

Leah giggled, and Sierra stifled a laugh. Mae looked between them, shaking her head as a smile pulled at her. Being the butt of the joke didn't sting when it came with an invitation. "I would love to."

"Surprised you have time," Jeremiah said with a chuckle. "That wedding's coming up quick, right?"

"Two weeks." She knew it was soon, in the way that she could look at a calendar and count the days. But mentally, it felt so distant and hazy. Like it was a whole other world away. A world that wasn't here in her grandma's creaky, old house, surrounded by relatives casually insulting her cooking.

She loved that other world, too. It was a world where Connor waited for her at the end of the aisle, probably with that goofy smile he got on his face whenever their eyes met across the room. A world where she could start calling him her husband, where that feeling she got when she was around him—like she was home—was cemented in law. But that world and this one were strangers to each other. She needed the barbecue to bridge the divide.

"How's that white boy of yours?" Wendell asked.

Mae started to smile, touched that Wendell would care to ask about Connor at all. She thought about the box she'd opened from Connor just that morning with calamine lotion, hydrocortisone cream, and a silly note. "Connor's good. He sent me a mosquito bite care package today. And he's been scrambling because his parents are making him assemble all the boxes they ordered for the wedding favors. The other night, he stayed up until 2:00 a.m. folding three hundred tiny cardboard boxes." She'd woken up to his texts, becoming more and more loopy as the evening wore on. She'd read them from bed, feeling a burst of affection, wishing she'd been beside him when he finally collapsed into their sheets at home.

"He did that all by himself?" Phyllis said. "While you're out here making a hundred batches of mac and cheese?"

Mae's smile faded. Put like that, she did feel like a monster. "Yeah," she said dully. In the silence that followed, she looked down at her plate, traced a line through the congealing cheese sauce.

"So, how'd he propose?" Jeremiah asked.

Mae looked up, grateful for the distraction. "Um…he didn't."

"You proposed?" Sierra asked.

"I don't know; it's hard to say. Neither of us did. Both of us did." When she was met with baffled looks, Mae launched into the story.

The non-proposal had happened well over four years ago. Connor was finishing up his first year of law school at the University of Maryland, where he'd enrolled after spending a few years working in law offices post-college. Mae was working for an association in downtown Baltimore. She'd been spending most nights at Connor's place, returning to her apartment every few days to water her basil plant.

"Our six-month anniversary's coming up," he'd said. He was at the stove monitoring her omelet while she washed blackberries at the sink. Mae hated making omelets. One messy flip and raw egg went splattering all over the kitchen. But Connor was more patient, knew how to coax a gentle turn.

"Yeah?" Mae replied.

"Two weeks."

"Nice." Mae turned off the faucet and reached into his cabinet for a bowl, then noticed Connor watching her. "What?"

"Are you…happy? With this? Us?" It was such a strange question that Mae laughed. "What?" he asked.

"I'd think that's something you should know, isn't it?" Mae popped a blackberry into her mouth.

"I *should* know. But you're a closed book. No." He pointed his spatula at her. "You're not even a closed book. You're like that book from *The Mummy*—a locked book. Except your book doesn't awaken mummies. But I don't know, maybe it does. I haven't read it."

She clamped her mouth shut to keep from laughing again. "That metaphor kind of got away from you."

"It did," he agreed. "So? Will you humor me?"

Mae softened. She was still getting used to how sweet Connor was. Her ex had been more of the opposite, clever and cocky and always ready with a quip, no matter at whose expense. But Connor was good-humored, good-natured, *good*, period. He never made her feel like a punchline.

Of course she was happy. That was old news, really. She'd known three weeks in that she wanted to marry him. They'd been headed to a concert in DC one night, but a pile-up on I-95 put them in standstill traffic for three hours. Somehow that time flew by, the conversation ping-ponging from jokes to anecdotes about their week to stories about their childhoods to favorite movies to deepest fears to the pros and cons of pineapple on pizza. They'd missed the concert, ended up getting dinner at McDonald's instead of the sushi restaurant they'd planned on trying. And it had never been clearer to Mae, when she was giggling in traffic hell with Connor and then gazing at him over Big Macs and fries in a McDonald's parking lot, that he was the person she wanted to spend her life with.

But apparently, on account of being a locked book, she'd failed to let him in on that fact.

She set the bowl down and leaned against the counter. "Connor. I'm happy. I'm very happy. I would marry you tomorrow."

Connor held her gaze, his mouth partly open. He shook his head slightly, his brow creasing and then smoothing out again as a slow smile came over him.

"What?" she asked.

"I would also marry you tomorrow."

They stood there, staring at one another across the kitchen. Mae felt herself smiling too, something just as wide as Connor's blooming all over her face. She was about to ask if they were doing this, if they should look up the nearest courthouse and go from there, but then he made a face.

"Um. My parents. They've always wanted me to get married at their winery. Do a whole…big thing. Unless you don't—"

"No," Mae interrupted. "That's fine." She'd take whatever route resulted in less conflict, less scrutiny on her as the outcast.

"Okay." Connor used the spatula to peek under the omelet, then did one of his perfect, guided flips. He turned back to Mae. "They'll want to start planning as soon as they find out, and I don't want to deal with that while I'm in law school, so…can we tell them after I graduate?"

"Fine by me." And he'd rolled her omelet onto a plate, and they'd moved to the table to eat breakfast like they always did. Mae had looked over at him more than once, trying to figure out what just happened. If they were engaged or just daydreaming.

But later that afternoon, he said he needed to grab a book from the campus library and headed out. When he came back, he placed a small, velvet box on the table in front of Mae. She looked at the box, then at him, saw the content look on his face. And she knew, without even opening it, that there was a ring inside, that they were engaged, and that Connor's word should never be doubted.

Mae moved her basil plant to his apartment the next day.

"Engaged at six months," Wendell said, giving a low whistle. "That's a choice."

"But it worked out," Phyllis replied with a decisive nod.

Leah leaned forward on her elbows, meeting Mae's eyes across the table. "I think it's romantic."

"It's cute," Ariel conceded with a tilt of her head. "Kinda boring." Which, coming from her, was high praise.

"White boy sounds like he's pretty special," Jeremiah said, looking at Mae with a gleam in his eye.

"He is," Mae agreed, melting into her seat with a smile. Falling under the spell of their relaxed faces, this companionable moment, she felt brave enough to add, "You could meet him yourself if you come to my wedding on the eighth."

She bit her lip, not sure if this reminder would thicken the air with awkward silence or spark a flurry of muttered excuses.

But the tranquil atmosphere didn't change. Jeremiah only laughed, exchanged a look with Phyllis, and said, "We'll see what we can do."

And Mae, who hadn't expected anything besides another joke about their early engagement, delighted in her first possible RSVP from the Townsends.

CHAPTER FOURTEEN

An afternoon spent shopping with her cousins felt like reaching the pinnacle of cousin bonding—until Sierra pulled into the parking lot of a three-story apartment building Mae had never seen before and asked, "Do you want to come inside?"

Mae let out an incredulous laugh, which did not mirror Sierra's casual tone in the slightest. "Really?"

They'd just dropped off Leah and Ariel, and Mae had expected Sierra to take her to Althea's next. She felt like a burden already, hitching a ride with Sierra while her car was in the shop. The idea of Sierra inviting her burden inside took some getting used to.

Sierra cut the engine and shrugged out of her seat belt. "I have some old clothes I was gonna donate to Goodwill, but you can go through them if you want, see if you want anything."

"Oh." Mae sat in the surprise for one more moment, but as Sierra opened the car door and stepped outside, she rushed to follow. "I'd love to. Thank you." She trailed Sierra to a door on the first floor, quickly taking in the details of Sierra's apartment complex: the grassy landscape, the bright-blue fence, the tree-lined path where a woman was walking a small Pomeranian.

"I know the boutiques we hit didn't really have much for you," Sierra said.

Mae leaned against a pillar while Sierra unlocked the door. "I didn't mind. It was still fun."

The shops they'd gone to were either geared toward teens or primarily stocked vintage, unique clothing with high price tags. Ariel came away with some cute sundresses and Leah with a few one-of-a-kind pieces that got her fashion designer creativity whirring. But nothing Mae saw was fit for her purposes, namely lounging, working, cooking, and, as Ariel teasingly remarked, spilling food on. Mae hadn't minded falling into the role of offering opinions on fitting-room looks and holding an ever-growing pile of clothes for Leah and Ariel while they shopped. Sierra had done much the same, and Mae enjoyed feeling like she was taking a page out of Sierra's book, learning how to be a good elder to their younger cousins.

Sierra unlocked the door, then tossed Mae a mirthful look. "Even Dandelion?"

Mae laughed. Just the name brought back flashes of straining to see in the dim light, gagging on the strong, perfumy odor that permeated the store, avoiding eye contact from the terrifyingly aggressive teens who ran the sales counter. "Okay, Dandelion was a nightmare," she admitted, following Sierra into the apartment. "But that was where I found out I'm a fashion icon, so I can't be too mad at it."

Sierra groaned. "Not the fashion icon thing again."

In Dandelion, Ariel had held up a dress that she said resembled the one Mae wore in the picture on her wedding invitation. When Mae asked how she remembered it, Ariel had shrugged and said Leah had it on her corkboard. With a few questions posed through a fitting-room curtain, Mae discovered that Leah's corkboard displayed a variety of pictures that matched the aesthetic of her current sewing project. The notion had occupied Mae's every thought until they dropped off Leah and Ariel and she got to see Leah's room for herself. And there, on the corkboard above Leah's desk, amid magazine cutouts, printed pictures, and a sketch Leah had made of a dark olive dress, Mae found herself in the bottom right corner: she and Connor posing together, Mae in an olive-green dress and Connor in a button-down, wedding details listed below them.

Mae had stood there for a while, staring and marveling, floating with a weightlessness that she could still feel now. Even if she was only on this board because the color of her dress vaguely matched the color palette Leah had in mind for her next sewing project, it still meant something that she was up here. It was proof that the Townsends thought about her. Like Mae wasn't alone in the way she'd saved that photo of herself and Sierra from that Thanksgiving all those years ago. The Townsends had been saving scraps of her, too, in their own way.

"Look, when you're a fashion icon like me, then you'll understand," Mae said, making Sierra groan again. Sierra dropped her keys onto an end table by the door and disappeared down the hall.

Mae stayed by the entrance, looking around. In the living room, a blue velvet couch sat against the wall. On a small ledge under the coffee table were two blankets, one of which looked like it had been knitted. Mae wondered who had made it, if anyone in their family had that skill. Her grandma Doris had loved knitting. And Mae had cherished those memories of the day her grandma taught her and Madison how to knit, the three of them side by side on the couch. But it was different now. Now, when she pictured her grandma teaching her how to loop yarn on her knitting needle, the memory played on a cracked screen, the colors muted, the sounds warped.

"You coming?" Sierra called out.

Mae shook her head free of her grandma and followed Sierra's voice down a hallway. Sierra stood in a cozy-looking bedroom flooded with sunlight, sorting through clothes in her closet. The mix of modern and vintage pieces in the room—the mint-green metal bed frame with a curlicue pattern, the sleek white dresser, the blue-and-gold steamer trunk at the foot of the bed—gave her bedroom an eclectic feel.

Mae perched on the edge of her bed. "I like your room."

"Thanks." Sierra kept rifling, every now and then throwing a shirt over her arm. "I love a good thrift shop. I would have taken you to one today, but Ariel really wanted to hit the downtown spots." Sierra turned and dropped an assortment of shirts onto the bed. "Let me know if you want any of these."

Mae reached for a black scoop-necked shirt, feeling the soft fabric between her fingers. "These are perfect. Just simple things I can cook and garden in. I'll take all of these if you're giving them away."

"All yours." Sierra sat on the other end of the bed by a tasseled throw pillow. She played with its edges, then lifted her head, her eyes hungry with curiosity. "So, you're gardening?"

"I am," Mae said, pride blooming in her chest. "I did some research, and I'm gonna plant tomato, cucumber, radish, and zucchini. Which I know might be pointless or whatever since they're selling the house, but—"

"I don't think it's pointless," Sierra said softly. She picked up a white ribbed tank top and folded it in her lap. "Grandpa planted zucchini for me. When I was like twelve, I told him I wanted to make zucchini bread, and next thing I knew he'd planted a whole row of it. I found out later he doesn't even like zucchini," she said, dipping her head toward Mae. She moved on to the next shirt, coaxing it off its hanger, and looked back up. "I like thinking whoever buys the house next will keep the Herb garden going."

Mae nodded, her heart swelling. "I like that, too."

In a peaceful silence, Mae helped Sierra coax the shirts off their hangers, and then Sierra stood to rummage through her dressers, muttering about some shorts she'd been meaning to donate.

Mae's phone buzzed with a text. She pulled it out while Sierra continued opening and closing drawers. Connor was with his parents today, helping out at a wedding they were putting on at the winery. He'd canceled her dress fitting quietly, but she wouldn't have been surprised if his parents had found out somehow, if they had weekly squash games with the seamstress just to check up on wedding dress happenings.

But no, no messages from Connor. There were, however, three from Madison.

MADISON: Southwest Airlines is having a sale on fall flights right now! Just FYI if you want to book your flight for my baby shower.

MADISON: Unless you're still mad at me about the fact that maternal death affects women of ALL races lol

MADISON: Anyway, I hope you can come! I haven't seen you in so long 💜

Madison's words pricked at her, but that goddamn heart emoji weakened her defenses. She started typing a reply, then stopped, deleted it.

"What's up?"

Mae turned, surprised to see Sierra watching her. "Oh. I have this cousin on my mom's side who's...kind of a bitch."

Sierra's eyebrows went up, and she returned to her spot next to the throw pillow. "Okay, now I have to hear more."

Mae found Madison's post that had started this whole tiff and passed her phone to Sierra, whose brow deepened with a frown as she read. Then Mae pulled up Madison's latest message for Sierra to read.

"Wow, okay." Sierra handed Mae's phone back to her. "She sounds like the worst."

Mae gave a dry laugh. "She is. I mean—" It didn't feel right, calling her own cousin the worst. This was the same Madison who played Monopoly with her on quiet Saturdays when they had nothing to do: Madison always the hat, Mae always the boot, because it made them laugh, these random pieces of clothing trotting around the board investing in real estate. Without siblings to grow up with, and Madison living just a few blocks over, she was as close to a sister as Mae had ever known.

"She didn't used to be this bad," Mae said. "Or maybe she was, and I just never really noticed it, I don't know."

"Tell me you're not flying out for her baby shower."

Mae screwed her lips to the side. "I'm not flying out?"

"You don't sound sure."

"I'm not going," Mae said, with more determination this time. And she believed herself. She hadn't flown back to Bakersfield in over five years; it would be silly to break her streak over a baby shower she didn't even want to attend. But it was hard to be firm when confronted with a direct question from Madison. She'd never been good at standing up to the Parkers. All those secret looks she'd shared with her dad, those moments of choosing to find amusement in ignorance, had trained her to ignore these comments, let them roll off her back. But now she was realizing that all she'd actually done was let those words sink into her skin while teaching her relatives it was okay to say whatever thoughtless remarks popped into their heads.

"Good," Sierra said, seeming to register Mae's decisiveness. "You gonna tell her to fuck off?"

An uncomfortable chuckle left Mae. It was probably the smart thing to do, and yet the mere suggestion of such a blunt approach felt like heresy. "Is there a politer way to phrase it? I cordially invite you to fuck off?"

Sierra laughed. "Perfect."

Mae glanced at Madison's message one more time, then closed the app. "No, but I won't respond."

"Coward."

The jab was toothless, friendly even. Mae stuck her tongue out at her, Sierra grinned, and she returned to digging around in her dresser, the atmosphere between them loosening with what felt like friendship—or cousinship, rather. Mae could probably even get away with calling her *cuz*, all carefree and casual like how Jayla referred to her cousins. But she tucked that temptation into her back pocket. This easiness spreading between them— how Sierra could hold up a pair of floral shorts with the price tag still attached and roast her past self's ambitious fashion choices— was perfect as is.

With enough clothes in her arms to last her through the

barbecue and then some, Mae headed into the living room to wait for Sierra, who'd ducked into the bathroom. Sierra had said she'd drop Mae off at Althea's, and Mae was already thinking about how she might extend the afternoon into evening, ask Sierra if she wanted to grab dinner, keep the fun going. While her mind worked on the best way to issue that invitation, Mae explored more of the living room, examining the photos on the wall beside the television. One of Sierra and three women around her age, their arms around one another. A picture of what looked like the entire Townsend clan on Christmas, except for Mae and her dad. Then there was one of just Sierra and Mae's dad. Her heart skipped a beat, seeing his face when she hadn't expected it. It must have been taken when he'd come here for his annual Fourth of July trip. Sierra was about ten in the photo, wearing a tank top and cutoff shorts. Her dad had an arm around her. The photo seemed relaxed, candid, as if someone had approached them with a camera while they were talking and they fell into a natural pose for the picture. Mae's heart ached, picturing him coming out here, being so seamlessly part of this life she was trying to fit herself into.

Mae swallowed the lump in her throat and went back to the wall, looking for more clues into Sierra's life. She spotted a postcard showing a city skyline and a sign reading *Welcome to Las Vegas*. Mae's dad had visited Las Vegas once for a work retreat. He'd sent Mae a postcard with the city skyline on it, too. Mae set her pile of clothes on the couch and carefully unpinned the postcard from Sierra's wall. She turned it over and, sure enough, his thin, scratchy handwriting was on the other side.

She read eagerly, devouring these new words from her dad. It was just a few lines—an explanation that he was here for work, a complaint about all-day meetings, a joke about trust falls. But still she savored them—until she reached the bottom, and then her breath caught.

Love, Dad.

Her eyes flitted to the address just to make sure. Sierra's name and address stared back at her. The *Dear Sierra* at the top of the postcard taunted her.

Dear Sierra. Love, Dad.

Mae's brain froze as she stood, staring and blinking, grasping for an explanation. It couldn't be a case of mistaken identity— this was definitely her dad's handwriting, with the ill-formed letters that required deciphering half the time. His *R*'s that looked like dashes, the loop in his *E*'s so small that they were nearly identical to his *C*'s. Every characteristically sloppy pen stroke was accounted for.

Her mind was working on overdrive, trying to make it make sense. She and Sierra had the same dad? But that couldn't be, because Barbara was Sierra's mom.

Except...Sierra always called her *Bee*. Mae had taken it for a cute nickname then, some term of endearment she wouldn't understand. But it made sense now, this discovery that didn't make sense at all. Sierra didn't call Barbara *Mom* because Barbara wasn't her mom. Barbara was just...the aunt who raised her?

But why?

Unless Mae was misinterpreting things, somehow? Suppose *Dad* was a nickname, an inside joke they shared?

At the sound of footfalls, Mae hurriedly pinned the postcard back into place, her head still a foggy daze. She stepped back from the wall just in time to see Sierra enter the room.

"We can head out now," Sierra said.

Mae's eyes drifted to Sierra's nose. No wonder she and Sierra had the same nose.

And her chin. Sierra and Mae's dad both had the same chin, square and narrow.

Her frame, tall and slender. Just like her dad. *Their* dad.

"What?"

Mae raced to meet Sierra's eyeline. "Hmm?"

"What are you looking at?"

"Nothing," Mae said quickly. She robotically scooped the clothes back into her arms. "I'm ready."

The question *Do we have the same father?* loomed in Mae's head on the drive to Althea's, but her brain couldn't process it. Asking it outright felt wrong somehow. It was so obvious a fact that she might make herself look ridiculous for not knowing. Or maybe it wasn't a fact and her nickname theory was actually correct, but that would also make her look ridiculous, thinking her cousin was her sister based on a nickname. Except, Mae thought, taking another glance at Sierra's nose, chin, frame, she was pretty sure it wasn't a nickname.

Whatever the truth was, Sierra wasn't the person Mae needed to go to for answers. Not today, anyway. Not after they'd spent a perfect afternoon together, when they were just starting to grow closer, when Sierra was helping her figure out the mac and cheese recipe and kindly driving her around while her car was in the shop. Not when Sierra was pulling into Althea's driveway and Mae's head was full of identical noses and E's that looked like C's.

And not when Mae wasn't sure she was ready to know the answer at all.

"Thanks for the ride," Mae said. "Um. I'll see you Monday." With another glance at Sierra (that *nose*), she shuffled out of the car in a distracted fog. The fog followed her inside, growing larger by the second. She collapsed onto the couch and closed her eyes, willing it away until she could make sense of the question marks that weighed heavy in her head.

But still the fog remained.

CHAPTER FIFTEEN

Mae awoke to light and shadows.

The room was slowly darkening as the sun prepared to set. The shadow from the lamp in the corner seemed to stretch before her eyes.

Her mind was still full of questions, but the fog was clearing. She'd gone over and over the puzzle pieces of her life as she'd lain on the couch turning them over, looking for gaps. At some point, she'd fallen asleep, but the puzzle was still waiting for her, right where she'd left it. And it was missing several pieces.

An explanation for why her dad never let her go to Hobson with him.

The real story of that Thanksgiving she'd shared with Sierra and Barbara.

The answer to what her mom and Barbara had been whisper-fighting about all those years ago at her dad's funeral.

The reason for every uncomfortable moment or knowing look that always seemed to crop up when Mae was around the Townsends.

Mae slowly sat up, stretching stiffness out of her spine.

She picked up her phone to call the person who owed her these answers. As the ring sounded in her ear, she took a steadying breath. She wouldn't let telltale pauses or vague responses slide this time. No matter what it did to her father's memory, that shiny 99 percent she and her mom upheld so loyally, she needed to know the truth. All of it.

"Hello?"

Mae opened her mouth to speak, but the flurry of half-formed thoughts and missing puzzle pieces whirling in her head didn't offer anything concrete to say, just words like *sister* and *dad* and *secret* and *why*.

"Mae?" her mom tried. "You there?"

She pictured that incomplete puzzle, zoomed out to the big, blurry picture, and hurled the question like a spear, heavy with hurt and accusation. "Is Sierra my sister?"

Part of her expected her mom to scoff and ask where she got that idea from. The rest of her wasn't surprised when her question was met with silence.

"Who told you?"

A shiver passed through her. There was no doubting it now, not with her mom's tone so serious.

"No one. I was at Sierra's and I found a postcard from Dad. He signed it *Dad*." When another silence followed, Mae asked, "So it's true? We're sisters?"

"Half sisters, yes."

Mae ran a hand up and down the goosebumps chilling her arms. As still more silent seconds ticked by, Mae let out a huff of breath, bristling with a spike of annoyance. "This is the part where you explain."

Her mom gave a deep sigh. "When I met your dad, he wasn't

as…together as he was when you knew him. We were teenagers, and he was figuring out how to be a father. He and his girlfriend had Sierra when they were seventeen. But things were messy. He got a job at Super Foods, and Barbara and their mom were usually the ones looking after Sierra. His girlfriend—his ex-girlfriend, by then—would watch the baby at first, but she came by less and less. When your dad got home from work, he'd spend a few hours with Sierra, then leave her with Barbara and go out with his friends. And then—well, you know how we met, at that party at Duke. I didn't know about Sierra until our second date. He said he had a daughter, and her mom was out of the picture."

Mae crossed to the fridge and pulled out the half-eaten batch of mac and cheese she and Sierra had made a couple of days ago. She took a large bite, chewing without tasting. None of this made sense. Her dad had always been caring and attentive. She couldn't imagine him flogging her off on someone else and then leaving to hang out with his friends.

"I think being a parent was a lot for him to take in," her mom went on. "He leaned on Barbara more than he should have. I *let* him lean on Barbara more than he should have. And then when I got pregnant with you…" She went quiet.

Mae's mom had gotten pregnant toward the end of her senior year at Duke. Mae knew how the story went: her mom finished out the year, graduating with a barely visible belly under her gown, and then a month after graduation, she and her dad moved to Bakersfield so Mae's mom could be closer to her family. They'd leaned heavily on Mae's maternal grandparents, living with them for the first few years of Mae's life until they could afford to buy a house of their own, relying on them for childcare while Mae's parents were still getting their lives in order.

This was the story Mae had always been told. She'd loved it then, looking at her mom's graduation photo and knowing she was part of that day. But that was before she knew there was another baby involved. One her dad had left behind.

"We wanted to bring Sierra with us," her mom said. There was an apology in her tone. An apology Mae knew wasn't meant for her. "But Barbara wouldn't hear of it. She went off on us, saying Rodney could barely handle one kid as it was; she wasn't going to let him whisk Sierra away when Barbara had been the one who'd looked after her for so long. She didn't believe him when he said he could take care of her now. And when his mom found out we were going to be staying at my parents', she went ballistic, saying how dare he even think about taking Sierra from her family to live with 'the racist who made her life hell.'" Mae could hear the air quotes in her mom's voice, the way the words sharpened. But there was no derision in it, no denial. Just a weighty regret.

"So, we decided we'd move out there, get settled, and come back for Sierra. Your dad thought that if Barbara saw we were taking this seriously, she'd change her mind. So, we moved to Bakersfield. Your dad got a job. We had you. Except...it was harder than we thought. Raising a baby, working, saving up for a down payment on a house. Even with my parents helping out, it took us a while to start feeling like we were ready for Sierra. But we *got* ready. We really did."

Mae felt her mom's desperation to be believed, the truth piercing her words. "Okay."

"He didn't end up flying out for Sierra until her next birthday. She was five by then. He got out there, took her shopping for a suitcase. She was excited, at first." Her mom took a deep breath. "But when they were packing, she realized Barbara wasn't coming with her," she said quietly. "She screamed her head off. She refused to leave Barbara. Barbara was the only person who'd been in her life consistently, every day, since she was a baby. Barbara said it would be better if we didn't uproot Sierra, if Sierra stayed with her permanently. And your dad agreed."

"Just like that?" Mae asked. She couldn't imagine her dad shrugging and handing his child over to someone else, relative or not. He'd been so involved in every part of Mae's life: dance recitals and parent-teacher conferences and the silly father-daughter dance her school had put on in third grade. He hated dancing, but he'd put on a suit and tie, taken her out onto that dance floor and let her step on his shiny shoes anyway.

"He thought he was doing the right thing, Mae," her mom said softly. "Letting her live with the person she was most comfortable with."

Mae scoffed. If he'd truly thought it was right, he wouldn't have kept it a secret. "Okay. Then what happened?"

"For the first few years, we visited back and forth as much as we could. But then...they came over for Thanksgiving one year. And after that, they didn't visit us anymore."

Mae sat up straighter, her pulse quickening. "Why? What happened at Thanksgiving?"

"It was silly," her mom prefaced, though Mae doubted it was anything of the sort. "Sierra was helping me check on the pies in the kitchen. She said she liked our curtains. They were those green curtains with the oranges on them, do you remember? And I told her it was her kitchen, too. I asked her if she might want to live with us. It was something your dad and I were going to talk to Barbara about, seeing if maybe Sierra would want to live with us for part of the year. But Barbara overheard me talking to Sierra and she went *off*. She said I was trying to steal Sierra and rip her away from the only home she's ever had." Her voice grew incredulous, reeling from the accusation even now. "Then she said she'd never want Sierra to have to put up with my 'racist family,' as she called it. She'd obviously been holding a grudge about my mom. Barbara was shooting daggers at your grandma all night."

Mae's stomach tensed. "Grandma was there?" she asked.

"Yes. It was Thanksgiving."

"Did Grandma say anything to her?"

"I don't know. 'Happy Thanksgiving'? 'Pass the yams'? Nothing you wouldn't say at the dinner table."

"She didn't say anything else?" Mae asked.

"Nothing unusual. Why?"

Mae kept silent. Her grandma was an expert at saying the wrong thing and dressing it up to sound perfectly normal. She could easily imagine her grandma complimenting Barbara about her articulate way of speaking and Mae's mom not picking up on it.

"Nothing," Mae said. "What happened after that?"

"Barbara and Sierra left the next morning. And then they never visited for holidays again. So, your dad always went to see them. He flew out every year for Sierra's birthday."

Mae frowned. "He flew out for the Fourth of July barbecue."

"Sierra's birthday is July fifth."

"But…" Mae's weak protest faded to nothing when the realization hit her. All this time, she'd built up the Fourth of July barbecue as a momentous event in Townsend lore, when in reality, it was probably a run-of-the-mill backyard barbecue. How silly she must have looked to the Townsends, insisting they continue the tradition, taking it upon herself to plan it because she'd been so naively convinced it must have been the cornerstone of Townsend tradition. Knowing her dad was really flying out to see his secret daughter on her birthday had her head spinning. Mae could have been part of it, too, if she'd known. She could have tagged along with him. Or made her a card at the very least. But she'd been oblivious. She'd spent her entire childhood being oblivious.

No, not oblivious. Lied to.

"Why didn't you ever tell me?" Her voice came out low.

"We were going to, honey. We were waiting for the right time. The right age. We didn't know what the right age was. And then..." She fell into a silence that spread before them like a black hole. Images of that night, the hospital, the wrecked car, flashed through Mae's mind. She blinked them away.

"Why didn't *you* tell me?" she asked. "After?"

"I didn't know how, Mae. I knew you would see him differently, and I didn't want that for you. You were going through enough. At first, I thought if we could get through the funeral and let some time pass, it would be easier to tell you after. But then I didn't see the point in dropping it on you out of the blue. I wanted you to remember him as you knew him."

Mae's mind flashed to that funeral memory she'd never understood. "Is that why you and Barbara were fighting at Dad's funeral?"

"We weren't *fighting*, but...yes. She asked me why the program didn't mention Sierra as his daughter, and I told her you didn't know, and I wasn't about to let you find out at your dad's funeral. She didn't take it very well."

Mae wanted to laugh. How could anyone take this news well? Barbara had every right to be upset by Mae's mom trying to quietly erase Sierra's connection to her dad—and to Mae. Her mom had prioritized Mae's feelings at the very high cost of

utterly disregarding how it would affect Barbara and Sierra. At
the cost of keeping Mae in the dark for the rest of her life.

Anger coiled deep within her. A lifetime of lies blurred her
vision. "So, you were just never going to tell me? That Dad was
a liar, and a terrible father—"

"He was an excellent father," her mom insisted.

"To *me*. He was an excellent father to *me*. And Sierra just got
a visit every year? Jesus, Mom. No wonder she hates me."

"I doubt she hates you."

"You have no idea how she feels about me!" Mae exclaimed.
"You don't know anything about her, because dad *left* her to run
off with you. And me," she added with a sardonic laugh.

"Your father wasn't perfect, Mae."

"I don't want to do this," Mae said. "Um. Thanks for finally
being honest with me, I guess."

"Mae—"

"I gotta go."

Mae tossed her phone on the other side of the couch and
laid back, staring at the ceiling. Sierra's attitude toward her made
sense now. Mae got their father year-round, and all Sierra got
was an annual visit.

She combed through their interactions in the last week,
looking for hints she'd missed. Sierra had never called Barbara
Mom, only *Bee*. But Mae's assumption that they were mother and
daughter hadn't been too far off. Barbara was the only constant
parental presence in Sierra's life. Barbara was, for all intents and
purposes, Sierra's mother. And their dad was the man who visited
once a year. He was basically Santa Claus.

No wonder the Townsends had been awkward around her at
the funeral reception. It wasn't just because of Althea's history

with Doris. They probably knew Mae had been oblivious to her connection to Sierra as a child and felt uncomfortable tiptoeing around the truth in case she still didn't know. She could picture it easily: Phyllis and Wendell slipping off into the kitchen during the reception to whisper with Barbara, their heads bowed as they dissected the moment and tried to figure out what Mae knew. Wendell peeking out of the kitchen to sneak a glance at an utterly oblivious Mae, loading up on potato salad and making more introductions that rattled their family.

And soon enough, all the tense looks and missing pieces snapped into place. That time at the family dinner when Mae said she'd always wished she could join her dad when he flew out for the barbecue every year. Of course Sierra would have prickled at the suggestion that their dad wasn't flying out for *her*. No wonder she'd scoffed. It was all making sense now.

And a few nights ago, when Phyllis was talking about Herb's calm demeanor and Mae brought up her dad getting Mae's mom pregnant out of wedlock. Phyllis had hesitated—because it wasn't even the first time Mae's dad had gotten a woman pregnant. If there was ever an incident that had challenged Herb's composure, it would have been that *first* time, when her dad dropped the news that he was going to be a father at seventeen. But Phyllis couldn't say that, because she hadn't been sure what Mae knew.

Mae's buzzing phone interrupted her thoughts. She picked it up, ready to tell her mom off. But Connor's name peered back at her. She answered the phone with a subdued, "Hey."

"Hi! Oh. Uh. Hey." She could hear him hurriedly downgrading his cheerful mood to match her tone. "What's wrong?"

"I found out Sierra's my sister and that my mom and my dead dad lied to me my entire life."

"Oh." More adjusting. "What?"

Out spilled the whole story. Connor listened attentively, his reactions a comforting validation of her anger and confusion.

"You should talk to Sierra," he said. "Barbara, too. I bet their side of the story is totally different."

"Yeah." Mae let out a heavy sigh and trained her eyes on the ceiling. "I'm done talking about my weird family secrets. Tell me what you've been up to."

"Well, I called to tell you Harlan's Market is finally carrying the tortilla chips I like. But your news kind of trumped mine."

She gave a distracted laugh. "Sorry about that."

"That was my big highlight of the week. I don't have anything else to report. Um. Christopher Walker said my foxtrot has promise, and he wants me to practice fifteen minutes a day. The stuff my parents ordered for the favor boxes just arrived, so now I'll get to spend my nights filling three hundred tiny boxes with tiny candles and chocolates."

"Thank you." Guilt tugged at her at the reminder of everything Connor had been doing while she was here dealing with mac and cheese overdoses and family drama. "I'm sorry you've had to do all this wedding stuff without me."

"It's okay. I'm sorry your whole life is a lie."

Mae laughed. "It's okay."

After they hung up, Mae slowly sat up, arching her back. She texted Jayla, who sent back a flurry of responses, each one wildly different in tone:

JAYLA: Oh my god

JAYLA: I'm so sorry this was kept from you. This whole thing is unfair. For you and Sierra both

JAYLA: Why was your teenage dad running around trying
to populate the Earth like some kind of low-budget Nick
Cannon

JAYLA: Sorry is it insensitive to call your dad a low-budget
Nick Cannon

JAYLA: I know this is a lot to process now, but if we forget
about the shitty way this was handled, this is also really
cool. You have a sister. Any kids you have are gonna have
an aunt

It *was* cool, if Mae thought about it that way. But her mind was too scattered to think about anything but the way she felt right now.

She brought the dish of now-cold mac and cheese closer and shoved a forkful into her mouth. Tomorrow, she'd figure out how to approach the conversation with Sierra, craft an opening more nuanced than *Hey, just found out we're sisters. Wanna bond?* And she'd decide what to do about the Fourth of July barbecue she'd been running around planning like an idiot.

But for now, she needed to turn her mind off. She picked up the remote on the coffee table and flipped through channels, pausing at a *Say Yes to the Dress* marathon. As if Connor's parents had engineered it themselves, a reminder that she would make it down that aisle no matter what. She set the remote down, picked up her fork, and settled in.

That night she dreamed about dress fittings, about lies and barbecues and gnarled family trees. Sierra was somewhere in there, too. Mae didn't see her, but it was a feeling so powerful she couldn't doubt it: Sierra had been there all along.

CHAPTER SIXTEEN

Mae didn't know how to act around Sierra anymore.

It felt different now that she knew they were sisters. Should she be acting differently? More sisterly? How did sisters act around one another? Why hadn't she watched a few episodes of *Sister, Sister* yesterday to prepare?

Sierra must have noticed something was off, because the first thing she did when Mae swung open the door was say, "Why are you smiling so weird?"

"I'm not," Mae quickly said, adjusting her smile by a few watts.

That was the other tricky part: pretending she wasn't a mess inside. She'd spent all yesterday in a haze of frustration and Postmates. Tackling the barbecue prep items on her to-do list had felt so useless. What was the point? She must have looked so silly prattling on about the barbecue all this time, making such a fuss over a standard Fourth of July party that actually meant nothing.

So, she'd pushed the barbecue out of her mind and focused on taking comfort wherever she could. Which meant ordering pecan pancakes from a place she'd found on Yelp and drowning them in maple syrup while watching *Iron Chef*. Falling into a food coma and taking a midday nap while Alton Brown discussed the merits of sturgeon. Ordering a pulled-pork sandwich for dinner and moving on to *Chef's Table*. But no distraction was big enough to fully wrench Sierra from her mind. In bed that night, she'd scrolled through Sierra's Instagram for clues she might have missed, as though she could simply pull up that throwback picture of Sierra and her dad at the barbecue and spot a hashtag she hadn't seen before, like #AlsoThisIsMyDad. But the few photos of relatives Sierra posted between cakes and cookies didn't come with explanatory hashtags or family tree diagrams. To Sierra, it was just family, simple as that. Meanwhile, Mae was quickly learning that family was even more complicated than she'd thought.

"Did you hear me?" Sierra asked.

Mae stopped grating the block of cheddar and turned. Sierra stood at the counter, a brick of cream cheese in hand. "Hmm?"

"How much should we add?" Sierra held up the cream cheese.

This, Mae remembered, was what they were testing for today's batch. Their earlier batches had gotten them closer, with the extra Velveeta and sharp cheddar improving the texture and flavor. But the Townsends had said it still needed to be creamier and that the flavor was missing something. Sierra had shown up today with cream cheese, saying she thought it might improve the texture. But it was hard to focus on anything now.

"Maybe half?" Mae guessed. When Sierra didn't argue, Mae went back to grating the cheddar. This she could do. This made sense. All she had to do was focus on the concrete tasks before her, and Sierra would leave, and she could go back to trying to figure out how to be a person.

"You okay?"

Mae stopped grating and looked up. Sierra's eyes were searching hers. Mae gritted her teeth. She couldn't very well say no, she wasn't okay, she'd been lied to all her life. She couldn't say she'd only just learned two days ago that Sierra was her sister, not when she didn't know what Sierra knew. But she had to say something.

"I feel kind of stupid for making such a big deal out of the Fourth of July barbecue," Mae said, setting the cheese down. "I was so excited about the idea of it, and I've never been, and I just wanted to make it happen. I got it in my head that if we didn't have it this year, the family would drift apart or something. I feel like I didn't give anyone a choice."

Sierra's silence had to mean she agreed. Mae swallowed the shame and turned to start back on the cheese.

"Forcing everyone to come to a family barbecue is totally a Grandma move," Sierra said, a sad smile on her face. "I think she would have liked it. I think everyone secretly wanted an excuse to do something that felt normal."

"Even you?" Mae asked, flicking a glance at her.

Sierra gave her a wry grin, like she knew exactly how aloof she'd been. "Even me. I think I was trying to convince myself that it didn't matter if we don't have our family get-togethers anymore because I'm moving to Seattle anyway. But...it would be nice to have one last one before I go."

Mae drew in a breath, her tense muscles loosening. So it wasn't all in her head that this barbecue meant something. Even if the Fourth of July didn't have any special significance for the Townsends, it still offered an opportunity for the family to get together, and that was something worth celebrating—especially with Sierra's move on the horizon. The reminder nagged at her unpleasantly.

"You're still set on moving?" Mae asked lightly, plucking a shred of cheese from the grater.

"I better be," Sierra muttered with a dry laugh. "I just got the lease for my new apartment yesterday." Despite her joking tone, her half-smile was more like a grimace.

An urge to latch onto that reluctance and convince Sierra to stay in Hobson came over her, but Mae let it pass. Sisters or not, it wasn't her place.

It was easier to putter around the kitchen with Sierra after that. She still had to tiptoe around her newfound knowledge that she and Sierra were sisters, but it became more manageable as the afternoon stretched on. While the mac and cheese baked in the oven, Sierra asked how Mae felt about *Nailed It!*, and then they were sitting on the couch together, laughing about crooked cakes and melted frosting faces.

When their test batch was ready, they moved into the kitchen and stood across from one another, digging forks into the still-hot pan.

"The sauce is definitely creamier," Mae said. "The cream cheese is a win."

"Agreed." Sierra went in for another forkful. "But the flavor still needs something."

Mae leaned against the counter, contemplating the flavors on her fork. "I think we need to experiment with the cheeses. Try adding some new ones into the mix?"

"Good idea."

Hearing praise from Sierra filled Mae with warmth. She met Sierra's approval with a timid smile and spoke a *thanks* so quiet that it was almost inaudible.

When she went to the living room to add their latest testing comments to her notes, her phone was alight with activity. She picked it up to see five missed calls, instantly sending a bolt of panic through her. Had she accidentally skipped an important work meeting?

Seeing Connor's name next to each one of those missed calls, the brief note of relief was immediately replaced by a slithering dread. Connor wouldn't call that much unless something was wrong.

Mae climbed the stairs to the guest room and called Connor. She held the phone to her ear, apologies at the ready.

"Everything is a nightmare," Connor said breathlessly. "The bakery canceled our order and my parents are freaking out. My dad decided we have to drive to every bakery in a ten-mile radius and personally beg them to make a wedding cake on short notice. I'm not kidding. They sent me a list of like a dozen bakeries they want me to drive to today."

Mae buried her hand in her hair, interpreting his flood of words. "They canceled the wedding cake order? Why?"

"They're canceling all orders from July out. Some company bought out their lease so they could turn the store into a hipster coffee shop or something. My dad's pissed they took the buyout."

Mae remembered meeting the bakery owner, a kindly man with ruddy cheeks who had brought them endless flavor combinations at the cake tasting. His cream cheese frosting had been divine, but Connor's parents had steered them toward the blackberry lavender. Mae had kept her distaste for floral flavors— which she'd always thought had an unpleasantly perfume-y taste—to herself. It wasn't like she was paying for the cake.

"And guess what?" Connor continued. "Kaufman and Stout want me to come in for a final interview on Wednesday. Because the world has decided my life isn't stressful enough right now."

The *tick-tock* of a blinker sounded through the phone. "Are you driving?" she asked.

"Yep. I'm going to Costco."

Mae went still. "Costco?"

Costco was where Connor went when he felt like his life was falling apart. He'd gone there when his uncle died. When he was stressed about studying for his 1L finals. When he didn't feel in control of his life, he'd told her, there was something satisfying about wandering wide aisles and looking at comically large bags of chips, plastic sample cup in hand, taking in the wonders of bulk goods, pretending his biggest problem was working out how to hypothetically fit a six-pound lasagna and ten pounds of chicken wings into his freezer.

"Costco," Connor repeated. "I'll try the bakeries later. But right now, I really need to eat a hot dog and stare at a giant can of beans." His voice was painstakingly measured, as though if he didn't treat his words with care, he'd go off the rails and start shrieking.

"I understand," she said.

"I need you here, Mae."

The pleading in his voice made her ache with guilt and longing. "I know. I'm sorry."

"No, I'm... I know you need to be there, but *I* need you *here*, and this guy just rolled a shopping cart into the space I was about to pull into, but *it's fine*, I'll find another one."

She chewed on the inside of her cheek, trying to think of a way to ease the situation. She almost decided to change course and drive back tonight, barbecue be damned. But it would have felt wrong, giving up on everything she'd come down here to find. Another idea came to her instead, floating down before her like a feather from above.

"Sierra could bake the cake," she said.

"What? How?"

Mae was still piecing that part together, but when she opened her mouth, she had the answer. "She's a baker. Not professionally, but she's really good. I'll text you her Instagram. She told me she wants to start a bakery; she's just afraid of failing. This could be the push she needs."

It was all coming together, making sense. Baking this wedding cake could jump-start Sierra's baking career. If all went well, this experience could give her some money to get her bakery off the ground, plus Rutherford wedding industry contacts that could lead to future baking gigs. And it would be easier to pull in clients when she already had one successful commission under her belt.

And best of all: starting a bakery in Hobson would mean Sierra wouldn't have to move to Seattle—a move Sierra was on the fence about anyway. Sierra could stay in Hobson, just five hours away, and she and Mae could have all the time they needed to figure out how to be sisters.

"That would be amazing. And you're sure she'd be up for that?"

"Definitely," Mae promised. And, yes, that was a lie. But she'd have said anything to ease the worry out of Connor. She'd find a way to make this work.

"You're saving my life. Thank you."

"How are you doing now?" she asked. "On a scale from one to Costco?"

"Better," he said. "If Sierra's making the cake, that helps. But I'm in the parking lot now, so. I'm gonna go get a hot dog anyway."

"Go get your hot dog. I'll talk to Sierra. And hey, congrats on the interview."

Mae actually felt useful after they hung up. Connor had spent the last week navigating the wedding mess alone so she could take this trip to Hobson, and now she could finally return the favor, prove to him that she was still invested in their relationship.

She glanced at the doorway, toward the sound of water running and plates clinking—Sierra washing dishes, oblivious to what Mae was plotting right now. It was an outlandish request to ask her to make a wedding cake with two weeks' notice. But this could get Sierra started on a new path—one she'd long fantasized about. Mae just needed to make her see that.

She'd take Sierra out to lunch this afternoon, her treat. They'd talk, bond a little more. When the moment was right, Mae would casually ask Sierra if she wanted to bake her wedding cake.

And with any luck—if there was any hope at all of saving Connor from spending the next two weeks roaming the Costco aisles muttering about bulk beans, any hope of keeping her newfound sister from moving across the country for a job she didn't care about—Sierra would say yes.

CHAPTER SEVENTEEN

As Mae sat on Veggie House's outdoor patio, the wedding cake towering in her mind cast a shadow over her every thought. She tried to scan the menu, but her gaze kept flitting around, bouncing between the leafy plants on her left and the brick wall on her right while she mentally rehearsed her pitch.

"Rainbow salad looks good," Sierra said, setting her menu down. "All this mac and cheese is making me crave vegetables." Sierra punctuated this with a laugh, which Mae didn't register until a few seconds later. She laughed to keep up, and Sierra gave her a puzzled look.

When a young woman came to take their order, Mae picked the first item she saw on the menu, then went back to preparing her question for Sierra.

"Did our grandma ever tell you about this place?"

Not that question. It just slipped out.

Sierra made a face like she was suppressing a laugh. "No. This is not her scene at all. But I would come back here," she added, looking around with an approving nod. "It seems cool."

"Marlene's nephew opened it," Mae said, relishing the fact

that she knew this, had something to share about Althea's life. When Sierra cocked her head curiously, Mae dove into the story of finding *Veggie House* in Althea's address book.

"That sounds like her," Sierra said with a sentimental smile. "Amazing how she could be so predictable yet full of surprises at the same time."

"Aren't we all." She'd meant it as a throwaway comment, but the more she considered it, and the longer the silence stretched on, the more her bouncing knee under the table urged her to get the question out now. "We had a surprise this morning," Mae forced out. She threw on a smile to cover up her shaky voice.

"Really?" Sierra stirred the paper straw in her water glass.

"Our bakery canceled the wedding cake order. Connor and his parents are freaking out."

"Jeez. That's a lot."

"Yeah." She cast a nervous glance at Sierra. "They were going to hit up bakeries all over town to see if anyone could make them a cake on short notice. But then I thought...what if you made it? Hear me out," she was quick to say when Sierra's eyes widened. "If any part of you is still thinking about starting a bakery, this is your perfect opportunity." She started counting off the reasons she'd rehearsed. "My fiancé's parents pay well, so that's money you could use to start your business. They have a ton of contacts in the wedding industry that they could introduce you to. Everyone will want to hire you to bake their cakes after they see yours. I've seen your Instagram. I know you could do this."

Sierra gave a dumbfounded laugh. "Those are just simple cakes I play around with for fun. I can't make a wedding cake for—how many people are coming to your wedding?"

"Three hundred," Mae mumbled.

"Three *hundred*?"

"Okay, but I'd help you, and you could charge whatever you wanted. My fiancé's parents are so desperate that they'd pay anything. And if it goes well, you wouldn't have to move to Seattle. You could stay here and do the thing you've always wanted to do." She refrained from babbling more when their waitress came by with their food. Mae leaned back as a colorful, veggie-filled rice bowl was placed in front of her. She snuck a glance at Sierra to see how she was taking it all.

Sierra sucked in a breath through her teeth and twirled a cucumber ribbon around her fork. "I don't know. That's a lot of work."

"I know, but…" Mae ran a hand over her curls, desperately searching for another reason. *We're sisters* sat on her tongue, but it had too much potential to backfire.

"I would really love the chance to spend more time with you," Mae said, choosing her words carefully. The safest option was nearing the subject without actually naming it. "It would mean a lot to me if you did this."

Sierra's brow crinkled. "But why are you so interested in spending time with me *now*? You had your whole life to do that. Why should I have to make your wedding cake just because you've decided you want to get to know me *now*, when it's convenient for you?"

Mae let out a deflating breath. "It's not like that. I've always wanted to get to know you. It's why I stalk you on Instagram. It's why I applied to Duke for college. It's why I invited you all to my wedding. And…" She hesitated, not sure how much to reveal. Not sure what Sierra knew. If Sierra still didn't know their dad had kept their connection a secret, she would be devastated.

But Mae couldn't let Sierra go on thinking she had always known they were sisters and just hadn't reached out—as if Mae could possibly be apathetic about having a sister. She needed to get it all out on the table, make Sierra understand how much she cared about her.

"I only just found out we're sisters a couple of days ago, when I saw that postcard from *our* dad on your wall," Mae said. *"That's* why I want to spend more time with you. If I'd known, I would have reached out to you a long time ago. But I didn't. Not until the other day."

Sierra's expression froze. Her eyes swept over Mae, but the rest of her was immobile. "Dad never told you we were sisters?"

Mae grimaced. "No. He was always secretive about his whole side of the family. He just said his parents didn't approve of my parents getting married, so I assumed no one wanted anything to do with me. My mom said they were waiting for the right time to tell me. But after he died, she wasn't sure how."

Sierra's face twisted into hurt. "Okay," she said, hard as stone. "Got it."

Mae felt an urge to reach out, maybe put a hand on her arm. But the edge in Sierra's voice kept her where she was. "What are you thinking?"

"Nothing. I *love* knowing my dad kept me a secret."

"You weren't a secret; I just thought you were my cousin. I always wondered about you." Mae thought back, clawing for a memory. "I had this picture of the two of us at Thanksgiving, from when I was like three? We looked so happy. I always felt like if we spent Thanksgiving together once, you must be pretty special."

"Not special enough for you to know who I am."

"I'm sorry for springing this on you. I know it's weird to be mad at someone who's dead. That's all I've been thinking about the last few days. He should have told me about you. He should have done more for you."

Sierra pulled back. "You don't know what he did or didn't do for me."

"I don't," Mae said quickly. "I just—" She wasn't sure how to word it. She'd been trying to acknowledge that Sierra had gotten the short end of the stick. That Mae got their dad every day while Sierra got a yearly visit and her existence tucked away into a secret. But Mae could see, from the defensiveness etched in Sierra's features, that Sierra didn't need that acknowledgment, particularly when it went hand in hand with pity. "I don't know," Mae finished.

Sierra sighed and looked down at her untouched salad. "I think I'd rather just eat this at home. I'm gonna get a box."

Mae tried to protest, but Sierra was already calling their waitress over. Silently, they packed up their food. Mae paid the bill. They got in Sierra's car without saying a word.

The ride to Althea's was silent, the tension thick between them. When they reached the driveway and Mae unclicked her seat belt, she noticed Sierra was staying put.

"You're not coming inside?"

Sierra shook her head. "I'm gonna go home."

Her head a muddle of defenses and apologies, Mae grasped for something to say. "Could we get together tomorrow to work on the recipe? I think we're close."

"We're not close," Sierra said. "We're nowhere near close."

"All the more reason to keep trying," Mae joked. Her smile wilted under Sierra's stare. "Even before I found out we were sisters, I've been dying to get to know you better. And now that I know…we have so much lost time to catch up on."

"That sounds like a waste to me."

Mae absorbed the blow without comment. So, this was what they were back to, the guarded Sierra she'd met on her first day here, who'd confronted her at the funeral and made her feel like she didn't belong. Gone was the open-hearted Sierra who'd become her recipe-testing partner, who watched baking competitions on the couch with her and came to join her on the side of the road just so she wouldn't have to wait for a tow alone.

Mae walked up the driveway heavy-hearted and lost in thought. She tossed her keys onto the coffee table, and they landed on the carpet with a jingly thud. She didn't bother picking them up.

She pulled her phone from her back pocket, blinking at the unsuspecting messages lighting up her screen.

> **JAYLA:** Strawberry yogurt, six days expired. Still fine to eat, right?
>
> **CONNOR:** Any word? • •

For Jayla she managed the appropriate level of lighthearted deliberation. But replying to Connor would be another matter. Mae didn't have the heart to respond that Sierra would definitely not be making their wedding cake. She didn't want to send him spiraling into another Costco panic when he was dealing with so much wedding nonsense on his own already. And she didn't want to admit, not even to herself, that she'd bungled her relationship with Sierra. Not yet.

Mae dropped onto the couch. A few minutes to collect her

thoughts, maybe a snippet of *Say Yes to the Dress*—it was oddly addicting, actually—and then she'd call Connor. She didn't have it in her to field his questions right now. Not when she was blinking back tears as the word *sister* echoed over and over again in her brain.

CHAPTER EIGHTEEN

Connor took the news well, in that he wasn't hyperventilating or rambling about Costco. After Mae informed him that Sierra would not be baking their wedding cake and would also probably never talk to her again, he said he'd start approaching bakeries the next day.

"Only twelve days 'til Paris," he said. "That's what's keeping me grounded right now. In twelve days, we'll be together in Paris, and we'll only be going to bakeries for baguettes and macarons, not ridiculous wedding cake requests."

"Twelve days," Mae murmured. It almost didn't feel real, that twelve days from now she and Connor would be wandering the streets of Paris with all their problems behind them. Though, if things with Sierra stayed the way they were now, she doubted she'd ever be able to leave that particular problem behind.

"What are you gonna get into tonight?" he asked.

"I-I don't know," Mae said. She could work on the mac and cheese recipe herself, but doing it without Sierra felt wrong. And showing up at Sierra's door telling her to forget her complicated feelings about their father and think about mac and cheese instead felt stupidly naïve. Mae had tried texting Sierra a few times since the incident at Veggie House, just asking to talk, but Sierra hadn't responded.

If Sierra refused to work with her, and if Mae wouldn't work on the recipe without Sierra, she'd be breaking her promise to the Townsends that she'd have Althea's mac and cheese at the Fourth of July barbecue. But what was a family barbecue if the relative you most wanted to see wasn't talking to you?

It wasn't even an important event for the Townsends. Jeremiah and Phyllis would probably be thrilled to resume their original plans of going to the lake over Fourth of July weekend. Desiree and Scott would be relieved that they wouldn't have to make the three-hour drive from Asheville with two small kids. If anything, the heated discussion with Sierra had illuminated just how much Mae was inconveniencing everyone by insisting upon the barbecue. To truly be selfless, Mae should respect Sierra's wishes and stop pestering her, and respect the Townsends' time and stop trying to force the barbecue on them.

The thought unlocked something in her brain. After she got off the phone with Connor, a plan took shape of its own accord, details snapping into place without her. She could leave for Baltimore tomorrow after work, put Hobson and the barbecue in her rearview mirror, get home by midnight, help Connor prepare for their stupid, obnoxious wedding, and go on with her life. She'd gotten her car back just that afternoon, brand new head gasket and all; she had everything she needed to take off. The Townsends would forget about her, and that was okay. She'd gotten this far without knowing them. Besides, she'd have the Rutherfords. Who probably weren't racist.

Presented neatly before her, the plan made more sense than her crumbling barbecue fantasies ever could. With a resigned sigh, Mae started typing out a task list for things she'd need to do before she left tomorrow: pack her things, do dishes, clear out the fridge, return the keys to Phyllis, fill up on gas. Once she was back in Baltimore and feeling less fragile, she could tackle canceling the barbecue.

In a fit of optimism, she added *Make up with Sierra*. She stared at it, then deleted it several long seconds later. That was one task too immense to handle.

Mae was still trying to push Sierra out of her mind while she sat at the dining table the next day, responding to a slog of emails. One of their clients, a jewelry shop, had reviewed the marketing plan they'd sent yesterday and torn it to shreds. Mae reviewed it, seeing with guilt that some of the details they'd taken issue with—the inconsistencies in header fonts, the differences in tone from one page to the next—were things Mae should have picked up on. She typically always reviewed deliverables before sending them out. But she'd been wrapped up in barbecue preparations, and so she'd passed it off to their brand associate to handle. If Mae had been paying attention, she would have caught those issues.

This was surely something her boss would hear about and bring up during her next performance review, she thought with a sigh. But that was so hazy and faraway. What felt more tangible, more pressing, even as she scheduled meetings about the new marketing plan, was the thought that just three miles away, Sierra was sitting in her apartment with a jumble of complicated feelings about Mae and their father.

Mae kept working, kept dodging thoughts of Sierra. When

Connor called at lunchtime, she leapt at the chance for another distraction.

"Hey," she said. "How's the bakery hunt going?"

"Two bakeries laughed at me. Another said they could do some sheet cakes but that we wouldn't be able to control the flavors. Which I'm fine with, but it's not good enough for my dad." He heaved a deep sigh. "And I think I accidentally threatened an old lady? My dad said I should namedrop him because, as he puts it, he's 'very influential in the wedding world.' But it came out wrong and I think she thought I was saying my dad would, like, put a hit on her if she didn't bake our cake. Her face got all pale, and I realized how it sounded and I apologized and panicked and bought four pies."

Mae gave a sympathetic laugh. "I'm sorry. If it helps, I've decided I'm driving up tonight so I can help you out." She refrained from mentioning her thoughts about canceling the barbecue. She wasn't in the mood for a pep talk.

"Really? That would be great. But, um, that's not why I'm calling. Your mom sent a package."

"She did?" Mae's first thought was that it held more secrets her father had kept from her, maybe evidence of a secret son. "What's in it?"

"Can I open it?"

"Yeah." She stayed on the line, hearing sounds of tape ripping. "There's a note," he said. "'Dear Mae, I looked through your dad's things and couldn't find the recipe. But I found these old cookbooks on our bookshelf. They're not mine, and I wonder if they might be your dad's. Please call me when you get this. Love, Mom.'"

Mae swallowed past the thickness in her throat. "Cookbooks? My dad didn't cook."

"Yeah, there are three cookbooks here. They all say *Southern Home Kitchen* at the top. They look really old."

"When were they published?"

"Let me check. Oh, wow, this one's from 1961."

"They could have been my grandma's," Mae said. Strange how she could be so mad at her dad one minute and the next be struck with an odd homesickness like a punch in the gut. If her dad were alive, she could have asked him where these cookbooks came from, why he'd held onto them, what they meant to him. And he could have told her. Everything he'd ever wanted to say, everything he'd been saving to share later, back when he thought he had all the time in the world, he could have told her.

"I'll leave them on the table," Connor said. "You can go through them when you get here."

Mae's first thought, after they hung up, was to tell Sierra. This could be the breakthrough their recipe search needed. But none of that mattered when they weren't speaking, when Mae might be leaving tonight.

But there was one family member she could make something right with. She scrolled through her texts with her mom, which used to be simple and straightforward—her mom sharing news of a sale at Sur la Table, Mae sending pictures of dinners she was proud of or snapshots from day trips with Connor. But since the Sierra revelation, there were just a few lonely texts from her mom with no response, apologies and pleading requests for Mae to return her calls.

Seeing her mom's unanswered texts pulled at her. The past day had taught Mae an excellent lesson in how awful it felt when someone froze you out. She typed out a text and sent it off.

MAE: Connor said the cookbooks arrived. Thanks for sending them. I can't wait to go through them when I get back 🖤
MOM: I hope you'll tell me all about it. I love you.

Mae went back to work, forcing herself to pay attention. She fixed the marketing plan's formatting issues and met with her project director to finalize the timeline for the new deliverable. She attended a meeting to discuss e-commerce and budget impacts. She responded to the emails that had gone unanswered while she'd been preoccupied with Althea and Sierra and barbecues and macaroni and cheese.

Finally, at nearly six o'clock, she closed her laptop and tucked it into her bag. Her brain was mush after working for nine hours—longer than she'd worked during any one day since she'd gotten here. And now it was time to finish up the rest of the tasks on her list. She'd tackled the dishes and the fridge that afternoon, and her suitcase and messenger bag sat neatly packed beside the dining table; she just needed to lock up the house and drop off the keys.

Mae walked to the sliding glass door across from her and tested the handle. It slid open easily. Instead of closing and locking it, she stepped into the backyard like it was summoning her. Warm, humid air enveloped her like a hug. She looked around at the crookedly mowed lawn, the trees, the wooden fence. Richard, after throwing a ball to a panting Jelly, waved at her from his backyard. Mae waved back, parted her lips to tell him she was going home tonight, but no sound came out.

Her eyes fell on the Herb garden in the corner, the soil dark with the fresh fertilizer she'd added just a few days ago. She could still see the little indentations where she'd planted her tomato, cucumber, radish, and zucchini seeds, the rows marked by Herb's faded Popsicle sticks. If she left now, she'd never see them sprout. They wouldn't even get a chance to sprout unless someone was here to water and check on them.

Mae bit her lip, a swell of shame rising in her. Sierra had said Herb would have liked to see his garden live on, and here Mae was, giving it a breath of life and promptly killing it a few days later.

None of this was in line with the glimmering barbecue fantasy she'd conjured in her head. An empty yard with a dead garden wasn't the plan at all.

She chewed her nail, considering her options. When she handed the keys over to Phyllis tonight, she could ask her to drop by and look after the garden. Phyllis already had a green thumb. She wouldn't need to scour gardening books and watch tutorials like Mae had.

But that didn't feel right either, starting something and then thrusting it into someone else's hands. Why start any of this— the garden, the barbecue, the mac and cheese, connecting with Sierra—if she wasn't going to see it through?

Then again, what was the point of following through with it all if Sierra refused to speak to her, if the barbecue didn't matter, if she was just making life difficult for everyone around her by being here?

The sting of a mosquito on her elbow spurred her to action. Mae swatted at it, then dashed inside to grab her car keys. Sorting through this mess herself hadn't gotten her anywhere, and Sierra wasn't interested in talking—but there was someone else who might be able to help.

Barbara had always been her ally here, had given her a chance when she needed it most. Barbara could help her decide what to do now.

And, Mae couldn't help hoping as she started her car, Barbara might just convince her to stay.

CHAPTER NINETEEN

Barbara seemed to know Mae had a lot on her mind. She'd taken one look at Mae and ushered her inside, no questions asked. Mae followed her to the kitchen and hovered by the stove.

"What are you making?" Mae asked, looking into the sizzling pan. Onions were just starting to soften.

"Stir-fry. You want some?" When Mae didn't speak, still entranced by the onions, Barbara decided for her. "You're having some."

"Okay." Mae looked over the food on the shiny granite countertop: cubed chicken on a cutting board, raw green beans in a colander, a glass measuring cup holding a brown sauce mixture, a small bowl of minced ginger and garlic. She picked up the bowl and breathed in the aromatics like they were smelling salts with the power to calm her mind: garlic warm and welcoming, ginger sharp and spicy.

"I'll give you two a moment alone, but I'll need those in a few seconds."

Mae forced a laugh and handed it over. While Barbara dumped it into the pan, Mae picked up the sauce next, gave that a sniff, too. She caught soy sauce and sesame oil, but the rest was a mystery.

"You really don't know how to keep to yourself, do you?" Barbara commented.

"I was just curious." Mae set the cup down. Then she gravitated to the colander and plucked out a green bean.

"If you don't stop touching my food and sit yourself down…"

"Sorry, sorry." Mae scurried to the table and took a seat. She crunched on the green bean and thought about the last time she'd been here, at the funeral reception. Sierra had spread their grandmother's recipe scraps all over this table that day, hunting for the mac and cheese. They'd come so far since then. And yet, after all the progress they'd made, their fight had walked them right back to estrangement and maybe worse.

"I heard from Sierra yesterday," Barbara said when she joined Mae at the table, two steaming plates of chicken stir-fry and rice between them.

"You did?"

Barbara gave a knowing hum. "I still don't know what the hell your parents were thinking, keeping that from you."

"*Thank* you." Mae picked up her fork. "That's why you and my mom were fighting at my dad's funeral, right?"

"We weren't fighting," Barbara replied, which almost made Mae laugh, despite everything. That was exactly what her mom had said when Mae had asked her about it last week. As though the idea of fighting at a funeral was too appalling to admit to.

"Fine, emphatically whispering," Mae said. "Better?"

"Better." Barbara took a drink of her water. "And yes, that's what we were discussing. I asked her why Sierra's name wasn't mentioned in the program as Rodney's daughter, and that was when she told me you didn't know Sierra was your sister. And I just saw red." Even now, Barbara's eyes flashed with anger. "Rodney keeping Sierra a secret. Your mom wanting me to play along with it to spare your feelings? Like *your* feelings are more important than Sierra's?" She shook her head. "But it explained some things. Like why Rodney always came here alone every summer. We just thought you and your mom didn't want anything to do with us."

Her heart sank. They'd spent all these years apart, each side thinking the other had something against them. So much time lost, grudges and insecurities that went nowhere. All because her dad was too ashamed of his shitty teenage parenting to tell her the truth.

"Then what happened?" Mae asked. "After your...emphatic whispering?"

Barbara shrugged. "I didn't want Sierra finding out her dad kept her quiet like that, especially not at his funeral. So, I played along, and the next day I got us out of there. And the more time that passed, I didn't see the point in telling Sierra the truth. It would just hurt her for no reason. It wasn't like you were gonna show up and enlighten her." She gave a dark chuckle.

"And then I did," Mae finished. She speared a piece of chicken, then hesitated before bringing it to her mouth. "How's Sierra?"

"She's processing." Barbara said it carefully enough to make Mae wince.

"Sounds like a euphemism."

Barbara met Mae's self-deprecating laugh with a tender smile. "It's a lot to take in."

"I know." Mae took a bite. Everything she'd smelled in the

kitchen had come together, married by a sweet, spicy sauce, though there was a familiar flavor she couldn't place. If this were just a few days ago, when sitting around the dinner table with the Townsends was starting to feel comfortable and easy, she could have asked Barbara what she'd used to round out the flavors in the sauce. But now, all she could do was swallow and say, "I just wish she'd talk to me."

"She'll get past it in time."

Something about Barbara's kind expression made Mae's eyes sting. She didn't *have* time. She had a barbecue in seven days that she was on the verge of canceling. She needed to start driving in the next hour if she wanted to get to Baltimore before 1:00 a.m. and help Connor with wedding stress. She needed to know the magic words she could say to Sierra before she left Hobson for good, the words to both say goodbye and guarantee that Sierra would remain in her life. She didn't want to be part of yet another divide in her family. She was sick of divides.

"What happened at that last Thanksgiving when you and Sierra came over?" Mae asked, looking up from her plate. "My mom said you called her family racist?"

Barbara exhaled in a huff. "Indeed, I did."

"My mom said it came out of nowhere."

"She said that?" Barbara cocked an eyebrow. "It did *not* come out of nowhere."

"I believe you," Mae said. "What happened?"

Barbara leaned back and took a long drink from her glass. "Well, we were all at the dinner table. It was fine at first. We were eating, making conversation. Your grandma was talking about...I think *The X-Files*?"

Mae smiled. "That sounds like her." And she didn't know what to do with this fondness that curled inside her, this sudden flash of memory: spending a rainy Sunday at her grandma's, eating a peanut butter and jelly sandwich, while *X-Files* reruns played on TV. She wanted to compartmentalize, box up the feeling and put it somewhere so she could focus on Barbara, but still it remained, effortlessly slipping through every crevice of her mind.

"Then Sierra got up go to the bathroom, I think, and your grandma leaned in and told me Sierra's hair was looking 'a little unkempt.' And I *know* that girl's hair was perfect. I'd detangled it just that morning, put it in a cute little afro puff, added a headband that matched her dress. But because her hair was kinky and curly instead of thin and straight, that woman decided it looked 'unkempt.'"

Annoyance rose up to join that fondness, because Mae knew her grandma had all sorts of opinions about Black hair. The day Mae had gotten her hair relaxed for the first time, her grandma had fawned over her and told her how pretty she'd looked. It was easy to look pretty when the alternative was unkempt.

"What did you say?" she asked.

"I just said, 'No, it's not.' You'd think I dumped the gravy boat in her lap. The conversation turned to other things, but I couldn't get my mind off it. So sometime after dinner, when your grandma had cornered me to ask how everything was back in Hobson—she wanted to know if the movie theater on Dunning was still there—I told her, 'That pharmacy where you accused my mom of shoplifting is still there, how about that?' That wiped the smile off her face real quick."

"I bet," Mae said with a dry chuckle.

"Then she said something about how it was all so long ago, and I said it didn't feel that way to my mom when she had that accusation hanging over her head for so many years. And then she said, 'I was raised to do the right thing.'" Barbara shook her head, her jaw set. "I had to leave the room. And right at that moment was when I walked in on your mom asking Sierra if she wanted to live with y'all, and I lost it. I wasn't about to let Sierra spend a minute more in that environment."

Mae played with a grain of rice on her plate. She could see how, from Barbara's perspective, it was a dangerously close call. A glimpse into the life she'd almost subjected Sierra to and the impetus for her decision to escape it. But Mae couldn't help but consider that Barbara's choice came at the cost of leaving Mae behind. And even though there was no logic to her feeling this way—even though she knew Barbara couldn't have just grabbed Mae's tiny hand that night and run away with the both of them—some part of Mae wished Barbara had protected her too, stood up for her when it felt like no one else did.

"I don't know if it was the right call," Barbara said. "But it felt right at the time."

The acknowledgment alone was enough to soften the hurt. Barbara was doing what she felt was best. And Mae already had two parents looking out for her full-time. Barbara's top priority had to be Sierra.

"You were looking out for Sierra," Mae reminded her. "That seems pretty right to me."

"There are a lot of ways to look out for someone. Doesn't make all of them right." Barbara was looking away at first, toward the window over the kitchen sink, but when her gaze came to settle on Mae, there was a pensiveness in her eyes. As if she was still retracing her steps, searching for the perfect response to use on that Thanksgiving night.

"Do you regret it?" Mae asked.

Barbara chuckled. "I don't do regrets. But I'm sure I coulda done something differently."

"So could my dad." Saying it felt like she was betraying his memory somehow, crossing an invisible line. Mae rolled her lips into her mouth—but Barbara didn't react.

"So could Rodney," she agreed.

Mae played with her fork, lost in thought. The great family divide seemed even more pointless now. Barbara had her reasons for stopping the visits, but those reasons came with doubts attached. There had to be time to fix it still. It was too late to confront her grandma, or her dad. It was too late to meet her other grandma and make up for lost time. But as long as they were on this earth, there was time.

"Do you think you'll be able to come to the wedding?" Mae asked.

The abrupt change in subject had Barbara looking at her askance. "I haven't thought about it," she admitted. "I might."

"My mom'll be there."

Barbara looked Mae over, a small laugh leaving her. "*That's* a selling point?"

"Yes," Mae said with a firm nod. "We could all move past this, if you talked it out." Seeing Barbara's amused skepticism, she continued, "Whether you like it or not, you're family. If you don't see each other that way, *I* do. When I think about getting married and what I want my family to look like, I want a family where people can spend time together and it's…easy." That was the best word to describe it. Casual dinners laughing over sitcoms with her parents. Chatting in the kitchen with Connor over morning omelets and spontaneous late-night meals. Teasing taste tests with the Townsends.

"I don't want grudges or secrets," Mae said. "All that ever did was make me feel lonely, and different, like I didn't belong." Her voice caught. She looked down at her plate, then back up at Barbara, who was watching her intently. "When I have kids, I'm not telling them they can't see their family because of some fight from before they were born. I'm done having relatives who are basically strangers. I love my mom, and I love *you*, and I'd really like for us all to be able to move forward."

Mae thrust a forkful of rice into her mouth to distract herself from the heartfelt, hopeful honesty she'd just spilled all over Barbara. And it wasn't even all that honest, really. She had no intention of going back to Bakersfield to subject herself to feeling like an outsider around the Parkers. And she'd been avoiding the Rutherfords for fear of history repeating itself. So, truthfully, she wasn't doing all that great a job at achieving that unified family image she'd just rambled about.

But if she ignored that, the rest was true. She did want to see her mom and Barbara smooth over the conflict that had hung over them for so long. She did want to weave the Townsends into her life, make sure their time together didn't end with this visit—or with her wedding, for that matter.

"All right."

Mae looked up. Barbara was smiling in a begrudging sort of way. "You'll come to the wedding?" Mae asked.

"I'll come to the wedding."

And, yes, she said it like she was doing Mae a favor, but Mae didn't care. The promise of Barbara's presence—and the glittering possibility of the united family Mae had always envisioned—was well worth the cost of feeling like she'd just browbeaten her aunt into attending her wedding. Mae and Connor weren't even all that thrilled about going. Thinly veiled reluctance was basically part of the dress code.

Mae threw her arms around Barbara with a tight squeeze. With Phyllis and Jeremiah as maybes and now Barbara agreeing to come, Mae might not only fill the two seats she'd lied about on the seating chart but have an extra guest on top of that. Susan probably had a binder somewhere on how to accommodate extra guests.

"I can't come if I'm dead," Barbara choked out, laughter in her voice.

Mae stepped back, feeling like a weight inside her had been lifted. "I'm really glad you're coming. Um." She paused. "Should I still have the barbecue?" she asked tentatively. "With Sierra and everything, I started thinking maybe I should cancel. I know I was forcing it on you all anyway."

Barbara jerked her head back with a frown. "Do you know what Patty would say if you canceled an event you'd already invited her to?"

Mae laughed. "She was already unhappy that I invited her with only two-weeks' notice."

"I know it. She called me after to say they must not teach manners out in California."

Mae couldn't help marveling that just last week when she was texting the Townsends about the barbecue, she'd felt left out reading their exchange about Patty—Ariel calling her a bitch, Barbara calling her *particular*. It had been yet another thing the Townsends were part of that Mae wasn't privy to. But now, she and Barbara were sitting at the dinner table joking about Patty, and she was *in on it*. She was part of something.

Giving up on the barbecue just because she'd hit a roadblock with Sierra wouldn't be right. They could move past this. They just had to talk it out.

"Thank you for dinner," Mae said. "It was delicious." She pointed at her plate, now mostly empty save for a few grains of rice and a small puddle of sauce Mae would have licked off the plate if she were alone. "What was in the sauce?"

Barbara, shaking her head, dutifully recited the ingredients. After one last question and a detour in which Barbara showed Mae the brand of Shaoxing wine she'd used, Mae hugged her again and bounded off to her car to see Sierra.

Sierra didn't seem surprised when she opened the door; she just eyed Mae warily. Mae guessed Barbara had sent her a warning beforehand, cautioning that an exhausting optimist was on her way over.

"Hey," Sierra said.

At least they were on speaking terms.

"Hey," Mae replied. "I want to talk to you. Can I come in?"

Sierra stepped aside. Mae entered the living room, then stopped when she noticed Sierra was staying by the door. Standing awkwardly next to the couch, one hand playing with a belt loop on her shorts, Mae dove into her apology.

"I'm sorry. I shouldn't have sprung that on you. I just really wanted you to know that I would have reached out to you sooner if I'd known we were sisters. But I didn't think about how it would affect you to know our dad didn't tell me about you. I can't imagine how that feels. I'm really sorry."

Sierra nodded, lips tightly pressed together. "Thanks."

"And I'm sorry for trying to pressure you into baking my

wedding cake. It's super short notice and I totally understand why you wouldn't want to do it."

"Well…" Sierra looked down at her nails. "I was thinking that I *will* make the cake, actually."

Mae let out a sound that felt like a cross between a laugh and a gasp. "You will?"

Sierra stepped back, like she feared Mae's enthusiasm might be contagious. "*Only* for the money," she said. "And to keep my options open."

"Oh. Okay." She scanned Sierra's face, trying to get a read on her. Her tone was spiky, but this had to mean something. Mae tried to work some lightness into her voice when she said, "I can't thank you enough. It's such a huge help. Connor and his parents are gonna be thrilled." Her hopeful smile wavered under Sierra's disinterested shrug.

Mae was starting to get the message. Sierra wasn't going to turn down an opportunity to get her bakery started, but she was making it damn clear that she wasn't doing this for Mae.

She took in a breath and decided to try again. "There might be a break in the mac and cheese case. My mom sent me some cookbooks that she thought might have belonged to our dad." *Our dad*, what a strange yet exhilarating thing to say. "Except he doesn't cook, so I wonder if they might have been our grandma's? They were called *Southern Kitchen* or something."

A flash of interest crossed Sierra's face. "*Southern Home Kitchen?*"

"Yeah, I think so. How did you know?"

"Just…sounds familiar. I don't know."

Mae waited for more to come. But Sierra had retreated back into her shell. "I could bring them to you once I get them," she offered. "We could go through them to look for clues to the recipe."

"I don't need to see them." Sierra's tone was as curt as her words.

Mae shrank back. "O-okay. I just thought it would help us figure out the recipe."

"I just think working on the cake is a better use of my time."

Which was fair. Baking a wedding cake for three hundred people on short notice was a massive undertaking. But Mae had to wonder if there was an underlying meaning in Sierra's words. A suggestion that she had no interest in spending any time with Mae ever, cake or not.

"I understand," Mae said. After a pause, she tried one last time. "I could help you with the cake."

Sierra let out a sigh, bringing a hand to rub the back of her neck. "Look, I've had a lot to...process...these last few days. I just need some time to be alone and work through all this. And baking helps me think, so it's a good thing I have a giant cake to make."

Mae's last withered hope roused a little. "Then you're welcome," she joked weakly.

Sierra's lips turned up in a humorless smile. "Was there anything else?"

"No." Mae took the hint and turned for the door. When she stepped through the frame, she turned to say goodbye, or at least wave, but Sierra closed the door on her as soon as she was outside.

She breathed in the warm summer air. She was back to walking on eggshells around Sierra, vying for approval, reaching out and getting little in return.

But Mae had won her over before, and she could do it again.

And as Mae and her grandma well knew, the best way to bring people together was with food. She'd do whatever it took to nail the mac and cheese recipe in time for the barbecue. Sierra would see how much effort she'd put in, how much she cared, and she'd thaw enough to let Mae back into her life.

Mae headed to her car, already composing a grocery list in her head. Getting her sister back started tonight.

CHAPTER TWENTY

Connor's voice was a soothing balm of relief when Mae called him with the news.

"I can finally stop harassing bakeries," he said. "I can stop buying pies out of politeness. Mae, I've had to eat so much pie in the last few days."

Mae grinned. At least she'd made something right with Connor. She wedged her phone between her ear and her shoulder as she put away the groceries she'd picked up on the way home: milk, butter, elbow macaroni, six pounds of assorted cheeses, and enough Velveeta to prompt a slightly alarmed cashier to ask after her well-being.

"Why pies?" she asked.

"I don't know," he admitted. "It just felt like the most respectful dessert. Oh, hold on." She heard muffled voices, and then Connor came back on. "My parents want to know what the cake's gonna look like."

"Oh." Mae stopped, one hand on a brick of sharp cheddar. Connor must have been having dinner with his parents. "I-I don't know. Like a wedding cake, probably."

This did little to assuage the Rutherfords' concerns. The background voices grew in urgency as Connor put the call on speaker.

"Mae, it's John. You didn't discuss the cake design?"

"Well—she *just* agreed to bake the cake, like, half an hour ago. We haven't had a chance to go over the details yet." She refrained from saying she doubted Sierra would be very open to discussing anything with her. "But we will," Mae lied. She set the last of the cheese in the fridge and shut the door.

There was a muffled sound, and then Susan's concerned voice came on. "Did she at least say whether she could do blackberry lavender?" Mae could picture Susan reaching across the Rutherfords' dining table to grab the phone in her frenzy for information.

"Um…I'll ask her. I'm sure we'll get the specifics worked out soon."

"And you're sure it's not too much for her?" John said.

"We're sure," Connor said firmly. Though Mae couldn't tell how much of that was a belief in Sierra and how much was a desperation to never have to plead with a baker again. "Right?"

"Right," Mae agreed. "She's an amazing baker. She's thought this through. She has a plan." Probably, anyway.

"Those pictures Connor showed us *were* beautiful," Susan relented.

"I'd just feel better if I could talk to her," John said.

Mae winced at the thought of ambushing an already reluctant Sierra with a phone call with the Rutherfords barking questions and requests in her ear. "She's pretty busy."

"When's she coming here?" Susan asked.

"Uh…" Another thing she and Sierra hadn't discussed. She couldn't well leave before the barbecue now that Mae had decided not to cancel it. "The fifth, I guess." Also known as Sierra's birthday. From dropping hurtful revelations about their dad to making Sierra work on her birthday, Mae was really disrupting Sierra's life in all sorts of ways this summer.

The silence on the other end signaled that waiting until July fifth to grill Sierra about the cake was unacceptable.

"Why don't we come down for a visit?" John suggested. "This weekend. We'll take a quick trip down, grab some lunch, go over the cake details. It'll put my mind at ease."

"I'd love that!" Susan exclaimed. "I could bring my cake binder."

"O-okay," Mae found herself agreeing. Though it was hard to imagine the Rutherfords in Hobson. She pictured Nosy Posey writing down the license plate number of John's shiny black Lexus and pulling him aside for questioning. Susan declining Marlene and Joan's offers of sweet tea and Taco Bell and asking if they had a 1992 Cabernet Sauvignon instead.

Connor let out an incredulous laugh. "I was gonna come anyway for the barbecue."

"That's right! You're throwing a barbecue, aren't you, Mae?" Susan asked, an unsettling level of enthusiasm in her voice.

Mae cringed. It was harder still to imagine the Rutherfords in Althea's backyard, surrounded by a gaggle of Townsends. Setting the Rutherfords loose at the barbecue after all the family unpleasantness Mae had worked so hard to smooth over felt like tempting fate.

But it was too late now. The conversation was barreling to its inevitable conclusion. John said they didn't have plans for the fourth. Susan asked if Mae might be able to make room for them at the barbecue. Mae stammered out an invitation.

And so it was official: the Rutherfords were coming to the Townsend family barbecue.

MAE: Head count update: Connor's parents are coming to the BBQ! Also, I'm taking menu suggestions. So far I've got mac and cheese, potato salad, baked beans, burgers, veggie burgers, hot dogs, ribs, Herb salad, and Jell-O. Any requests?

LEAH: lollll jello

WENDELL: I'll be making the ribs

JEREMIAH: I'm on burger and hot dog duty!

SCOTT: Is Richard bringing his cider?

MAE: Yep! Also Patty said she's bringing her famous tea cakes, if that means anything

ARIEL: It doesn't

MAE: I'm making some more batches of mac and cheese today. Anyone want to come by later and try them?

WENDELL: Sorry, working late tonight

BARBARA: I need to lay off the heavy foods before the barbecue

JEREMIAH: Phyllis and I are staying in tonight. She has a migraine :(

MAE: Sorry to hear it.

MAE: So no one can taste test?

LEAH: Isn't Sierra helping you?

Mae set her phone on the kitchen counter and surveyed all the ingredients she'd optimistically set out for what she'd expected to be her biggest taste test yet. A large pan rested on the stove, ready to melt butter and create a roux. Blocks of cheese sat stacked in a tower next to the grater, still waiting to be shredded and turned into a creamy sauce.

But she couldn't make test batches without anyone around to try them. Mae didn't know what Althea's mac and cheese tasted like. And, as Leah unknowingly reminded her, she couldn't count on Sierra's help either now that their relationship had reverted back to its cold, distant beginnings. Their only interaction since last night was a text Mae sent to let her know the Rutherfords were coming to town to discuss the cake. Sierra hadn't even texted back. She'd just sent a thumbs-up reaction. The impersonality of it felt worse than no response at all.

She sighed and plodded around the kitchen, putting ingredients away. She'd try again tomorrow. But, as her fingers tapped restlessly on the counter, she knew she couldn't do nothing either. The barbecue was less than a week away, and the Rutherfords rolling into town this weekend was bound to distract her from the recipe. Even if she couldn't make mac and cheese for anyone to try tonight, she could at least search for a clue. Going through Althea's cookbooks, nightstand, and file cabinets hadn't turned up anything useful, but maybe there was something here in the kitchen. Something she hadn't found yet.

Mae began opening the kitchen drawers, checking each one. Utensils. Knives. Foil and saran wrap. Ziploc bags. And then what she'd deemed Althea's junk drawer: a mess of expired coupons, rubber bands, and other odds and ends. She pulled out a piece of paper, smoothed it out to see that it was an old Food Lion receipt for—she peered closer—dish soap.

Mae stared at the receipt, an idea coming to her. She'd already scoured this drawer for Althea's recipe scraps and hadn't found any. But suppose one of the old receipts in here held a clue?

She hefted the whole drawer onto the counter and started sifting through it. Flyers from junk mail inserts. Loose pens and coins. More receipts. Mae pulled out every one she could find—some crumpled, some crisp, all faded. A few went as far back as ten years. She laid them out on the counter and started reading.

It was hard to know what to look for. Any number of groceries Althea bought could have conceivably gone into the mac and cheese. Mae picked up a pen and started going through each receipt, circling anything unique that could have worked in her recipe. Celery salt. Chives. Taco seasoning would have been a weird choice, but why not; she circled it.

On a wrinkled receipt from November 2015, Mae spotted two of the most beautiful words in existence: *elbow macaroni*.

Her pulse quickening, she went through the rest of the list. Further down, she saw *Colby, cheddar,* and *jack*. These had to all be ingredients in her mac and cheese. Mae hadn't been using Colby and jack in her recipe.

She drew asterisks next to the cheeses and took a picture of the receipt, then texted it to Sierra.

MAE: There's been a breakthrough in the case!!!

Her heart leapt when three dots danced with Sierra's response. And then the dots disappeared. At last, a thumbs-up reaction appeared next to the message. The only way Sierra was willing to communicate with her now, apparently.

Well, she'd have to talk when they met with the Rutherfords on Saturday. Unless Sierra found a way around that too, invented some kind of thumbs-only sign language just to spite her.

Mae gave up on staring at their texts and swiped over to her recipe-testing notes. Sierra could give her the silent-thumb treatment all she wanted. She'd change her mind when she tasted Mae's mac and cheese. From now until Saturday, her only focus had to be making a batch good enough to win Sierra back—no matter how many it took.

CHAPTER TWENTY-ONE

Connor smelled like home: the clean scent of their laundry detergent, the peppery sharpness of his deodorant, the faint peppermint on his breath from his favorite tea.

The second Mae spotted him at the Raleigh-Durham International Airport, she'd leapt into his arms, breathing him in. She stood on her toes to kiss him, then pulled back to get a look at him. His sandy hair was in its usual state of dishevelment and his lopsided grin was the same, but the dark circles under his eyes belied the wedding stress he'd been under lately. In those shadows, she saw dance lessons, three hundred manually folded favor boxes, canceled dress fittings, desperate pleading with bakeries, everything she hadn't helped him with.

But Connor didn't say any of that. Nor did he comment on how tired she probably looked, a result of staying up too late making far too many batches of mac and cheese in what now felt like a fever dream. He just kept looking at her, his eyes warm, his expression content.

"Hi," he said, threading his fingers through hers.

"Hi." They shared a smile, but before they could speak further,

John and Susan came up behind him, and then began the ritual of hugs, pleasantries, asking about their flight, and then whisking them to their hotel in downtown Durham to meet Sierra for lunch.

Mae knew better than to expect hugs or pleasantries from her sister. Sierra, already seated at a table by the bar, gave Mae a taut smile and obligatory nod but heaped all her charm on the Rutherfords, standing and shaking John, Susan, and Connor's hands and thanking them for coming. Mae, feeling like a stranger, had to look down at her shirt, a faded purple cotton top Sierra had given her just a week ago, to remind herself they hadn't always been this distant.

They took places at the table, John and Susan on one side, Mae and Connor on the other, Sierra at the end like a high-powered executive, with her pale-blue sleeveless collared top and her hair swept into a neat ponytail. When Susan pulled a binder from her purse, Mae shot Sierra an apologetic look—but Sierra, ignoring it, just pulled out a folder of her own.

While Mae sipped her ice water, Sierra slid forth a pencil sketch of an elegant, five-tiered wedding cake. Pale pink roses ran down the tiers in a diagonal stripe, like the cake was wearing a floral sash. Small white pearls dotted the outside of the second and fourth layer, and lace adorned the bottom tier.

"It's beautiful," Mae breathed. "Is that edible lace?"

"Mmhmm."

"I didn't know that was a thing. I need to watch more baking shows." Mae laughed tentatively. Sierra didn't so much as crack a smile.

Susan put on her reading glasses and leaned over the sketch. "These pearls look just like the beads on Mae's wedding dress. Sierra, this is stunning."

"Thank you so much." Oh, *now* Sierra smiled, something wide and gracious that she'd never throw Mae's way.

With drooping disappointment, Mae stared vacantly at the sketch as John and Susan exclaimed over the details. Her eyes fell on the flavor written off to the side: red velvet. She looked up at Sierra in wonder, but Sierra didn't meet her gaze.

"The roses are lovely," Susan said. "You know, we've gone with peonies for the centerpieces. Would you be able to work those in?"

"I'll be honest with you; roses are the only flower I know how to make. Basically, if you want flowers, you're getting roses."

While Susan, John, and Connor laughed, Mae resigned herself to studying the menu. This Sierra, with her humor and charm and softness, wasn't meant for Mae. All she could do was press her lips together and wait for John and Susan to notice the flavor written off to the side—and hope they wouldn't bulldoze over it with their blackberry lavender expectations.

"Roses will be perfect," Susan said.

"Red velvet?" John read.

Sierra tossed a glance at Mae. Mae conjured the words in her head, but her mouth wouldn't form them. A beat of silence passed, then another. Sierra soldiered on. "Yeah, it's Mae's favorite," she said, making Mae's chest twinge.

"Oh," Susan said, turning to Mae. "I didn't know that."

Mae shrugged, because apparently she was a mime now. But her eyes remained locked on Sierra, aching to ask what this meant, if she still cared.

"The only hiccup is that the menus have already been printed with the original cake flavor," John said. "Blackberry lavender."

A moment of silence followed as Sierra absorbed John's

expectant stare, giving him absolutely nothing in return. Mae's muscles clenched.

"But we can print new ones," he said. Mae's muscles relaxed, and the conversation moved on. They worked out logistics, the Rutherfords sharing that they'd take care of Sierra's travel arrangements and expenses for the wedding. Mae watched them exchange phone numbers, an uneasy feeling building in her at the thought of Susan and John having unfiltered access to Sierra.

Throughout lunch, Mae picked at her Caesar salad while her head swiveled back and forth between Sierra, Susan, and John like she was watching a tennis match and not listening to a light-hearted discussion about the merits of buttercream over fondant. Not even Connor's hand sneaking its way to Mae's in her lap, tracing smooth circles on the inside of her palm, could keep her from her vigilance.

At one point, Mae caught Sierra watching her. She stared back, curious for the reason, but Sierra just took another bite of her beet salad and asked John and Susan how long they'd been running their winery.

By the time the bill arrived, Mae was no closer to winning Sierra over. Susan and John were signing the receipt, chattering about exploring downtown Durham, and in a few moments they would all be standing, Sierra would leave without another word, and all Mae's mac and cheese testing last night would be for nought. Mae's gaze flickered to Sierra, a question burning in her brain, but her voice stayed mute.

"Thank you for a lovely lunch," Sierra was saying. More thanks and civilities echoed around the table. Chairs scraped against the floor. Cloth napkins were tossed onto the empty tabletop. Connor's hand left hers as even he stood to leave. Only

Mae remained seated, refusing to admit defeat. The question grew frantic, straining against her lips as her heartbeat thundered in her ears.

"Sierra, do you want to come over?" Mae blurted out.

Four heads swiveled to look at Mae.

She pushed on, forcing the words out in a rush. "Connor brought those cookbooks that might have been our grandma's— and I need your opinion on some batches I made." Against Sierra's uncertain glance, Mae twisted the cloth napkin in her lap, imploring Sierra to say yes, come over, give her a chance to close this chilly distance between them once and for all.

"You should!" Susan said, filling the silence with cheer. "Don't worry about John and me. I'm making him take me to the botanical gardens. You three have fun!" She led the charge in a round of hugs, and then she and John disappeared out the door, leaving Mae and Connor to await Sierra's response.

Sierra studied Mae in silence. Mae stared back, bursting with hope. Connor grew interested in the ceiling tiles.

"Okay," Sierra said. "Just for a few minutes." And even though her words were tightly coiled in reluctance, Mae let out a slow breath of relief. She had her chance. She just needed to not mess it up.

On the drive to Althea's, Mae kept checking the rearview mirror to confirm that Sierra's silver Honda was still following behind them, as if any second Sierra might swerve into a side street and ditch them completely. But all the way down the turnpike and through Althea's neighborhood streets, Sierra remained behind them.

"I went a little unhinged last night," Mae confessed to Connor as she pulled into Althea's driveway.

"Unhinged how?" he asked with a laugh.

She put the car in park and leaned against the headrest. "I made more batches of mac and cheese. Like…a lot."

Connor paused. "How many?"

"Twelve."

"*Twelve?*"

"I wanted to get it right! But I also don't want to scare her off." Mae craned her neck to watch Sierra park at the curb. "So just act like it's normal," she hurriedly instructed on her way out of the car.

Naturally, this resulted in Connor loudly remarking, "Oh, how normal!" when he and Sierra followed Mae into the kitchen. The sink, counters, and stove were a mess of dirty pots and pans, crumpled grocery bags, empty milk cartons, used forks, puddles of bechamel. Grated cheese dotted the counter, and Mae suspected the kitchen was going to smell like cheese for the next week at least.

"Is this blood?" Sierra inspected a reddish stain on the counter.

"Maybe?" Mae dabbed it with her finger. "No. This was when I was experimenting with hot sauce."

"Why would you think it was blood?" Connor asked slowly, his eyes roving the kitchen.

"I said it wasn't."

"Right, but—"

"You weren't sure at first," Sierra said.

"Which suggests there's blood somewhere in this kitchen," Connor finished.

"Lawyers," Mae joked to Sierra, pointing a thumb in Connor's direction. When their serious faces held firm, she sighed and said,

"There was an incident with the grater, but I cleaned it up. It's fine." She waved it off, then noticed Connor and Sierra's gazes zero in on the bandage on her finger. "Are we ready to taste test?"

Connor and Sierra stood silently watching Mae conjure more and more foil loaf pans of mac and cheese from the fridge like a harried magician.

"What?" she asked when she set the last one on the counter. "I promise there's no blood in these." Which perhaps wasn't the most reassuring thing to say when offering someone food.

"Why did you make so much?" Sierra asked.

"Not that it's not a normal amount," Connor interjected.

"I just..." Mae toyed with the edge of one of the foil pans, bending it back and forth, searching for the words. "I knew I was gonna see you today, and it felt like my only chance to try to make things up to you. So I stayed up 'til five a.m. trying different ingredients and proportions of cheeses." She looked up at Sierra and dropped her arms to her sides in a helpless shrug. "I know this recipe means a lot to you, and *you* mean a lot to *me*, and I really, really wanted to get it right."

Sierra was quiet at first, staring at Mae in disbelief. "You did this for me?" Her voice was soft, tentative.

"Of course." Mae found herself blinking more than usual, her dry and tired eyes suddenly stinging with emotion.

"You know," Connor said, "I was thinking when we got here that the grass looked a little long, so I'm gonna go...make myself useful." He gave Mae's elbow a squeeze on his way out of the kitchen.

And then she was left watching Sierra, hoping the wondering expression on her face meant what she thought it might.

"You didn't have to do all this," Sierra said.

"No," Mae agreed. "But I wanted to."

"You're so extra." Sierra shook her head, her eyes glistening, then crossed the room and pulled Mae into a fierce hug. "And I'm sorry," she said. "That day you dropped that news on me, I was surprised and upset, and I took it out on you because...the person I wanted to yell at isn't around anymore."

"I know the feeling," Mae admitted. "And if you ever do want to talk, or yell...I'm here."

Sierra nodded, a smile growing across her face. "I know."

Mae exhaled, feeling all her restlessness from the past few days leaving her. "So...are we good?"

"We're good." Sierra looked Mae up and down, from the bags under her eyes to the Band-Aid on her finger. "Are *you* good? Do you need to, like, sleep? Or get stitches?"

"The only thing I need," Mae said gravely, pulling a fork from a drawer, "is for you to try my mac and cheese."

"You're ridiculous." Sierra took the fork, twirling it in her fingers as Mae prepared a plate to heat up for her.

"You know you love me," Mae retorted. Ordinarily, she might have panicked at letting an assumption like that slip out, felt it was too much too soon. But she didn't dwell on it now. It felt too true not to say it.

And Sierra, who rolled her eyes with a fond smile but didn't dispute it, seemed to agree.

CHAPTER TWENTY-TWO

Batch number eight from Mae's frenzied, twelve-batch, late-night cooking session turned out to be closest, Sierra determined. Its proportions of Colby and jack created a smoother texture and a different kind of cheesiness that complemented the Velveeta and cheddar.

"I'd say this is the one," Sierra decided. "Still not as creamy, and the flavor's not completely right, but it's pretty close."

"*Pretty* close isn't good enough." Mae scrolled through her notes.

"Mae." Sierra lowered her chin, her voice taking on a *be real* tone.

"The barbecue's in three days," Mae said. "I promised I would figure out the recipe."

"Yeah, within reason. This"—Sierra circled her hand in Mae's general direction—"is not reasonable."

"Hey, Mae?" Connor's voice came from the front entrance. "Can you come vouch for me? I was in the garage looking for the lawn mower and this guy came up and started asking who I am and why I'm here? And I know logically I shouldn't have to answer him, but I feel weirdly compelled to?"

Mae caught Sierra's eye over the table, and that was all it took to send them both into a laughter that made her lungs feel ecstatically full. That feeling remained after she introduced Connor to a suspicious Nosy Posey and retrieved the cookbooks from Connor's suitcase.

"Will you just go through these with me?" Mae asked Sierra. She spread the cookbooks out on the dining room table. *Southern Home Kitchen* was printed at the top of each one, followed by a unique theme. *Appetizers Aplenty. Feeding a Crowd. Holiday Traditions.* "If we don't find anything, I promise I'll stop."

Sierra traced the words on one of the covers. "Grandma had tons of these."

"She did?"

"They were her favorite. I took the whole stack from her house after she died, looking for the mac and cheese recipe. I couldn't find anything."

"Wow," Mae said. "I guess that's another reason to be mad at our dad. Breaking up the set."

Sierra smirked. "We'll add it to the list."

Methodically, they checked the index in the back of each one, then went through every page, looking for a recipe that had gone unindexed, or perhaps a handwritten note in a corner somewhere, some sign that their grandma had left a clue behind. There was nothing.

"I knew it would be a long shot," Mae said, more to the disappointment curling around her ribs than to Sierra.

"Your version is good," Sierra said. "I promise." They shared a smile, and Sierra idly began flipping through one of the cookbooks. "So, Connor's parents are coming to the barbecue?"

"Yeah, they sort of invited themselves. I hope that's okay."

Sierra let out a bemused laugh. "It's fine. I swear you act like this barbecue is a bigger deal than it is."

"Agree to disagree," Mae said, making Sierra grin.

"Can I ask you something?" Sierra paused at a recipe for deviled eggs, then kept turning the pages.

"Sure."

"Why are you weird around Connor's parents?"

"What? No, I'm not."

Sierra gave a low chuckle. "Yes, you are. You were all quiet and tense around them at lunch."

Mae was silent for the next few moments, getting used to the idea that her hesitation around the Rutherfords wasn't just a feeling that lived in her head. She only hoped Connor hadn't picked up on it. She wasn't sure she had any answers for him.

"I wasn't tense," she objected weakly.

"Oh, come on!" Sierra laughed. "Look, you're getting married in a week. If they've spat in your face when no one's looking, or if they've openly talked about lynching you, I need to know so I can tell you to run."

Mae lifted her eyebrows. "Spitting and lynching? That's the scale?"

"That's the scale. Which is it?" Sierra's unrelenting stare wore her down.

"Fine. Um." Mae studied her hands in her lap. "It's nothing. I was at the beach with Connor and his family a few years ago, and I was putting sunscreen on, and his mom asked how dark my skin gets in the sun."

She lifted her eyes, half-expecting Sierra to tell Mae she was overreacting. Or joke that this was what she got for marrying into a white family. Because hadn't Mae brought this on herself when she fell for Connor? Weren't comments like these her price to pay for marrying a white man? That illogical feeling had kept her quiet about that day on the beach, prevented her from telling even Jayla—whose husband was Black—for fear that her feelings weren't warranted since she'd basically brought this on herself.

But Sierra wasn't shrugging it off. Her mouth twisted in a sympathetic wince. "How'd she ask it? Was it like, 'It better not get any darker, negro,' or was it like, 'I don't know how Black people work and this is my awkward way of trying to figure it out'?"

Mae let out a relieved breath. "Exactly! That's the thing. I couldn't tell. I'm sure it's the second one, but I keep wondering if it's just the tip of the iceberg. My mom's family always said stuff around me that made me feel different, and I don't want it to be like that with Connor's family. I don't want to be their token Black person they ask all their weird questions to. I don't know how to give them a blanket statement, like, 'Hey, don't ask me anything weird from now until forever, thanks.'"

"What does Connor think?"

"I…never told him."

Sierra arched a brow, her expression shifting into amused disbelief. "Jeez. No wonder you were trying to *Runaway Bride*."

"I wasn't *Runaway Bride*-ing!" Mae said. "I just—I don't know. It's hard to bring up. I did try once, though."

"Yeah? How'd that go?"

"Well." Mae tipped her head to the side. "It was after we'd been dating for a few months, and we were driving to meet his parents for the first time. I asked him what his parents had been like around his ex-boyfriend, who's Mexican. But then he talked for the rest of the drive about how his parents didn't seem to understand his bisexuality, and I didn't have the heart to tell him I was actually asking about race."

"You're useless," Sierra said around a chuckle. "What'd you say to his mom, then? When she said the thing about your skin?"

"I stammered like an idiot, I said 'It depends,' and then I pointed at a seagull."

"Smooth," Sierra remarked. She grew serious as she regarded Mae. "You should talk to Connor. Or you'll always obsess over it."

"Okay." It was practical advice, or it would be if she knew how to broach the topic to him. Mae went back to staring at her hands.

"What's holding you back?" Sierra pressed.

Mae sighed and looked up. "What if he doesn't see anything wrong with what she said? What if he takes her side?"

Sierra suppressed a laugh. "Mae. I have known that sweet, beautiful, Saltine of a man for one day, and it is very obvious that he would do anything for you. He folded all those wedding favor boxes so you didn't have to, didn't he?"

"That's just because his parents wanted him to. He'll do anything his parents ask."

"Okay, but he'll do double-anything for you. Do you think I didn't notice that he held your hand all during lunch just because he missed you? Even though it meant eating with his left hand the whole time? And going by the entire field of lettuce he dropped in his lap, he is not left-handed."

Mae's efforts to keep a straight face failed as Sierra went on. "That's true."

"I know. So, stop obsessing, and get the conversation over with."

"Okay, okay," Mae relented. "I'll talk to him."

"Before the wedding," Sierra said, pointing at her.

"Before the wedding," she agreed.

Sierra nodded, satisfied. "That said, if he pulls that hand-holding shit again, I'm leaving. It was cute the first time, but I have my limits."

"Understood."

Sierra went back to perusing the cookbooks, a comfortable silence settling between them. When the roar of a lawnmower sounded, they turned their heads to see Connor in the backyard, using the old mower from the garage. Sierra gave her a knowing smirk. Mae just smiled and shook her head.

The mower went quiet a minute later. Mae watched Connor wipe sweat off his brow, nodding and listening to someone who must have been talking to him over the fence, and knew immediately that Richard was intervening again. A dreamy smile came over her at the prospect of her worlds colliding.

"You use a bechamel in the mac and cheese, right?" Sierra asked.

Mae turned from the window. Sierra was staring at a page in the cookbook. "Yeah."

"What's in it?"

"The usual," Mae said, speaking slowly. "Butter, flour, milk. Why?"

Sierra looked up, her eyes roving around like she was piecing something together. "What kind of milk?"

"Whole. Again, why?"

When Sierra returned to the cookbook, Mae sped to her side of the table, reading over her shoulder.

"Bechamel?" she said.

"But it uses evaporated milk," Sierra replied. "And look." She pointed to a sentence in the recipe introduction. *Using evaporated milk results in a richer, creamier bechamel.*

Mae's mouth fell open. "The cookbooks weren't a dead end!"

"We don't know that," Sierra warned, but Mae was already dashing across the kitchen to rummage through the cabinets.

"Aha!" She pulled out a can of evaporated milk and held it up. "One more batch?"

After her twelve-batch mania from the night before, Mae cherished having Sierra by her side, returning to that coordinated rhythm they'd developed in the kitchen, the easy back and forth. Sierra turned the heat up on the pan while Mae dropped a cube of butter into it. Mae rummaged in a drawer in search of a clean spoon, and Sierra gently swatted her hand away and handed her the wooden spoon she'd just washed.

Mae looked from the spoon to Sierra, her heart swimming in gratitude. She reached for the spoon—then stopped. "You stir the roux this time," she said.

Sierra looked at the spoon like it might bite her. "But the gravy—"

"You're not gonna burn this. I trust you." She ignored Sierra's outcry, turning instead to the butter foaming in the pan. "You better hurry." Mae picked up the small bowl of flour Sierra had measured and threw it into the butter, which greedily sizzled around it.

Sierra gave a panicked squeak and flew to the stove, stirring vigorously. "It's lumpy."

"That's fine. It'll even out." She looked on with satisfaction as Sierra's stirring became slower, more self-assured, and the roux took on a smooth, golden hue, giving the kitchen a toasty smell. "You ready for the secret ingredient?" Mae held up the can of evaporated milk.

When Sierra nodded, Mae poured it into the hissing pan. Sierra stepped back but didn't stop stirring. She kept at it, maintaining her cool as the mixture thickened, as Mae threw in the cheeses and then the macaroni. Only when they turned the burner off and poured the pan's contents into a foil pan did Sierra relinquish the wooden spoon, setting it on the counter with a dazed look.

"Look at that," Mae said, beaming at her. "You stirred a sauce and it didn't burn."

Sierra's lips curved into a self-conscious smile. "I *know* Grandma's turning over in her grave right now."

"I bet she's proud of you," Mae countered, sprinkling grated cheese over the dish with abandon. "*I'm* proud of you. I'm proud of *us* for cracking this recipe."

Sierra shook her head slowly, like she hated every second of this—but her broad grin betrayed her. "Let's not get ahead of ourselves," she said as Mae slid the mac and cheese into the oven.

"Too late." Mae nibbled on a stray piece of cheddar, her eyes on the oven. She took a step closer and switched on the oven light, then dropped to her knees to watch through the door. The cheese on top was just starting to melt, little shreds softening into a uniform sheen.

"You don't need to babysit it," Sierra said.

"Oh, come sit with me. It's fun."

Sierra looked like she was considering it, but her phone rang before she could make up her mind. A strange look crossed her face when she looked at her screen.

"What?" Mae asked.

"Nothing. I just…have to take this." She disappeared upstairs, leaving Mae to watch the cheese bubble on her own.

When Sierra returned a few minutes later, she planted herself next to Mae and sat cross-legged on the kitchen floor. Though she seemed more interested in sneaking looks at her phone, and then at Mae, than in watching what was happening in the oven.

"*What?*" Mae said.

"Nothing."

Mae frowned at her but went back to monitoring the oven. When the cheese topping was bubbling and starting to brown, she pulled it out. It didn't look or smell any different. But that didn't mean anything. This could still be the one.

"Here goes," Sierra muttered when they dug their forks into the still-steaming dish. Mae closed her eyes and chewed.

All the same flavors were present and accounted for. It was still rich and cheesy, the sharpness of the cheddar balanced by the blend of milder cheeses, the spices adding a hit of flavor. She chewed past the crackly top layer and into the macaroni underneath, trying to focus on the texture. Then she took another bite, one without the top layer. It could have been placebo, but she felt like it was slightly creamier. It was silky. Velvety.

Mae opened her eyes to gauge Sierra's reaction. Sierra was chewing—she must have also gone back for more.

"Did we do it?" Mae said, speaking over the food in her mouth, manners be damned.

"Patience." Sierra took another bite and chewed thoughtfully. Her eyes roamed the kitchen, finally coming to rest on Mae. She swallowed, a flash of something Mae couldn't read passed over her face, and then Sierra broke into a smile. "We did it."

"Oh my god!" Mae threw her arms around Sierra in a tight

embrace. "So, this is what it tastes like? The famous mac and cheese?"

Sierra nodded and went for another forkful. "It tastes like home."

Mae took another bite, too. As if she could train her brain to conjure up this association after the fact, summon thoughts of holidays with the Townsends. But this wasn't a bad memory either, she thought, with a glance at Sierra. Eating mac and cheese that reminded her of standing in her grandma's kitchen with her newfound sister while her fiancé mowed the backyard under the supervision of a meddlesome neighbor sounded like a wonderful memory to her.

Although she hadn't heard the mower in a while. Enough time had passed that the lawn should have been done by now, meddling neighbors or not, but Connor was nowhere to be found.

"Have you seen Connor?" she asked.

"No. Why would I know where he is?" Sierra grabbed a sponge and busied herself with wiping down the counter. But there was something exaggerated about her words, her movements. Almost theatrical.

Before Mae could call her on it, Connor opened the back door and poked his head into the kitchen. "Hey, Mae? Can I show you something in the backyard?"

Mae gave Sierra a suspicious glance over her shoulder as she followed Connor outside.

"You went to Bojangles?" Mae asked him, spotting the yellow cup in his hand.

"Joan did. She saw me mowing out front and we got to talking. Want some?"

Mae laughed. "I should have known." She took a sip, ice-cold sweet tea lighting up her taste buds. She handed it back to Connor with a curious look. "What did you want to show me?"

And then she saw it. A simple white arch stood against the backyard fence, a web of string lights hung along the frame.

"Where did that come from?" she asked. Yet her skin tingled with goosebumps as though she already knew the answer.

"I bought it," Connor replied. "From Party City. Not the classiest place, but it's hard to find a wedding arch on short notice."

"And why did you buy a wedding arch?" Again, some part of her must have known, which had to be why she couldn't keep from smiling. But the pieces weren't quite coming together in her head, and she needed to hear it from Connor.

"Well." Connor took a long sip from his straw. "Sometime between watching you talk to that Brian guy, and hearing Richard tell me about helping you mow the lawn, and seeing Joan drive-by-deliver me a drink I didn't ask for, and sitting on the porch with her and Marlene, being force-fed cookies...I started to understand how much this place means to you—why it was so important for you to be here. And I know the barbecue is a big deal to you, and I know you never wanted the big wedding my parents are throwing. So I wondered...what if we had a different wedding first? What if we got married at the barbecue?"

For the second time that day, Mae had to blink back happy tears. Her eyes shifted from Connor's sweet, sincere brown eyes to Sierra watching them through the kitchen window. "Is Sierra in on it too? Is that why she was acting so weird a few minutes ago?"

He nodded, grinning. "I asked her if your family would be cool with it. She said yes. I also checked with your mom, and she's willing to change her flight."

Mae shook her head in wonder, glancing between him, Sierra in the window, and the arch. "I—"

"One more thing," he interrupted. "I never really got a chance to officially propose, and I always kind of wanted to. So, humor me." He dropped to one knee, taking Mae's hand in his. "I know we're getting married in a week, but will you marry me on the Fourth of July? I don't have a ring, but I can offer you Bojangles." He held out the yellow cup.

Mae was smiling so widely she thought her face might split in half, though it felt impossible to think about anything other than this wonderful person kneeling before her, and this backyard that was going to host her beloved barbecue and, miraculously, a wedding in front of the family she cared about most.

"Yes."

When he stood to kiss her, a corner of her brain was already whirring with to-do lists detailing the particulars of spontaneously tacking a wedding onto a barbecue.

But even that corner gave in to her feeling of contentment here and now: Connor's arms, his lips, the taste of sweet tea, the warm air, the smell of freshly cut grass. Every detail was perfect. And she knew, without a doubt, that their backyard wedding-slash-barbecue was going to be perfect, too. *Her* version of perfect, a version that couldn't be found in bridal magazines or Susan's binders. This backyard, this town, the presence of people she'd come to care so fiercely about—these were the ingredients for a perfect wedding.

CHAPTER TWENTY-THREE

MAE: If you haven't heard the news, the barbecue will also include a wedding!

DESIREE: Yay!!!

JEREMIAH: Can't wait!

WENDELL: That's fine as long as we're still eating at 2. My ribs are on a very specific timetable

PHYLLIS: I forgot Wendell's an expert chef in addition to being an expert plumber

BARBARA: Ha! Expert timekeeper too

DAWN: He's a man of many talents!

WENDELL: THANK YOU Dawn

WENDELL: Or were you mocking me too?

DAWN: 😄

ARIEL: Will there be cake?

LEAH: Do you have a dress?

All good questions. The to-dos for a spur-of-the-moment backyard wedding were overwhelming on paper, especially with just two and a half days to pull it off. But slowly, surely, everything started to come together. Mae's mom changed her flight, and Mae and Connor woke up early the day before the barbecue to rush downtown to Hobson's county clerk's office right when it opened to get their marriage license.

Now they stood in the kitchen, drinking coffee, while Mae went over her list of remaining tasks. "I still need to get a cake," she said.

Connor froze, mug halfway to his lips. "Asking bakeries to accommodate last-minute requests doesn't go well in my experience."

Mae tried her best to keep a straight face. "I'll handle the bakery." She went back to her list, her eyes falling on *Ask Sierra to officiate*. She hoped it would be a straightforward task. Sierra was on her way over to help Mae prepare the final batch of mac and cheese for the barbecue. She'd find the right moment to ask her.

"Giant foil pan, at your service," Sierra said when she arrived a few minutes later. She held up the pan in one arm and readjusted the straps of the cloth bags on her shoulder with the other. "I've got extra Velveeta in the bag."

"You're amazing, thank you!" Mae helped Sierra carry the bags to the kitchen. "Patty called me when I was getting groceries yesterday and I got distracted."

Patty had been the only non-Townsend who hadn't answered the phone when Mae had called to inform them the barbecue was now a wedding. Patty reprimanded Mae for calling while she was in church, then grumbled about the rudeness of holding a wedding with two days' notice. Mae tried to object when Patty said that now she had to go out and buy a gift, but Patty wouldn't hear it. Then Patty asked if Connor was a Christian, scoffed when Mae said he wasn't, and muttered *Lord help you* as she hung up the phone.

"Patty's a distracting person," Sierra deadpanned.

"Hey, is there a bakery you'd recommend?" Mae asked. "I need to get a cake today."

"No need," Sierra said. "I've got it covered." Only then did she reveal the contents of another bag she'd brought in: three bunches of bananas, two boxes of Nilla wafers, and a dozen eggs.

Mae took a moment to piece the ingredients together, warmth flooding her when she made the connection. "Banana pudding," she murmured. Flashes of the dish's significance came to her: her dad buying it from the bakery they used to go to and waxing poetic about Althea's banana pudding. That Instagram post Sierra had made when Althea died, sharing that banana pudding was the first thing Althea ever taught her to make. And now all the makings were here on her counter.

"I know it's not a cake, but—"

"It's perfect," Mae said. "Thank you." There could be no better dessert to represent tomorrow's day of family coming together than this dish that meant so much to Mae's dad, to Althea, to Sierra—and now to Mae. And to Connor, who was so grateful to be spared from revisiting his bakery trauma that he'd thrown his arms around Sierra in a relieved hug.

Mae leaned against the counter and crossed *Cake* off her list. "I still need to get a dress, but I can figure that out later."

"No need," Sierra said.

"What?"

Sierra just gave her a shrewd smile. "Nothing."

Before Mae could press her on it, Connor's phone rang. He glanced at the screen, then looked up. "It's Kaufman and Stout."

"Who?" Sierra asked.

"Law firm," Mae explained while Connor answered the phone. "He's up for a job."

Mae listened intently to Connor's polite responses, though it was hard to tell from his professional demeanor which way the conversation was going. But when he hung up and turned to Mae, his stunned expression told her exactly what he was going to say next. A sense of foreboding loomed over her.

"I got the job."

And there it was.

"Congratulations," Mae tried. Was she smiling right? Was it too wide? Not wide enough?

"Congrats!" Sierra exclaimed. Mae searched her face for clues on how to look happy for someone. Sierra gave Mae a strange look, then turned back to Connor. "What's the job?"

"Associate attorney for a law office in DC," Connor said, still sounding like he couldn't believe it.

"Your parents live there, right?" Sierra asked. "Are you gonna commute or move?"

"I'm hoping to move. If Mae's willing. She hasn't made up her mind yet."

Mae caught Sierra's eye. She guessed Sierra had a good idea of where Mae's reluctance stemmed from. When Mae glanced away, she noticed Connor watching her. She gave him a hasty smile.

"My head is a mess right now with all this wedding stuff, but we'll definitely figure it all out after the wedding," she assured him. And then, to make sure she was being the right level of supportive, she added, "They'll be lucky to have you."

That seemed to do it. Connor grinned and kissed her cheek. Mae gulped down her coffee.

Sierra's mysterious comment about the dress took on meaning a few minutes later, when Leah, Ariel, and Wendell burst through the door. Wendell was carrying a sewing machine, Ariel a fabric basket, and Leah several dresses on hangers in her arms.

"What's happening?" Mae asked.

"You said you didn't have a dress," Leah explained matter-of-factly.

"You the fiancé?" Wendell asked, looking Connor up and down.

"Yes." Seeing Wendell's scrutiny, Connor's relaxed posture slowly straightened. Wendell was looking at Connor as though he could hunt down every skeleton in his closet through eye contact alone. Connor gave him an awkward smile in return. Mae had to suppress a laugh.

"He's not supposed to see your wedding dress," Ariel said, giving Connor a suspicious look.

"Well, I didn't know you were gonna come in here with Mae's wedding dress," Connor pointed out. His smile stiffened under Ariel's firm stare. "But I should have," he added. "I will...go upstairs."

"You're not gonna decorate the backyard for the wedding?" Ariel asked.

"I mean, I put in the arch...but it's not enough," he said slowly, trying to read Ariel's expression. "I will...get some decorations?" He hesitated, as if waiting for permission.

"Good." Ariel frowned, like she was confused as to why he was still there. "Go do that."

"Yes, ma'am." Connor set his half-drunk coffee on the counter and reached around Mae to grab her car keys, mouthing *What just happened?* when their eyes met. She held back a smile as she watched him head out. Sweet-natured Connor was no match for Ariel's assertive personality.

"Okay," Leah announced. "I have a few mostly finished dresses that might work. This one's probably the closest thing to a traditional wedding dress." She held up a white dress with fluttery sleeves and a sash around the waist.

White probably wasn't the actual color, though. Mae remembered the wedding dress she'd picked out last year, an embroidered, champagne-colored gown that had made her feel simultaneously like a princess and a doily. *Champagne*, such a fancy name for a color Mae would have called beige-ish. It wasn't until she was shopping that day with Jayla and Susan that she discovered just how many shades of white there were. She still remembered the serious tone the sales associate had used to correct her when Mae dared utter the word *white* to describe what was actually a very obvious *milk*.

"That's pretty," Mae said. Leah's lips pursed as she looked at the dress, whatever shade of white it was. "What?"

"Well, we're gonna be at a barbecue, with food around, and..."

"You're a messy eater," Ariel finished, prompting Sierra to burst out laughing.

"No, I'm not!"

"You do have a stain on your shirt right now," Sierra pointed out.

Mae looked down, spotting a dime-sized splotch near her belly button. "That's from cooking! It's cheese sauce."

"Okay, then you're a messy cook, too," Ariel amended.

Mae laughed. She had to admit they had a point. She could easily picture barbecue sauce dripping down that white dress, leaving a stain the sales associate probably would have called *garnet* or *mahogany*.

The next few dresses Leah held up were colorful and summery: one a tiered midi dress with a pale-blue floral pattern, another a green cotton fit-and-flare with an eyelet design. But the one that caught Mae's eye had a yellow checkered pattern with a sweetheart neckline and a matching tie-belt around the waist.

"It kind of reminds me of the red checkered tablecloth in the pictures I've seen of the barbecue," Mae said, feeling the soft, cottony fabric between her fingers.

"You want to be a table?" Ariel asked dryly.

"Let her be a table if she wants to be a table," Leah hissed.

Mae much preferred this scene to the day-long affair of picking her wedding dress in the boutique in DC. Then, she'd been overwhelmed with options, fabrics, bright lights, mirrors. Associates running around fetching dress after dress, pushing free champagne and cupcakes on her even though she was still full from breakfast. Mae peeking at price tags and dying inside. But this, standing in the kitchen while Leah took measurements and Ariel served as her grumbling assistant, listening to Sierra chastise Wendell for eating one of her bananas, was the ideal wedding dress shopping experience.

While Leah set up camp in the living room to work on tailoring the dress, Sierra and Mae started on the mac and cheese. It felt strange to be making it in such a large quantity after all the small test batches they'd made—but it felt right, too. Exciting to finally reach this stage, where they weren't testing a recipe but feeding a crowd. Just like Althea did.

When Connor came in loaded down with bags bearing the Party City logo, Ariel abandoned her seamstress assistant duties, leaving Wendell to pick them up in her stead, and followed Connor into the backyard to help decorate. From what Mae could see through the kitchen window, the role Ariel assumed involved a lot of pointing, and then nodding or shaking her head while Connor hung up decorations, dragged out the long table and mismatched lawn chairs from the garage, and looked for her approval. Slowly, the backyard was taking shape, starting to become what she'd seen in pictures. Starting to feel real.

"Ready to make the banana pudding?" Sierra asked, and Mae nodded eagerly.

Sierra walked her through the process of making the pudding, and Mae wondered how similar this scene was to that time some thirty years ago when Althea taught Sierra to make this dessert, probably in this very kitchen. Was Althea standing in the same spot where Sierra stood now when she taught her how to separate egg yolks from the whites? Was this old wooden spoon Mae was using to stir the thickening custard the same one a six-year-old Sierra had used to make this pudding for the first time? She followed Sierra's instructions on how to layer the banana slices, Nilla wafers, and pudding in the large foil pan, enjoying the feeling of being a student much like a young Sierra had been. After Sierra guided her through piling on the foamy egg whites and making the textured swoops Althea liked to do, they slid the pan into the oven, then leaned against the counter waiting for the topping to brown.

"Have you talked to Connor yet?" Sierra asked. "About his parents?"

Mae stiffened. She'd vaguely broached the topic that morning, in the car on the way to the county clerk's office. She'd asked him, "Do I act different around your parents?"

Connor had shrugged, tossing her a glance as he slowed to a stop at a red light. "Yeah, a little."

"What am I normally like around them?"

The light turned green. The car rolled into motion. "You're polite. A little quiet." Another glance. "Why?"

Mae took a breath. "Does that bother you?"

"No. As long as you're not quiet around me, what do I care?" He gave her a puzzled look at another red light. "Is something up?"

She shook her head, relief coursing through her. Sierra's insistence that Mae talk to Connor about her fears hadn't felt so crucial anymore. Connor had just confirmed that however she was around his parents, he didn't care. And Mae hadn't felt like getting into it anyway, not when they had a day of barbecue-wedding-related errands to run.

But here in the kitchen with Sierra, that reasoning started to feel ineffectual. "Not yet," she admitted. "But I will."

Those last three words felt like a lie. From the way Sierra eyed her, she seemed to feel the same way. But then the egg whites were starting to brown, and it was time to take the dessert out of the oven and move on to the next task, and the conversation fell away.

They set about making the Jell-O next, Sierra making Mae giggle with memories of the decades-long rift between Althea and Nosy Posey. Leah came by to have Mae try on the tailored dress, which now zipped up her back with ease. She'd just finished changing out of it when Connor and Ariel rapped on the sliding glass door and told them to come outside.

Mae had to smile when she stepped into the heat to admire their handiwork. String lights and red, white, and blue crepe paper were strung along the wooden garden fence enclosing the backyard. They'd even wound the crepe paper around the branches of the dogwood tree in the corner and hung an oversized patriotic ribbon on the tree. Two large, crepe wedding bells were hung on the fence, placed on either side of the arch. The table from the garage, now positioned near the fence, was covered with the worn, red checkered tablecloth. Even with these changes and over-the-top decorations, this piece of Althea would still be with them.

This was almost exactly the setting she'd imagined in her head when she thought about the Fourth of July barbecue her dad always attended: festive, fun, maybe a little shamelessly gaudy.

"It's perfect," she said, grinning when Connor and Ariel high-fived. In the glow of the moment, this magic coming together, she turned to Sierra. "All I need now is an officiant."

Sierra's brows rose as she regarded Mae with laughter in her eyes. "You're asking me?"

"Yeah, if you're willing. I already looked into it, and I can send you the website to get ordained. It just takes a couple minutes, and you don't need to give a speech or anything. But..." She shared a look with Connor. "We need someone, and I really want it to be you."

Sierra nodded slowly. "If I don't, are you gonna stay up 'til five a.m. making twelve batches of mac and cheese to win my approval?"

"Yes."

"Please don't," Connor interjected.

"I do kinda wanna see that again," Sierra said with a devious look. "But I'll be nice and say yes."

"Thank you!" Mae wrapped her arms around Sierra's shoulders, hugging her sideways despite Sierra's grumbling. Sierra groused some more when Connor and Ariel joined in, but her laughter told a different story.

"Just seven days now," Connor said when it was just him and Mae in the backyard, after Sierra and Ariel went inside for something to drink.

"Hmm?" Mae's eyes were busy following the path of string lights along the fence.

"Our honeymoon." He put an arm around her and gave her shoulder an affectionate squeeze. "Not long now."

"Yeah. Right." Her gaze was still trained on the backyard decor, but her mind was trying to work out why the reminder of their honeymoon put an unpleasant feeling in her gut.

And then the answer came to her, sudden as a drip of barbecue sauce on a champagne dress: she had no idea how much PTO she'd used up during her time in Hobson.

Her stomach lurched. She'd told Connor she wouldn't use any, that she'd work during the day and get to know her family in the evenings. But then she'd gotten swept up in planning the barbecue, making batches and batches of mac and cheese, forming a tentative bond with Sierra. Work had sort of just fallen by the wayside.

She'd done *some* work. She'd logged at least a few hours every day. Most days. But she had no idea, running the mental calculations now, how much she'd actually used. How much she had left.

Mae muttered an excuse to Connor about needing to check her work email and sped inside. Ignoring the playful chatter drifting from the living room, she raced upstairs to perch on the guest bed with her laptop. She navigated to her company's benefits website and logged on.

She scrolled down to PTO. Clicked it.

A whoosh of air left her lungs. Three days. She had three days left. And between spending July fifth driving the five hours from Hobson back to Baltimore and helping Sierra with cake preparations in the days leading up to her wedding on the eighth, she was likely to use all three of those days this week. Even if by some miracle she managed to hold onto them, worked on the long drive using her phone as a hot spot, worked every second she wasn't helping Sierra with the cake, that would still leave her only three days for their two-week vacation.

Connor had put up with so much lately. Reminders of dance lessons and favor boxes and panicked Costco runs closed in on her. All he'd wanted was a relaxing vacation at the end of it. Two weeks of Paris, pastries, togetherness, no more wedding drama, no stress. Just the two of them walking along the river Seine, crepes in hand, not a care in the world.

He'd asked her to be mindful of her PTO while she was in Hobson. That was his one request. And she couldn't even do that for him.

That night, while Mae and Connor snuggled on the couch watching TV, she tried to push the thought out of her mind, focus only on the feel of Connor's heartbeat as she leaned against his chest. She breathed in, breathed out, tried to calm her own rapidly pounding heart to match the slow, rhythmic beats of his.

But the thought only grew bigger, looming over her every impulse, taking over her mind. Pulsing with a threat.

Three days.

CHAPTER TWENTY-FOUR

Mae's head was clear when she opened her eyes the next morning.

After hours of tossing and turning, thoughts of Paris and PTO spiraling around her, a simple solution came to her somewhere around 2:00 a.m. She could call her boss the day after the barbecue and ask for more time. At her last job, she'd been able to go into a negative PTO balance of up to forty hours. That was five days right there. Add the three she had left and that was practically the full ten days she needed. She and Connor would be so blissed out on chocolate croissants and fresh brie that he wouldn't bat an eye if she was working from her hotel room for two measly days. He could use that time to see Disneyland Paris. He loved Disneyland.

And so, she didn't need to worry. She could spend today celebrating: her wedding, the barbecue, seeing her family getting along. Hopefully.

She was up early, creeping downstairs while Connor slept to start making the baked beans, potato salad, and Herb salad for the barbecue. She should have been more tired after getting just four hours of sleep, but it was an energized sort of tiredness, the same kind that had her waking up at dawn on Christmas as a kid. It was like her body knew the excitement of the day overshadowed everything else and held back the droopy eyelids and foggy head.

Getting ready was simple. No one sticking an eyelash-curling contraption in her face like at the makeup trial Susan had insisted upon a few months back. No rigamarole of making sure Connor didn't see her wedding dress. Connor zipped up her dress and helped her make sure the tie-belt was centered; she straightened the collar of his short-sleeved blue button-down. She noticed he'd even tucked a scrap of yellow checkered fabric into the front pocket of his shirt. Mae fingered the fabric, smiling when he told her Leah had given it to him yesterday as a makeshift pocket square.

As the barbecue's start time inched closer, she put the mac and cheese and baked beans in the oven, and soon the house filled with the sweet smell of barbecue and a subtle, cheesy richness. Just as she had the night she'd hosted her first family dinner in this very house, Mae planted herself in front of the living room window, scanning the road for arrivals.

Althea's church friend Harriet arrived first, walking slowly up the drive, her face shielded by a large sun hat. Mae vaguely remembered seeing her at the funeral reception. She'd been awkward then, closed-lipped in Mae's presence. Now, she greeted Mae and Connor with warm hugs and held out her foil-covered paper plate of cornbread.

Others slowly trickled in: Jeremiah heading into the backyard with Phyllis to start the grill, Scott chasing Ethan around the living room while Desiree looked on from the couch with Amara in her arms.

"Here we go," Desiree muttered with a glance at the window. "Here comes Patty."

Mae turned to see an elderly woman in a patterned blue and white dress and matching cardigan come walking toward the front door. With her sharp eyes and thin line of a mouth, Mae could easily match her face to the prim reprimands Patty had given her over the phone. In her arms, she balanced a gift-wrapped box atop a large Tupperware container of her promised tea cakes, which resembled pale cookies.

Even as she threw on her most welcoming smile, Mae braced herself for a lecture when she opened the door. "Patty! I'm Mae. Thanks for coming. Can I take anything off your hands?"

"Thank you for the invitation," Patty sniffed, holding out the gift and tea cakes. "Even if I had to move some things around to come on such short notice." She lobbed a piercing glance at Mae as she stepped inside.

Mae fought back a laugh. Patty was so perfectly *Patty*. "I'm sorry again about that."

"That's okay. I know it's your nature." She stopped to coo at Amara, fawning over her in a gentle voice she definitely hadn't used to speak to Mae.

Mae stared after her, trying to decipher her words. "What do you mean, 'my nature'?"

Patty, one finger tapping a squealing Amara's open hand, said, "Thea told me how you were born. Your mama went into labor during a movie, didn't she?" She looked Mae up and down. "I suppose you've always had a knack for disrupting schedules."

A wondering laugh escaped Mae. "She talked about me?" Her dad's letter was proof that he'd told Althea the story of Mae's birth, but nothing suggested Althea had paid any mind to it.

"Of course," Patty said. "Every Halloween, she'd remind me you were born during one of those horror movies. Tasteless films, if you ask me." She gave Mae another meaningful look, as though she expected Mae to apologize for not picking a better movie to be born to. And Mae could only stand there, open-mouthed in astonishment, tears glistening in her eyes, and think to herself that Patty wasn't as bad as everyone said.

The smoky smell of the first burgers hitting the grill lured the early arrivers to the backyard, and the barbecue kicked off. Mae left the front door unlocked and opened the back gate to let people come as they pleased. Slowly, the table filled with more food beyond Mae's contributions: Harriet's cornbread, Patty's tea cakes, a burger and hot dog station Jeremiah had set up, Phyllis's coleslaw, collard greens with pink flecks of ham from another of Althea's church friends, a watermelon and cucumber salad from Marlene and Joan, and more. In the ice-filled coolers Mae and Connor had set out, people were helping themselves to sodas, beers, water, and—once Richard arrived—homemade cider.

Beyond the food table, the Townsends, neighbors, and family friends were all mingling. Jeremiah was manning the grill, burgers and sausages sizzling. Ariel was playing with Ethan under the overly patriotic tree. Phyllis was deep in conversation with Harriet and Desiree. Leah was laughing about something with Tyrese. Patty was talking to Scott and Dawn by the food table. Barbara was sitting in a lawn chair in the shade, chatting with Marlene and Joan. Connor stood by the drinks with Richard, a bottle of cider in his hand, and she could just hear Richard's baritone voice walking Connor through the brewing process.

It almost didn't feel real to finally be here. Mae took a sip of her seltzer and thought back to the moment she discovered her dad had actually been flying back to Hobson for Sierra's birthday. How she'd thought herself silly for mentally making the barbecue bigger than it was. But what could be bigger than this? Family, friends, and neighbors coming together to celebrate a summer day, enjoy each other's company, eat good food and share it with others?

"Be cool," a voice said from behind. Mae spun around to see Sierra, dressed in a simple black tank and jean shorts.

"Be cool?" Mae repeated with a laugh.

"Your best friend just walked in."

Mae looked around—then laughed when she saw Brian Posey weaving his way through the yard, casting furtive looks in every direction. "He showed!"

"Yeah, and he's heading right for you."

Sure enough, Brian parked himself in front of Mae, peering down at her shrewdly. "No unusual activity so far. Plates all check out."

"O-oh. Thank you." Next to her, Sierra disguised her laugh as a cough. Mae elbowed her in the side.

"Anything you need me to keep an eye on?" he asked.

"No, nothing. Just have fun." She should have known, from the deep frown Brian gave her, that this was a silly thing to say.

"I'll do another lap around the perimeter in fifteen," he said gruffly. He gave her a nod and turned away, leaving Mae and Sierra to exchange amused looks.

"See, I was smart to invite him," Mae said. "Free security."

"Watch him bill you for his services."

"Worth it." Mae kept looking around, soaking it in. "So, this is what it's like, huh? The famous barbecue."

"It's really not famous," Sierra said. "It's just something we've always done."

That was strange to imagine, too, how Sierra wouldn't think

twice about something Mae had spent so much time fantasizing about. Today was a day of things finally happening. A day where she grew her family through marriage and reunions and the magic of a backyard barbecue.

Though that magic didn't stop her from tensing when Susan texted that they were five minutes out. She wound and unwound her dress's tie-belt around her finger, eyes shifting to the street every so often, waiting for signs of the Rutherfords' arrival. At last, when she spotted Susan and John walking up the drive, Mae wove through the house—passing Wendell in the kitchen, fussing over his ribs in the oven—and opened the door, silently praying that the Rutherfords wouldn't pick today to say something unsettling.

She was greeted with the sight of a poster-sized board with nine wooden pegs poking out of it. Mae stared, trying to make sense of it.

"It's a donut board!" Susan explained, peeking her head over the board. "The one at the big wedding will be much bigger, but we found this online and couldn't resist."

A surge of love came over Mae as she looked between Susan's excited face, the donut board she held, and the box of donuts John presented to her. And yes, the donuts were fancy in typical Rutherford fashion, probably secured from a high-end bakery rather than the greasy donut shops Mae tended to frequent. One donut was topped with a whole macaron, another with fresh raspberries and a mint leaf, another with flecks of what looked like actual gold. But John and Susan had remembered that bizarre donut wall request she'd tipsily made at that wine-tasting lunch over a month ago, and they were making it happen twice over. Hell, even if they hadn't—even if they'd shown up empty-handed—their eagerness to attend this barbecue spoke volumes about how much they cared about her. How desperate they were to be part of her life, if she would only let them in.

Mae wrapped her arms around Susan, not caring that the pegs on the donut board poked into her chest. Next, she hugged John, nearly jostling the box of donuts in the process. "Thank you," she said. "I love it."

"We're just happy to be here," John said, beaming down at her.

Mae led them to the kitchen, where Wendell was peeking into the oven. He stood and gave the group a wary look. "Ribs need another five minutes before they're ready for the grill," he said, as though they'd come to interrogate him about the state of his ribs.

"I love ribs," John said. "What sort of dry rub do you use?"

This turned out to be the key to Wendell's heart. He started talking spices and rubs, and Mae and Susan moved into the backyard, leaving John and Wendell to talk in the kitchen.

While Connor helped Susan hang the donut board on the fence, Mae saw her mom walking up to the back gate. She wore a pink wrap dress, brown hair down at her shoulders, one hand on the gate as she scanned the yard nervously. Mae greeted her with a hug, then grabbed her by the elbow and steered her in Barbara's direction.

"Time to bury the hatchet," Mae said.

"I'm just worried about *where* she'll bury it," she muttered.

"Barbara!" Mae shouted before her mother could change her mind. "My mom wanted to say hi."

Barbara glanced up, then stood with a polite smile. "Stacy. It's been a while."

"It really has. You look great."

"Oh, I don't feel it," Barbara said good-naturedly, and the two of them laughed. Mae shot Connor a curious glance across the backyard. Were they getting along?

"Are you still living in that beautiful house?" Mae's mom asked.

Barbara let out a sigh. "Let me tell you about that money pit." She began a long story about termites and exterminators, and Mae slowly edged herself toward Connor until she'd done it: Barbara and her mom were having a conversation all on their own, without a third party to force them into it.

In fact—she looked around. Susan had joined Phyllis's gaggle of ladies. John was at the grill with Wendell, Jeremiah, and Nosy Posey himself. And her mom and Barbara were lost in an animated conversation, talking and laughing in equal measure.

"We did it," Mae whispered. "Our families are here. They're getting along. No more separation."

"*You* did it," Connor corrected her. He put an arm around her shoulders and pulled her in for a kiss.

"Gross," Ariel said, coming up to them.

Connor cleared his throat and removed his arm. "Very sorry. Won't happen again."

"Hm." Ariel shot the both of them apprehensive looks. "My dad wants to know if you can do your wedding thing now, while his ribs are grilling. You have seven minutes."

"Seven minutes," Connor repeated. "Starting now?" Already his eyes were widening with distress.

"Starting whenever my dad told me," Ariel said with a shrug. "*Patty* got in my face when I was coming over here. She wasted at least a minute telling me my shirt's uncouth." She rolled her eyes and gestured to her oversized Demon Slayer T-shirt.

"So, it's actually six minutes?" Connor swiped around on his watch.

"I like your shirt," Mae said. "But I like Patty too," she added with a smile.

Ariel gave a dissatisfied hum. "Traitor."

"I feel like we should maybe do the wedding now?" Connor suggested, his voice rising in pitch. He held up his watch, a timer blinking that five minutes and forty-five seconds remained.

Mae grinned. The spontaneous countdown might have stressed her too, once upon a time. But nothing could touch the sense of peace she felt today. "That's plenty of time." She wouldn't have had it any other way, a hurried wedding set to the timetable of Wendell and his ribs. "Wedding starts in one minute!" she announced, cupping her hands around her mouth.

Her announcement brought looks of amusement from most guests, though she caught Patty's displeased frown. Nosey Posey squared his shoulders, standing a little straighter at his post near the open gate. When he caught Mae's eye, he lowered his chin in a somber nod. She did the same, fighting to keep her expression serious.

"A minute?" Sierra said with a groan. "I *just* bit into my veggie burger."

"Take it up with Wendell."

"And I have to pee," Sierra grumbled. She set her plate on the table and stalked into the house.

"Um, I also have to pee," Connor whispered in Mae's ear, a note of grave concern in his voice. "But..." He held up his watch. "We're almost down to four minutes."

A laugh parted her lips. "Go ahead. We'll make it work."

While Connor scurried inside, Mae took her position by

the arch. She glanced from the attendees before her—who were mostly standing and enjoying their food, still chatting among themselves—to the house, looking for signs of her groom and officiant.

"Do you need anything?"

Mae turned to see Susan at her side, rifling through a clear, zippered pouch.

"I've got a sewing kit, bobby pins, tissues, Band-Aids, Q-tips, deodorant, baby wipes, Advil, lotion, lint roller, mints…" Susan raised her head, seeing Mae's look of surprise. "With all the weddings I throw, I try to be prepared."

Mae smiled. "Thank you, but I—" Something about Susan's earnest expression made her stop reciting the usual polite decline she trotted out around the Rutherfords. The donut wall had made it clear already, hadn't it? Susan was here because she cared. Here in North Carolina, here at this barbecue, here in front of this wedding arch where Mae stood alone. Susan *cared*, and Mae letting her fears push away the people who cared about her was no way to be a family. With a glance at the donut wall just past Susan, Mae took a breath and a cautious step toward family. "Actually, I would love a mint. Thank you."

Susan brightened and pulled out a small tin. Mae plucked out a mint, letting the sharp peppermint flavor dissolve on her tongue.

"You know what, I'll have one, too," Susan said, taking one for herself. There was something endearing about the conspiratorial way she said it—like they'd decided to go in on bottomless mimosas at brunch, not eat mints in a backyard. But Mae liked thinking this moment meant something to Susan, too.

"Quickest pee of my life," Connor said as he sidled between them.

"Charming," Susan commented, sending Mae into laughter.

"I had to race to the top floor because Sierra was in the other bathroom," he protested, still out of breath, but Susan was already making her way back to the crowd. He raised his watch into Mae's eyeline. "We're at three minutes."

"It'll be fine," Mae assured him, lowering his wrist. Spotting Sierra coming through the sliding glass door, she said, "There's our officiant now."

"How are we on time?" Sierra asked, prompting Connor to let out a labored breath.

"He thinks Wendell's gonna murder him if we mess up his ribs schedule," Mae said.

"Oh, he will," Sierra said. "He doesn't mess around with ribs." Over Connor's delirious laugh, Sierra raised her voice and addressed the group standing before them. "We ready for a wedding?" Amid a smattering of cheers, she clapped her hands together and started speaking.

"I remember when I was seven," Sierra began. "Bee and I were in California visiting my dad. It was the night before Thanksgiving. The adults were talking in the kitchen, and I'd just sat down in the living room and turned on the TV. And then this three-year-old girl in a plastic pink tiara came up to me and said, 'You come to my tea party.' I just wanted to get back to finding the Disney channel, but she grabbed my hand and dragged me to her room. She had these two teddy bears sitting at a little table. She pointed at an empty chair and said, 'Sit.' So, I sat. We drank invisible tea. And for the longest time, that was my clearest memory of my sister Mae. The bossy tea party bitch."

The people around them laughed, but Mae could only stare incredulously at Sierra, quietly absorbing the fact that she had an entire memory of that Thanksgiving locked and loaded.

"I saw her another time after that, years ago, but we didn't really talk." She cast her eyes downward, and Mae felt a pang at the reminder of their father's funeral. Then she lifted her chin, her gaze settling on Mae. "And then she showed up at our grandma's funeral a few weeks ago. No invitation. *I* didn't want her there. But I shouldn't have been surprised. Mae has always been headstrong. Kind of like our grandma, actually," Sierra said wistfully. "Turns out I'm glad she came back into my life. It's important to have someone there who fights for what they care about. Mae fought to come down here and connect with us. She fought for this barbecue, she's fought like hell to try to get Grandma's mac and cheese right," she added to knowing laughter from the Townsends. "She's even fought for me, trying to get me to stay in Hobson and open a bakery, which is starting to feel more like a possibility." Sierra gave Mae a meaningful smile. "And now that I've met Connor, I'm pretty confident that they're both willing to fight for their family, for what they love, and for each other."

A sound of a throat clearing made them turn their heads. Wendell swirled his finger in a *Wrap it up* motion.

"Okay, damn," Sierra muttered. "Skipping ahead. Connor, do you wanna marry Mae?"

"I do," Connor said, his twinkling eyes on Mae.

"Mae, do you wanna marry Connor?"

Mae had to stifle a laugh at the jarring transition from beautiful speech to rushed officiation. "I do."

"There you go. I pronounce you married."

Mae pulled Connor into a kiss just as his watch chimed to signal the end of the countdown, and the crowd broke into scattered applause from those who weren't holding plates or cups. Mae turned to Sierra, whose wide grin betrayed her nonchalant officiation. Then she turned back around, looking for the familiar faces. Connor's parents were beaming and clapping. Jeremiah was tapping his tongs together like a happy crab. Her mom and Barbara, now sitting side by side in lawn chairs, were applauding. Wendell was very occupied with setting a large plate of ribs on the table.

This was the perfect wedding. She wanted to bottle this moment: being surrounded by family, by good food, by all these symbols of their love for her. The donut wall on the fence, Sierra's banana pudding in the fridge, Leah's tailored dress around her waist. More love than in any backyard barbecue she'd ever imagined.

"Thank you for indulging us," Connor told the crowd. "Wendell, all you!" he called. Wendell gave him a satisfied nod and announced that his ribs were ready to eat.

With the wedding over with, Mae was free to fully relax for the rest of the barbecue. She had a burger, ribs, and every side she could fit on her paper plate. She got to see the Townsends' reactions to the mac and cheese: a slow nod from Wendell, a thumbs-up across the backyard from Tyrese, a look of pleasure from Scott, a hand teetering in a *so-so* gesture from Ariel, who was perhaps her harshest critic.

But Connor's reaction was her favorite: first an eyebrow raise, then a crease in his forehead, like he was trying to figure something out, then his eyes growing wide with wonder. The Townsends knew what Althea's mac and cheese was supposed to taste like, and they knew when it fell short. But Connor didn't.

For the first time, she got to witness the reaction of someone who had no point of comparison.

She wondered when her grandma had this moment—if, many decades earlier, she'd sat Herb down with a steaming dish of mac and cheese and watched him fall in love with her food.

The afternoon passed in what felt like snippets, snapshots of moments spent with her family, each one of them perfect. Playing Slapjack with Connor and Ariel. Listening to her mom and Barbara tell a story about when a two-year-old Mae projectile-vomited all over their table at Outback Steakhouse. Kneeling over the Herb garden with Phyllis, who fingered the soil approvingly and said she'd keep an eye on the plants in Mae's absence. Nodding solemnly as she and Sierra listened to another report from Nosy Posey, who had at least loosened up enough to help himself to a plate of food—including the Jell-O, they were delighted to notice. Posing with Connor so that John could take a picture of them cutting into Sierra's banana pudding, even though there wasn't really anything to cut. Eating her serving with gusto, thinking about how her dad would have loved the way the salted caramel rum sauce Sierra served alongside it played beautifully against the creamy pudding and softened Nilla wafers. Leaning toward Sierra to say, "This definitely belongs in your bakery" and basking in the coy smile taking over Sierra's face.

The barbecue lasted well into evening, when the sky dimmed, the twinkling lights glowed, and fireworks lit the sky in starry explosions. Mae had forgotten, briefly, that this was a holiday for anyone else at all, that this wasn't just a day for her, for Connor, for their family.

Their family. What a wonderful phrase that was. One pronoun and one word to sum up all of these marvelous people.

CHAPTER TWENTY-FIVE

A rehearsal dinner seemed an odd thing when one had already gotten married.

Standing before the entrance to the Rutherfords' beautiful winery, watching guests in flowy dresses or dapper ties stream through the tall glass doors, Mae couldn't help but think tonight's rehearsal dinner was sort of a sham. She and Connor had gotten married three days ago. What was there to rehearse?

"Ready?" Connor asked, gripping the door handle. She nodded and pasted on a smile. Which she'd been doing a lot over the past few days.

First, there was the whole PTO issue she hadn't yet figured out how to break to Connor. Her attempts to solve the problem hadn't gone as planned. She'd woken up early the day after the barbecue, in a sunny glow of post-wedding optimism, and called her boss while pacing the backyard, sure she could find a way to smooth it over.

"You know I've been busy staying in North Carolina, seeing my family after my grandma died," she'd begun. "I had to stay for longer than expected, and I ended up using more PTO than I planned."

"I know," Kevin said. "My heart goes out to you."

They were off to a good start, then. She had his heart. That sounded like a plus.

"I was actually supposed to be saving all of that PTO for, um, my honeymoon, for next week and the week after next. I'd already told my project teams I'd be out during that time."

"Oh, that's tough. Best-laid plans," he said with a chuckle.

Mae laughed back in confusion. His detached attitude was starting to border on alarming. "Right. So, I wondered if there was a way to get an advance on my PTO? At my last job we could go into the negatives, up to two weeks"—a little embellishment never hurt anyone—"and I wondered if that's the case here."

A pause. "My understanding was that you'd be back to working your regular hours for the next couple weeks, *because* of all the time you've taken off," Kevin said, his tone noticeably chillier. "We've all done our best to let you work on your own schedule, but things have been slipping. Three of your project directors have told me they have concerns about the quality of your work. There were those formatting issues in the Cardio Center marketing plan, you've been missing meetings, and your teammates have been scrambling to pick up the slack.

"I know you've got family stuff, and I really feel for you, but we need you back, working your regular hours, by Monday. You don't have my permission anymore to use PTO next week, and we don't have a negative PTO policy, so if you don't log on ready to work on Monday, I'll assume you're giving your notice."

Mae had abruptly stopped pacing. Indignation rose within her, but she wasn't sure who to direct it toward. She'd have loved to go off on Kevin, but it wasn't his fault she'd gotten Townsend tunnel vision and become unreliable lately. She couldn't blame her project directors for snitching on her subpar work without realizing she'd simply funneled her organizational skills into a different project altogether. They didn't see the immaculately planned barbecue she threw, her timelines and spreadsheets with every detail accounted for. The only person she could be mad at was herself, for dropping everything to pursue what felt important and expecting the world to alter itself to suit her.

She would have loved to call his bluff, tell him she wouldn't be showing up to work on Monday, that she had a honeymoon to get to, thank you very much. But she couldn't risk losing her job when the lease on their rowhome was expiring soon. Connor was eager to move to DC—which, okay, Mae still hadn't wrapped her head around—and they might have a hard time finding a place to rent without both their salaries, especially with DC's high cost of living.

So, really, no matter what choice she made, she'd be letting Connor down. Skip the honeymoon and log on for work on Monday, and she'd be robbing Connor of two weeks in Paris. Quit her job to take the honeymoon, and they might have to move into a shoebox in the outskirts of Oxon Hill when their lease was up.

If forced to choose between honeymoon and job, she had to pick job.

"I understand," she croaked. "I'll be ready on Monday."

"I'm glad to hear it. We'll talk more next week." He hung up without saying goodbye, leaving Mae staring at her phone in a dismay that still hadn't left her, even three days later.

Second, Mae was starting to come to terms with the fact that her idyllic backyard wedding had done little to solve her family hang-ups. Yesterday, when she was helping Sierra bake wedding cake layers in her kitchen, she'd scrolled through her notifications as the cakes cooled. Likes and congratulations had been rolling in from her Instagram post boasting pictures from the wedding. Townsends had followed her and tagged her in more photos, and celebratory comments kept coming.

And then she spotted a Venmo notification. From Madison.

Along with a gift of one hundred dollars, Madison had sent a note:

> Congrats on the wedding! Some of that food looked a little weird lol. Have a real wedding dinner on me!

The message had sent her crashing back to reality. What was weird about burgers and ribs? The whole point of a barbecue-wedding was that it was casual. Or did Madison find certain dishes weird, the soul food cookout staples that the Parkers would have never served at a barbecue—the collard greens, the cornbread, the potato salad that was more yellowish-red than white?

Mae had thought, however naively, that seeing her mom make up with Barbara, watching the Rutherfords and Townsends getting along, had set her on course for a future where her family would lift her up, not find subtle ways to tear her down. But as long as relatives like Madison were in her life, she would always be laden with these insecurities.

Cutting Madison out of her life couldn't be a real solution, though. It was basically cheating, taking a shortcut. She owed something to Madison, didn't she? After all those sleepovers, movie nights, and Monopoly games? Madison's Venmo message needed some work, but she'd still sent a wedding gift. She was still trying. And if Madison's trying made Mae feel like she didn't matter, then that was Mae's problem.

And so, Mae had decisively pressed the like button on

Madison's message. Except it left a sour taste in her mouth that even red velvet cake scraps couldn't counteract.

"You okay?" Connor asked.

She blinked the thoughts away, looking around the winery's attached restaurant, already half-filled with people talking and laughing. Some sat at tables while others stood at the bar, getting drinks and mingling. Mae and Connor, tucked away in a corner of the bar, were supposed to be sitting at the table near the front of the room, but it was still empty. Mae's mom was on her way, Sierra was tending to the cake but had said she'd get there soon, and Connor's parents were somewhere in the crowd. About sixty people were coming tonight, mostly friends of the Rutherfords.

She watched Connor's uncle Rob come up to the opposite end of the bar and speak with the bartender. Noticing Mae, he flashed her a quick smile, then took his two glasses of red wine somewhere into the crowd. Probably going to his wife to gossip about Mae, a snaking thought speculated. She didn't bother dispelling it.

"I'm good," she told Connor, resting an elbow against the bar. "Just...a lot of people."

"I know," he groaned. "My parents have too many friends." Then, his tone brightening: "I see some of our people, though."

She followed his gaze to see Jayla and a few other members of their wedding party sitting at a table near the front. Connor's best man, a friend from law school, waved him over. Jayla, seeing Mae, ditched the group entirely and made a beeline for her. Her rust-orange dress seemed to shimmer under the lights, and she walked so quickly that Mae half-expected her box-braided updo to come tumbling down.

"I'm so glad you're here," she said, squeezing Mae in a tight hug. "Krystal's trying to get me to join her yoga cult."

"Class," Mae corrected with a laugh, glancing over at her bridesmaid Krystal, now talking animatedly with a groomsman.

"I didn't trust her CrossFit cult in college and I don't trust her yoga cult now." Jayla took a sip of her white wine. When she looked at Mae over the rim of her glass, her eyes were sparkling. "So how does it feel to be married?"

Mae gave an anxious chuckle. It was hard to tap back into that peaceful, buzzy contentment she'd felt at the wedding-barbecue.

"Good," Mae said.

"You sure?" Jayla asked, looking her over.

She let out a breath. "Just, um…I had a call with my boss about my PTO, and…" She trailed off at the sight of a familiar face passing through the glass doors. "*Madison?*" Mae choked out.

"Your cousin?" Jayla whispered.

"Yep." And now Madison was heading straight for her. Her blond hair was shorter, her face rounder, and her baby bump was prominent. But she was unmistakably the same person Mae grew up with, bright green eyes, dimples, and all.

"Mae!" Madison flung her arms around her, overwhelming Mae with the strong, floral scent of her conditioner.

"Hey," Mae said, trying to match her energy. "How are you…here?"

"Your mom and I are staying in the same hotel!" she chirped. "She said she was coming here tonight and I asked if I could be her date!"

"Wow," Mae remarked. She glanced at Jayla, who was looking at Madison like she was something to be studied.

"I didn't want to wait another day to see you," Madison said. "I missed you."

A strange sort of wistfulness rose within Mae. Madison had a tendency to say whatever entered her mind, which ran the gamut from sweet to blood-boiling to hurtful and back again. She had always loved when Madison caught her off-guard in a good way with compliments or heartfelt sentiments.

"Me too," Mae said, and somehow it felt like the truth.

"I've heard a lot about you," Jayla said. Her friendly smile slipped just enough that Mae caught an evil smirk sneaking through.

"Thanks!" Madison beamed. "Are you, um, Shaniqua?"

Just like that, the wistful feeling vanished.

"Did you mean *Sierra?*" Mae asked. "Either way, no, this is my best friend Jayla."

"Oh! Sorry. Pregnancy brain." Madison grinned angelically at them both.

While Jayla took the bait and asked how far along she was, Mae looked past Madison to the table at the front, where her mom was now seated, talking to Susan. Her mom probably hadn't thought anything of letting Madison tag along to the rehearsal dinner. And why would she? Mae hadn't given her any reason to.

"We were thinking maybe Maui for the babymoon," Madison was saying. "Where are you going for your honeymoon again?" she asked, turning to Mae.

"Paris," Mae mumbled.

Madison droned on, grilling Mae about every detail of her honeymoon and unknowingly twisting the knife even further. When Mae saw Sierra enter the restaurant and head in their direction, she perked up—but as Sierra drew closer, and Madison kept prattling on, Mae's eyes darted between the two of them, a sense of unease descending over her.

"Hey," Mae greeted her, stepping aside to make room. "How's the cake?"

"It's coming together," Sierra said, looking slightly frazzled. She'd been living and breathing all things wedding cake since the barbecue. Even on her birthday the following day, when Mae and Connor had taken her out to dinner at a trendy vegan place in Baltimore after making the trip up from Hobson, Sierra had been sketching minor tweaks to the design on her napkin. "I've got the tiers all frosted, and I'm finishing up the decorations tonight."

"I can't wait to see it," Mae said. Her smile faltered when Madison held out a hand and introduced herself with the air of a royal acknowledging a peasant. Mae noted the way Sierra's brow quirked when she heard Madison's name.

"I love your earrings," Madison said, pointing at Sierra's chunky black earrings, shaped like abstract curlicues.

"Thanks." Sierra tucked a curl behind her ear to show them off. "I got them on Etsy. There's this Black-owned business I get most of my jewelry from."

And when Mae saw a small wrinkle form in Madison's brow, the conversation filtering through her ears deadened to white noise. Something was coming. Another one of those secret club moments, something Mae and her dad would have shared a look over, was right there on the tip of Madison's tongue.

"I don't get why people make such a big deal over Black-owned businesses," Madison said. "I sell candles on Etsy and I can't call myself a white-owned business."

And there it was.

Sierra stiffened. Jayla's eyebrows shot up. Mae wanted to disappear behind the bar.

"Well…you can," Jayla said. "No one's stopping you."

"Right," Madison laughed. "Like that would go over well. I've just started avoiding businesses that say they're Black-owned or whatever-owned. Using your race to try to sell things just seems racist."

Mae felt rooted to the spot. She knew what would happen if her dad were here: they'd share a look, the conversation would move along, and the moment would pass. But with Jayla and Sierra here, silence didn't seem like an option this time. Their advice to call Madison on her ignorance came back to her—but when she tried to prepare a sufficient response in her head, some comeback to make Madison realize the effect of what she was saying, the words lost their shape.

Jayla and Sierra both glanced at Mae, then each other. Mae bit the inside of her lip. More silence passed. A knowing look settled over Sierra, her expression hardening as she turned to Madison with cool disinterest.

"Actually, *you* seem racist," Sierra said dryly.

"*What?*" Madison took a step back. "I'm not racist. How could you say that?"

Sierra lowered her chin and stared her down. "You literally just said you avoid Black-owned businesses, and you don't see how that's racist?"

"I didn't mean it like *that*. I just meant—" Madison shook her head, eyes sprinting around—and then she settled her gaze on Mae. "I mean, my *cousin* is Black; how could I—Mae, you know I'm not racist. *Tell her.*"

Mae's heart pounded as she glanced from Madison's wide-eyed desperation to Sierra's disdain. This was the moment when she was supposed to stand up for herself, back Sierra, tell Madison off. But her mouth went dry and fuzzy. Madison was still family. And no family was perfect.

"She—" Mae swallowed, tried again. "Madison didn't mean anything by it." Her words came out dull and monotone. Like they weren't her own.

"*Thank* you," Madison huffed. She glared at Sierra. "I don't know where that aggression came from, but you can apologize whenever you're ready." When Sierra said nothing, Madison rolled her eyes. "Fine. I'm gonna go sit with Aunt Stacy." With that, she marched off to their table.

"Wow," Jayla marveled. "I did not know it was possible to be that terrible."

Sierra's laugh was stiff, her mouth a tense line. She looked at Mae like she could see right through her. Jayla, seeming to pick up on this, excused herself to refill her glass.

"So, you took *her* side," Sierra commented.

"I wasn't taking sides; I was just…"

"Just what?"

"It's easier to let things go," Mae said. "Whenever Madison or my grandma or anyone on my mom's side said something stupid, Dad and I would just share a look and keep quiet. That's just how I deal with that sort of thing."

"Dad was a fucking coward," Sierra spat. "Keeping me a secret from you, letting your family say whatever they want to you? Following his example is not a good thing, trust me." She crossed her arms, looking Mae over. "Did you even talk to Connor about his parents? Like you said you would?"

Mae froze. Admitting that she hadn't sure sounded cowardly to her. Cowardly like their dad, apparently.

"I'll take that as a no," Sierra said.

"I'll tell him," Mae insisted. "I just need to find the right time. Everything got so hectic with the barbecue and the wedding."

"Right. The barbecue." There was something in her tone Mae couldn't make sense of.

"What?"

"Is that another way you're like our dad?" she asked quietly. "You'll drop by once a year, attend a barbecue, and forget about us the rest of the time?"

Mae frowned. "What? No."

"Okay. But you were *so* focused on that barbecue, and in the back of my head, I started wondering...what happens after that? You get the barbecue you wanted, you go back to your real family, and we never hear from you again? You wanted to surround yourself with Black people for a few days so you can feel better about yourself before you go home, marry into the whitest family in the world, and forget about us?"

Mae shrank back. "Sierra." The word came out quiet, strangled.

Sierra shrugged, still and serious. "Am I wrong?"

She was using such a reasonable tone. Like she was genuinely curious, putting forth a scientific hypothesis instead of cutting accusations.

"Yes," Mae said. But a shred of doubt crept in even as she said it. "I mean..."

Some small part of her *had* been dwelling on the reality that marrying into a white family meant giving up on that hope of never being the odd one out ever again. For all her lifelong yearning to connect with the Townsends, it would be a lie to say she hadn't also wanted to drive down and see them this summer *because* she was about to marry into the Rutherfords.

"So, I'm right?"

"No!" Mae let out an exasperated sigh. "I was hoping we'd stay in touch. I want you in my life. I've *always* wanted you in my life."

"Okay," Sierra said, again sounding so goddamn reasonable. "Well, if what just happened with Madison is any indication of what it's like to be in your life, I think I'll pass."

Her words sliced through Mae like a knife. "What are you saying?"

Sierra sighed, her gaze landing somewhere behind Mae. "Connor's parents are waving us over."

Mae turned to see that most of the guests had arrived and taken their seats. Their table—John, Susan, Connor, Mae's mom, and Madison—awaited them expectantly. "Can we please just talk first?" she tried.

But Sierra was already striding toward their table. All Mae could do was watch her go, take a shaky breath, and follow suit.

Mae begrudgingly took her seat between Connor and Sierra, training her face to look neutral and not like she'd never see her sister again. Connor's hand found Mae's under the table and gave it a reassuring squeeze. She took a gulp of water, keeping her head down, avoiding eye contact.

At the start of the meal, John announced to the room that Mae and Connor had gotten married spontaneously just a few days before. The guests burst into cheery applause.

But for Mae, hearing the words aloud, it just reminded her how much of a sham this rehearsal dinner was. Her table was full of people who had already seen Mae and Connor get married. They'd all been there. So why were they here? What was the point?

And yet, as Mae sat there trying to coax a capricious sprig of arugula onto her fork, it occurred to her that, actually, if anything was a sham, it was the wedding at the barbecue. Every family unit she'd wanted to unite had gathered in Althea's backyard and watched her get married, and Mae had taken that as some kind of sign that she'd finally brought everything, everyone, together. As if mac and cheese and donuts and a mint could solve her problems and erase her doubts.

But with Sierra's words echoing in her mind, Mae had to admit none of that was true. No one was united in anything. Sierra wanted no part in her life. Mae still hadn't been honest with Connor about her fears. She was starting to feel like the Townsends might never want to see her again once Sierra told them what a coward she was. It was all a sham.

Mae dragged an arugula leaf through a pool of peach vinaigrette as rehearsal dinner chatter continued around her. She was so focused on it, head bent, eyes down, that Connor had to nudge her knee with his to get her attention.

"Hmm?" She looked up. Connor was tilting his head in his dad's direction. "Yes?" she said, turning to him.

"Are there any museums you want to visit, Mae?" John asked. His eyes searched her, like he was trying to dig down and find that joyful, carefree Mae from the barbecue.

"Um…the Picasso one would be cool," she said, grasping onto one of the museums she remembered daydreaming about with Connor. That was enough to get John talking about the best days to visit museums, and how they were lucky to be in Paris over Bastille Day and they shouldn't miss the fireworks show at the Eiffel Tower. Every mention of another activity they wouldn't get to do next week was another thorn pressing into her.

Eventually, the conversation drifted to a less stressful topic. They moved from tourist season to wedding season, and Susan detailed wedding trends she'd observed at the winery.

"I've noticed a lot of bohemian themes," Susan said. "The last few weddings we've held here lately have had a rustic sort of look. Twine, ivy, boots, barrels." She leaned closer to Mae's mom. "It's not really my preference, personally. Mae and I prefer the classic look, don't we, Mae?"

Mae gave her a strangled smile and reached for her water glass. "Mmhmm."

"I can't imagine all the weddings you've seen," Mae's mom said. "I think I've been to two in the last decade. Your dad would have been happy about that." She glanced at Mae, looking wistful. She toyed with the gold bar bracelet on her wrist, a gift from Mae's dad that she wore on special occasions, then turned back to John and Susan. "It's funny. When Mae's father was alive, there was one year where we went to six weddings. And he *hated* weddings."

Mae's nails dug into her palm. She didn't know why this bothered her so much. She and her mom loved talking about him. Sharing their favorite stories about him was their way of keeping him alive. The time he'd passed by a pet adoption event and come away agreeing to foster two dogs, even though he was allergic. Or how he'd make a bowl of microwave popcorn every Friday night and burn it a quarter of the time because he always got distracted by something. She liked that they could talk about him now, in front of Connor, to give him a glimpse into her dad.

But what her mom said wasn't true.

And her words were a cutting reminder that even now, there were still things about him—about their family—that Mae's mom was entirely unaware of. What a privilege it must be, to not have to carry that burden around with her—a burden that had weighed Mae down for as long as she could remember. And she was so tired of lugging it around.

"Dad didn't hate weddings," Mae said.

Her mom's brow creased. "Yes, he did," she said with a chuckle. "He was always going on about how he could go the rest of his life without hearing the wedding march ever again."

"No, he didn't," Mae said more firmly. She set her fork down. "He hated going to *your* family's weddings. Because it meant being around a bunch of white people who were just subtle enough to keep their racism discreet."

That did it. Susan froze. John took a long drink from his wineglass. Connor's gaze steadied on Mae, a haze of uncertainty in his eyes. Madison jerked her head back. Sierra watched her, looking vaguely curious. Her mom stared, mouth open.

"It was inevitable," Mae continued. "Whenever we had to be around the Parkers. Someone would always say something borderline. Dad and I would exchange a look, like, *Here we go.* Every wedding, every Christmas, every Thanksgiving, every Easter, we would sit across from each other at a table full of white people and share our silent little looks."

Her face was burning. Every pair of eyes at the table was laser-focused on her. Even Jayla, sitting one table over with the wedding party, was staring. Mae's mom opened her mouth, which just reminded Mae she had more to say.

"I wish you'd told me about Grandma being racist to Althea."

It was mortifying, spilling her guts in front of her in-laws, but it was freeing, too. Like she was invincible. Like even though she was about to wreck her entire life, at least no one could stop her. You couldn't stop a hurricane.

"You said you didn't want me to feel different around her, but, Mom, I already did. And I wish you'd told me I had a sister. Do you know how much less alone I would have felt, knowing Sierra was my sister? Being around family that looked like me? Instead of a grandpa who said the n-word in front of me when I was eight? Or my husband's mom asking me how dark my skin gets in the sun?" Susan paled. "Or a cousin who—you know what, Madison," Mae said, catching her eye across the table, "it *is* racist to say you refuse to shop at Black-owned businesses, and I shouldn't have defended you when Sierra called you on it." Madison's cheeks reddened, and she looked like she was going to object, but Mae wasn't done. "Is it any wonder that I would drive to Hobson and sacrifice *so much* to stay there, burning through all my PTO, giving up my entire honeymoon, because I finally had a family that didn't make me feel out of place?"

Her hurricane of invincibility couldn't last forever. Mae was left taking ragged breaths, her vision blurring, feeling naked in front of the six shocked faces before her. In an instant, she shrank into feeling the way she inevitably did around the Parkers: out of place and helplessly alone.

"Excuse me," she mumbled. She stood, her chair squeaking against the tile, and stalked off for the exit.

CHAPTER TWENTY-SIX

Searching for solace in food truck nachos perhaps wasn't the best plan. Especially when Mae discovered too late that she'd left her wallet and phone back at the winery.

Inwardly cursing her gauzy floral dress and its lack of pockets, Mae stepped out of the line for Buenos Nachos and looked past the throng of happy, chatty people on the sidewalk for a new hideout. A closed Starbucks, a lively bar, and a brightly lit CVS weren't all that appealing given the whole no-wallet thing, but they were better than trudging back to the winery and facing the repercussions that awaited her.

So, browsing the aisles of CVS it was. Maybe something in the magazine aisle would tell her what to do. Like she could flip through a copy of *Essence* and come upon an article titled "5 Avoidance Strategies You Haven't Tried Yet!"

She was stepping toward the crosswalk when a figure in an orange dress came quickly toward her, heels clicking, arm waving like she was trying to flag down an airplane.

"Don't you go anywhere!" Jayla called. "I'm not taking another step in these heels."

Mae melted into relief on the spot. Jayla she could talk to. She hadn't dropped any tactless surprises on Jayla tonight. She stayed put as instructed until Jayla folded her into a hug, enrobing Mae in the familiar smell of cocoa butter and lavender.

"What are we doing?" Jayla asked, taking a step back, her hand firmly on Mae's shoulder. "Are we running away? Do we need a snack? What's going on?"

"I—" Mae lifted a hand, dropped it. "I got in line for nachos, but I left my wallet at my table."

Jayla held up her beaded black purse and raised her eyebrows teasingly. "So let me buy you nachos."

On a bench outside the closed Starbucks, tray of nachos between them, Mae crammed a chip loaded with cheese, black beans, guacamole, and crema into her mouth. The chip's toasty warmth was soothing, and its loud crunch echoed in her ears in a satisfying way. She reached for another.

"You good?" Jayla asked. Mae nodded, chewing. "So, what the hell just happened at your table? Who do I need to fight?"

Mae winced. "How much did you hear?"

"Enough to know you got secrets."

Fixed with Jayla's imploring brown eyes, Mae came out with the story and all its fraying threads: how a single question on the beach had festered inside of her for so long, how the Parkers had spent years wearing her down and calling it love, how she'd used all her PTO chasing a barbecue in Hobson and left Connor with nothing, how she'd bungled her burgeoning sisterhood with Sierra in an instant.

"Okay, so I'm fighting a buncha people. Let's start with Madison, and then I'll move on to Connor's mom." Jayla made a show out of scanning the street, as if she could spot them from four blocks away. Mae giggled and pulled her forward.

"I don't wanna think about Madison. And Connor's mom probably didn't mean it the way it sounded." Mae used a chip to scoop up a jalapeño slice.

"What did she say when you confronted her about it tonight?"

Mae busied herself with chewing before she admitted, "I didn't really give her a chance to respond. I sort of just said everything and ran away."

"Not the best way to have a conversation," Jayla said with a laugh. Her expression grew serious, eyes searching as she studied Mae. "So why didn't you tell me what Connor's mom said? I remember you going on that trip. You got me a shot glass and tried to convince me I'd like ceviche."

Mae smiled at the memory. She'd gushed to Jayla about how the ceviche she'd had at an upscale seafood restaurant on that trip had tasted so fresh, like she was eating the ocean itself. "That ceviche *was* really good."

"It's squishy fish. You know how I feel about squishy fish."

"I do." Mae's smile faded. "Sorry I never told you. I felt like...I brought it on myself? Like, this is what I get for marrying into a white family?"

Jayla shook her head. "Now I gotta fight *you* for being stupid."

Something about her serious face and mournful tone made Mae burst into a cackle.

"I'm serious!" Jayla said through laughter. "Okay, now I'm serious." She cleared her throat and pulled back her shoulders. "No stupid shit anyone says or does to you is your fault. Ever. Okay?"

The words were logical. The sentiment was something Mae

had tried telling herself before, but in a rote, thinking-without-feeling way. Believing them was another matter.

"Okay," she said quietly. "But it still seems like this is the cost of choosing Connor. And I have to accept that."

"You don't have to accept shit," Jayla insisted. Her gaze flickered somewhere off to the side, then returned to Mae, eyes dark and serious. "If Connor's parents—or anyone in his family—say something weird again, you can't just bottle it up and obsess over it for years. You have to tell people. You have to tell me and Connor, so we know who to fight."

A sad chuckle left her. "Connor wouldn't fight his family."

"For you, he would. For you, he'd stand around on a street corner holding your sparkly purse just in case you needed it."

Mae narrowed her eyes. Then, when Jayla jutted her chin somewhere behind Mae, she turned around. Connor stood in the glow of the CVS, one hand in the pocket of his suit jacket, the other holding the long strap of Mae's purse on his shoulder. When their eyes met, he gave her a small, reassuring smile that made Mae's heart skip with a hopeful flutter.

"You stay there," Jayla shouted across the street. "We're still talking!"

"I got nothing but time!" Connor called back.

"He can wait," Jayla said, turning back to Mae. "He just saw you at your first wedding. He's fine. What else you wanna talk about?"

Looking between Jayla and Connor, Mae felt a blanket of peace drape over her. For all these unknowns, all this mess, she had two people fiercely on her side. Maybe even more, if she could summon the courage to go back to the winery and face the scene she'd left behind.

Mae moved aside the nachos and scooted closer to Jayla, leaning her head on her shoulder. "I love you."

"I'm very lovable."

Mae allowed herself one more minute like this, to sit on a bench in companionable silence with her best friend, postponing the inevitable conversations that lay in her future. But they would go fine, she reminded herself. No matter what happened, everything would be okay.

Mae lifted her head. "Okay," she said. "I'm ready."

Jayla brought her in for another hug and picked up the nachos, telling Mae she'd hogged them long enough. And as Jayla walked off, Mae strode to the curb and pressed the crosswalk button, her eyes on Connor.

She'd avoided emotional conversations long enough. She'd married him once with that pile of unresolved baggage hidden behind her. The least she could do was avoid making that mistake again tomorrow.

And, for all her dragging her feet about the absurdity of tomorrow's elaborate wedding—the ice sculptures, the chocolate fountains, the orchestra, the too-many guests—the thought of getting through it with Connor, the two of them back to being a united front, sounded oddly like a dream.

The crosswalk flashed green. Mae stepped off the curb and started toward Connor, hoping against hope that he felt the same way.

CHAPTER TWENTY-SEVEN

The very first thing Connor did when she reached him was pull her close and wrap his arms around her. She crumpled into him, legs wobbly.

When he pulled back, and she met the tender concern in his eyes, she instantly knew they were going to be okay. She wasn't sure how, but that instinct remained, a truth she could feel with every beat of her heart: they were going to be okay.

"You wanna walk?" Connor asked.

She slipped her hand into his, and they started down the sidewalk—not toward the winery, Mae realized with relief, but somewhere else, away from all this, their own path.

"I didn't know my mom said that to you," he began. He rubbed his thumb back and forth over his other thumbnail. "I'm really sorry that happened. But if it's any consolation, I don't think she meant anything by it—not that that makes a difference," he said hastily.

Mae watched his fidgeting fingers. It was strange, hearing him try so hard to choose his words. He usually knew exactly what to say.

"Why didn't you tell me?" he asked.

"I didn't want to make a big deal over something that's probably nothing."

"But it's not nothing. Anything that affects you like this isn't nothing."

They passed a small park, a span of trees and grass and a fenced-in basketball court. In the darkness between streetlights, Mae weighed her words.

"I know. I guess it made me worry I could be repeating history. Surrounding myself with a white family where I'm always going to be the only Black person around. Listening to people who say things without thinking and don't realize how it affects me."

He stopped fidgeting. "Do *I* ever…?"

"No." She nudged his arm. "I wouldn't have married you if you did. But I've wondered…if someone in your family says something to me about my skin, or touches my hair without asking, or makes a comment about race…would you notice?" She kept her eyes on the glow of the streetlight just ahead, pushed on despite the waver in her voice. "And if I told you about it, would you say something?"

He stopped walking, dropping her hand to face her. "Mae. Look at me." She did as he asked, meeting his serious eyes. "I like to think I would notice, but honestly, I can't be positive. But if you tell me—and I really need you to tell me—I will make it very clear that it's not okay. I don't care who it is. Not if it's my mom, or my dad, or anyone else. You come first. Always."

She could only blink. Something about the grave conviction in his voice made her want to cry. Like it was proof that her feelings mattered. When she'd spent so much time, as a child, trying to convince herself that they didn't. As though she could have folded her feelings into a square so tiny that it would eventually disappear, and here he was, unfolding that square and framing it and hanging it up like it mattered.

"Have I ever done anything to make you think you don't come first?" he asked. His eyes were searching, like he was afraid of the answer.

"Not explicitly, but…you always seem to do what your parents want. I thought you'd take their side."

"I do what they want how?"

She traced a crease in his tie. "You help out around the house whenever they ask for it, you went along with the wedding they wanted, you agreed to the dance lessons."

His forehead wrinkled. "But I asked you when we got engaged if the wedding would be a problem. You said no. I never would have gone along with it if you'd told me you didn't want to do it."

Mae had to play his words back twice before they sank in. It almost didn't make sense, the idea that she could have declined without issue, that he would have listened. But when she dug deeper, tried to figure out why she couldn't get her mind around it, she realized it was only because she'd spent so long convincing herself her opinion didn't matter.

"Really?" she asked.

"Yes. You can't decide I'm not putting you first just because you weren't honest with me when I asked what you thought. I'm not a mind reader."

Mae smiled, remembering what he'd called her the morning they got engaged. "You can't read a locked book?"

"Exactly," Connor said, the memory lighting his face. "Look, I'm always gonna help my parents out. But you take priority, always. Okay?"

"Okay," she agreed, feeling anchored by his words.

"And will you tell me?" he asked. "If my parents say something out of line?"

"I will."

"Good." He hesitated. "Is there anything else you want to talk about? About my family, or anything?"

"No. I'm sorry I didn't tell you sooner. Sierra said I needed to tell you before we got married, but I kept putting it off."

A hint of surprise flashed over his face, but he didn't comment. "Is it true, what you said about the honeymoon? You used all your PTO in Hobson?"

Mae swallowed. "Yeah," she said quietly. "I'm sorry. I was trying to avoid using it, but then stuff kept coming up, and I lost track. I didn't know how to tell you."

"Apparently there's a lot of things you don't know how to tell me," he said, looking skyward with a bitter laugh.

"What does that mean?"

"Nothing."

She tried to catch his eye, get a read on him. "Connor."

He breathed in and out through his nose in a long, controlled sigh. "We're married. You know we're married now."

She frowned. "Yeah. I'm pretty sure I was there."

"Well, I need you to act like it. You can't keep hiding things from me. If you want to talk to Sierra about it first, then okay, but you need to factor me in eventually. I feel like I've been very patient these last few weeks."

"You have," Mae agreed.

"Okay, so…" He ran a hand down his face. "You need to let me in on things. You won't give me a straight answer about moving to DC. If you don't want me to, I need to know why.

I want to know what you're thinking—about DC, my job, my family, everything. You've been so focused on yourself, and your family, and I feel like I'm not part of it. I want to be part of the things that are important to you. Can you just…include me?"

At the sound of his pleading voice, shame gripped her, tightening its hold at every reminder of how much she'd pushed Connor aside in the past few weeks.

"I will," she said. "You're right. And the thing with DC was just…I was afraid that if we lived so close to your parents, it would be like it was around my mom's family, where they'd be around a lot and make me feel like an outcast."

"Okay." He nodded, like everything was decided. "Then we'll stay in Baltimore. I'll commute."

"No." Mae put a hand on his arm, gave it a gentle squeeze, tried to be reassuring, if she could remember how. "That was just me being stuck in my head. After everything we've just talked out, I don't think it'll be an issue."

"But let's make *sure* it's not an issue. I can commute. I've done it before."

"And you hated it," she reminded him. "Connor. You don't need to do that. I'm fine moving to DC."

"I want you to be more than fine," he said. His gaze was serious and unmoving.

She let out a breath. The right words had to be out there somewhere, but her depleted mind couldn't find them. "Can we sleep on it and talk about it later? Maybe Sunday, after the wedding? I want to make sure we get this right."

"Okay," he agreed. "We'll talk Sunday." But he was still looking past her.

"Is there more you want to say?" she asked.

Another sigh. "I feel like I can't be mad about Paris. After everything you've been going through."

"You can be mad," she said.

He met her eyes, one side of his mouth listing up cheerlessly. "I'm just sad."

"You don't want to go for mad? Mad is on the table."

Connor chuckled quietly. "Maybe later."

"Okay." She watched him stare ahead, aching to lift his spirits and undo her mistakes, find a way to retroactively be there for him all the times he'd needed her. "Are we okay?" she asked.

"Yeah," he said, but his smile was still dimmed. He looked around, as if he'd only just noticed they were in a darkened park. "You feeling up to going back? My parents want to talk to you."

Mae nodded, his hand found its way in hers, and they began the walk back in silence. She squeezed his hand. He squeezed back. And she knew she could handle whatever came next.

When they made it to the winery, the restaurant was as lively as ever, tables filled with people talking and eating. Except for their table, where Susan, John, and her mom sat in silence, glumly sipping wine or staring out the window. Mae had never seen the Rutherfords look so out of place in their own winery before. She looked around for signs of Sierra or Madison but didn't spot them.

Susan was first to see her approach. She waved Mae over frantically. With a glance at Jayla one table over—who, unbeknownst to the Rutherfords, was currently pointing two fingers at her own eyes and then pointing at John and Susan in a silly threat of surveillance that made Mae laugh—Mae returned to her seat, Connor sliding in next to her.

"Mae," Susan said, "I just want to say, I am so sorry about

asking you that stupid question. It was in no way meant to be racist. I think I was just making conversation. I was admiring your skin and I wasn't thinking. And I was wrong."

This was all she'd needed, Mae realized, a long, relieved sigh leaving her. None of the defensive denials the Parkers always jumped to whenever Mae's mom called them on their overtly racist comments. No attempts to convince Mae she was the problem, like Madison did during their tiff on Instagram. Just an apology and an acknowledgment of her feelings. Was this what it felt like to be validated? After all her stressing and burying, was it really as simple as this?

"It's okay," Mae said. "You can have the best of intentions and still slip up. But I know you didn't mean to. And if I wasn't so afraid of confronting you, I could have just told you about it instead of stewing over it for years."

"We would really like it if you would feel comfortable enough to tell us," John said.

"That seems to be the Rutherford consensus," Mae said, glancing at Connor with a small smile.

"If we haven't said it lately, we're so excited you're part of our family," Susan said. "You can call us on our crap. You can say no to us. John was telling me once that he didn't think you liked white wines, since you never seemed to go for them unless I poured you a glass, but I told him that can't be true, because you'd tell me if you didn't like it. But now..." She looked at Mae uncertainly.

"I hate *all* wine," Mae said. "Please stop serving it to me."

John was first to react, an involuntary guffaw erupting out of him. Susan burst into laughter next, perhaps thinking about the times Mae had gotten drunk in front of them because she didn't know how to turn down a glass. Mae met her mother's gaze across the table. She was smiling, but her eyes were sad.

"Let's grab ourselves a drink at the bar," John said, looking between Mae and her mother. Connor put a hand over Mae's before getting up from his seat.

"And we won't bring you anything." Susan winked and squeezed Mae's shoulder on her way past.

Alone with her mom, Mae felt like she was out of words. She'd said so much already, and not at all kindly.

"Where's Madison?" Mae asked.

"I sent her back to the hotel. I never would have let her come tonight if I'd known…" She shook her head. "You were always playing together when you were kids."

"Until we weren't," Mae said simply.

"I didn't know it was that bad for you, or your dad. My parents, my brothers…they said some borderline things sometimes, but I always called them out."

"Not all of them," Mae said. "And you weren't always around to hear them."

She sat with that fact, seeming to take it to heart. "And you're right. I should have told you about Grandma. I didn't want you to think it would mean she'd treat you differently, but she did, didn't she? I just didn't see it?"

"Pretty much."

"And Sierra." Her mom went quiet. She fiddled with her bracelet, turning it over and over on her wrist. "I was trying to honor your dad's memory. I wanted to give you that, if I couldn't give you him. I didn't think it would matter since we never saw his side of the family much. I thought you would think of them as strangers. But they're not. Family is family. Except." Her mom frowned, an awareness coming over her. "I guess that's not always true. I hope you know you come first. Over everything. If there are relatives you don't want around anymore, they don't have to be around."

Mae smiled. "*Mom*. Are you threatening to murder your family for me?"

"Mae!" Her mom scoffed, then gave a nervous laugh, glancing around as if the FBI were in earshot. "Absolutely not. I'm just saying I want you to be comfortable, always. And I'm so sorry there was so much I didn't notice." Her expression became tentative. "Can you tell me what sorts of things they said to you? You said your grandpa called you—"

"No, he didn't call me that; it just slipped out when he was fixing the car once. Then he tried to turn it into a lesson about the history of the phrase *jury-rigged*." She wanted to roll her eyes, but she couldn't, still. Because she couldn't divorce that moment from everything else about him: the warm hugs, the mint-tobacco smell, the way he'd pull her into his lap and read her the Sunday comics.

"God," her mom muttered. "What else did they say?"

Mae tilted her head. She felt like she was coming up empty in the best possible way. The words her relatives had lobbed at her were right there in her head, clear as ever, but that confused mess of hurt that usually accompanied them didn't spring forth this time. There was only a budding sense of clarity.

"Just…things they shouldn't have," she finally said. Met with her mom's imploring expression, Mae almost laughed. "It's been a long night. We can talk about it another time."

"Only if you want to." Her mom fixed her with a misty-eyed stare, then leaned over to hug her.

In the companionable silence that followed, Mae revisited that vestige of clarity. She was starting to feel she could make peace with it all. Stop trying to cram her memories of her grandparents into boxes labeled *Good* or *Bad* and just call it what it was: complicated. Her grandma made her other grandma's life a living hell as a teenager. She also spent a month sewing Mae a butterfly costume when Mae wanted to be a butterfly princess for Halloween. She once told Mae that her messy, knotted hair made her look as though she'd stuck her finger into an electrical socket. She also took Mae to see *Toy Story 2* in theaters two weekends in a row because Mae had loved it so much.

Mae didn't have to make sense of any of this. She could give herself permission to cherish the memories she held dear without excusing anyone's shitty behavior. She could keep the memories of Sunday comics, Monopoly games, *Toy Story 2*, knitting lessons, Oreo Blizzards, *The X-Files*. But everything else, every ugly word or harsh reality, she could throw at them, hold up a mirror and reflect their words right back. She could take that burden she'd lugged around all her life, that tangled mass of words she'd packed up and carried, and launch it into the sun.

And she didn't need to see the Rutherfords through this lens, either. She'd let Susan's one comment grow and grow, gaining more power, more weight, until it sucked every gasp of air out of any room they were in together. But neither John nor Susan had said or done a single thing since then to make Mae think they might be like the Parkers. As exhausting as it was to be on edge around them all the time, expecting words that might not ever come, it had felt like the easier choice. Harder would be finally letting her muscles unclench around them. Letting herself think it might be different this time. But Mae was starting to believe it actually would be.

And even if it wasn't—even if John or Susan made another borderline comment one day, something else said without thinking—Mae could tell them, straight up, because they had asked her to. And if she couldn't, she had a secret weapon.

Mae turned around for a glimpse of him. Connor was sitting at the bar, his back hunched over. His parents were beside him, heads close together, talking. John had a hand on Connor's shoulder. At one point, Mae might have jumped to the worst conclusion, taken this huddle to mean they were obviously talking about her. And they might well be after all she'd said tonight. But it wouldn't be anything nefarious or hurtful. They loved her, all three of them, and it was different this time.

She surveyed the room again, feeling a pang at the prospect of Sierra leaving before they'd had a chance to make up. And then she saw her: a slim figure in a simple black gown standing on the balcony, leaning over the railing, staring at the city. Sierra had stayed after all.

Mae wasted no time in making her way to the balcony. The air was warm on her shoulders when she stepped outside. Sierra turned at the sound of the door opening but didn't seem surprised to see Mae.

"How did I know the tea party bitch would come barging out here?" Sierra quipped.

Mae let out a watery laugh and joined her at the railing. "You know me well." She looked down at the glimmering lights strung up in the courtyard below, piecing her thoughts together. "I'm sorry I took Madison's side," she said. "I was a coward. Just like Dad."

The admission felt like treachery. She'd grown up thinking those secret looks she and her dad had exchanged were their way of showing how cool and unbothered they were. She didn't like thinking that they actually signified her dad's unwillingness to stand up for himself, or for his daughter. For his daughters, plural.

"But not anymore," Mae continued. "I talked to my mom, and I talked to Connor, and his parents. It's all taken care of."

A smile graced Sierra's lips. "Good." Her gaze returned to the balcony view, then back to Mae. "And you're not a coward. You had your own shit to work through. I didn't realize how bad you had it. With your mom's family. I've heard the stories from Bee and Grandma, but…it must have been hard."

"It was," Mae said quietly. "And everything with our dad must have been hard for you."

"It was," Sierra echoed. They locked eyes, sharing a quiet moment of understanding.

Mae turned and leaned her back against the railing, tossing a sidelong glance at Sierra. "I hope you know you're never getting rid of me. I'm gonna be blowing up your phone. Coming to see you. Hobson, Seattle, wherever you are."

Sierra didn't acknowledge the unspoken question in Mae's voice, but a light flickered in her eyes. "Sounds like a threat."

"It is."

"Okay. And, you know…" Sierra gestured toward the city lights surrounding the balcony. "DC's not hideous. I could come here sometimes."

Mae nudged her arm. "You're always welcome." She chewed her lip, growing thoughtful. "But you know who's not…" She dug her phone from her purse to put into action the thought that had been growing louder in her mind for the last few minutes.

Sierra looked on curiously while Mae unlocked her phone. Her chest tightened at the sight of two new messages from Madison, but she just laughed when she read them.

MADISON: It was really unfair of you to say that stuff to me tonight

MADISON: I came all this way for your wedding and now I'm not even sure I want to go

No remorse, no apology, no attempt to see things her way. It made her decision an easy one. Mae pressed *Block this caller*, and Madison was gone.

Sierra gave Mae an approving nod, and Mae took a deep breath in. It was freeing, like loosening her belt after a big dinner. She kept scrolling, looking for more Parkers. Her cousin Amber had always been thoughtful and kind to her; she could stay. But anyone who ever made her feel out of place: blocked. In her phone. In every form of social media she had. In her life.

This was more than freeing, actually. It was powerful. All her life, she'd let her relatives hold a power over her—the ability to make her feel small. But Mae was the only person who could decide how people made her feel. That power had been hers all along, and she'd just never known it.

Mae lifted her head, catching sight of Connor through the window. He was sitting alone at their table, contemplating the glass in front of him. He looked up, met her gaze. Instinctively, his lips curled into a smile. His eyes were tired, and etched with traces of sadness, but still he had that habit of breaking into a smile when their eyes met across a room. She couldn't help but mirror it.

A light feeling of possibility and promise swam through her. This was fixable. Family wasn't always fixable, Mae knew. It could be complicated and messy. Some bonds, like those she'd had with her grandparents, would be too complex to ever make sense of. But Mae believed in *her* family, the people who had her heart. Her mom, Connor, Sierra, Jayla, the Townsends, the Rutherfords. Neither disputes nor distance would ever tear them apart, not after what she'd been through to put them all together. She wouldn't let it.

CHAPTER TWENTY-EIGHT

The ride home was quiet. Connor insisted he wasn't upset, but his tone was melancholy.

"I'm gonna head to bed," he said when they got home, even though it was barely 10:00 p.m.

"Or I could show you how to make my grandma's mac and cheese." Mae leaned against the front door, tapping her fingertips together in exaggerated anticipation. It might be a silly gesture, but she wanted him to know she was done keeping him in the dark. Showing him her grandma's recipe—the recipe she'd spent the last three weeks chasing—was the best way she knew.

He studied her in confusion for a moment, then broke into a puzzled smile. "Okay."

She pulled out cheeses and ingredients one by one. He'd been with her when she'd thrown all the requisite cheeses into their shopping cart on a grocery run a few days ago, mostly because not having the ingredients on hand felt wrong after the last few weeks. But now she walked him through the role each cheese played in the recipe, the discoveries she and Sierra had made in their testing. She taught Connor how to follow the steps that had become second nature. Boiling water. Grating cheeses. Measuring spices. They worked together, Connor checking with Mae at every stage to make sure he was following the process correctly. Like he knew exactly how special this recipe was. He sprinkled grated cheddar over the dish with great consideration, making sure no corner was neglected. And when he put it in the oven, he turned to Mae with a triumphant grin that made her wish she'd included him in the process so much sooner.

Tomorrow's wedding floated into her mind, but it didn't unsettle her calm. The three hundred guests, the peonies, the attention. It was one day. One day when her in-laws could throw their son the wedding they'd always wanted for him. One day when she could marry her husband for the second time, kiss him at the altar knowing they'd done this before, knowing this fanfare wasn't them and not really caring.

They sat at the kitchen table, the steaming dish cooling between them. They had only enough patience to wait a few minutes before digging in.

Connor breathed a happy sigh as he chewed his first bite. "Do you think my parents would be mad if I brought this to the wedding as my dinner?"

"After all the money they spent on that caterer?" she said, recalling the caviar cones and truffle bruschetta they'd endured at the tasting John and Susan had dragged them to. "Absolutely."

"They'll get over it." He lifted his eyes to meet Mae's. "Thank you for teaching me how to make this."

A warmth came over her. It was like they were back to being themselves. Honest conversations and late-night food and mooning at each other over the table.

"I'm sorry about everything—staying for so long, and the

honeymoon, and not knowing how to let you in. I promise I'm going to be better about that."

"It's okay," he said. "I know you've always wanted to know your family. I wouldn't want to stand in the way of that."

"You're never in the way," she said intently.

His hand found hers across the table. "I know."

Mae watched their clasped hands, Sierra's observations about Connor and his hand-holding running through her mind. "You can still go to Paris, you know," she said. "You deserve it, after—"

"I'm not going without you. Besides, everything's refundable. We can go next year. Paris isn't going anywhere."

She held his gaze, that warmth giving way to fluttery anticipation. "Paris might not be going anywhere, but we are."

Connor tilted his head, a question in his eyes.

"I want you to take the job," she said. "And I want to move to DC. All those worries I mentioned had nothing to do with your parents. I was just projecting my own family stuff onto them. And I know, after tonight, that it's not gonna be a problem. Will you take the job?"

He hesitated, still searching her. "You're sure?"

"I'm sure."

A slow smile came over him. "Okay. I'll accept the offer on Monday. And I think I'll take a couple weeks off between jobs and just sleep. Recover from wedding stuff. Bug you while you're working."

"Sounds perfect."

They locked eyes, basking in the joy of the next step that awaited them. For the first time, she let herself feel excited about the prospect of moving to DC. She could return to the city she'd fallen in love with in college, visit all her favorite restaurants whenever she wanted. Her in-laws would be minutes away, but—thinking of John and Susan's assurances that night, their presence at the barbecue-wedding, every kindness they'd ever shown her in the nearly five years she'd known them—that was a good thing.

As Connor went back to eating, Mae glanced at the fork in front of her. He was holding her dominant hand. She thought about letting go to continue eating, but she wanted to take a page out of Connor's book tonight. Be that same pillar of sweetness and support he'd always been for her, shine it right back at him. He deserved every bit of it and more.

She picked up the fork with her left hand and used it to scoop up some macaroni. As she inelegantly brought it to her mouth, a noodle falling on the table in the process, she noticed Connor watching her with a knowing smile. She grinned right back.

CHAPTER TWENTY-NINE

Mae was beginning to understand why *skip your final dress fitting* and *eat mac and cheese for three weeks straight* did not come recommended in any bridal magazine.

Her beautiful, beaded champagne dress had been so forgiving once upon a time. It had eased down her body, hugging her curves while giving her plenty of room to breathe. Now, it seemed, breathing was ill-advised. At least it was if she wanted to fit into her dress. And with her mom and Susan looking on in alarm from the corner of the bridal suite, Mae was getting the idea that fitting into her wedding dress was not optional.

It was starting to make sense why Susan had gently suggested Mae try on her wedding dress now, hours ahead of the ceremony. Though Mae suspected that squeezing into this dress would take far more than a few extra hours.

"Sometimes you just need to break it in," Susan said, circling Mae for a better look at the back, where Mae was sure she had a perfect view of the zipper that had given up at the halfway mark. Mae imagined she resembled a partially peeled banana.

Mae made a face at the word *break*. "Aren't wedding dresses, like, delicate?" She pushed her shoulders back and forward a few times to try to stretch the material. The firm fabric remained committed to constricting her ribs.

"Why don't we try again?" Mae's mom suggested. "This time, I'll hold it from the back, and Susan will—"

"No." Mae sucked in her stomach and carefully eased the dress down her hips until it gratefully collapsed in a pool at her feet. She let out a relieved sigh, her stomach pooching back out. "Luckily, I have another wedding dress at home." She caught Susan and her mom's puzzled looks as she changed back into the shorts and tank top she'd arrived in. Mae didn't bother to elaborate. The yellow dress she'd worn to the barbecue counted as a wedding dress. She'd gotten married in it, after all.

She dashed off a text to Jayla, hoping she hadn't left for the winery yet. Jayla had a spare key to her home.

MAE: Any chance you can pick something up from my place?
JAYLA: What do you need?

Mae crossed the hall to the room where Connor was getting ready. She poked her head in to see Connor biting into a bagel while frowning at the three-piece suit hanging across the room.

"I can't fit into my dress," she announced.

"Don't worry. Everyone will be so busy watching me die of heatstroke that they won't even notice." Another twist the day had brought them: a high of 104 degrees and not a cloud in sight.

"I'm asking Jayla to get my dress from wedding number one," she told Connor. "Want anything?"

His eyes lit up, a sly grin passing over him. "I would also like my outfit from wedding number one."

Mae and Connor's second wedding was, in many ways, far from what his parents had envisioned. They rushed through their vows, too hot to focus in the dizzying sun. The official photos of the bridal party would show that Mae and Connor were severely underdressed compared to everyone else, their cotton casuals against a sea of ties and chiffon, her yellow dress and his blue shirt clashing with the pale pink color scheme the rest of the party wore.

At the reception, once they were indoors breathing in the refreshingly cool air conditioning, the scattered seating revealed how Mae had slightly overpromised and underdelivered as far as guests were concerned. Neither Madison nor her parents showed up, which Mae attributed to last night's events and, perhaps, some strong words from her mom, going by the innocent smile her mom gave when Mae asked about them. And the seating chart she'd signed off on a lifetime ago had promised a couple of Townsends, which wasn't quite the truth. But it wasn't quite a lie, either—Mae *had* had Townsends at her wedding. Just not this one. No need to make them drive hours to see her get married a second time. It felt miraculous that Mae had even one Townsend with her, that Sierra was sitting at her table, in accordance with the seating chart Mae had made up. As if Mae had lied her into reality.

Christopher Walker's dance lessons were also a bust. Mae and Connor had optimistically hoped that the lessons Connor took would be enough to make up the difference. He would lead, and she would follow, and no one would know she hadn't taken a single lesson. But, as they discovered in real time while their guests looked on, it was actually the opposite. Mae's clumsy ignorance became the dominant force, and every practiced move Connor tried was met with a full-body freeze that made him stumble in return. At last, they gave up and resorted to basic middle-school-style swaying. Out of the corner of her eye, Mae saw John, holding up his phone to perhaps take a video for Christopher, slowly lower his phone and sink into his seat.

The wedding cake was anything but a disaster, though. It was tall, imposing, and exquisite, five tiers artfully stacked and draped in cream cheese frosting, edible lace adorning the bottom tier while a garden of handmade, pastel-pink gum paste roses ran up the cake in a diagonal stripe. It filled Mae with pride to stare at it and see her sister's talents laid bare.

But the part she loved most was the two figurines at the very top. They were simplistic in design, each one a round circle of a head on an oval body, but the details were intricate. One figure was a brown-skinned woman with a swoop of dark hair. Her oval body was white, like a wedding dress, tiny pearl sprinkles dotting it like beads. The woman's face was painted with such care: dark eyes, red lips, two patches of blush on her cheeks. The figure next to her was a blond, white man dressed in black: Connor in a tux. Sierra had even managed to capture his crooked smile, how one side lifted higher than the other.

Mae liked knowing these miniature versions of her and Connor were looking down at them from their sugary perch throughout the wedding. Every time she glanced their way, she could see all the care and love Sierra had poured into them.

Mae enjoyed herself more as the atmosphere loosened and people began paying more attention to wine and the dance floor than the bride and groom. Left to their own devices, she and

Connor took a photo in front of the donut wall, her one drunken mark on this event. The wall boasted dozens of colorful donuts neatly arranged and ready to be devoured. She picked a glazed donut off the wall and sank her teeth into it, savoring its soft texture and luxuriating in the power of night donuts.

While Connor went off in search of savory food, Mae used her free, non-donut-bearing hand to grab another slice of cake from the dessert table.

"Amazing job, Sierra," Susan was saying when Mae returned to her seat. "The cake is absolutely perfect."

"It really is," Mae said, going for a bite of her second slice of cake. The sweet, chocolatey flavor was perfectly balanced by the tangy cream cheese frosting.

"We'd like to add you to our list of recommended vendors," Susan said. "Is that okay? You'd have to come up here for the occasional cake tasting, but it could mean a lot of business."

"Especially now that we're no longer speaking to Bruce," John grumbled, making Mae fight off a smile. John's grudge against the baker who canceled their original cake order was holding strong, but Mae loved him for it. Bruce and his cancelation had given Mae the excuse she needed to bring Sierra closer into her life. Mae owed Bruce a thank-you card.

"I'd love that," Sierra said, a soft surprise in her voice. "Thank you."

"Thank *you*. We appreciate everything you've done for us. I know this was a lot of work on very short notice." Susan passed Sierra an envelope, then patted her hand before getting up to dance with John.

Sierra opened it and peeked inside. Her eyebrows quickly shot up.

"What?" Mae asked.

"They way overpaid."

"They know quality when they see it." Mae grinned at Sierra's shy, reluctant smile. "So, if you're on their list of recommended vendors, does that mean you're staying in Hobson and starting a bakery?"

Sierra was quiet for a moment, lips pursed. Then she nodded, her eyes sparkling with excitement. "Yeah. I want to try it and see what happens. And it helps that I have some seed money," she said, holding up the envelope.

A fizzy joy leapt through Mae. "Thank you for letting me be your first customer."

"Thank you for having rich in-laws."

As they laughed, Connor took his seat beside her, a familiar-looking Tupperware in hand.

"Told you I'd bring it," he said.

"You seriously brought it from home?"

"It's very important to have a backup meal on deck when your alternative is crudites and crostini," he said solemnly.

Mae watched him peel the lid off the container. "Is that even safe to eat?"

"I put it in the fridge when we got here." Connor brought a bite to his mouth, closing his eyes. "It's even good cold."

Mae wanted to laugh at his newfound obsession, but it just made her all the more content. It felt right that Connor should come to love the dish she'd spent the last few weeks obsessing over. He was part of her family now. And in this family, they took their mac and cheese very, very seriously.

As much mac and cheese as Mae had eaten recently, she couldn't resist hefting a small serving onto her plate. She was too proud not to. It had taken so much work to get the recipe to this point.

Sierra couldn't resist it either. She reached over, using a fork to steal a bite from Mae's plate. As Sierra chewed, her brows dipped together slightly—and then a slow dawning came over her.

"What?" Mae asked.

Sierra leaned in, peering at Mae's plate. "There's frosting on your plate."

"Well, yeah. I only lick my plate clean at home. I'm very proper."

"You are the most proper person with frosting on her face in the whole world," Connor said. Mae met his twinkling gaze and smiled while he gently brushed her lower lip with his thumb.

"Yes, I get it, you're adorable," Sierra remarked. "But listen. The bite I had—it tasted *right*. Like the way Grandma makes it."

Mae frowned at her plate. "I refuse to believe our grandmother put frosting in her mac and cheese."

"I know, but...I think our recipe needed a tiny hint of something sweet. You don't notice it when it's there, but you notice when it's gone. That's what it's missing."

Mae's jaw dropped. "Wait, how can something be missing when you said I got the recipe right?"

"Not important," Sierra said, waving her off.

"You *lied?*" Mae's mock outrage fell away as the implication hit her. "You *lied*," she teased, a grin spreading across her face. "You lied because you love me."

"Oh, get over it." Sierra wrenched her lips to fight off a smile. "Can you think of anything sweet that could go in mac and cheese?"

Mae took out her phone and searched for that picture she'd

taken of Althea's receipt with the handful of mac and cheese ingredients. Sierra bent her head over Mae's phone, the two of them wordlessly studying the picture.

"There!" Sierra poked a spot on the receipt. "Condensed milk. I bet that's it. She probably only uses a tiny, tiny amount, but I bet it makes all the difference."

"Really?" Mae stared, dumbfounded, at the clue she never would have guessed. She stabbed a piece of macaroni with her fork and copied Sierra, dipping her bite in frosting. She chewed, trying to keep an open mind. "All I taste is sugar."

"We'll make another batch with a smidge of condensed milk, and you'll get it." Sierra sat back and let out a satisfied sigh. "We did it. For real this time. We finally solved it."

Mae held Sierra's gaze, feeling warm and content and *whole*. Like every missing piece of her was finally filled in. She had Sierra and the Townsends. Connor and the Rutherfords. Her mom had made up with Barbara. She could see the bridges she'd built, connecting all of them.

There were no more factions now. There was only family who made her life better and family who made her life worse. She was still wrestling with her feelings about her maternal grandmother—how she could feel love and nostalgia and disgust toward her, all in the same, confusing muddle. But that was okay, too. She would stop letting them define how she carried herself. And she would stop pretending her feelings toward the Parkers weren't valid.

As for the family who made her life better, that was easy. She'd embrace them—all of them. She'd stop hiding and worrying about what they'd think about her or if they were talking about her or when was the right time to come into their lives.

Always, that was the answer. She couldn't go back in time, couldn't confront her dad and make him tell her the truth, couldn't plant Sierra into her childhood memories retroactively. She couldn't go back to that day on the beach with Susan and save herself years of anxiety and accidental drunkenness.

But for all the lost opportunities the past held, there was so much to appreciate here in the present. No worries or musings or clenched muscles. No swallowed hurt or silent acceptance. This was family the way family was meant to be. Just love. Comfort. Honesty.

Mae watched Sierra lean in to say something to Connor, who laughed. This was just the beginning of their union, the Townsends and the Rutherfords. She could picture so much more to come. Sierra getting her bakery off the ground and staying with Mae whenever she came up to DC to consult with a client. Mae and Connor going to Paris next year. Going down to Hobson and seeing the Townsends for special occasions or just-because weekend trips throughout the year. Her grandma's mac and cheese at the table at every barbecue, every holiday, every event. Kids down the line who would know both sides of their family and never, ever feel out of place. They would feel everything Mae felt now: full and loved and wonderfully, wonderfully whole.

READING GROUP GUIDE

1. Discuss Mae's initial perception of the Townsends and their annual barbecue. Did she romanticize them? In what ways did they fall short of her expectations?

2. Characterize Mae and Connor's relationship. What do you like about it?

3. Imagine your own family's potluck. What dishes set the scene? What would you bring?

4. Consider Mae's reasons for distrusting Connor's parents. Why is she so concerned about becoming a part of their family?

5. There are a few reasons for the rift between Mae's parents' families. Which is the biggest reason for their discord?

6. Discuss the ways, large and small, that racism appears in the book. How does Mae handle it?

7. Mae is desperate to feel like a part of the Townsend family. What are a few of the ways she tries to win them over?

8. Althea Townsend was the heart of the Townsends. Is there one person who sits at the center of your family?

9. Compare Mae and Sierra. In what ways are they similar?

A CONVERSATION WITH THE AUTHOR

This is your third novel. What inspired you to write it?

About a decade ago, my dad told me my grandmother had died and asked if I wanted to come with him to her funeral. I considered it, tempted by the idea of seeing and/or meeting my extended family members…but I also knew that meeting them while they were grieving someone I'd never met might not be the best timing. I ultimately decided not to go, but that concept of showing up at a funeral to meet your family (and all that could unfold from there) has always stayed with me.

Mae has to contend with varying degrees of racism, particularly from people in her own family. Folks don't always think of that kind of negativity coming from the people closest to us. Can you talk a bit about that?

Everyone has blind spots—even the people who love you most in the world. Having honest conversations about the ways our lived experiences differ—and understanding how what may seem innocuous to one person can be harmful to another—can go a long way toward reaching understanding.

Food is integral to this story. What made you land on that as a theme?

I love food. I spend so much time thinking about food. It was only a matter of time before it made its way into one of my books.

What are some of your favorite reads lately?

People Person by Candice Carty-Williams is a recent favorite. I love its unconventional and very compelling portrayal of family. It's creative, unique, funny, and I enjoyed every second of it.

Connor and Mae have a rock-solid relationship. Why did you choose to write them that way?

Look, Mae has enough issues to sort through. I couldn't have Connor adding on to the list. Connor would never.

You populate Hobson with so many quirky but lovable folks. (We're looking at you, Nosy Posey!) How do you go about crafting those kinds of characters?

I wish I had an intelligent, thought-out process to share. The truth is that they just sort of pop into my head. Nosy Posey, for example, didn't become part of the book until the third draft, when I wanted to flesh out the neighborhood a bit more and decided a nosy neighbor might be a fun addition. One detail very quickly built on the next, so as soon as I decided he was nosy, the rest followed suit, from his distrust of Neighborhood Watch to his decades-long rivalry with Althea.

Are you more of a "lavish vineyard wedding" or a "backyard barbeque wedding" kind of person?

Neither! As far as my deeply introverted self is concerned, weddings are parties and parties are nightmares. Since DC allows self-uniting marriages, I got to marry my husband without any witnesses, and I served as our officiant. It was perfect. And no one saw it.

What do you hope readers gain from Mae's story?

Admittedly, my primary goal is always to write the book I want to read. So I hope the reader I wrote this for (me) gains satisfaction from the fact that this book exists now (I do!).

But for people who aren't me, I hope readers can relate to Mae's story in some way, whatever that means for them. I hope readers come away knowing that family should make you feel loved, accepted, and whole. And, if that's not the case, that choosing a family of your own making is a perfectly valid way to create the support system you need.

ACKNOWLEDGMENTS

Thank you to my fabulous agent and editors who loved this book back when it was nothing more than a blobby idea I wasn't sure about. Katelyn Detweiler is the best agent I could ever ask for, and MJ Johnston and Jenna Jankowski always know how to ask the right questions and offer suggestions to make a book sing.

I'm grateful to Sam Farkas, Denise Page, and the rest of the team at Jill Grinberg Literary for all that they do. And thank you to Pam Jaffee, BrocheAroe Fabian, Cristina Arreola, Valerie Pierce, Ashlyn Keil, Caitlin Lawler, Katie Stutz, Margaret Coffee, Jessica Thelander, Madeleine Brown, Anna Venckus, and everyone else at Sourcebooks for all they've done to support this book and my previous books. And thank you Gianni Washington for copyediting!

Thank you to the writing community at large and to the Lit Squad for your wisdom and the endless laughter you bring. Special thanks to Jas Hammonds (who was kind enough to read an early draft), Camille Baker, Bethany Baptiste, Gabi Burton, Sami Ellis, Elnora Gunter, Déborah Kabwang, Avione Lee,

Britney Lewis, Allegra Martschenko, Melody Simpson, Halley Sutton, KJ Micciche, and Eden Robins.

Kate Reed read the very first version of this book and has listened to me rant about it since its inception (and about every book and about everything in my life for the last twenty years). Whatever the topic, whatever the crisis, she never fails to make me laugh. Thank you for existing.

Barbara Singhakiat wanted a character named after her—I hope you like her! Thank you for your friendship (and for letting me steal details about your car trouble to use in this book. Your massive inconvenience is my convenient plot point).

For anyone hoping Althea's mac and cheese recipe actually exists, I'm sorry to say it doesn't. But I did take inspiration from many recipes that can be found in reality, especially Tobias Young's Southern Baked Mac and Cheese.

Thank you to my family for their support and for being aware that this is a work of fiction! Growing up with only my immediate family around did make me wonder what it would have been like to know my extended family on either side, and the fun thing about writing is that anything can happen. I've met my mum's side of the family, the Rodgerses in Australia, only a few times— some people just once and others not at all—but the memories I do have are filled with love and laughter. My memories of my dad's side of the family, the Robinsons in Louisiana, mostly boil down to one long-ago visit, but I do remember love and kindness from that trip. My other memory of my paternal relatives is one I hold dear: a phone call with my grandfather, Charles Robinson, Sr., which has long cemented him as my favorite grandparent, both because that call made him the only grandparent I can ever recall speaking with and because he sounded like a very kind man. But social media offers new opportunities to connect with faraway family, and I'm glad I've now gotten connected to relatives on both sides through Facebook (but also, apologies for rarely being on social media).

And then there's the family I married into. The Hockers, Fitzsimmonses, and co. have been supportive and thoughtful for as long as I've known them, and I'm so glad to have them in my life. (I'm also glad they didn't subject me to the wedding chaos Mae's in-laws did so I could forgo a wedding entirely!)

And to Matt Hocker: thank you for listening to me think out loud about this book, for brainstorming with me, for pep talks and laughter and unwavering support.

ABOUT THE AUTHOR

Photo © Rachel E.H. Photography

Shauna Robinson writes contemporary fiction with humor and heart. Originally from San Diego, she now lives in Virginia with her husband and their sleepy greyhound. Shauna is an introvert at heart—she spends most of her time reading, baking, and figuring out the politest way to avoid social interaction.